D0045448

DARKNESS AT CHANCELLORSVILLE

RALPH PETERS' NOVELS PUBLISHED BY FORGE

Cain at Gettysburg (Boyd Award)

Hell or Richmond (Boyd Award)

Valley of the Shadow (Boyd Award)

The Damned of Petersburg

Judgment at Appomattox

Darkness at Chancellorsville

The Officers' Club

The War After Armageddon

The Hour of the Innocents (writing as "Robert Paston")

RALPH PETERS' CIVIL WAR MYSTERIES PUBLISHED UNDER THE PEN NAME "OWEN PARRY"

Faded Coat of Blue (Herodotus Award)

Shadows of Glory

Call Each River Jordan

Honor's Kingdom (Hammett Prize)

Bold Sons of Erin

Rebels of Babylon

and

Our Simple Gifts: Civil War Christmas Tales

Ralph Peters is also the author of numerous books on strategy, as well as additional novels.

DARKNESS AT CHANCELLORSVILLE

A Novel of Stonewall Jackson's Triumph and Tragedy

RALPH PETERS

MAPS BY GEORGE SKOCH

A Tom Doherty Associates Book
New York

This is a work of fiction. All of the characters, organizations, and events portrayed in this novel are either products of the author's imagination or are used fictitiously.

DARKNESS AT CHANCELLORSVILLE

Maps by George Skoch

A Forge Book
Published by Tom Doherty Associates
175 Fifth Avenue
New York, NY 10010

www.tor-forge.com

Forge® is a registered trademark of Macmillan Publishing Group, LLC.

The Library of Congress Cataloging-in-Publication Data is available upon request.

ISBN 978-0-7653-8173-6 (hardcover)
ISBN 978-1-4668-8403-8 (ebook)

Our books may be purchased in bulk for promotional, educational, or business use. Please contact your local bookseller or the Macmillan Corporate and Premium Sales Department at 1-800-221-7945, extension 5442, or by email at MacmillanSpecialMarkets@macmillan.com.

First Edition: May 2019

Printed in the United States of America

0 9 8 7 6 5 4 3 2 1

To Dr. James S. Pula,
in honor of his pioneering work
on the vital, dramatic, and long-slighted roles
played by immigrants and freedom fighters
from central and eastern Europe
in our Civil War.

And it will come to pass, when some of them be overthrown at the first, that whosoever heareth it will say, There is a slaughter among the people that follow Absalom.

—2 Samuel 17:9

DARKNESS AT CHANCELLORSVILLE

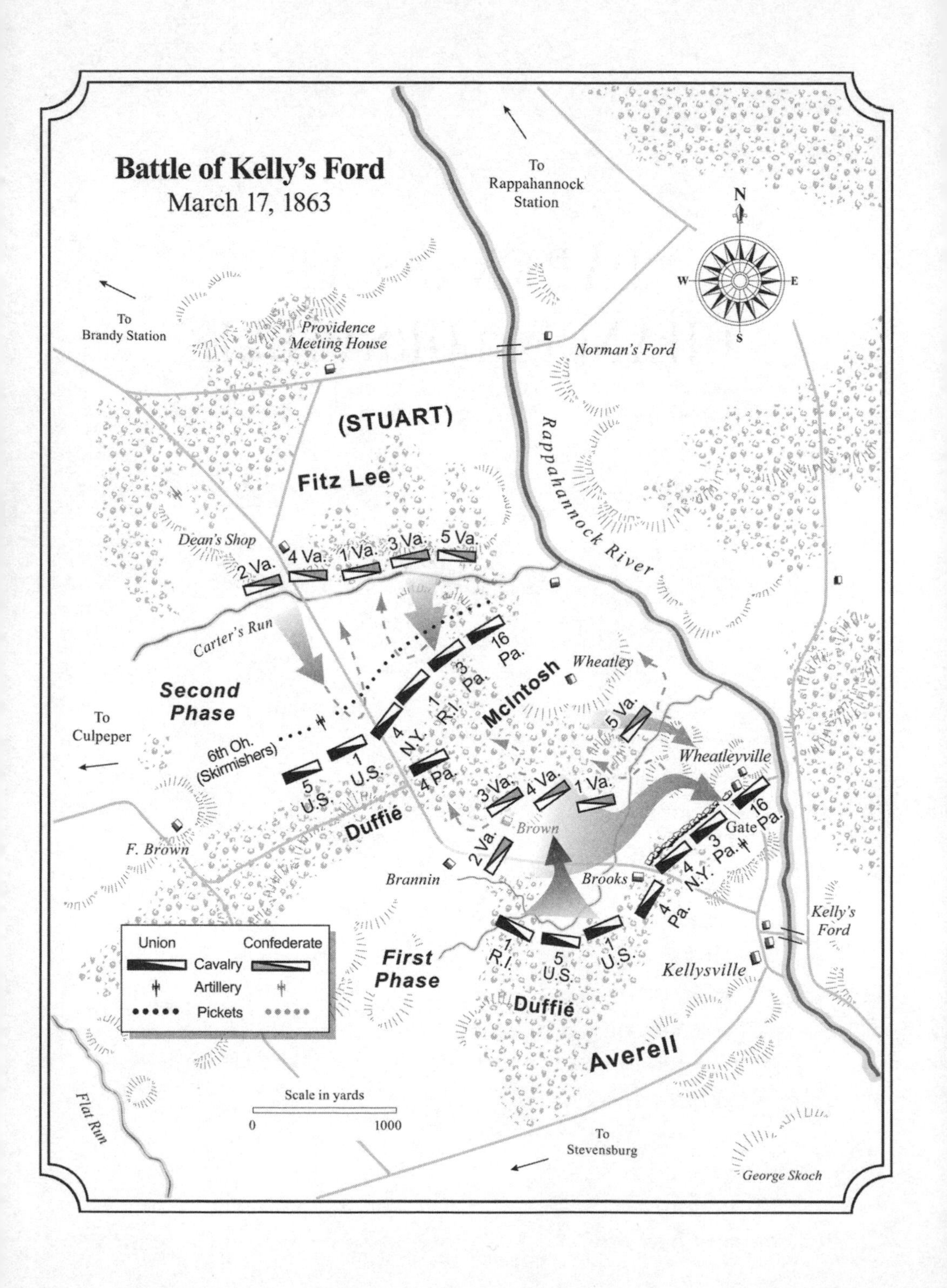
Battle of Kelly's Ford
March 17, 1863
To
Rappahannock
Station
To
Brandy Station
Providence
Meeting House
Norman's Ford
(STUART)
Rappahannock River
Fitz Lee
Dean's Shop
2 Va.
4 Va.
1 Va.
3 Va.
5 Va.
Carter's Run
16
Pa.
3
Pa.
1
R.I.
4
N.Y.
Wheatley
Second
Phase
McIntosh
To
Culpeper
6th Oh.
(Skirmishers)
1
U.S.
5
U.S.
4 Pa.
5 Va.
Wheatleyville
3 Va.
4 Va.
1 Va.
16
Pa.
Gate
3
Pa.
4
N.Y.
Duffié
Brown
F. Brown
2 Va.
Brannin
Brooks
4
Pa.
Kelly's
Ford
Union
Confederate
Cavalry
Artillery
Pickets
First
Phase
1
R.I.
5
U.S.
1
U.S.
Kellysville
Duffié
Averell
Scale in yards
0
1000
Flat Run
To
Stevensburg
George Skoch

PROLOGUE

Saint Patrick's Day 1863
Kelly's Ford, Virginia

Sam Chamberlain fired his Colt at his own men as they retreated, at the Rebs on the far bank who'd turned them back, and at all the worthless world.

"Goddamned cowards. . . ."

With his face shot through, the words emerged as grunts. Blood chilled and clotted on his jaw, his neck. Doused in icy water, his uniform sheathed him.

The revolver clicked empty. A last cavalryman's horse gripped the mud of the bank and spattered past, its rider mad-eyed.

Chamberlain spit out another tooth, maybe a splinter of jaw bone. Lowering his pistol in disgust, he watched the river's current tug his dead horse from the shallows. Determined to save his saddle roll, he entered the water again.

Even the river betrayed him. The carcass fled downstream.

Hatless and drenched, with high boots bucketing water, he coughed out more bloody pulp and cursed again. The wind combed strips of face-meat.

Never was a beauty. Less of one now.

He stared across the river as cold water scoured his groin. Shivers gripped him, uncontrollable, strong.

"Go on home, Yank," an unseen Johnny called. "You just go on home now."

Had the ford not been deepened forbiddingly by melt, Chamberlain might have crossed that river on foot and gone at the hidden graybacks with his fists. Find them and flush them out, every last one.

Only saw them when they rose to fire. Behind the slashings. Some in a ditch, others in that brush.

Twice, he'd tried to lead a detachment from the 4th New York to clear the far bank. And twice the men had lost their nerve midstream and turned their horses. Then he'd called up soldiers he'd believed better, lads from the 1st Rhode Island. They, too, had quit, although one had tarried long enough to free him from tangled reins.

Pain swept him. Monstrous pain, delayed then delivered with interest. His face had burst like a pig's bladder poked with a knife. He could have howled.

But Chamberlain only gummed out more obscenities, wiping blood from an eye with a sodden glove.

Staring across the swirling brown water, he felt frozen inside and out. Unable to move or be moved. Outraged beyond human compass. Helpless.

A hand gripped his upper arm.

A bullet tore past. Then another.

"General says come back right now, for God's sake."

Bill Averell watched his chief of staff stomp through the mud, face so mutilated that Chamberlain was more recognizable for his bad temper than his features. A sergeant tried to drape a blanket over the major's shoulders, but Chamberlain cast it off with the growl of a beast.

Sorry shit of a morning. Averell had dispatched an advance detachment of a hundred men to secure the ford, and the effort had failed utterly. Now here they were, in the full morning light, his two brigades held up by a handful of Rebs.

Fitz would gloat when he found out. Damn him.

Old Fitz. Fitzhugh Lee. With those ain't-you-small-now? eyes that put every man in his place. Chums at West Point, neither one a scholar. But friends or not, Fitz always had that knack of reminding you that he was a Lee of Virginia—and not from a lesser branch of that august family. As a cadet, Fitz had been the queerest mix of merriment, mischief, and snobbery that Averell had encountered among the Southerners. And he'd had some competition.

Now he and Fitz ruled opposite banks of the Rappahannock River, but Fitz had crossed over one too many times, ending his last foray by leaving that snot of a note:

> *Dear Billy,*
>
> *I wish you would put up your sword, leave my State, and go home. If you won't go home, return my visit, and bring me a sack of coffee.*
>
> *Fitz*

This day had been chosen for the return call. But his men couldn't even get across the river. Averell was tempted, again, to call up his rifled battery and blast the Johnnies, but with the bulk of his command still hidden, he didn't want to reveal his strength to the Rebs: Cavalry alone signaled a patrol, but artillery meant that someone had come to fight.

He did want to teach Fitz a lesson, though. *Had* to do it. Matter of pride. Not just personal vanity, but the honor of his command, the restoration of the cavalry's tattered reputation. He'd promised Stoneman and Hooker his men would show well, that he'd raised his newly acquired division to a higher standard. And Hooker had licensed him to show its mettle.

Now this slipped-on-dog-shit start. High water swept heavy limbs downstream and the ford's approaches were already hoof-cut. Each new assault grew more difficult and slower. The river's current stole the lives of his wounded, and one blue-jacketed corpse had snagged on a branch, a discouraging display for men going forward.

In sheltered spots across the ford, snow bandaged the earth. Cold air scraped. And two thousand men waited uselessly in the mist.

Not so gently mocking Averell's upbringing, Fitz had entertained their classmates by dramatizing the differences between a Virginia plantation and an uplands New York farm, drawing everyone in with his patter and mimicry, his cavalier's velvet disdain. Averell would regret to the end of his days revealing to Fitz that he'd worked in an apothecary shop before getting his appointment to the Academy.

He was about to call up the battery, plan be damned, when Lieutenant Brown nudged his gelding forward, risking a black-tempered blast. Sim Brown was all right, an eager boy. But Averell reserved the right to rip his darling head from his youthful neck.

"General Averell, sir? I can get across, I can do it. I watched, I know where the bed's good. Let me take volunteers. I can do it, sir."

Averell snorted. "After Sam Chamberlain couldn't?"

The lieutenant had spoken his piece and now he waited.

Well, why not? If the lad wanted to hurl himself into eternity—by way of an ice-cold river—wasn't that war?

"All right, Lieutenant. *If* you can get those stump-fuck skedaddlers to follow you, give us all a lesson in how it's done." Smarting under the day's embarrassing start, Averell added, "And God help you, if you make a mess of it."

Brown led eighteen men toward the river. He'd expected more volunteers, but the boys were spooked: another hard-luck day for the Cavalry Corps. Didn't see how he could back out, though. After his show of bravado in front of Averell.

Well, Averell was a decent sort, when he wasn't in a temper. He'd write a pretty letter to his mother. "I regret to inform you that your gallant son . . ."

Wasn't quite the way Brown had imagined ending up. Never had bedded a woman. Now he regretted not taking advantage of Washington's well-drilled whores.

His little party emerged from the skeletal trees and faced the river. Afraid to look back and find himself alone, he left his revolver holstered and drew his sword.

"At the gallop, *charge!*" he cried. His voice seemed too weak by half. Puny.

His mount defied the mud, though, almost leaping the distance to the water.

Reb rifles blinked from the far bank. Behind Brown, supporting fire crackled, augmented by shouts of encouragement.

His horse struck the river with a clumsy splash. Spray pecked Brown's face. The water topped his right boot, flooding its depths.

Christ, the water was cold.

Fighting the current, his horse seemed to grow stronger, as if it had become one giant muscle. Half kicking the bottom, half swimming, it shook its head and blew its nostrils open.

Brown believed—hoped—that he heard other riders by him.

Don't look back. Don't think. Keep going.

"Come on, boys!" he shouted, voice still little more than a child's cry. All of him a-shiver. The unbelievable cold of the river. Plus the chill of fear.

Bullets hissed past. The Rebs yelled, crazed. His volunteers responded, the Irish among them bellowing curses and taunts to frighten death. Sudden gasps pierced the uproar.

The far bank seemed impossible to reach, ever receding.

"Come on, we've got them!" Brown shouted. A leader, a liar.

Icy water leapt to scorch his lips.

He would *not* turn back. Damn it. He would not do it.

Waving his useless sword, all but begging the Rebs to empty his saddle, he clung to his horse's mane with his left hand, a thing forbidden by the riding masters.

Nearby a soldier blasphemed with fury, but the voices were fewer.

His last command.

A sergeant surged past on a huge black horse, racing Brown to the bank. An instant later, blood and meat and bone tore from the man's shoulder.

That, too, spattered Brown.

Just keep going. . . .

There were no more words thereafter. Only an animal howl that surprised him as it erupted from his throat. Rage gripped him, vanquishing thought. Now he longed to kill, to take men's lives.

Spurring his horse, he pointed his saber straight at the far bank, hardly feeling its weight.

"Come on!"

Abruptly, his horse stopped floundering. Hooves bit mud. The animal lifted itself and its burden, mounting that unreachable bank, streaming water. Free of the river, the beast neighed triumphantly.

Astonished to find himself alive, Brown looked back at last. Only three of his volunteers had survived the passage. But they joined him.

And that was all it took. A miracle unfolded. Instead of shooting the riders down, the Rebs leapt from their hides, scooting up the slope by the dozen, quitting.

A cheer went up from the bank Brown had left behind. But there was no time to revel in it. Surely the Rebs would get over their moment of panic. . . .

Rising in his stirrups, Brown waved his sword, shouting and gesturing: *"Come on, come on!"*

The morning's mood had been transfigured, a man felt it like a sharp change in the temperature. Disorganized at first, blue-clad riders sloshed into the river to reinforce him, soon followed by a regiment advancing in column of fours.

Guiding his horse into the underbrush, Brown leaned over the animal's neck and vomited.

Yankees want another thrashing, by God we'll give it to them."

Fitz Lee's rich voice rang above the hoofbeats, a voice that might have belonged to a bigger man. He'd been taken by surprise and didn't much like it. He'd believed the Yankees would lie low a stretch longer, let the river go down while they licked their wounds.

Stuart had taken word of the crossing well, there was that, at least. No hint of recrimination. On the contrary, Stuart seemed to be enjoying himself, accompanying Lee's column for the pleasure of it, as jovial as if off to a parlor call. Of course, riding out to trouble Yankees was considerably more pleasant than another day of court-martial duty, which Stuart had only the day before declared to be his bane. Not like Jackson that way. J. E. B. Stuart preferring cajoling men over judging them. Not like Tom Jackson at all.

After a pause, Stuart bantered back, "Even Yankees can't stay in their burrows forever. Had to come out for some air." He sniffed the gray morning. "Good a day as any to go visiting."

"Ain't that just true," Tom Owen put in. The colonel's 3rd Virginia Cavalry followed behind the generals, trailed by the rest of Lee's Virginia Brigade. "High time they come out."

With Brandy Station and the railroad behind them, the horsemen made for Kelly's Ford at a trot, careful of their none-too-well-fed horses. There'd been a lull in the firing from the ford, still miles away, but the pickets at the river had held long enough to get word back to Culpeper—and for Lee to call in his regiments.

Raw weather, though. Still no hint of the Virginia spring. Their mounts steamed and men breathed white. Whenever they passed a farmhouse, wood smoke teased them: Breakfast there had been none.

Nor coffee, a hot dose of which would have been a tonic, after Judge Shackleford's Saint Patrick's Eve soiree.

Stuart didn't imbibe, of course, and had gone off to bed early. Now his excellent spirits were a bit trying.

The road rose slightly, changing the pitch of the hooves to a dry-dirt clap. Spend enough years in the saddle, a man learned all the sounds a hoof could make, harmonized with the landscape and the weather. Out west, men lived or died by the hammering of shod government mounts or the tap of Comanche ponies.

Out west. Lee's once prized U.S. Army career and his life had almost ended in that vastness, with an arrowhead through his body and the shaft stuck in his guts. Broke off the tip and had them draw out the rest. Screamed just once and wasn't ashamed of it, either. Damn, if he couldn't still feel it sometimes, the oddest sensation, the body violated. He'd reckoned he was dying, all of them had. But Lee blood ran strong. Two hundred miles of jostling in a litter across Texas and he survived. To find himself on horseback this brute morning.

The old blue uniform had gotten fair value from him. He'd paid back his West Point schooling in full, indentured to the Second Cavalry.

Billy Averell had bled out there, too, with the Mounted Rifles. New Mexico Territory, with the Navajo stubborn and hard atop their mesas. Billy had been cut up so bad he'd been placed on the invalid rolls. Came back to fight when the war began, God help him.

Fitz Lee did hope Averell commanded the column passing the river. Couldn't help it, he just delighted in yanking down Billy's pantaloons. Always had. It wasn't meanness, exactly. Just the manly, Christian order of things. Poor old Billy, hatched in Nowhere, New York, born to milk cows and mix salts for a quack. No grace to a life like that, no dignity. Wasn't a wonder the Yankees were heathen jealous of the South, of all things that had grace and showed refinement.

Lee's long beard lofted. Billy was in for a dogging. Love to take him prisoner, see his face.

Hadn't seen Billy face-to-face since Carlisle and the Cavalry School.

An eager horseman overtook them.

"Well now," Stuart hailed the rider, voice pleased with the day, "if it ain't young Pelham himself." His smile widened. "I'm gratified that Miss Shackleford released you, I'd begun to fear that Samson had his hair trimmed."

Raw-eyed, the major saluted. It had indeed been a late night at the judge's.

"Just looking to my responsibilities, General." Pelham's Alabama drawl lazied a sentence out to nigh on a paragraph.

Stuart raised a hand to the rim of his hat, shielding his eyes against an invisible sun. "I *do* see Major Pelham. That is a certainty. But I do not see his guns. It was my impression that he commanded and directed my artillery. Of which we may shortly find ourselves in want. . . ."

"Breathed's on the way, sir. I came on ahead, didn't care to miss the pleasantries. In case the Yankees aren't inclined to stay."

"They won't be so inclined," Fitz Lee told them all.

He was just coming off a bout of the camp trots, nastier turn than usual. Didn't put a man in the best of moods. If that was Billy Averell out there with his pack of clerks, Billy was going to go home well-instructed.

Wasn't even proper sport in it, fighting Yankee cavalry. Almost wished they were better horsemen, showed more grit. Just to keep things lively.

A rider appeared on the road ahead, galloping back toward them. Lee spurred his horse to meet him.

The scout looked jaundiced and starved, but his eyes burned. "Beg to report, sirs . . . Yankees, they're across, all right. Done crossed, all of them. Best part of a division."

"They coming on?" Stuart demanded.

"Not to a muchness, can't really figure 'em that way. But they're across."

Stuart smiled. And the smile became a grin. "Halloo the fox, boys!"

Gilded by youth, Pelham hooted. The major had been dubbed "gallant" by no less than Lee's Uncle Robert. "The Gallant Pelham," adored by maidens. Leaving Fitz and most everyone but Stuart a tad jealous—if Stuart ever felt jealous of any man, it didn't show.

Even Jackson liked Pelham. Indulgently so.

And the major was a splendid artilleryman, none could gainsay it. Brave to an excess, the best gun-monkey in the entire army. Despite that Alabama tone falling just short of a gentleman's.

"Let's get this done," Lee said.

The stone wall was the key. Averell saw that much immediately. Advancing his division cautiously and in good order, he had refused to rely solely on his scouts. The West had taught him to study the landscape personally, trusting no man's eye and no man's word.

He'd been looking out for terrain that would let him fight the way he wanted to fight, the way he believed he could take his revenge on Fitz—and dent the renown of the vaunted Confederate cavalry.

Now he saw that ground.

Despite the setback at the ford, his men were good and capable, Averell knew it. The problem was that his men were better than they themselves believed: better equipped, better mounted, and better trained. They only wanted confidence. The cavalry of the Army of the Potomac needed to win to convince itself that horsemen in gray could actually be defeated.

That queer stone wall, stretching away from a farmyard, was the perfect anchor for the line he envisioned. It not only offered protection for dismounted men but stood too tall for a cavalry charge to risk jumping it as a body.

The Rebs had seen it, too. They'd gotten to the wall first, but with a party too small to hold it. Now they were trying to bluff him until their main force arrived.

He reined in his horse and summoned the two brigade commanders he'd chosen for this day's work. No pair of colonels could have been more unlike: John McIntosh had been, of all things, a midshipman during the War with Mexico, then a man of business; and Nattie Duffié, a still-youthful French aristocrat, had graduated from the Saint-Cyr military academy, commanded light horse in French Africa, been decorated in the Crimea, then wounded at Solferino, only to come to the United States to fight and marry well. McIntosh had the suffering look of a Presbyterian with constricted bowels, but the man was stalwart in a fight, while Count Alfred Napoléon Alexander Duffié might have played a hero on the stage and fought with flair.

"John," Averell began, "you take that wall, drive off those Rebs. And you take it from them the first time you try, do it quick. I don't want any galloping back and forth, this isn't the camp races. Dismount the men you need and do it on foot. No more faint hearts." He tightened his features. "That goes in spades for the Fourth New

York. Tell Cesnola if I see another one of his men run, I'll see him cashiered."

"Yes, sir."

"Then tuck a regiment—a good one—in among those farm shacks. The Rebs will have to come through that gate, after they've tried all else. When they do, we need to hit them from three sides. Then post your other regiments along that wall. Every man dismounted." He gave McIntosh a listen-here-now look. "No fires, no coffee. I want every man who isn't a horse-holder standing behind that wall with his carbine ready."

"Boys do get uneasy . . . fighting on foot."

"Well, they're going to learn better, damn it. Biggest advantage we have is the breech-loading carbine. Man on foot's a better shot than a fool bouncing on the back of a moving horse. And that horse is meant to carry them *toward* the enemy, not away from a fight." He began to turn toward Duffié but reversed toward McIntosh again. "Nobody runs. Shoot them, if they try."

McIntosh nodded.

Averell understood how the men reasoned. They were used to getting whipped, and a man on a horse had a better chance of escaping the enemy than he had on foot. Nor had it helped that, upon crossing the river, they'd captured a few dozen Rebs before they could reach their own horses.

His men were not about to run this day. He turned to Duffié.

"Nattie, your men will extend the line to the left, beyond that wall. But your brigade stays mounted. Mounted, but stationary. Mask them as well as you can along that tree line. If assaulted, deliver carbine fire from the saddle. Otherwise, hold your position. Until you get my next orders." Envisioning it all, he added, "The Rebs will go for the wall, they'll misjudge it. Fitz has got more confidence than sense, and his temper's going to be up. All right, *move*."

The Frenchman offered a sharp salute, McIntosh a reserved one.

"Damn it, John, get going," Averell told the latter. "You grab that wall. And not one step back thereafter."

He intended to maintain control. He'd seen too many promising starts dissolve into chaos and loss. This was going to be a disciplined fight, and Fitz would not set the terms. Fitz would attack impetuously, expecting to sweep all before him. And Fitz was about to face steadied carbines that could outshoot and outrange by far the revolvers the Rebs relied on in the attack.

Oh, they made a grand show, the Johnnies, coming on howling and firing. But a Reb-mounted charge was better at frightening men than at killing them.

Averell intended to do some killing.

Tom Owen had gotten his orders from Fitz Lee, but the plan wasn't working. The generals and colonels heading the column had spotted the Yankees clinging to a stone wall, afraid to advance. Fitz had ordered the 3rd Virginia forward, specifying that Owen precede his charge with skirmishers who would ride forward, dismount, and fire to keep the Yankees' heads down.

But his skirmishers had not fared well. It was a fool thing to send them to fight in the open against blue-bellies behind a wall and quick with their carbines. Cursing their own unwieldy arms, his skirmishers fell back having barely started. Theatrically usurping Owen's role, Stuart had ridden forward himself to rally them.

And Stuart had failed.

Well, he'd been ordered to charge those Yankees, and Tom Owen meant to do it. A charge made more sense than fooling with skirmishers, anyway—that was infantry fighting, slow and timid. Owen had yet to encounter a Yankee defense his boys couldn't ride right through, around, or over. Nor had he met Yankee cavalrymen afoot who had the vitals to stand up to a mounted charge.

Owen told his bugler, "Toot your horn, Darby." Raising his Colt, he led the regiment forward, still in column of fours, as he tried to spy out the gap that had to be there. Every wall had its openings.

Go right over it if they had to, though.

As the horsemen moved through a canter and swelled to a gallop, the old, familiar thunder rattled the world. Hooves found solid ground beneath patches of snow, biting the earth. His men began yipping and yelling. Instinctively, Owen bent forward, whipped by his horse's mane. He rode with his right elbow cocked, ready to extend the pistol when the moment came.

His men became one mighty beast, a behemoth formed of hundreds, irresistible. Drawing abreast of Owen, Major Carrington rode with his reins in his teeth and two pistols drawn.

Owen had to turn the column abruptly, confronted with a rail fence that a fold in the ground had concealed—too risky to jump en masse. He'd spotted a derelict gate, though, broken and left ajar. Jerking his horse rightward, he led the way. But the gateway could not pass more than two men abreast.

Nothing to be done. Owen and Carrington pounded through the gap. Yankee artillery, a hidden battery, opened.

Rounds shrieked toward them, fused to burst in the air. Its impetus broken, the regiment jammed up and funneled through the gate, jostling boot against flank, spur chiming off spur. The best-mounted men backed off to get a good start and leapt the fence.

Determined to regain momentum, Owen kicked his horse forward the moment he judged he had gathered half his command, ordering his men to re-form on the move. Had to accept some disorganization and put his trust in spunk.

He could see the stone wall clearly now, running left from the route he'd been forced to take. It was higher than he'd judged from across the fields. And he did not see an opening, a gate.

On his right, a rifle shot distant, mounted Yankees waited in perfect alignment, the ultimate size of their force masked by swales and windrows. But they had no wall to protect them.

He was tempted to go right at them, horse to horse, numbers be damned.

But Owen had been ordered to take that wall, and he meant to do it. Anyway, dismounted Yankees were quickest to break. That wall could protect them but couldn't make them brave. And Owen reckoned they'd cling to it too long.

Might take a nice haul of prisoners. And some much-needed remounts.

As more riders joined him, he wheeled the regiment leftward, bearing down on the wall at a slant, seeking out the gate that had to be there.

Carbine fire exploded, knocking riders down.

"Sumbitch," he snarled.

There *had* to be an opening. . . .

The Yankee artillery shortened its range. Men flew from their saddles. Mounts twisted and shrieked.

Surely there was a way. . . .

As far as John Pelham was concerned, the three finest things on God's earth were a well-bred horse, a yellow-haired woman, and Yankees bending over to take their licking. Wasn't at all certain he'd be able to settle himself on Pap's holdings along Cane Creek, once all this was over. How could a man of spirit endure the calm of a farm dressed up for Sunday and calling itself a plantation? Might have to leave Alabama and go west, at least to Texas. Or even to Mexico, where the pot was stirring.

His lead section was up, but Breathed could place it. Pelham reckoned he had some time for sport. And when Fitz Lee ordered the 5th Virginia forward to help Tom Owen, Pelham asked leave to ride along and didn't wait for an answer.

Yankee artillery was shooting well, but his men would see to that.

Rejecting Owen's flawed line of advance, Colonel Rosser led the 5th leftward, around the end of a fence, before unfolding his column to charge the Yankees. Owen's boys had been stymied by that wall, and Rosser inclined his regiment to avoid mingling the commands as long as possible.

Little else of what Pelham saw made sense. No one seemed to have a clear objective. Riders skirted the wall and got shot down, their revolvers all but useless against massed carbines. Amid growing confusion, commands contradicted each other.

An artillery burst in midair left a horse streaming gore, its rider cast down and trampled.

Despite Rosser's stab at maneuvering, the regiments collided. There was just no place to go, with that man-killing wall in the way. No one had scouted things properly: They'd just done the thing that had always worked before, pitching into the Yankees.

Now their plight would take some serious fixing.

Pelham steered his gray through the muddle. The firing was so intense a fog of gun smoke obscured the Yankees, their presence revealed only by muzzle blazes and toppling Confederates. The frustrated troopers cursed the Yankees, emptying their revolvers and making clumsy efforts to reload on horseback.

Gun-smell, horse-smell, man-smell. Blood steaming in the cold, freezing in puddles.

Something was happening, though. Abruptly, there was movement on the left.

Carrington of the 3rd waved a revolver. *Over here.*

They'd found a gap in the wall, a gate uncovered. Pelham fol lowed a breakaway band of riders heading straight for it, muscling their way through.

Yankees were going to pay now, going to pay dearly.

Despite the morning's chill, sweat gripped his back.

His horse reared and resisted, a rare thing. As if it didn't want to carry him forward. He gave it both spurs.

His mount obeyed and bore him toward the gate.

A Yankee shell burst overhead and Pelham fell to earth.

Owen had found his gap. But as his men poured into the farmyard, they took Yankee fire from three sides, from doors and windows, corners and thrown-up barricades, a terrible volume of fire, sudden and lethal: a perfect ambush.

His men could not press through the opening swiftly enough to mass in sufficient numbers. The Yankees even advanced on foot, startlingly confident, firing their carbines with dexterity, out for revenge of their own. Gray-clad riders yanked their horses about, looking for a chance to turn the tables, revolvers clicking empty.

Separated from his bugler, Owen rode through the stink of smoke and manure, waving his men back, shouting, *"Withdraw . . . withdraw . . ."*

He squeezed back through the gate himself, ashamed and outraged.

Major Carrington reached him as Owen struggled to bully his men into order.

"Carried off Major Pelham, sir. Hit back of the neck."

"Serious?"

"Unconscious. Can't really tell. Not much blood, but . . ." Carrington waved his hand and looked away.

Owen shook his head. "What was the damned fool doing out here?"

Pursued by Yankee artillery, Yankee carbine fire, and Yankee cheers, he led his disordered command back across the field.

He's dying," the regimental surgeon said. "Penetrated the nape of the neck, the brain."

Stuart looked down at the litter, robbed of words. His eyes glittered.

"Take him back to Culpeper," Fitz Lee ordered. "Do what you can. Get him to Judge Shackleford's, Gilmore can see to it. Do all you can."

Sabers!"

At Duffié's command, every cavalryman within the range of his voice scraped his blade free. In moments, the remainder of the brigade imitated their comrades.

The colonel told his bugler: "Sound 'Forward.'"

Bright notes pierced the battle noise as no man's voice could do. A thousand riders emerged from black-boned trees, horses at a walk.

Duffié had seen a splendid opportunity. With at least two Reb regiments engaged and flailing about, the remaining two or three holding back were fixed in place, facing the fight. They offered him a miraculous chance to strike them on the flank, to rout them with superior power and numbers.

With no obstacles in his path of the sort that had frustrated the graybacks, the colonel nodded to the bugler keeping pace. Different notes pierced the morning.

As the host rose to a canter, the earth complained.

Across the long field, the Rebs awoke from their trance. Duffié could not hear, but well imagined, the frantic commands of their officers. The Confederate horsemen shuffled clumsily, misaligned.

Again, Duffié gestured to the bugler. And this time he thrust out his saber and added a shout:

"Charge!"

Still maintaining their long, successive lines with handsome discipline, his regiments spurred their mounts and roared, *"Hurrah!"*

The ground shook beneath them. Duffié could feel it right up through his saddle.

Sabers. *L'arme blanche*. "Cold steel," as Americans put it. Duffié respected every weapon put in the hands of his horsemen, but he still believed, with a conviction resembling profound religious faith, that a saber charge at the proper moment cut to the cavalry's soul.

He recalled the magnificent charge at Solferino. His wound had been nothing measured against *la gloire*.

The distance between the forces closed in seconds. Formed into ragged ranks, the Johnnies spurred forward, attempting to gain momentum of their own.

Despite the gloom of the winter's day, a thousand sabers gleamed along Duffié's lines. Howling, the Rebs plunged toward them, some lofting sabers, others relying on pistols.

Duffié curled his wrist and leaned into his horse's neck, preparing to slash to the right then hack left. He'd been not the best, but the second-best man with a saber at Saint-Cyr.

The blade was truth.

The lines collided with a shock. Horses overturned and riders tumbled. Pistols spit. Blades clanged. Shouts. Screams. Driven beyond words, men growled like animals. Those slow of hand or unlucky splashed enemies and comrades alike with blood.

In perfect control of his saber, Duffié turned a Johnny out of the saddle, striking so deftly the man shot himself in the leg. Then Duffié rose in his stirrups and twisted leftward. Meeting steel with steel, he parried a new opponent and gracefully slashed open the fellow's skull.

Amid the general fury, a gaunt-faced boy raised his pistol toward Duffié's chest.

Before the lad could pull the trigger, Duffié severed his hand at the wrist. The Reb stared in wonder at the spurting blood where his paw had been.

Saber fighting, if properly done, rivaled the ballet at the Paris Opera. Although men, Duffié knew, were not half as cruel as those women.

Bludgeoned, the Johnnies began to pull back, first in small bands then by regiments.

Duffié's bugler remained near, horn slung and pistol smoking.

"Sound 'Recall,'" Duffié told him. "Quickly."

He knew the Rebs. They were far more adept than the Austrians. They'd come back at his men swiftly, hoping to seize the upper hand with a countercharge.

Duffié never forgot his lessons: All the lamp-lit texts had revealed their worth over the years. And one maxim drilled into every cavalry cadet was that a squadron was most at risk when disordered by success.

The Rebs didn't waste a second. With Duffié's men hastily reforming amid crazed horses, the fear-eyed wounded, and the astonished dead, the lean regiments of Johnnies turned back and charged with a howl.

Hooves threw dirty snow and clots of mud.

"Charge!" Duffié bellowed. His bugler spread the command.

This time, the Johnnies held the edge in momentum. The impact was ferocious. Reb pistols aimed into faces, chests, groins, thighs. Some revolvers were batted away, but others found their targets.

Then revolvers clicked empty, and graybacks were struck down in turn. Nor had their leaders calculated well. Duffié's large brigade flanked them on both ends.

Again, the Rebs pulled back. Duffié could feel their anger, their shock. He imagined glaring eyes and blasphemies.

They wouldn't come back for a third bout. Not on this ground. They'd want to do it, yearn to hit back right now. But their ranking officers would come to their senses at last and start to think. Their next charge would come on terrain the Rebs selected.

The withdrawing Johnnies didn't halt but passed into a grove. That drew a cheer from Duffié's men, from winter-raw throats. The fighting had all but ceased on the right as well. By the long stone wall.

A Union gun fired a last round and fell silent.

Colonel Alfred Napoléon Alexander Duffié, late of the 4th Chasseurs d'Afrique, re-formed his men for a second time and waited for new orders.

Averell rode up, trailed by his retinue, and he was livid.

"Christ in a corncrib, Duffié, I told you to hold your position!"

The Frenchman shrugged. "It seemed an opportunity, *mon Général.*" He gestured at the dead and wounded, at his men who had taken this ground from the Rebels and held it. "It was not badly done, I think."

"This isn't a cathouse, damn it, *you* don't get to choose. You will adhere—strictly—to my plan from this moment on." He grunted. "Don't they teach you to obey orders in France?" Another grunt. "Colonel, you won't wipe your nose without an order from me. Or you will be relieved of your command. Do you understand me?"

Their horses pawed, impatient of human quarrels.

Again, Duffié shrugged. "I do my best. If this does not suffice . . ."

Exasperated, Averell searched the faces of the gathered officers—none of them eager to approach much closer. "You, Reno," he called out to the captain commanding the Regulars, "explain military discipline to the Count of Monte Cristo, would you?"

Without waiting for an acknowledgment from the captain, Averell turned back to Duffié. "Hold this position until McIntosh moves up. When his men come on line with yours, you can go forward. Advance at a walk, and don't halt until ordered. Then don't move another step until further ordered. Understand?"

In the distance, from the direction of Brandy Station, a locomotive shrieked.

"Hear that?" Averell demanded. "That could be their reinforcements."

The colonel shook his head. Mildly. "But this is an old trick, General. Always with the trains, the commotion, to make us believe they are stronger. If they bring more men, I think, the train does not make such a noise to warn us."

Aflame in the cold, Averell told him, "It may be some damned trick, or it may not. But I'm the one who decides which chances this division takes. And this command will move and fight with discipline. Understand?"

Duffié offered an indulgent, impeccable smile: There was always another army, another war, another adventure—although he quite liked the United States, where even a count's youngest son was regarded by society as an archduke. In France, he could not have married such great wealth—and the girl was handsome.

"All this is clear," he told his commanding officer. "Now it is most clear. *Je comprends.*" He reached out toward Averell, as if about to pat him on the wrist. "I regret that I have made you unhappy, *cher Général.* But I think that the Rebels are more unhappy, *non*?"

Fitz Lee was unhappy. Damnably so. And furious. Seething. Bowels clenched as tightly as his jaw. His mount seemed to cower under him, reading his mood.

On top of it all, he'd lost his left glove. Wouldn't say a word about it, but the raw cold bit.

His gloves had been a Christmas gift from the best woman on earth.

Around him, his men withdrew sullenly, awaiting the command to halt and fight. They'd had to leave their wounded behind, a rare occurrence.

Only Stuart bothered to feign high spirits. "Reckon we leapt before we looked," he announced. Banishing thoughts of Pelham, he even grinned. "Learned ourselves a lesson, I'd call that useful. Do better this afternoon. Teach the Yankees something they can show Mammy. . . ." In a voice redolent of banjos, Stuart added, "Anybody can stand behind a stone wall. Let them come on out and they'll get their licking."

Mistrustful of his likely tone, Lee did not reply. But he thought: Wasn't the damned wall. Fool business to go right at it, that was true, but that wasn't where the trousers pinched. No, it was that charge the Yankees made. And the ease with which they had repelled his countercharge. No blue-bellied outfit had ever performed like that, not on horseback in an open fight. . . .

He knew the rule that it took two years to mature a cavalryman. Now the Yankees had had almost two years.

He shook himself, intent on shedding the twinge of alarm. One charge didn't portend much, after all. Just a hard-luck morning. He ordered himself to believe it, as the ghost of that last bout of camp trots plagued his innards.

Stuart tried again to lift his spirits. "Fitz, you look like you've been run out of the kitchen without your cornbread. Myself, I blame those carbines. Downright unfair. Have to capture us more of them, even things up." He chuckled. Falsely, falsely.

Neither man spoke of Pelham. His loss was too near, too dispiriting. Sorrowing had to be set aside as long as there was fighting to be done.

And there was going to be more fighting.

Lee spoke at last: "I'm going to drive them. By God, I'm going to drive them."

"That's the spirit, that's my Fitz. How's that next stand of trees look, fix ourselves there? Get a little elevation and clear lines of sight, give our own guns a chance." Stuart licked flaking lips. "Excellent ground for maneuver, to my eye."

Lee regarded the line of bare trees, the snow left in the lees. Then he scanned the open ground with a killer's eyes.

"I'm going to cover that field with Yankee bodies," he promised Stuart.

Marcus Reno would have been a colonel, had he made the jump to the Volunteers, but he loved the Regular Army and he was stubborn. He'd loved the Army's traditions since West Point, where he'd done worse than some and better than others. Now he cherished the gunmetal mornings, the savage bite of coffee cooked in haste, and the waking light. It had always been thus, the delights carved out of misery. His memories were scented with campfires curling smoke in the Washington Territory, and with temptations to which he had sometimes succumbed: No man who had passed through for a single night forgot San Francisco, its raw whores, murderous drams, and voracious bedbugs. His garrison had been elsewhere, though, in the godforsaken scants of Walla Walla, and the duty of the 1st Dragoons had consisted of fruitless pursuits through boundless timber. Now all that seemed a lifetime away, although it was hardly two years, since men now divided had shared their bottles and sins.

What a different, innocent world it had been, their debauchery that of children, their ambitions petty. He recalled his pride in minor commendations, in a major's stingy praise for a brevet lieutenant on payday parade at a forlorn post the paymaster finally remembered, the impoverished spectacle watched by broken Indians unable to comprehend the white man's rituals. Nearly two years into this war, Reno remained astonished that a soldier could lose a blanket or even his rifle and not face a board of inquiry. On the frontier, lieutenants had feared the quartermaster's logs and signature chits far more than they feared Indians. This lurch from parsimony to abundance had been a greater shock than the general slaughter.

The Army was his life, it never wavered. Even this war was but another interlude, and his Regular captaincy would count for something out on the Plains, where the Army's postwar rump would surely find itself.

No, he would not join the Volunteers, for whom service was an onerous necessity. He felt himself at his best flanked by old sergeants, sour-mouthed fellows who cherished their trade, old before their time and scarred by service, cored by every disease from the pits of vice, men who kept their weapons flawlessly clean, even if water rarely met their bodies. The bugle sounding reveille was Gabriel's call to Reno, and he ate poor food with zest. The Army was a calling that could not be reasoned out, but duty rewarded those of sturdy faith. A Regular captain, he commanded two regiments this day—the 5th U.S. and his old 1st Dragoons, rechristened the 1st U.S. Cavalry—and he led them with a firm hand and masked affection.

So when Averell, after a slow advance that gnawed the afternoon, ordered them all to halt and extend a division line facing the enemy, Reno took his position on the flank without reservation, curling the 5th U.S. to master the ground. But the next order, shouted by a puffed-up aide, was surprising and rigid: When the Rebs attacked—which they certainly would, and vengefully—each cavalryman was to steady his mount and hold his ground, not one step forward or backward, and greet the Johnnies with a volley from massed carbines at one hundred yards. After that, every man would fire as rapidly as possible. There would be no retreat, but no charges, either.

Reno shrugged, conditioned to obedience. He'd taken his share of orders he didn't like, and that, too, was the Army. Averell was just ill-tempered today and far more cautious than usual, but independent command sat heavy on some. And if Averell was no genius, he was no fool. He'd keep them out of trouble. Still, Reno would have liked to combine Averell's approach with a dab of

Duffié's dash. The Frenchman would have been a caution in the peacetime Army, but he shone on the battlefield. If only you could take the best of both. . . .

Reno passed on the order: *Steady your mounts, rely on your carbines, and don't move an* inch *until ordered.* His first sergeants, all whiskers, broken teeth, and rotten loins, snorted their distaste but saluted smartly. One merely observed, "Ain't we got horses beneath us to move us handsome, Captain, sir?"

"No mouth from you, Brady. And remind your men to aim at the chests of the horses. They just might hit something."

Well, there seems to be a lot of them," Stuart observed. "Out in the open now, though."

"Line's long," Lee allowed. "But only one deep. Hit their center hard, punch right through." He closed his fist around the tip of his beard, a nervous habit. "Then it'll be a race back to the ford. Which they will lose."

"Surely," Stuart said. After a pause, he added, "I recommend you put everyone in this time." Lee noticed that his commander's lips were cracked to bleeding. It had been a long winter and didn't want to quit. "Only a recommendation, of course."

Miles to their rear, the locomotive shrilled again, announcing another arrival of nothing at all. Lee did wish he had another brigade. For the surety of it. But he'd made do before, with less. And his boys had their dander up now, gone surly and hard.

He intended to do it properly this time, though. Let Jim Breathed show the Yankees how to handle a battery. Deploy skirmishers in good order. Then he would, indeed, put everyone in.

Reno couldn't figure it. The Reb horse artillery was always aggressive, but rarely reckless to the point of folly. Now their lone battery begged for destruction, without any good effect, and Reno could not understand it.

The Reb guns had been driven out of successive positions, outranged and outshot by their Union counterparts. They seemed to have a problem with bad ammunition, too: Many Confederate shells just plowed up dirt. The impacts barely made horses shy.

The duel dragged on, though, through peak afternoon, as the two small hosts held their ground a half mile apart, bound to their saddles, each waiting on the other.

Were the Johnnies scared? That was unlikely.

The advantage in numbers did tilt blue, though. That much seemed clear enough.

Were they prodding Averell to attack them? Did they have a surprise waiting, some hidden reserve? That didn't feel right, either. With more men, the Johnnies would have attacked already. And made it stick.

The Rebs were masterful bluffers, of course: They played fine battlefield poker. And Reno's instinct said they were bluffing now. Had he been in command, he would have ordered a general attack.

Duffié was itchy, too, it was so obvious it was almost laughable. Kepi atilt and mustaches perfect despite his early saber-work, he trotted up to "inspect the flank," but, really, for a chat. The French were supposed to be devious, but the colonel was a simple man to read: He loved to fight, although it was poor form to say so.

Duffié had a prince's air and a workman's wrists. A man who fought with sabers needed two things to survive: quick reflexes and strong wrists. During the first year of the war, the cavalry had lost more new men to broken wrists than they'd lost to Rebel bullets.

"You have done well," the Frenchman told him. "You and your men. The charge this morning was properly done, I applaud you." He drew out a silver case, offering a cheroot.

Reno accepted: Good tobacco was rare now, and Duffié's would be fine. "We ought to charge them again. This minute."

The colonel shrugged and sighed, searching his greatcoat for a lucifer match. "General Averell has his plan. His plan must be our plan. *La vie militaire . . .*"

Reno bent from the saddle toward a shared light. The first suck of tobacco came rich and welcome. "Fool's errand just to sit here. Time's on their side, not ours."

"You see this as I do, of course," the Frenchman said. "But we make no difference." Across the fields, the Reb guns tried again. Union artillery replied immediately. "I think they will attack soon," Duffié went on. "They must settle things. Their pride."

Just as Duffié spoke the last word, a grand line of horsemen emerged from the far groves and swelled over low crests. It looked to Reno as though the Johnnies were going to send in every man they could.

"You see?" Duffié asked. "Their pride, it is always their pride."

Major General J. E. B. Stuart led the right wing of the attack himself. He smiled and teased those around him, making a grand display of confidence as every regiment present advanced at a walk.

The Yankee guns had their range, and their shells paced the advance. Stuart felt, again, the loss of Pelham. Young Breathed would do fine, in time. Medical doctor, of all things. Just needed time. But time was an item running short today.

The Yankees had to be punished, humiliated. Beaten down like chicken-killing dogs. Stuart would say it to no man, but he knew the Yankees could not be allowed to build up confidence. Nor could his men doubt their invincibility. So he laughed at untold jokes and remarked, "I do wish the Yankees had brought them along a band. Wouldn't mind a tune, something with spirit."

"Catch 'em up and make 'em give us'ns a concert," a good soul said. "One of them fat German bands."

"Germans do make fine musicians," Stuart agreed. Letting Lee set the pace, he waited for the bugle call. Fitz was trimming things awfully fine: Yankee guns were finding targets.

They *had* to give the Yankees a proper whipping. Send them running. *Had* to do it. The way they'd done it dozens of times before.

The bugle sounded. The line broke into a canter.

Stuart scanned the Yankee position. Hoping they'd come out. Expecting it. Desiring to meet them head-on in the open.

But the Yankees remained as still as if on a parade ground.

What were they up to now? They had no stone wall here.

The canter became a gallop. The wild yelling challenged the foe, a blood-remembered battle cry from ancient moors and glens.

The Yankees didn't move. But for the shake of a horse's head or pawing hooves here and there, the Union line might have been frozen to a man.

Eight hundred riders neared the Union line at full gallop.

Two hundred yards.

One hundred fifty.

Shouting, Stuart pointed with his saber.

One hundred twenty . . .

"Carbines up!" The command, repeated instantly, rang down through brigades and regiments.

The Rebel tide seemed about to overwhelm them, unstoppable. But the cavalrymen in blue obeyed their orders, fitting carbines to their shoulders and taking aim.

"Fire!"

The noise punched ears harder than recoils punched shoulders. The artillery discharged canister. The effect was immediate.

Trailing guts, horses shrieked. Forelegs caved, men flew past bridles. Gore swabbed the air. Bleeding riders fought to master their mounts. The luckiest and bravest Johnnies fired useless pistols.

Fresh rounds thrust into chambers. A second wave of carbine fire rippled then roared. Troopers reloaded with once unthinkable speed, firing at will as the Rebs sought to recover.

Saving his pistol's ammunition for the countercharge that would surely be ordered, Reno watched as two flanking guns and his Regulars' volleys bit into the Rebs. A burst of canister tore off a horse's leg and the leg of its rider, hurling the severed limbs into the chaos. Reno's lines were not even assaulted—the Rebel front didn't stretch far enough. Elsewhere along the Union line, it didn't appear that a single Johnny got within eighty yards.

Rebs in a confusion of uniforms emptied last rounds from their cylinders and shook their fists. Reno had never seen the Confederate cavalry so easily trounced.

Why didn't Averell's bugler sound the charge? With the 5th Cavalry alone, Reno could have struck the Rebs' flank and rear, could have swept them up. He'd not had such a chance in the entire war. . . .

"Parker," he shouted to his adjutant. "Ride to Colonel Duffié. Tell him I need permission to charge, I can finish them."

The lieutenant needed no encouragement. He spurred his horse to draw blood.

Seconds mattered. As the Union line poured out fire, the Johnnies struggled to restore their order. Their vulnerability would disappear in a blink.

No Union bugle sounded.

Reno was tempted to order a charge on his own authority. But he simply could not do it, he could not disobey a lawful order. Too damned much of an Army man, he thought ruefully, determined never to stand before a court-martial.

He wanted to lash out with sabers, to hack right through the Rebs, cut them all down.

What was Averell thinking? They could sweep them all up right now, for the love of God.

The Rebs began to withdraw. Pulling their horses about and spurring them. Galloping back toward safety.

Reno rode out in front of his line, struggling with himself. Tempted again to give the order to charge, career be damned.

A shell fragment—from the one Reb shell that exploded—struck his horse's eye, exploding meat and blood and bone.

The animal dropped sideward.

Reno went down with his mount. The beast pinned his right leg.

"Get it off me," he shouted. "Get the damned thing off me."

He didn't feel pain. Not yet. Only desperation.

Sergeants and nearby privates dismounted and rushed to coax up the horse, but the animal died, its bowels and bladder emptying. The weight on Reno's leg felt as though it had doubled.

"Are ye hit, Captain, sir? Are ye hit, man?" a flush-faced sergeant with lethal breath demanded.

"Just get it off me. Get this goddamned thing off me."

Men tugged and pulled, their actions a grim comedy.

Reno felt the weight begin to lift. Impatient, he yanked his leg with all his might.

"God!" he howled. Something had torn in his groin. He clutched himself, pain-shocked. "God," he called again, this time with a moan.

All he could think was that they should have charged.

The Rebs abandoned their position a second time, riding off slowly.

Pestered, Averell watched them go.

"General," Duffié tried again, "we are letting go a great chance. Permit me to take my brigade, at least. Only my brigade, if you—"

"We should *all* go." That was McIntosh. "Both brigades, every man. Hit them with everything. They're whipped, we could crush them now."

"It would be a great victory," the Frenchman added.

It was already victory enough, Averell believed. He didn't say it, didn't try to explain, but this was just the victory he wanted. Perhaps they could do more, but he could not bring himself to take the chance, to throw away what this day had achieved: The cavalry of the Army of the Potomac had beaten off every charge of the proudest horsemen in Confederate service, Fitz's Virginia Brigade. He knew that much from the prisoners taken, men bleeding and bewildered. He knew for certain that Fitz was on the field. Some Rebs insisted that Stuart was present, too. And both men had been beaten.

He didn't intend to give Fitz the least chance to get his own back. Averell's men had learned what they could do—and they believed they could do still more, the evidence was here in these rambunctious colonels.

But the day was fading and soon the light would go. He wanted his men back across the river by dark. Not that he looked forward to the swim. Christ, he did recall the cold of that water. Still not dried out, boots and stockings sopping.

"That's enough," he told his brigade commanders. "Return to your men."

Scouts reported that the Rebs had halted a mile away, behind a minor stream called Carter's Run.

"Plenty of them just hopping along on foot," a sergeant reported. "Lost them plenty of horses. Keep on dropping, too, sorry-looking horseflesh."

When the war began, the Confederate mounts had been splendid. And plentiful.

When Averell didn't reply, the sergeant added, "We could grab us up a pack of prisoners, sir."

Averell was tempted. Not just to gather in prisoners, but to order a grand attack, after all. But the impulse was fleeting. He had his plan and he intended to stick to it.

Turning to his bugler, he ordered, "Sound the division recall."

By the rules of war, it does count as your victory," Stuart consoled him. "The Yankees abandoned the field."

They rode through the twilight, horses stepping gingerly amid the generous trash left by the Yankees. The blue-bellies did enjoy lives of abundance.

When Lee did not reply, Stuart tried another approach—he couldn't have his key subordinate brooding.

"We just didn't have the numbers, Fitz."

The evening promised an overnight freeze.

"Never needed numbers before."

Stuart forced a smile. "You know what Napoléon said. 'God's on the side of the big battalions,' something like that." Instantly, he regretted saying it. If the Lord truly sided with the big battalions, the South was doomed.

Lee didn't reply. His sulk approached rudeness. Stuart let it go.

Bad day all around. Although it didn't do to say it out loud. It counted as a near miracle that the Yankees had not come at them with all they had right at the end. Easy enough to pretty up his report, though, give Fitz credit, boost him a touch. After all, the Yankees *did* retire.

As the pair of generals and their retinues neared the now worthless stone wall, Lieutenant Ransom rode in from the ford. He'd been on a scout, at Stuart's suggestion and Lee's sour command.

"Yankees all run off?" Stuart asked, lightening his voice.

"Yes, sir. All back across." Man and horse panted. "Excepting some of their wounded, the bad ones. Yanks left two surgeons with them. Not far off, y'all want to parley some."

"I reckon the surgeons are busy," Stuart allowed.

The lieutenant turned to Lee. "One of the docs said this was left for you, sir." He swung out a half-filled burlap sack.

Lee took it and undid the string. Instantly, he smelled coffee, dark and lascivious.

There was a note stuck in the bag as well.

"Strike me up a match, Lieutenant," Lee ordered. "Lean it over here."

The note read:

Dear Fitz,

Here's your coffee. Here's your visit.

How'd you like it?

Bill

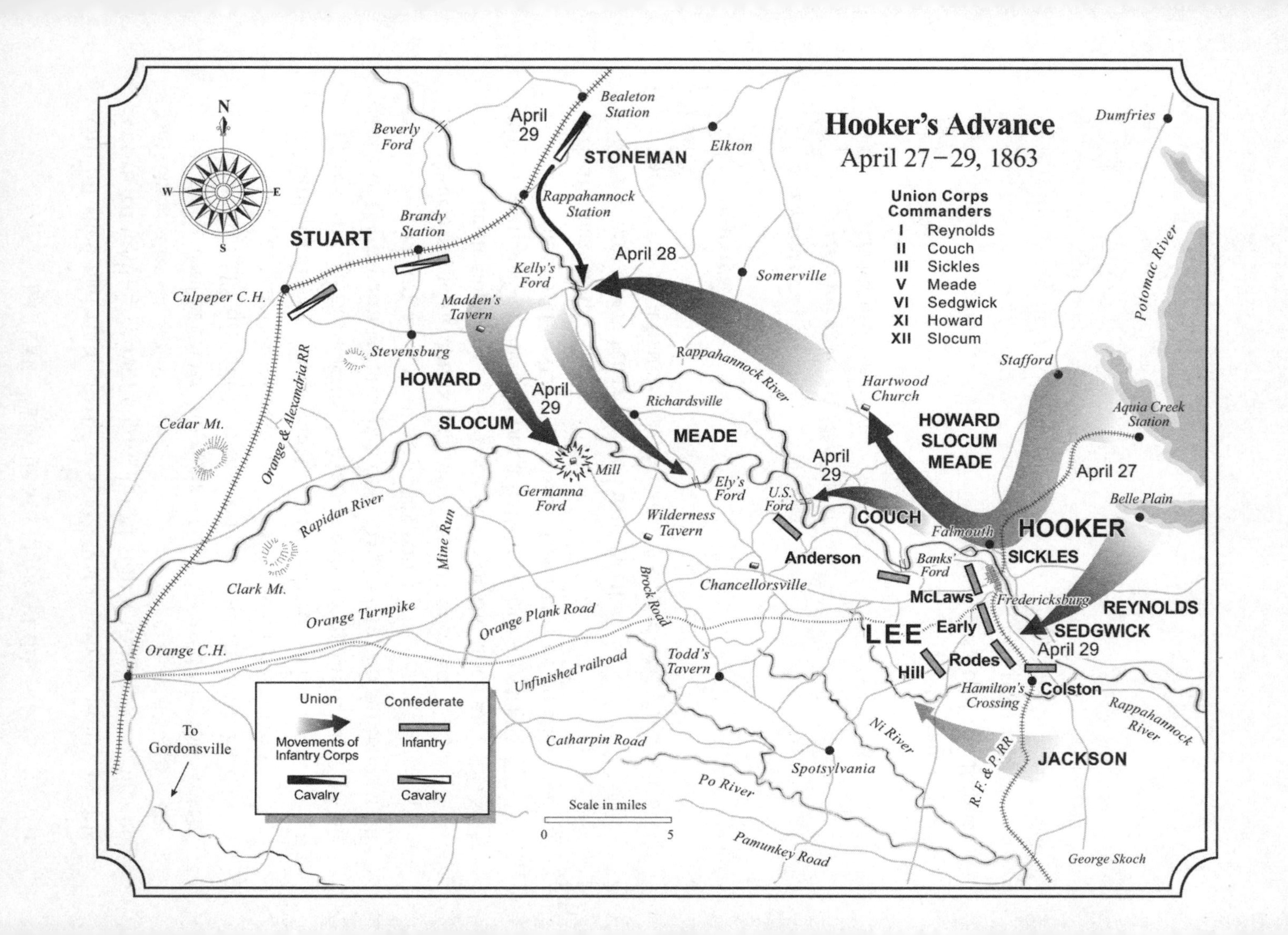

Hooker's Advance
April 27–29, 1863
Union Corps Commanders
I Reynolds
II Couch
III Sickles
V Meade
VI Sedgwick
XI Howard
XII Slocum
Union
Movements of Infantry Corps
Cavalry
Confederate
Infantry
Cavalry
Scale in miles
0
5
To Gordonsville
Orange C.H.
Orange Turnpike
Orange Plank Road
Unfinished railroad
Catharpin Road
Po River
Pamunkey Road
Spotsylvania
Ni River
Todd's Tavern
Brock Road
Clark Mt.
Cedar Mt.
Culpeper C.H.
Orange & Alexandria RR
Rapidan River
Mine Run
STUART
Stevensburg
Brandy Station
Beverly Ford
HOWARD
SLOCUM
Madden's Tavern
Kelly's Ford
April 29
Germanna Ford
Mill
Rappahannock Station
Bealeton Station
STONEMAN
April 28
Richardsville
MEADE
Wilderness Tavern
Ely's Ford
Elkton
Rappahannock River
Somerville
Chancellorsville
U.S. Ford
Anderson
April 29
COUCH
Hartwood Church
HOWARD
SLOCUM
MEADE
LEE
Hill
Rodes
Early
McLaws
Banks' Ford
Falmouth
Fredericksburg
SICKLES
HOOKER
Stafford
April 27
Aquia Creek Station
Potomac River
Dumfries
Belle Plain
Hamilton's Crossing
Colston
April 29
SEDGWICK
REYNOLDS
R. F. & P. RR
JACKSON
Rappahannock River
George Skoch

ONE

Late morning, April 29
Germanna Ford on the Rapidan River, Virginia

Amid green leaves and birdsong, in a world scented by sawdust and quick water, Corporal Bill Smith watched and listened and waited, letting the officers have their way with the visitor. Didn't do any good to interfere, but he had to know what the fuss was all about. The pair of captains—two men assigned to do the job of none—weren't always inclined to share what little they knew, even with each other. And Smith had a bridge to build, since nobody with rank on his collar seemed able and willing to do it.

The withered farmer shifted his weight from leg to leg, a parody of a soldier undone by the camp trots.

"Yankees, I tell you," the old man all but shouted. "Passels of 'em, crossing at Kelly's Ford ever since last night."

In that disdainful voice of his, a voice bred to raise hackles, Captain Tyler said:

"Sure now. We're grateful for your concern, sir." He touched his hat as if to tip it, but didn't. "Any Yankees this side of the Rappahannock won't be nothing but scouts wearing out their horses."

The old man flushed crimson. "Damn me, boy . . . I seen me enough of you folks and them'uns to tell a man on a horse from one afoot. And I'm telling you Yankee *infantry* come across, thick as the legions of Hell. And they're headed this way, fast as cloven hooves can bring 'em along." He reached out to calm his sweated mule, which had taken up his excitement, then turned back to the captain with fresh fierceness. "You been warned, boy. Be it on your head. You done been warned."

"Had any Yankees crossed that river in force, we would've had word." Tyler's voice cut, managing to imply not only that the farmer was a fool, but that he might have made his breakfast of applejack.

To soften the sting of Tyler's tone, his fellow captain—another of the army's abundance of Smiths—told the old man, "Warning taken, sir. Much obliged. We'll keep us a proper lookout, thank you kindly."

Rope-muscle forearms quivering, the farmer all but spit. "You don't believe me neither, sonny. Figure me for an old fool." He shook a head carved by decades of sun and wind. "Ain't none so blind as them what will not see."

The farmer jacked himself back into his saddle. His mule still heaved. "Reckon I'll go on home and see if the Yankees et what little was left." He cast a hard look at the pair of captains. "And thank you for your fine defense of Virginia."

Corporal Smith didn't share the disinterest of the officers. Mannerly rivals one to the other, Tyler of his scorned 12th Virginia and Captain Smith of the 41st had been detailed because they could best be spared by their regiments. The party had been dispatched the week before, at the Cavalry Corps' request, two understrength companies, along with a handful of carpenters and pioneers entrusted to Smith and his stripes, and a shiftless pack of Posey's Mississippians. A hundred and forty heads when the roll was called, their task was to erect a new bridge on the foundations of one destroyed in the last year's campaigning. The captains treated the mission as a lark, a chance to call at neighboring plantations, and even the sergeants weren't much minded to help, so the serious doings had fallen to Smith and his boys.

And Corporal Bill Smith didn't trust the Yankees. He'd learned in fights behind the schoolyard privy not to trust man or boy he couldn't see plain to his front. He knew the country folk around these parts, too, he'd studied them in his ranging. They weren't much given to fits like town folk were. That old farmer had seen enough of something to launch him ten hard-rump miles atop a mule.

Smith nodded at the captains, not quite saluting, and turned back to his task. Stuart's staff had sworn to provide the plans and guide the construction, but Captain Collins, the Cavalry Corps' engineer, had contented himself with pointing out the plain-to-see old foundations before taking himself off to Culpeper again.

That was what came of handing over infantrymen to the cavalry: nothing good, ever.

Left to themselves with inadequate tools, Smith's men had peeled off crusted shirts and turned the run-down mill on the south bank into their workshop as well as a headquarters, a laboring few as the many watched. Now, at last, the stringers were placed or readied, the final planks trimmed, and the first two spans completed from the north bank, almost a wonder. He'd had to bring down the full weight of his not-much-of-a-rank to get even the best men to work with vigor, though, since the ford was a pleasant refuge, far from the usual duties, with apple and peach blossoms prettying the world and the river an invitation to bare-ass tomfoolery as men soaked off layers of filth or soothed their itches.

An odd bunch they were, his fellow Virginians, especially the Southsiders: They'd fight like demons, but faced with manual labor they grew indolent, an attitude Smith himself had never adopted. Couldn't afford to, not like those white-glove boys. Born Southside himself, he'd gone west, to Nashville, for new chances and honest work, returning only when the war came calling.

The only thing that had made the soldiers move with manly speed had been the abrupt discovery of a wasps' nest.

Mindful folk contended that the South—the true South—began below the James, and Bill Smith believed they were right.

Of course, the Mississippians were far worse, prideful and front-porch lazy to a man. Fight a duel before they'd pick up a shovel. And not just the gentlemen. As soon kill a slightful cousin as a Yankee.

"Carey, Nelson," the corporal barked at a pair working on the third span, "pull that plank back up and lay it right. Darkies would do a better job than that."

Bare-chested and scarred and Irish as Saturday sin, Private Carey teased him back: "Ain't none of your black bucks left you, Corporal dearie. They're all traipsed off up north to Yankee heaven."

He grinned with amber teeth.

Wonder if I shouldn't take ten or twelve men and have a look," Captain James Smith, Jr., told his rival company commander. "Push out two, three miles along the road. Just to be certain."

"Might not be unwise," Captain Tyler agreed.

"Could be a raid."

"Reckon that's possible." Tyler put on an among-us-officers smile. "Corporal Smith won't be happy, you take any men away from his precious work, though. Best holler back to the mill and roust some do-nothings."

Captain Smith waved off the concern. "Take too long. Besides, Billy Smith thinks all officers walk on water. He won't fuss."

Noon, and the warmth had thickened, drawing the last winter's chill from a soldier's bones. Corporal Smith had no intention of letting the work detail rest, though. Hadn't earned their bacon. They could curse him all they wanted, complaint was a soldier's right. But the bridge was going to be finished sooner, not later.

He'd been relieved when Captain Smith drew off ten men for a picket. That farmer. Couldn't get the fellow out of his head. That's all they'd need, to get surprised by a multitude of Yankees.

He decided to shuttle his crew back to the south bank a few at a time, to take up their arms and come back again. Wouldn't pay to leave his best men defenseless and caught on the wrong side of the river. If some Yankee patrol with high ambitions did try to spring a surprise, his men could see them off, Smith reckoned, as long as they had their rifles close to hand. But hammers and saws wouldn't do.

He didn't intend to raise the matter with Captain Tyler. Just do everything quiet-like. If Tyler noticed and got up on his high horse, he could say, "Sir, I tried to do what I knew you'd do, have the boys ready. Been studying on your lessons, trying to learn some."

Tyler would gobble that up like cherry pie.

Only officer Smith much cared for was Little Billy Mahone, a man hard enough to regulate Southsiders. Serving under Little Billy might not be the safest spot in a war, but it was satisfying.

The brigade commander wasn't anywhere close, though. And trouble of some dimension was headed their way, if Smith was a judge. Maybe not today, maybe that farmer had been seeing spooks, after all, but the weather had turned at last and that meant trouble. Despite on-and-off rain, the roads were firm enough to carry artillery. The Yankees wouldn't sit still, no matter the licking they'd taken at Fredericksburg. Memories didn't stretch that far in a war.

Just more and more of the blue-bellies, that was the curse, as if those Northern mills could turn out men as easy as they made woolens. He'd watched their numbers swell all winter, across the Rappahannock, Yankee soldiers thickened by fine greatcoats. While his lean brethren shivered.

The corporal noted that Captain Tyler had lingered out in the road, staring after the vanished detail, arms folded and pondering.

An officer with nothing to do was a danger to man and beast. Smith decided to entertain the captain before Tyler turned his attention to the bridge and fuddled the doings.

As the corporal neared, the captain said, "Ah, Smith! We making progress? Looks like it, to my untutored eye."

There was something about Tyler that just made a fellow want to knock him down. But Smith only nodded. "Right fine progress, Captain. Done tomorrow, Lord willing."

Tyler's eyes took on a strained look that any corporal could read: The captain was in search of a question that would demonstrate concern and show authority.

"The bridge . . . it *will* bear the weight of artillery, Corporal Smith?"

"Wouldn't drag siege guns across it, sir. But she'll bear up under horse artillery well enough."

"That's all that's been asked." Tyler squared his shoulders. "You're to be commended."

Smith knew exactly who would be commended, if things went well. But he nodded his thanks.

A horseman emerged from a far grove at a gallop.

"That's not Jimmy Smith," Tyler declared.

No, it wasn't Captain Smith returning, but someone in a gray coat who'd taken enough of a fright to ruin his horse. Coming on as if pursued by an army of ghostly riders. In naked daylight.

The fugitive was a junior engineer from Stuart's staff, Lieutenant Price, whom the men had renamed "Priceless." Every few days he rode out to find a flaw in the bridge's construction.

Now the lad was transformed. Hat lost, coat blackened by sweat and flesh scared hot, the lieutenant took to shouting like a fool.

"Yankees! Yankees coming! Yankees!"

His horse bled at the flanks. Green foam spattered Smith and doused the captain.

"Calm down, Price," Tyler ordered. "And gentle that horse, for God's sake."

"Yankees . . ."

"Talk sense. Cavalry? Infantry? How many?"

Smith held out his canteen. Price gulped water and choked, but calmed himself.

"Cavalry, sir. A right plenty."

Smith gestured for the lieutenant to hand back the canteen: A good canteen was ever harder to come by. Price took another swallow and gave it over.

Tyler looked at Smith but questioned himself. "How the devil did they . . ." He turned again to the lieutenant. "Didn't you see Captain Smith? He—"

"Didn't see nobody, sir. 'Least, nobody in gray."

Faced by the prospect of combat, the captain woke to his purpose. The Virginia gentry might not care to work but loved to fight.

Tyler pivoted sharply, barking orders for the work crew to stop and retrieve their arms.

Smith didn't tell him the order had been given, didn't want to break the spell of command. It was time to let Tyler earn his pay. If a paymaster ever showed up.

Ignoring the lieutenant now, the captain wheeled on Smith. "I'm going back over to set up a proper defense. You deploy the work crew around the bridge, keep any raiders from torching it. When they're set in, come over yourself. I want you by me."

"Might want to send someone else out to have a look, sir. In case Captain Smith . . ."

Tyler nodded, with no more fuss about rank. "Robertson's the best man on a horse."

The captain strode off toward the rowboat, snapping orders as he passed the men. Smith looked up at the still-mounted lieutenant.

"I was you, sir, I'd make my way on back to General Stuart, report what you've seen."

"I should stay and fight," the boy insisted.

Stepping close enough to get a noseful of horse stink, Smith said, "Lieutenant, there's a mile of difference between gallantry and stupidity. You go on back to Stuart and make yourself useful."

They beat back the Yankee patrol with surprising ease. Smith reckoned there were at least two companies of Union cavalry present, but even fighting dismounted they stayed near the road, as if preparing to flee from the very start. He'd been ready to recross the river, orders be damned, and fight beside his crew, but the men who'd been hauling and hammering minutes before proved sufficient to send the Yankees reeling back to wherever they came from.

"Not much to that, was there?" Captain Tyler said. "I suppose you can get back to work."

They stood on what remained of the mill's upper floor, looking northward through a skeletal window frame, past the river, over the fields, and into the scrub oaks and waste pines. There was nothing more to see, the Yanks had gone high-tail.

Pleased with the one-sided skirmish, Tyler added: "That poor old fellow meant well, he did his duty. But you can't rely on civilians to count soldiers." He smiled, almost as if Smith were his equal, a confidant. "Civilians do multiplication, not addition."

The corporal nodded. But the gesture was meaningless. He was fixed on thinking. Something didn't make sense.

"Didn't expect to find us here, that's plain," the captain continued. "Figured they'd use the ford and be on their way."

Smith dipped his chin again, another bit of nothing, then he said: "They went quits awful easy. I didn't see one man fall."

"They're on a scout, they weren't looking for a rumpus."

"Yes, sir. Still . . ."

The captain smiled warmly, pleased with the wonders of spring and his superiority. "Don't go getting the jumps on me, Corporal Smith. I rely on you to keep the men steady."

But Bill Smith had stopped listening. For a second that seemed a lifetime, he just stared.

"Oh, Jesus."

The captain followed his line of sight. Not one, but two Yankee infantry regiments had stepped from the far trees in a line of battle. With flags unfurled.

And that was the least of it. The mill stood at a loop in the river, outflanked on both sides from the northern bank. No one had ever thought they'd have to defend it.

Now the undergrowth teamed with blue-coated skirmishers who'd worked around the flanks.

It was not going to be a good day.

They fought. As long as they could. Longer than was sensible. Smith watched as the Yankees scooped up his work crew. On the south bank, the remainder of the detachment fired and reloaded as swiftly as experienced hands could work, determined to extract a price from anyone who tried to cross. But converging Yankee lines of fire drove heads down and hearts faltered.

"Where'd all them sumbitches come from?" The comment from a private summed up every soldier's thoughts.

Clouded with smoke, the ruined mill stank of gunpowder. Smith looked toward the captain, who clearly struggled with the only decision left in the world: whether to save what men he could or to continue defending the ford.

"Captain, it's useless," Smith told him. "They're everywhere, there's too many."

"They're not everywhere. Not yet." Tyler's voice sounded firm and determined. But his hands quivered as he tried to reload his revolver.

"Hell they ain't," Smith hollered, casting rank aside. A daring peek through the window frame revealed Yankees crowding onto the south bank, too. Closing the trap. "They're already over here, we've got to go, sir."

The captain nodded but couldn't form the words. Bullets stung the interior walls and ricocheted. Even the best soldiers cowered and made themselves small.

"Captain," Smith tried again, voice severe, "we have to get out. Someone has to tell General Mahone."

"Surely," Tyler muttered, as if pondering other matters entirely. Then he snapped back to life and shouted: *"Clear out. Everybody. Clear out, just run for it."*

A lieutenant added an eager voice to the order. Smith hollered, too. But the men clung to the walls, dazzled by the volume of bullets seeking them. Even hard kicks and curses couldn't move them.

A Mississippian knotted a dirty rag to his rifle's muzzle, prepared to give up if the officers wouldn't.

Smith broke from the rear of the mill, leapt a ditch full of huddled soldiers, and ran up through the campsite, past steaming kettles and unhitched wagons, darting away from Yankees thick as rattlesnakes in a den.

The firing slackened considerably as ever more men surrendered. Smith lost sight of the captain, of all but a few fleet privates.

"Give up, Johnny. You're got, give up. Don't want to shoot no Christian in the back."

But Smith ran on, heedless, determined, unreasoning, as if being taken prisoner would be worse than dying.

At last, bleeding and breathless, he got beyond the Yankee shouts and shots. He reckoned they'd bagged enough men to make them happy.

And they had the bridge. It was going to be finished, right soon, by other hands. It grated to think he'd built it for the blue-bellies.

As he gained a ridgetop Smith paused and glanced back to the ford.

On the roads and in the fields north of the river, it looked as if the whole Union army had come.

Late afternoon
Ely's Ford on the Rapidan River

You shouldn't be this far forward, General," the captain commanding the cavalry escort insisted.

George Gordon Meade stilled his horse and steadied his spectacles, turning black-bagged eyes on the worried officer.

"Captain, I shall go wherever I want. If you haven't the stomach to come along, this army has an abundance of other captains."

"Yes, sir," the captain said, chastised and mortified. "I only . . . those Rebs across the river might take a shot . . ."

"It seems to me, Captain, that the best way to prevent such an occurrence would be for you and your men to drive them away."

Meade knew immediately that he'd been too harsh. He often spoke more sharply than he intended, Margaret had admonished him countless times. War was no place for Philadelphia manners, of course, but he'd wronged the captain, who had no chance for redress.

The lad was as brave as any, but his job was to see to Meade's safety, not seek a fight.

For his own part, though, Meade had learned that he quite liked to fight. All the years of building government lighthouses and mapping waterways counted for nothing compared to war's exhilaration.

Grim it might be, but battle was almost voluptuous.

Charlie Griffin trotted up with his staff, outpacing his division. Dusty and fierce, with more mustaches than face, the former artilleryman was the sort who always rode forward, too.

"Expected to have to swim that creek to find you," Griffin said. "But here you are." He lifted his kepi by way of a salute. "Got the slows today, George? Thought you'd be biting Bobby Lee's ass by now."

"Griffin, that's no way for you to address your corps commander." But Meade found himself struggling against a smile.

"Hell, George . . . if I don't keep you humble, which one of these piss-cutters will?"

Griffin was a hard case who only revealed his humor to trusted comrades. But Charlie Griffin was honorable, too, which was something of a rarity these days. Charlie had stuck by Fitz John Porter throughout his court-martial, while others skulked off or lied to save their careers. To his soldiers, Griffin was profane and demanding, but he spared their lives when he could and his men adored him.

Meade didn't have that common touch and envied it.

He turned back to the cavalry captain and offered a more measured tone. "Thompson, go on ahead now. Clear off those Johnnies, there can't be more than a dozen. And catch one, if you can. I'd rather like to hear what he has to spill."

The captain looked doubtful about leaving Meade unguarded.

"General Griffin is bringing up his division. I think I shall be adequately protected."

Young Thompson, a 16th Pennsylvania man, saluted and set to the task. Perhaps relieved, Meade thought, to have escaped me.

"You'd think I was the crown jewels," Meade grumbled to Griffin. "Charlie, don't let them make you a corps commander. The palace guards want to watch you while you squat."

"Not a task for which I'd volunteer, watching you shit, George. I hear Slocum's across at Germanna Ford."

"Just heard myself, had a courier. His lead division's over. Seems the Johnnies were in a generous mood and left him a bridge."

Griffin soured his lips under his mustaches. "No such luck up here, of course. Have to wade the Jordan." He snorted. "Scouts report it's running deep. With a current."

Meade glanced at the heavens. A fine spring day was closing with a promise of rain in the night. "Men will get wet, one way or another."

Griffin shrugged. "Never saw a rusty soldier. They'll curse like micks, but do fine."

"I'll have my escort form a chain downstream, fish out anybody who loses his footing. Show the men the cavalry's good for something." He met Griffin's eyes—eyes as disdainful of folly as his own. "Just get your division across, Charlie."

"Just you get out of my way." Griffin grinned, showing rough teeth, and his face cracked into countless lines incised by the sun in the New Mexico Territory. "Isn't this something, though? Who'd have thought Joe Hooker had it in him?"

Meade smoothed his beard. "I'll grant you that I'm impressed. Joe stole a two days' march on Bobby Lee, which takes some doing. Might even stretch it and say three days entire." His fingers rose from his beard to resettle his spectacles. "I didn't understand it, not at first. Hooker's not a man for explanations. But things have worked out rather finely, haven't they? Three corps across the Rappahannock, with hardly a shot fired. And no resistance to speak of along the Rapidan. Take away Lee's river lines and you take away his primary defense." He dropped his hand to his saddle. "Can't believe they didn't catch on to us yesterday, at the latest. Stuart must be off in some opium slumber."

"Wouldn't mind knowing what Joe has in mind next, though. Never was one for guessing games."

Meade's horse whisked its tail and calmed again. "My bet is he intends a grand envelopment. We sweep east, Uncle John pushes west from Fredericksburg with Reynolds. Couch and Sickles reinforce where needed. And Lee's all but trapped, give us one more good day." Meade offered another rationed smile. "Joe's done all right."

"So far, so good," Griffin snorted. "Now let's see how Bobby Lee responds."

"Charlie, if Joe Hooker fights this army half as well as he's maneuvered it . . . well, isn't it about time someone did it? Gave Lee a thrashing? Show what this army can do when it's well led?" Meade thought for a moment. "I could be wrong about the plan, of course. I don't think even Butterfield knows the whole of it. And he's the only man that Hooker trusts."

"Well, if we don't know, maybe the Rebs won't know. For once."

Of a sudden, Major General George Gordon Meade, commanding the Fifth Corps of the Army of the Potomac, felt a wave of renewed urgency, a fresh sense of time's value, of minutes measured in blood.

He buried his smile. "Just get your division across that piss trough, Charlie. And get yourself to Chancellorsville in the morning."

Nine p.m.
Culpeper, Virginia

Stuart tried to put up a good face for his staff, to summon his smile. At least until he could close a door behind him. But at a banjo chord, his self-control quit:

"You want to claw that thing, you go outside."

When Jeb Stuart couldn't bear music, his mood was beastly. And the officers serving him knew it.

He slammed the door to the little room off the parlor that served as his sanctum, preferring to take his gall and wormwood alone. He tossed his hat toward a table. It missed and slapped the floor, plume shuddering, but he didn't pick it up. Instead, he dropped onto a hard chair, punishing a rump already sore: hemorrhoids, the cavalryman's plague.

One mistake after another. When he'd gotten the first report of Yankees crossing the Rappahannock, he'd assumed that it was just another raid, if a heavier one, headed south for the rail depot at Gordonsville. The night before, he'd sent a telegraphic message to Lee saying as much and reporting that one infantry division might be reinforcing the Union cavalry.

He'd gotten it utterly wrong. By noon, word had come in that the Yankees were not marching south, but had turned east by Madden's Tavern. And he'd disbelieved it, clinging to his notion of what was afoot. At least he'd had the sense to see for himself, riding out on a pleasant day that promised showers later.

His scouts had been right, the Yankees had turned east. Outflanking the much-reduced Army of Northern Virginia and Robert E. Lee.

He'd dispatched patrols to round up Yankee stragglers, and his men had returned with prisoners not from a single division but from three Union corps. Then Lieutenant Price had ridden in on a murdered horse that somehow was still breathing, hollering like a snake-bit missy that Yankees were in strength at Germanna Ford.

Stuart had hastened back to Culpeper to ensure that a corrected report was telegraphed to Lee.

Lee, whom he all but worshipped. Lee, whom he'd almost failed.

Lee. Of course, he'd long admired him from afar—they all had—when Lee was a colonel in blue and the West Point commandant. But their first intimate encounter had come thanks to good timing and John Brown. Stuart had been visiting the War Department just when Lee was ordered to Harper's Ferry to suppress a slave rebellion. Stuart had volunteered to go as his aide.

Brown's uprising hadn't amounted to much. At least, not then. No slaves had rushed to massacre their owners, and Brown, born to be hanged, had made an inept defense of an engine house. But Lee had commended Stuart for his role in a few spare words that had meant more than the rhetoric of famed orators would have done.

Lee had the gift not merely of greatness, but of discovering greatness in those around him.

He could not bear the thought of failing Lee.

When a knock braved his mood, Stuart answered, "No."

Didn't want to move, didn't even want to take off his boots. Kick that darkey in his cannonball head if he barged in now.

Convinced that he'd given Lee warning and made things right, he'd then learned that one of the telegraph stations along the patchwork of relays had shut for the night, with no one in attendance to tap the key. Lee would not learn of the scale and direction of the Union movements until the morning.

Stuart wondered if the previous night's message had been delayed, too, if matters were even worse than he'd believed, if he'd left Lee blind. Of course, the detachments on the Rapidan, scant as they were, must have sent Lee word of the Yankee advance.

He prayed it might be so.

Damn, though. They all had been seduced by copper wire, every last one of them. Lured by newfangledness and mechanical ease, the siren song of the telegraph. When a man on a horse was still the most reliable means of passing reports.

He'd sent two couriers off in furious haste, each with a copy of his latest message, but they'd have to ride roundabout to avoid the enemy. At best, they'd reach Lee an hour or two before dawn. And all the while the Yankees were on the move, surely across the Rapidan in force, with as good as nothing on Lee's left.

How had that scoundrel Hooker pulled it off, that drunken whoremaster? Even Lee, of retiring speech, had mocked Hooker's appointment to command, belittling his soubriquet of "Fighting Joe" by referring to him disdainfully as "Mr. F. J. Hooker."

Now Joe Hooker was closer by half to Lee than Stuart's cavalry.

Had Stuart been a drinking man, had he not sworn temperance to his mother and clung to that promise—along with the memory of his beloved, charming, worthless, drunken father—"Beauty" Stuart would have downed a bottle of whiskey and asked for more.

He could not fail Robert E. Lee.

Sudden rain dazzled the roof. Stuart glanced toward the unlit fireplace. The room felt queer, as if it were unknown to him. A place where he did not belong. And he *didn't* belong there, he belonged on horseback.

Rousing himself, he noted that in his rush to Madden's Tavern, he'd left in plain sight the poem he'd been writing to Flora.

Stuart rose, took up the paper, and crumpled it. He'd been writing poems when he should have been in the saddle.

When he had been snowbound on the prairie the winter before the war, his highest aspiration had been to publish his poems, at least a few of them. His grand ambition had not been to gain a general's star—such had seemed impossible in those days—but to be celebrated as "the American Wordsworth."

Now words weren't worth a lick. Only actions mattered.

Outside, the rain gushed. Mud, too, would slow his couriers.

He flung open the door and strode into the parlor. The room had been abandoned by all but the essential men of his staff.

"Pack up and get on your oilskins," Stuart told them.

Ten p.m.
Headquarters, Army of the Potomac
Falmouth, Virginia

Handsomest officer in the U.S. Army, that was Joe Hooker. Butterfield was envious, but only to a point: A man could be too handsome for his own good.

Women hurled themselves at Hooker, harlots, wives, and virgins. Cleaning out the camp for the campaign had stirred up a riot of petticoats, pouts, and impertinent demands—the latter not always from women in the trade.

Not that Daniel Butterfield minded a turn of quinny. He and Joe shared a taste for flesh and the devil, with Sickles making a third. In the presence of females, Hooker possessed the power of a magnetic device amid iron shavings, and he himself had the knowledge befitting a gentleman of the best establishments, from Manhattan to the reeking streets of Washington. He even knew a house or two in Boston, though they lacked vitality.

After seeing off Patrick, their dour provost marshal, Hooker bent over a map spread across a table. Mud gripped his boots. Butterfield joined him and pulled the oil lamp closer.

Hooker stank of horse, but he was gay.

"Properly done . . . wouldn't you say, Dan? Hardly thought I could pull it off myself."

"Nothing like it so far in this war."

"You should have seen them, though. The crossing . . . beautiful, and I don't use that word lightly. Even Howard's Germans made a good showing."

"Uncle John's across at Fredericksburg. A few delays early on, but he's over in strength, so both flanks are in order. Latest report has the Johnnies strengthening their lines opposite Sedgwick. Jackson's bunch."

Hooker clapped his hands. His teeth were not as impressive as the rest of him. That fine shock of graying hair and the ruddy skin suited him, the goodly bulk of the man, but Joe had whiskey teeth and a drinker's breath. Even now, fully sober.

"Splendid. Splendid, splendid, *splendid!*" Hooker straightened his back, his figure commanding. "If I don't compel Bobby Lee to do exactly what I want . . . I tell you, Dan, they can put me up against a wall and shoot me dead."

"It's a good start . . ." But there still was much to be done, Butterfield finished the thought to himself.

Hooker's spirits would not be tamed or tempered. If he was the army's finest-looking general, Joe was far from the humblest.

"A good start means a fine finish. You know the dictum, Dan. All but impossible to recover from flawed initial dispositions. Jomini wasn't a *complete* fool. To say nothing of Napoléon. Lee's dispositions leave him at my mercy." He gripped Butterfield by the biceps and gave him a playful shake. "I've *got* him, Dan. He's as good as cooked and on the plate."

Butterfield nodded. Matters seemed fine, indeed. Better than anyone had a right to expect, it was simply the truth. They'd been a good team, with Hooker the driving wheel and himself the brake, when necessary. And Hooker deserved credit, more than his jealous peers were apt to render. When Hooker had taken command after Burnside's wretched performance at Fredericksburg—the fellow had shattered the army—morale had been low and conditions beyond description. The Mud March, then the sicknesses in the camps. Bad rations and general lassitude, thieving quartermasters and pay in arrears. Hooker had fixed it in mere weeks, bludgeoning the War Department, reforming everything from field hospitals to the commissary, camp sanitation to hours fixed for drill. It had been little less than a miracle: By St. Patrick's Day—as wild a day as wanted—the Army of the Potomac had been restored and improved, in the mood for another scrap, in the mood for vengeance.

The only problem pressing was the looming expiration of enlistments for a full fifth of the men. The prospect of losing tens of thousands of soldiers—out of 150,000 present for duty—had demanded the earliest possible date for opening the campaign, and there had been hints of mutiny, quickly suppressed, as the spring rains forced delays.

Still, the force on the march was superb, unrivaled. For all his gifts and grandiose schemes, McClellan had never approached Joe's skill at hammering the army into shape and making it move. Butterfield's wound from Gaines' Mill attested to that, a memento of Little Mac's utterly botched campaign.

Beside him, Hooker yawned. "Believe I'll take myself off to the sleep of the just. If a fellow *can* sleep. . . . Isn't it all just grand, though? I'll have Lee just where I want him, he can either retreat on Richmond, or accept battle on *my* terms. Either way, he's buggered."

Butterfield rubbed the back of his neck, stiff from a long day of bending over maps, that necessary, lesser form of action. They all were tired, with the campaign barely begun.

"I'll stay up for a bit," he said. He did not add that he would have liked a drink. Hooker, who was a bully friend to a bottle, had sworn off his whiskey for the campaign's duration and Butterfield meant to help him keep his vow. There would be no accusations of drunkenness, not this time.

He had even, in Hooker's absence, made certain that no bottles remained either in the room Hooker used for private matters or in his tent, where he displayed himself as a proper field soldier to visitors.

As if reading his thoughts, Hooker added, "After all this . . . after we've knocked down Lee and strung up Davis . . . we'll have us a grand debauch in New York City, you can *really* show me around."

"You'll be my guest, Joe. You'll be celebrated."

And he would be, indeed. Hooker would blaze through the city's finest establishments, breaking the steely hearts of hardened whores. As Marsena Patrick had flushed the last of the wantons out of camp, a famed and ferocious *madame* from Washington City had resisted her dismissal, moony as a girl over Joe Hooker, if somewhat rougher in language and comportment.

Hooker deployed the lopsided smile he reserved for private exchanges. "And then you can teach me how to make a fortune. Damned if I ever figured it out myself. I'll go back to California and rub their faces in it."

Butterfield knew those tales, too, how Hooker had left the Army in California to amass riches but had amassed only debts, scrabbling about the brown fields of Sonoma, welcome in barrooms but ever less welcome in banks, feuding with greasers, and living in a cabin. If the war had killed many another man, the war had saved Joe Hooker.

The thing was that Joe really was a grand fellow, despite all, a talented soldier and jovial companion, sound in command and delightful when carousing. Nor was he a martinet or close-minded ass: Joe was a friend to any man's good idea. He'd readily backed Butterfield's propositions, the cap patches to identify the corps to which men belonged, the red, white, or blue flags to distinguish divisions and brigades—small matters, yet touches the men had embraced with pride. His bugle calls had found a welcome, too, even his schemes to support the campaign with deception.

Now they just had to win.

Rain arrived from the west, slapping walls and windows. Many a soldier would get a good soaking this night. Butterfield almost wished that he were out there, in rough camps beside them. As chief of staff, he was tethered to headquarters, imposing the order and discipline he'd mastered not at some stiff-necked academy but as the eastern superintendent of American Express, a company that was almost a family possession. The West Point men were fine in the field, but it took a man of business to run an army.

Midnight
Headquarters, Army of Northern Virginia

Robert E. Lee yearned to sleep. And the rain striking the canvas, diffusing the familiar mildew smell, could not be blamed for his wakefulness, no more than the old discomfort of his cot. He had lived with these things for two-thirds of his lifetime, and ease had only rarely been his companion. Nor was it the flutter in his heart or the worsening rheumatism that haunted him. The secret, inadmissible doubt was locked within. And there it would remain.

He had ever been a good keeper of secrets, revealing as little of himself as possible, constructing over decades the armor he wore in the battles of everyday life.

But he needed rest and found none.

Certainly, this retreat from sleep, this unwanted rearguard action at day's end, had partly to do with the chronic failings he battled, the hunger rations allotted to his soldiers, the lack of forage for horses, the unavailability of shoes or even laces, the regiments and brigades so whittled down. . . . Longstreet had been dispatched to Suffolk not as a strategic stroke but to feed his men off counties less chewed by war.

Lee felt the quirk in his heart again, the elusive flirt of pain.

He feared that he needed Longstreet now and had pressed President Davis to hasten the return of his two divisions, but a crisis looming on the Rappahannock somehow seemed less urgent on the James. At times, Richmond seemed immune to war's reality. The president always listened, but he often failed to hear.

The report from Stuart describing those people as marching on Gordonsville had arrived late and already disproven, and there had been no word from Stuart since. Lee's slight information had come in bits, from fugitive soldiers surprised on the Rapidan and from scouts retained by headquarters, and all that was clear was that great designs were afoot. The Federals were on the march against his left in strength, and he had watched another force pass the Rappahannock on the right, below Fredericksburg. He could not yet reckon where the main blow would fall, and that knowledge was critical. For the first time since that long afternoon at Sharpsburg, Lee felt trapped.

He had sinned the sin of pride, dismissing Hooker and mocking him. Now Hooker had leapt toward him, with startling skill. The Lord had chosen to humble him, to caution him.

But the Lord, he trusted, would not desert him truly, not if there was justice in his cause. His God was the God of miracles, of resurrections, a loyal God.

Robert E. Lee had come late to the Lord. For most of his life, attendance at church had been a social duty, pleasant or dreary, depending on the company. He had believed that he believed in the Lord, but he had not. Then, at his first gray hairs, the spirit had shaken him—not so grandly as was done unto Paul on the road to Damascus, but in a quiet knowledge, an unexpected awareness. His wife's concerns had been put to rest as Lee embraced his Savior.

He was no zealot, of course, his prayers were not shouted. He was a Lee, and Lees were not demonstrative. The Episcopal Church fit him as if specially tailored, as it had his forebears. He had none of Jackson's blaze, no trace of that Presbyterian ferocity, that broadsword faith. Lee's God valued good manners.

Jackson. Some had thought him mad, with his early-in-the-war demands to raise the black flag and slay every Federal, to take no prisoners but to fill the North with dread of massacre, forcing a war just begun to a quick end. His hand had been stayed as Abraham's had been, if not by the Lord then by decency and sense. And Jackson accepted his superiors' demurrals as if they had come from the Lord. He was a faithful servant.

Now no man was a greater aid to Lee. Not even Longstreet.

Brilliant, peculiar Thomas Jonathan Jackson, his right hand, this matchless killer.

And yet, at winter's end, Jackson had been distraught, almost unmanned, at the death of a little girl from scarlet fever, a child who was no kin. And to see him reunited with his wife and lofting his infant daughter had been to view a portrait of every tenderness. That morning, Jackson had been surprised, as they all had been, and he had been compelled to send off his wife and child in haste as he readied for battle. All the day thereafter, Jackson had appeared fierce and fixed and dutiful, but Lee had read the loss deep in his eyes.

He had never met a man as strange as Jackson, a hanging judge with a child's heart: earnest and awkward, implacable.

Well, Jackson would see to the right, to the Fredericksburg lines, as the situation developed. But all Lee had been able to do for his left, in the absence of certainty, was to dispatch Anderson and his division to slow those people and gather information. But Anderson was no Jackson. A brave man, but lethargic, he required detailed orders and stern tones.

Jackson had identified two Union corps on the right below Fredericksburg. Reports from the left suggested three corps advancing from the west. That left two entire Union corps unaccounted for—where were they? Nor was Stuart certain of the Federal cavalry's intentions. It was all aswirl, nigh on overwhelming.

Spies and the Northern newspapers granted Hooker an edge of three to one, impossible odds.

No, he must not think so. Nothing could be permitted to be impossible. And nothing was impossible for the Lord.

Was it blasphemous to pray for a miracle? In this fearsome, unwanted war? A war he had hoped might be avoided even after the first shots had been fired? A war his people *must* win?

He thought of poor old Scott, gargantuan, unable to rise without the assistance of an aide-de-camp. Venerable, with anger and tears in his eyes at once, so disappointed had he been in Lee. But Lee had not had a choice, Virginia needed him. That last ride back to Arlington House had been inexpressibly painful, a betrayal not merely of an oath but of his life entire.

So many ties had been broken, so much abandoned.

Rain slapped the canvas. The damp gripped. His bones ached.

Perhaps all things would seem clear in the morning, perhaps inspiration would present itself, an ingenious solution. . . .

Lee did not believe it. He had been caught out, that was the truth. In his pride, he had laid a snare for himself. Now he risked being crushed, like Pharaoh, between two great blue waves. And he and these lean-shanked men sleeping wet around him, these good men in their thousands, would have to spend their lives to save the army.

TWO

Eleven a.m., April 30
Germanna Plank Road, west of Chancellorsville

The rain in the night had summoned memories of another land, of a lost world Carl Schurz had fought to free, only to fail. Now, on the march and uniformed in the blue of his new country, he relived that youthful struggle again, an interlude—so brief—of wondrous hopes, of dreams that had ended in exile for the fortunate, leaving behind comrades fallen in unequal battles and others who had been shot by firing squads.

The lyrics of a cradle song assailed him, in damp daylight:

Schlaf, mein Kind, schlaf leis',
Da draussen geht der Preuss'
Der Preuss' hat eine blutige Hand,
Er schwebt es ueber das Badische Land . . .

How might he translate that whispered scrap to tell his new countrymen how fear reigned under tyrants?

Sleep, my child, keep still,
The Prussian comes to kill.
The Prussian has a bloody hand,
He waves it over Baden's land . . .

Not a literal translation, not fully, but the meaning was there. The fear, always the fear. Of the petty magistrate, of the wrong word caught by the wrong ear, of soldiers hammering on the door at midnight. Suddenly, in that glorious year of 1848, the dread had been vanquished with bewildering ease. Revolutions swept Europe, the people demanded freedom. Hardly more than a boy, if skilled with a pen, he'd hurtled forward as a disciple of Kinkel, his cherished professor, to join the Frankfurt National Assembly. And there, in the sweat of summer, the heartbreak began.

Germany had a free parliament at last. And Germans squandered the chance. There had been too many theoreticians, too many scribblers and cloud-dwelling idealists, and too few practical men who knew how to govern. The vision of a democratic union of German states had staggered under a burden of rhetoric, undermined by petty jealousies. By 1849, as the revolutions faltered one after the other, the king of Prussia—his overlord—had recovered his footing and set the army in motion. There had been nothing left for good men to do but fight.

He'd hurried southward with Kinkel then, from Bonn to Kaiserslautern, to join a Palatine people's army that was no army at all, merely a band of shopkeepers and artisans, of students and consumptive intellectuals, furnished with ancient muskets, fowling pieces, or swords recovered from attics. Lacking uniforms, trained in nothing, freedom's incompetent champions were sent reeling by regiments of well-armed, well-drilled Prussians. The staunchest retreated southward into Baden, where the duchy's small army had joined the revolution, where one sliver of Germany remained free.

He put on the uniform of a lieutenant of Baden. Witness to follies innumerable, he learned how a retreat becomes a rout. Outfought and outflanked again and again, he and his comrades finally were cornered at Rastatt, shut within fortress walls along the Rhine.

Kinkel was captured. The survivors faced a siege, its outcome predestined. As Prussian subjects, he, Kinkel, and many another rebel expected death.

But he had not died. When a surrender was agreed—to spare civilians—he had taken to the storm drains and the sewers, determined to escape and fight again, somewhere, someday. He and two companions almost drowned before nearly being captured by alert sentries. Driven back, they hid in a loft as Prussian lancers took up quarters below them. At last, they slipped back into the sewers and, on their second attempt, escaped and crossed the Rhine to France and safety.

Kinkel wasn't shot but imprisoned for life. Now, on this overcast morning an ocean away, as a different uniform dried between rinses of rain, Schurz remained astonished at the task he had next undertaken, at his daring, his madness. Only a brazen and foolish young man could have pulled off what he achieved—he lacked that fearlessness now. Safe and welcome among fellow exiles in Switzerland, he had chosen to make his way back across Prussia's borders, all the way north to Berlin. To his own amazement and the world's, he had all but single-handedly freed Kinkel from Spandau Prison and smuggled his friend and mentor onto a merchant ship bound for England.

At the age of twenty-one, Carl Schurz had found himself feted by London's babel of political refugees. He had thought only of Kinkel and the professor's matchless wife, of their needful children, and had become an incidental hero, the author of a victory for freedom. He married a splendid Hamburg girl and they left for the United States.

Greeted by German émigrés, he taught himself English from newspapers, exploring each unknown word, and his knack for accents quickly set him apart. Alone among the Germans he encountered, he could mimic the language of the native-born—a blessing when he moved west to Wisconsin, the latest promised land for Forty-Eighters.

He soon was drawn into politics at a time when the German vote went to the Democrats, despite the party's association with slavery. The faltering Whigs had been infected by anti-immigrant Know Nothings, and the *Deutsche Einsiedler* saw them as the enemy. Democrats seemed the lesser of two evils.

But not to Schurz. He aligned with the fledgling Republican Party, braving country roads and frontier tracks, embracing the roughhouse politics of a raw land, suffering defeats but moving forward, eventually speaking to eager crowds from Milwaukee to Boston. Equally persuasive in German and English, Carl Schurz preached freedom, freedom, and freedom. Along the way, he got to know a politician and railroad lawyer named Lincoln.

Now here he was, on horseback and wearing a general's stars. Liberty had a real army at last.

The column ahead stopped abruptly.

Schurz raised a hand to halt his division but let his subordinates call the order back through his brigades. The endless stopping and starting and stopping again was the fate of any trailing corps on a march, that was a given, but he did wish Howard's staff would keep him informed. He never knew when there might be time to let the men fall out and cook their coffee.

Not that he was fond of his present surroundings. The thickets and dwarf pines along their route were unsettling, the landscape the army had entered felt blighted and wronged, unlike anything Schurz had yet seen in Virginia. Nor was the road an engineering marvel.

He felt a child's urge to hurry on.

Schimmelfennig rode up from the First Brigade, huge beard flecked with mud. Sidling his mount near to his commander's horse, the brigadier unleashed a cannonade:

"Verdammt noch mal, Herr General, diese Scheisser haben doch keine Ahnung . . ."

Damn it, General, these shits have no idea . . .

Schurz smiled indulgently but didn't reply. Brigadier General Alexander Schimmelfennig was a fellow Forty-Eighter, but one with superior military credentials. They'd first met in Kaiserslautern, where Schimmelfenning had held the higher rank. An officer of the Prussian army and veteran of two famed regiments, he'd deserted to fight on the people's side, only to be wounded thrice and condemned to death in absentia. Fellow émigrés, they had become great friends over the years.

Schimmelfennig still had a whiff of the Prussian about him, though. In front of their subordinates, he was flawlessly correct when addressing Schurz. Only among their intimates—Forty-Eighters every one—would he call him "Carl." And Schurz had to rein him in now and then, explaining that this strange behemoth of an American army could not be ruled by discipline alone. These men, these new-made Americans, were volunteers, their youthful dreams of a better world reawakened. They were men who believed in liberty, in this remarkable Union that had sheltered them and let them prosper. But they also were older than most native-born recruits, not boys but men with families, solid burghers who'd left established professions for their ideals. They were brave, but their courage was of a settled sort; it was not the heedless daring of the young. Each man had much to lose and expected orders to make sense. But orders often didn't.

Schurz needed Schimmelfennig to tread lightly. He had doubts inadmissible to anyone about their new chain of command—about Howard, above all. He didn't need more discontent, since the men remained sour over Sigel's departure. "Kluger Franz" had been their ideal, and now that he was gone, they imagined virtues for Sigel he'd never possessed. Sigel was a good man who'd made a poor soldier, and Schurz intended to learn from the example.

For all that, his soldiers had endured the past night's soaking with no more than common gripes. And in the lulls between squalls, one *Sängerverein* after another had raised old melodies from their lost world, plaintive songs of snows and roses and impossible loves. Few things made Germans happier than melancholy music.

The march, the fresh air, the small successes . . . even the rain and the shared discomfort . . . it all seemed magically good for their morale. That morning, his sodden troops had stepped off with spirit, alight with a sense of purpose. His division would be fine. And so would the rest of the Eleventh Corps.

He had to believe that.

"Ist doch eine Schweinerei," Schimmelfennig tried again, in a mood to chatter. *"Die verstehen keine Marsch-Disziplin, keine Ordnung."* The brigadier shook his head. *"Ich frage Euch, Herr General: Was ist denn das fuer eine polnische Wirtschaft?"*

It's all a piggery. They don't understand march-discipline or order in the least. I ask you, General: What kind of Polish management is this?

"Don't let Kriz hear you speaking badly of Poles," Schurz cautioned. "Your fellow brigade commander might send you a challenge."

"Ach, *der* Kriz is a good man. I say nothing against him. He makes his brigade good."

"Better than yours, some say."

"Maybe he is good. But not *so* good."

The two men laughed.

"Well, he's Polish. Don't forget."

"*Der Herr Oberst* Krzyzanowski lets no man forget." Schimmelfennig nodded toward the wagons halted ahead. "And I would like to know, *bitte,* what the devil goes on now?"

"I'd like to know myself," Schurz admitted. "But I suspect that General Howard's rather busy."

All morning, they'd heard ripples of shots in the distance, but each exchange had faded into nothing. For all the annoying halts, the army's march was progressing impressively.

At the mention of their corps commander's name, though, Schimmelfennig glowered. His face seemed to retreat still farther behind the wall of beard. Schurz felt his smile swelling again—his true smile, not the one he'd mastered for politics. Alex was easy enough to understand: The red-faced silence masked a struggle between the former Prussian officer who would never dare speak ill of a superior and the new-made American aching to blurt out exactly how he felt about Major General Oliver Otis Howard.

Schurz felt trapped in the middle, bound by a formal loyalty that he struggled to feel in his heart. He leaned forward in his saddle and stroked his mount's neck.

"General Howard's a brave man, Alex."

"Any man can lose an arm," the brigadier spit out. Then he shrank back, appalled at his own words. *"Ich bitte um Vergebung, Herr General. Dass war unverschaemt."*

I beg forgiveness, General. That was shameless.

Schurz let it pass. But he put a slight chill in his voice. “If you want to get on with General Howard, I suggest you restrict yourself to English.” He turned to face his subordinate more fully. “He needs time, Alex. To get to know the corps, to settle in. Meanwhile, it’s our duty to support him, you know that better than I do. He just needs time.”

Schimmelfennig opened his mouth to speak but checked himself. Schurz knew what his friend had intended to say: “We don’t *have* time.”

There was nothing to be done and the words were best left unspoken.

His horse shied mildly and swished its tail. Schurz took off his glasses and held the lenses up to the light: impossible to keep them clean on the march. “The men have to accept the fact that Sigel’s not coming back. He called Lincoln’s bluff and failed. General Howard has the corps now, and he’s likely to keep it. Help the men face it, start with your officers.”

Schimmelfennig waved off a fly. “He may have the command, but he does not like it, the men see this.” He leaned closer, as if to tap Schurz on the knee, and lowered his voice so nearby aides wouldn’t hear. “You know what his staff *Burschen* say of us? They call the other regiments their ‘white troops.’ Even the Irish. What does that make us, then?”

“They’ll learn,” Schurz said. It wasn’t much of an answer.

It was, indeed, a strange corps, with its near equality in German and non-German regiments. Nor had it been long with the Army of the Potomac, making it doubly the outsider among the corps serving under Hooker. The Eleventh Corps had served in the Valley, where Fremont had botched things badly, leaving the Germans with a taint of failure.

Schurz tried again. “He’s proud. They all are, the West Point men. And General Howard has a legitimate complaint. He’s senior on the Army rolls, he expected to command a premier corps. And one much larger. Instead, he got us.”

"So terrible a thing, is it?"

"No. It's a fine corps. But it's also the smallest." Schurz's smile returned in force. "Full of Germans, too. Come now, Alex. The campaign's going well. Even the weather's set to improve, I think. Let him see us in a fight and Howard will come around."

The former Prussian officer grunted. "He only sees the new men, his men. Those he brings along with him." The brigadier all but snarled, "This Barlow, such an arrogant young *Schwein* . . ."

"Renowned for bravery, as well."

"I've known my share of brave fools." He looked at Schurz. "We both have."

The truth was that Schurz was tired of defending Howard. But it remained his duty. Nor did the fact that Howard treated him as an exception—a well-spoken, influential friend of Lincoln's—blind him to the accuracy of Schimmelfennig's remarks. Howard's coterie, imposed on the corps, made little effort to hide their disdain. A colonel had complained in his presence that "Germans all smell like piss."

The column ahead began to move, but Major General Carl Schurz, late lieutenant of the Baden-Palatinate revolutionary army and former United States minister to Spain, waited for the last teamster to his front to snap his whip. Only then did he wave his division on.

Turning to Schimmelfennig a last time, he said:

"None of it matters, as long as we fight well." Schurz forced another smile. "Now go back to your brigade, before it wanders off."

Eleven a.m.
Confederate lines, Fredericksburg

I can drive them into the river, General," Jackson said, kicking mud from a boot. "Put an end to this. I could do it now, before they cross more men."

Yes, Jackson could do it. Lee was confident of that. But at what cost? The Federal artillery massed on the heights across the river would slaughter any attackers who neared its bank. Better to leave a few hundred yards of ground to those blue hordes than to lose irreplaceable men without necessity. Terrain could be retaken, but men could not be resurrected before the Lord was ready.

Jackson was ever eager to fight, to smite an enemy viewed in Old Testament terms. Such enthusiasm was invaluable, but Lee could not spare soldiers, let alone more regimental officers, short of true necessity. The past year's casualty lists had been mortifying. Malvern Hill, Sharpsburg . . .

The answer was to let Jackson reckon the matter for himself. Lee's reply would have to communicate more than his words expressed.

"We faced the same dilemma in December, General Jackson. Their massed artillery. But for that, we should have destroyed their army." Lee paused, to let Jackson remember, while he chose his next words with care. "But if you think you can effect anything . . . I will give orders for the attack."

As slow of speech as he was swift in battle, Jackson nodded and said, "I'll study it. I'll make a study of it. I'll report to you, General."

Jackson had understood him. Tom Jackson was the one man who always did. Locking his hands behind his back, Lee said, "What presses upon us now . . . is the need to determine where General Hooker will strike. Where his major blow will be delivered."

"Won't be here," Jackson said. "Not the main attack." He gestured toward the busybody foe, some men stripped of their tunics and digging, others dressing ranks out of battery range. "That's Sedgwick, Sixth Corps. Supporting wing, my opinion. Sedgwick's trusted. Won't act foolish. Meant to tug on our ankles, fix us in place." Jackson pulled his cap's brim lower in conclusive punctuation.

Jackson's instincts about Hooker's plan reinforced what Lee suspected, that Hooker's prime attack would come from above, that his opponent meant to leap out of the Wilderness and approach Fredericksburg from the rear, trapping the army. But it did not do to suspect: He had to *know*. And the information he needed was slow to arrive and contradictory. Hooker had screened his advance with remarkable skill. And Stuart . . . had not been at his best.

Light rain teased their party and moved on.

Lee considered Jackson again, this ineffable man so many had thought incapable, even crazed. His altered appearance remained as jarring as it had seemed yesterday, when Jackson first appeared in a fine new uniform, startling those used to seeing him in rags. The only scrap that had survived the renewal was his battered kepi.

Finery did not suit the man, he looked like a child playing dress-up. Upon the handsome uniform's debut, staff men had laughed to tears behind Jackson's back. Lee had put a stop to that with one look.

"I have ordered General Anderson to entrench," Lee resumed, suppressing the rheumatic pain that came ever more often. "I've sent engineers to lay out positions and forwarded all the reinforcements at hand. He must purchase us time, to clarify matters." He looked earthward. "Should our apprehensions be realized . . ."

"Move quick as we have to," Jackson said. It wasn't a brag but confidence.

Jackson kept returning his gaze to the Federals along the river, these intruders in his realm, these Midianites. His desire to fight them felt all but uncontrollable.

Yet Jackson would control himself, Lee knew. The man's strength of will was remarkable, not merely iron, but steel. An odd man, Jackson, graceless, but touched with immense gifts.

The corps commander tugged his cap again. It signaled impatience, a yearning to act. At times, it seemed the weathered visor, drawn down over that vast expanse of forehead, would hide Jackson's face completely. Lee had, upon one occasion, indulged himself and asked Jackson why he wore his cap in that manner. Jackson had taken the question as seriously as a discussion of strategy. As guileless among peers as he was cunning on a battlefield, the fellow had answered:

"I slump, sir. Wicked habit. Unseemly. Pull the brim down, I have to stay bolt upright. If I mean to see anything."

Returning to the present, Lee said, "Inform me, General, if those people cross more troops. That would tell us much. Come to me later this afternoon, I shall welcome your counsel."

Jackson saluted, but his attention remained riveted on the Yankees. Like a cat tensed and ready to spring upon a bird.

Lee could not depart without a few courtesies, a touch of affection for this awkward Gideon.

"Mrs. Jackson is safely away, I believe?"

"In Richmond, sir," Jackson said, in a voice abruptly gentled. "With my little girl."

"Their visit adorned this army. We hope to see them again, when conditions permit."

Jackson shrugged, embarrassed.

Lee turned to go, breaking up a confabulation between Marshall, his military secretary, and Jackson's young man, Pendleton. Valiant, if a bit lumbering—not of the very best family, though respectable—Pendleton had been reported smitten by a local belle. Lee hoped the boy would live to enjoy a marriage. Many men would not survive this week.

It took all of Lee's self-control not to share his desperation, but his officers—even Jackson—had to believe that he was unshakable.

As Lee remounted, a string of Federal batteries opened up from the heights beyond the river, out of range and firing at nothing, with ammunition to waste. Yes, they mean to keep our attention, Lee told himself. Jackson's right, this crossing's a fraud.

It was time to turn his attention to the west.

Two p.m.
Chancellorsville

Slocum, I'm glad to see you," Meade called as his fellow corps commander rode up with his staff. Elated by the army's progress, the Philadelphian dropped his accustomed reserve. "Damn me if I've had a better day in this blasted army. . . ."

The instant he'd dismounted, Slocum pulled off his riding gloves and tossed them to an orderly. The women clustered on the porch of the big house caught his eye, missies in full skirts and full of temper.

"Don't look like *they're* glad to see me," Slocum said, with a nod to the belles.

Meade snorted. "Mad as hornets. Told 'em Joe would need the house for his headquarters. And didn't I get a lecture on Bobby Lee and how we'll all be scooting back north five times as fast as we came."

Slocum turned to his nearest aide and pointed to a yard pump. "See if the water's fit for a man to drink." He took off his hat, wiped his forehead, and swept back his hair. Slocum's look was that of an English border lord, old stock, with eyes ever a bit weary.

"We've got him, Lee's bagged," Meade continued. "My divisions are up, they're ready to go on." He gestured toward his three division commanders, assembled for further orders. "I can have Charlie's men on the move in twenty minutes." He felt almost gleeful. "This is splendid, Slocum, truly splendid. Hurrah for old Joe, he's done it! We're on their flank, with nothing in our way. Clear roads ahead, nothing but a scattering of bushwhackers." He stepped closer to the Twelfth Corps commander, his senior by date of commission. "You take the Plank Road for Fredericksburg, and my men can take the Pike. Or vice versa, as you prefer. And we'll get out of this Wilderness, hit Lee on better ground."

Meade noticed, belatedly, that Slocum wasn't smiling. On the contrary, he looked funereal.

A faint shake of Slocum's head ruined the day.

"George . . . we're not going anywhere, not today. This is it, we're done. My orders are to assume command upon arrival at Chancellorsville. Temporarily, of course. We're to take up a line of battle here and not move one step forward without Joe's orders."

Meade was astonished. Shocked. "Good Lord . . . that's insane. Henry, that's madness. A 'line of battle' here? In this jungle? We need to get out of these tangles as fast as we can. It's . . . it's pure—"

"It's an order, George." Slocum waved to his chief of staff. "Give me General Hooker's latest missive. No, hand it directly to General Meade."

Meade read the message in horror:

> *The General directs that no advance be made from Chancellorsville until the columns are concentrated. He expects to be at Chancellorsville tonight. The maps indicate that a formidable position can be taken there.*

"Good Christ," Meade said. He looked over their surroundings in disbelief. Except for the open field below the house, there was no terrain that favored a defense. One could not even see through the vegetation, let alone fight in it.

"Things do look different on a map," Slocum allowed. He glanced around dismissively. "Chancellorsville? One big, ramshackle house?"

"This simply can't be," Meade said. "We can't stop here. It's a gift to Robert E. Lee. . . ."

"Easy, George. Calm down. Joe hasn't done badly. You were shouting hosannas yourself a minute ago." Yet Slocum's tightened jaw warred against his words. "I'd wager he's got something up his sleeve. He must have."

"We've got a balled fist right here. Your corps, mine. Howard coming up. Second Corps crossing at U.S. Ford. Sickles close behind. That's five corps, we could smash Lee's army to bits." He felt almost faint, breathless. As if his winter fever had weakened his heart. "But not here. We can't stop here. . . ."

"Just follow your orders, George," Slocum told him, out of patience with the world around him, "and you'll keep us out of trouble." Fresh raindrops probed. He added, "Don't need more goddamned rain, either."

As Meade wheeled about to chew his rage alone, waving away his aides and striding off, the girls and women on the porch laughed savagely. As if they had heard and understood every word.

Four p.m.
Confederate lines, Fredericksburg

Samuel Pickens dried his feet, peeling off dead skin. Sometimes a man just seemed to be one big itch.

The remains of his stockings dangled from sticks placed shy of the played-out fire, and his once fine shoes stood propped at a well-judged distance.

Wet through for nothing. Again.

Squatting by the smoking embers, Bob Price said, "Man's feet are a burden unto him."

"Just as soon not do without them," Pickens replied. "And a man's more of a burden to his feet, it seems to me."

"Don't help to scratch."

"Plenty of things that feel good don't help."

"That's the Lord's truth."

He clawed himself, drawing blood. "Wouldn't I like a hot bath, though? If I had one wish?"

Lean as a willow switch, Bob said, "Choose me a plate of biscuits, with gravy hot to scald. If called on for wishes."

Pickens almost told his friend that he'd dreamed of biscuits that night, in his short sleep, but he held his tongue. No man cared to hear another's dreams. A given law of humanity, that was, and any right-raised progeny of Alabama knew better than to talk phantasms, as surely as a gentleman knew not to pick his teeth at dinner. Not with ladies present. Hadn't taken Charlottesville to teach him.

Oh, but that dream! He could've wept on waking. He had been home in Umbria, a house not as grand as many hereabouts, though it passed for fine by Greensboro. And this dream had not been a riddle of shards, of nonsensical disjunctures, but real as a man's lifeblood. He'd been man and boy at once in the dream, but everything else was plain: He sat there in the kitchen, like old times, eating Auntie Delsie's biscuits with fresh-made butter. His mother had not appeared in the dream, only Delsie, with her mahogany strength and glorious knowledge of what fixed up a stomach. He saw and sensed her so clearly, the suspicion in her eyes directed at everyone but him and her scent a comfort immense—not the reek that porch-talk assigned to niggers, not at all—and the way, of a sudden, she'd spoon up a gob of butter and eat it just so, in one smooth gulp, while she cooked and stirred and *hmmm-hmmmed,* telling him, "Butter do keep off the misery." And adding, ever cautionary, "Don't work for white folks, though."

Wasn't how it was meant to be at all, but Auntie Delsie was home to him in a way he could not limn. It was not, ever, that he'd been fetch-minded by her comely daughter, no, he'd never taken to dark folk that way. Nor, tell the truth, had the bone-shouldered local belles held his attention, weak-pale every one, with perspiration blistering faint mustaches and their smells of lye and lavender. They seemed composed not of flesh but of demands upon a man's freedom, ensconced in inveterate falsehoods, every one sly as a snake waiting up a tree. Their bank-clerk eyes alarmed him unutterably, that icy reckoning of the portion of wealth he would possess. No, not for him the petting hand of the female—which was but the condescension of a jailer—nor even a night call on a shanty slut, for dread of consequences and bare distaste: an uncle locked away among the mad, disfigured, and the gripping stink of woman-parts that sickened.

Delsie never smelled that way, just of vinegar and good sweat, and the fragrance of pies on the sill.

He reckoned he'd marry once he tired of fighting off the savages in crinolines, once he was cornered and had no choice but surrender, but he really didn't see much worth in a woman beyond the role of family brood mare. Just spoiled a man's good humor for their pleasure, women did. Their laughter unnerved him, their nails.

Rather take the dogs down in the live oaks.

Auntie Delsie, though. Never had felt safer or better than seated at her table, that splinter-edged realm where the house servants fed in their turn. "Ain't you just the eating-est chile in all of Alabama, ain't you just?" she asked of him always. And her own brood—assorted, half-assembled—sat there wide-eyed and envious, bound to be fed to fullness but conditioned, already, to fear and furtiveness, learning every day where the secret lines lay, as he had to learn, too, so that the world would turn smoothly on its axis, with all accommodated.

Folks who went on about slavery just didn't know. How mixed up everything was—complicated, befuddled, impossible, enduring—a world suspended between the Lord's ordained order and grievous notes held by the bank.

Looking back in longing, with a soldier's peculiar rue, the wide-awake, daylight Sam Pickens figured that the kitchen back home remained his favorite place that had a roof. The rest of the house did not aspire to the halls of the Virginia gentry, but the acreage was good—fine bottomland and more than one paid-off property beyond—with two hundred slaves to render all abundant.

"Fond of biscuits myself," he said, and he let it be.

Pickens had come late to the war, tardy to Company D and the 5th Alabama, but he'd entered the Greensboro Guards as a private in penance. He could have bought his way high, even raised his own company, maybe a regiment. Folks speculated that his mother wasn't only the richest widow in the state, but like to be the richest person, man, woman, or child. Not Virginia rich. And certainly not South Carolina rich. Not like the Hampton clan. But fitted up handsome to any sound man's needs.

Could've bought his way in or out, but he needed to be with his kith in Company D. And the 5th Alabama had needed new meat to satisfy the war's hunger.

He rubbed his feet, half-mad, but restrained his fingernails. And he said:

"I take it back."

Bob Price and the others edging the ashes turned toward him.

"Before a bath, I'd take a bottle of liniment. Bath could wait."

Eyeing Pickens' hind paws, Price told him, "More like a gallon. Or two. You need to visit the surgeon, Sam. Those feet are bad."

Pickens shot back a mirthless laugh. "Surgeon won't tell me anything Doc Cowin hasn't. 'Keep your feet dry and clean, change your stockings daily.'" He shook his head. "A man might as soon expect Abe the Ape to bring him a plate of fried chicken."

"Take me some chicken about now," Joe Grigg put in, stepping up to the circle, newly arrived, eternally gaunt and hound-eyed. "Fried, baked, boiled, or just half-dead. With feathers left on, be all right."

"Where's all that fish you and your skulkers was set to catch?" Bob Price asked.

"Fish weren't running."

"Well, then," Price said, fussing with his ever-resistant pipe, "I guess I'll just set here and eat the rations that didn't come and drink the coffee I ain't got." He narrowed his eyes at Grigg. All mischief. "Bet you ate all you caught on your dawdling way."

"I told you the fish weren't running. And we came back soon as called."

"Yankees aren't running, either, seems like," Bill Lenier said to ease things. Everyone knew that Grigg was easy to rile. And Price did love to rile him.

They all bumped along just fine, though. It had taken Pickens some time to decipher the rough-edged humor of soldiers, to understand that duels would not result from ribbings that grew jagged now and then. It was how soldiers beat down their fears and bursts of loneliness. Fact was that they'd die for one another. Just wouldn't ever say it, nor anything like.

A man couldn't.

Grigg looked down at nothing. "Why'd they want to cross that river, anyway? Just get themselves another whipping, like they got afore Christmas. Don't make sense."

"The ways of the Yankee cannot be known," Doc Cowin said, joining the forum, "for they are unfathomable and unbounded, lost to reason. Thought I smelled coffee, but I see I was deceived." The doc was a precious oddity, a physician who chose to serve as an infantry private—although he was not averse to lancing a boil.

"Likely just another fuss about nothing," Jim Arrington said. Big Jim mulled things more than was good for a man, and there was a wish in his voice. "Been across since yesterday and still haven't done a lick. Remember that 'Mud March' of theirs? Just fuddled themselves for nothing. Might be no more to any of this."

Compelled to honesty, Pickens said, "Feels different this time, Jim. Something's going on, officers are twitchy."

Bob Price folded his arms and considered the point. Then he took his friend's side. "Yes, sir. Yes, indeed. Something's boiling in the kettle this time. Take today now. Woken unneedful, in blind dark, and we're slop-marched and mud-grabbed for miles, then left to stand in trenches ankle-deep in—"

"Knee-deep," a voice corrected.

"—water. And then, when we're all but drowned, we're yanked back again, with General Rodes as confused and confounded as anybody, hollering, 'Y'all be ready now, boys, don't let your guard down. . . .' Him with his mustaches dripping, high on his horse. . . ."

"Hard man, but fair," Corporal Hutchinson judged.

"Rodes?" Price said. "Hard man, sure, but—"

"Never saw him do one fool thing," Hutchinson insisted, voice bearing his rank. "Leastwise, none that wasn't concocted and ordered by somebody else. Smart fellow, they say."

"Smart enough to move to Alabama, 'least for a time. Then fool enough to creep back to Virginia," Price declared, biting off a cackle. "I, for one, have had my fill of this magnificent commonwealth."

"Don't let Captain Blackwood hear you bad-talk Virginia."

"Then why'd he move to Alabama, too?" Price demanded.

"Schoolteacher, needed a job. Not that you were ever set to learn anything," Pickens said. His family knew every action taken by man or beast within fifty miles of Umbria. "Rodes now . . . he's an engineer. They go wherever there's engineering to do. Railroad man, that's his specialty. Brought him down our way. Took an Alabama bride with him when he left, Lord bless him. One less to pester the rest of us."

"I believe," Doc Cowin said, in that voice that spoke ever of good whiskey sipped on a front porch, "that our good General Rodes was, of late, a professor at the same noble institution as our General Jackson . . . who might be deemed the first useful Presbyterian in three hundred years."

"I'm still asking what poker trick put all of them Virginians over Alabamians," Price told them all.

"Pass me those stockings, Bob," Pickens said. "They dry yet?"

"I ain't touching them. Volunteer for burying detail first. Jesus healed the lepers, but he ain't here."

"Sam," Doc Cowin said, "I told you to report yourself sick, you're halfway on to gangrene. If blood poisoning doesn't strike first."

Pickens gave a shrug, sheepish. "After the fight. Not going to hide on a sick list with a fight coming."

"I had your feet," Price said, "I'd be first in line."

Cannon fire lifted chins and eyebrows. Faces turned northward.

"Been at it since yesterday," Corporal Hutchinson explained to Grigg, who'd been off on his failed detail. "Don't know who's got the jumps worse, our generals or theirs."

With a shake of his head, Bob Price tossed Pickens his stockings.

They still weren't dry.

Seven p.m.
Second Corps headquarters, Army of Northern Virginia
Near Hamilton's Crossing

The change in Jackson astonished Sandie Pendleton, so much that he'd slipped off to ponder miracles, along with a visit to the field latrine. When the general had ridden off to Lee's headquarters, Jackson had been as hard of mien as Joshua. Then he had reappeared, almost giddy, as if about to dance a jig of delight. It was hardly the general's usual behavior, even before the battles that he craved.

Orders went out as swiftly as they could be copied: The corps would march west at dawn, with Rodes' division followed by

Colston's and Hill's, while Early's boys, plus one brigade, remained to cover ten miles of front at Fredericksburg. It was the sort of risk that Jackson thrived upon, but this night he seemed to be almost enraptured. As if he had just learned a wondrous secret.

Well, Jackson was indeed a man of secrets, to the great frustration of subordinates, who often were left with no inkling of his plans. He'd driven General Ewell to the brink of fury before his wounding. And he and Powell Hill hadn't patched things up, not below the surface. Even relatives felt his unbending ire.

Yes, if that great and good man had a flaw, in Pendleton's judgment, it was his unforgiving character. He jailed generals and shot deserters without a wince of doubt, without remorse or mercy. He fit the Old Testament better than the New, a John Knox Presbyterian, not a mild Virginia Episcopalian.

When next he got home, Pendleton hoped to speak with his father about rigor versus mercy, about the theology of it. A part of him still felt called to the cloth, to follow the family tradition, and he needed to believe that Jackson was right, that his triumphs were godly, his harshest actions justified.

In any case, Jackson kept a Christian headquarters, overseen by the Reverend Doctor Lacy, who prayed more than most but still prayed less than Jackson. There was no shameful behavior, no foulness, no untoward language or tolerance of drunkards, and all men near to Jackson were properly churched.

Still, there were comic moments when even Pendleton had to bite back laughter. Just the day before, he'd overheard a soldier remarking on Jackson's habit of thrusting his right arm heavenward. The private had said: "Looks like Old Jack means to grab the Lord by the seat of his pants and set him to doing."

And then there was the way the human telegraph worked in camp, how the wildfire warnings of Jackson's approach made decks of cards disappear amid instantly purified language. The general was convinced that his soldiers were paragons of godliness, holy warriors, unaware that worship attendance in the brigades and regiments suddenly swelled when "Old Stonewall" decided to pay a visit. The staff, of course, was not above hinting a warning to the right colonel in plenty of time.

Not least among Jackson's virtues, Pendleton found, was his calm acceptance of mockery and taunts, whether from the cadets at VMI, who had christened him "Tom Fool" for his eccentricities, or over the Negro Sunday school in Lexington. The people, from the best sort down to the trash, had been set against the latter. Even Pendleton's father had been doubtful, despite his otherwise generous views. But Jackson had marched ahead anyway, defying Virginia law by teaching even slaves to read the Bible, leading the coloreds in prayer, and joining them in hymns in his off-key voice. The front-pew citizens had laughed, but Jackson had persevered, and the Sunday school had become an institution—even now, in the midst of war, Jackson sent home his monthly contributions, Pendleton knew.

Perseverance, that was the thing the Lord asked of the faithful, from Job to Paul. And Jackson just would not quit. He had no step-back in him.

And now he meant to go forward.

Boswell appeared in the freshened night.

"If I knew a good prank, I'd pull it," the captain said. "Hardly expected such levity today."

Pendleton shook his head in enduring wonder. "Surprise to me, too, Bossie."

"Well, glad I'm not Jed. We'll see how the general's mood holds up if the maps aren't done on time." He smiled, a friend and mock rival. "Any news from Miss Corbin, you old dog?"

Pendleton felt a blush rise. Kate was his darling, newly betrothed, won through the winter while the staff camped at Moss Neck. He was not a handsome man, he knew, not dashing like Bossie Boswell or Kyd Douglas. But Kate, who had a brain in her pretty head, had chosen him above other would-be swains.

"I expect she's fine, thank you. Doing her best to look after things, with all the servants run off. Hoping the Yankees spare the house, if things turn in that direction."

"I reckoned the ladies had all gone to Richmond by now."

"Not Kate. Not yet." And he was proud of it.

"Well, bully for you, anyway. You swept up the prize."

Yes. It amazed him still.

"When the war is over," Major Sandie Pendleton said, "you'll have to come visit us."

"Surely. And bounce a squad of young Pendletons on my knee."

Pendleton blushed again. There were thoughts he did not wish to have in another man's presence.

And no, Kate was not so old, that was wicked gossip. Nor was she plain, as declared by jealous tongues.

She was going to make him the happiest man on earth.

Laughter bloomed from the nearest tent, centered on Jackson's bray.

It was, Pendleton reflected, an age of wonders.

Nine p.m.
Field headquarters, Army of the Potomac
Chancellorsville

Sorry to keep you waiting, Swinton," Hooker told his favorite newspaperman. Grinning, he continued, "You understand, of course. Duty comes first."

William Swinton waved a hand at the noisy, merry commotion beyond the walls, the brass bands and the cheering. "The army seems in good form."

"Shouldn't it be? Masterful, that's what this is. Lee and his minions have never faced a campaign remotely like this." Hooker smiled generously. "Just took proper leadership."

A band took up "Camptown Races," competing with endless patriotic airs. The cheers were less explosive than they had been an hour before, when Hooker's general order had been read to the troops by their officers, but they still confirmed that the army was in high spirits.

With one of his well-schooled smiles, Swinton extended a copy of Hooker's evening proclamation:

It is with heartfelt satisfaction the commanding general announces to the army that the operations of the last three days have determined that our enemy must either ingloriously fly, or come out from behind his defenses and give us battle on our own ground, where certain destruction awaits him.

"Rather strong beer," Swinton commented. He drew a notebook from his pocket. "Mightn't one say? With the battle still to come?" The scribbler was some sort of bastardized Scotsman by way of Canada and reputed to be a Bohemian, but his paper had been a pillar of support. And Joe Hooker wanted no cracks in the pillar now.

"Don't go flat-foot on me, Swinton. Your *New-York Times* is about to get the greatest goddamned story of the war. Greeley will be sick to death with envy."

"I shall be glad of it."

Hooker straightened his posture, reinforcing his authority. "The Rebel army is now the legitimate property of the Army of the Potomac. I've said it before, and I'll say it again: They may as well pack up their haversacks and make for Richmond. And I shall be after them, Lee hasn't a chance."

"My readers will be delighted."

"All this army ever needed was a proper hand." Hooker stopped himself. "Don't quote that. No need to insult my failed predecessors."

"Indeed."

Hooker felt the newspaperman's rather too piercing eyes upon him.

"Well, then," Swinton resumed, "my congratulations, General. Oh, by the way: Not everyone seemed to be celebrating this evening. Meade seemed . . . shall I say 'morose'?"

"Meade's always that way. Constipated Philadelphia blueblood, you know the sort. Always contrary, always knows best."

"I hear he wished to assume an advanced position. There was a tiff."

Hooker bore down. "Listen, Swinton, the plan's been a grand success. Just look around you. And I mean to stick to the plan. Between us, Meade knows Lee's licked. He just wanted to grab the glory, claim he chased off the Johnnies by himself." Hooker shook his head. "High ambition on every side, I deal with it every day. It's a curse on this army."

Swinton opened his mouth then closed it again. He slapped shut his notebook, making a small drama of it.

"I'd buy you a drink, General. But there's an absence of desirable liquids."

Hooker smiled. "No spirits on this campaign. Only esprit."

"Then I shall take my leave. I need to get my dispatch back across the river and on to Falmouth—your telegraph seems a bit laggard."

Hooker waved that away. "New machines, new system they're trying out. Big improvement, Butterfield tells me. Just need to let the Signal boys do their work." He instantly smothered a newborn concern: His plan depended heavily on the telegraph. "Everything will be in order tomorrow."

"Indeed."

Hooker lay awake on the borrowed bed, thanks to a damnable headache. Since he'd cut off his drinking four days before, he'd had a few punishing interludes. Of course, there were also times when he felt just splendid. All in the natural order of things, he supposed. He'd soon work through it. He'd always been robust in every respect—ask a hundred women. And he had a great deal to celebrate, had he not? Even pleasures could give a man a headache. . . .

They'd all been wrong, every one of them. All those who'd thought him destined to end as a failure. If he wasn't already the most admired man in the entire Union, he would be in a matter of two or three days.

The best choice Lee could make would be to run. And running would not suffice.

Joseph Hooker's shame would be behind him, every shred of it. The bankruptcy, the poverty, and the sweat that had never been enough to save him. In California, he'd left the Army, expecting to make his fortune, but the soil of Sonoma had proven worthless, the small cabin with its off-kilter door confining, and the saloons by the presidio too alluring.

He'd failed at farming, yes. And government posts had disappointed both him and his benefactors. Yet he'd been a white man, and he'd assumed the greasers, at least, would know the difference. In Mexico, after the war, they'd known their place.

He'd loved her, that was the thing. Isabella. That was the damnable, shameful thing: He'd loved her. And her family, the Alameda-Castillos, hadn't had a proper pot to piss in, despite the airs they put on and the finery they dragged out for their church's feast days, the silver buckles and embroidered costumes. Welcomed on their ranch as a guest, he'd believed himself admired and properly valued. Not least by Isabella, with whom—in that elusive Spanish way—he'd been denied a single moment alone. He'd even endured their sickening food to breathe the same air she did. And when he had at last asked for her hand in marriage—doing it formally, their way—the appalled look on her father's face, the mortification evident on the features of a brown man who took better care of his beard than he did of his property, that look had stunned him. The old bugger hadn't bothered to be polite, merely stuttering, *"Pero . . . pero . . . no es imaginable, es imposible. . . ."*

And then, when the war had come to his rescue and patriotic friends in San Francisco had taken up a collection to pay his passage back to volunteer, one had declared, all too publicly, "I'd pay the whole fare myself to see the last of Joe."

Now here he was, commanding a vast army, an army that had cheered as he rode past, on the verge of a great victory. And Isabella, who'd soon been married off to a fellow greaser, could weep over her brown brats.

Midnight

Confederate Second Corps headquarters

Blessed he was in the women he had known, blessed in their flowering and grace. Only they could release him from his shyness, only they accepted him as he was. Men judged; women understood. Men mocked, but women soothed.

Perhaps, he thought, only women grasped the wonder of God's Creation, the beauty and sorrow, the majesty and the immemorial loss.

The Lord had never asked more of him than upon his Ellie's death, inflicting a loss he feared he was too weak to bear. Oh, the Lord had tested him then. He had not believed that a man could love more fully upon this earth than he had loved the wife of his first marriage. Only her sister, Margaret, had found the power to console him. They had grown to love one another, too, but their union was forbidden by the church, by God's own covenant. Still, Maggie had calmed his soul in his time of need, even as her glance inflamed his heart. Now she was wed to another.

But the Lord had remained his guardian, rewarding his submission and obedience by lighting his way to North Carolina to fetch home an earthly angel to take to wife, his matchless *esposa*. Anna, in her quiet way, brought him joy beyond measure. With her, he could cast off the haunting fear, the lifelong dread of inadequacy, of blunders and humiliations. He spoke to her with a fluency he never had managed when confronted by men, with an ease he'd only found when addressing Negroes. As he shut the front door at day's end, Anna's love untied his tongue. The Lord was his shepherd and had sent him a lamb.

How short the time seemed now, how cruelly brief, those days of a new marriage in the last bright years of peace. Casting off frugality, he had bought Anna a piano, and after pulling down the shades and closing the drapes with care, he would push back the furniture and dance, alone, ecstatic and thumping, as she played. Then, heedless, he would sweep her up and hum as they danced together, whirling until she was breathless, escaped from all judgment, in flight from a frightful world. He suffered when she visited her family, even missed her when she rose from their bed to use the pot.

Then she gave him a daughter.

He did not believe he would go back to the Institute after the war. Instead, he would farm, somewhere in the Valley, perhaps there in Rockbridge County, rendering the earth fruitful, enjoying the fulsome beauty of God's abundance, honoring Him through honest labor and prayer, and raising a family educated to reverence. If it were not blasphemous to say so, he and his wife and children would create an earthly paradise.

He rose from an hour of fitful sleep and reverie, kneeling first on the earth to offer prayers, thanking the Lord for His mercies and begging His aid in the undoing of His enemies.

Unwilling to wake his servant, Thomas Jonathan Jackson finished his toilet by candlelight and made ready to kill.

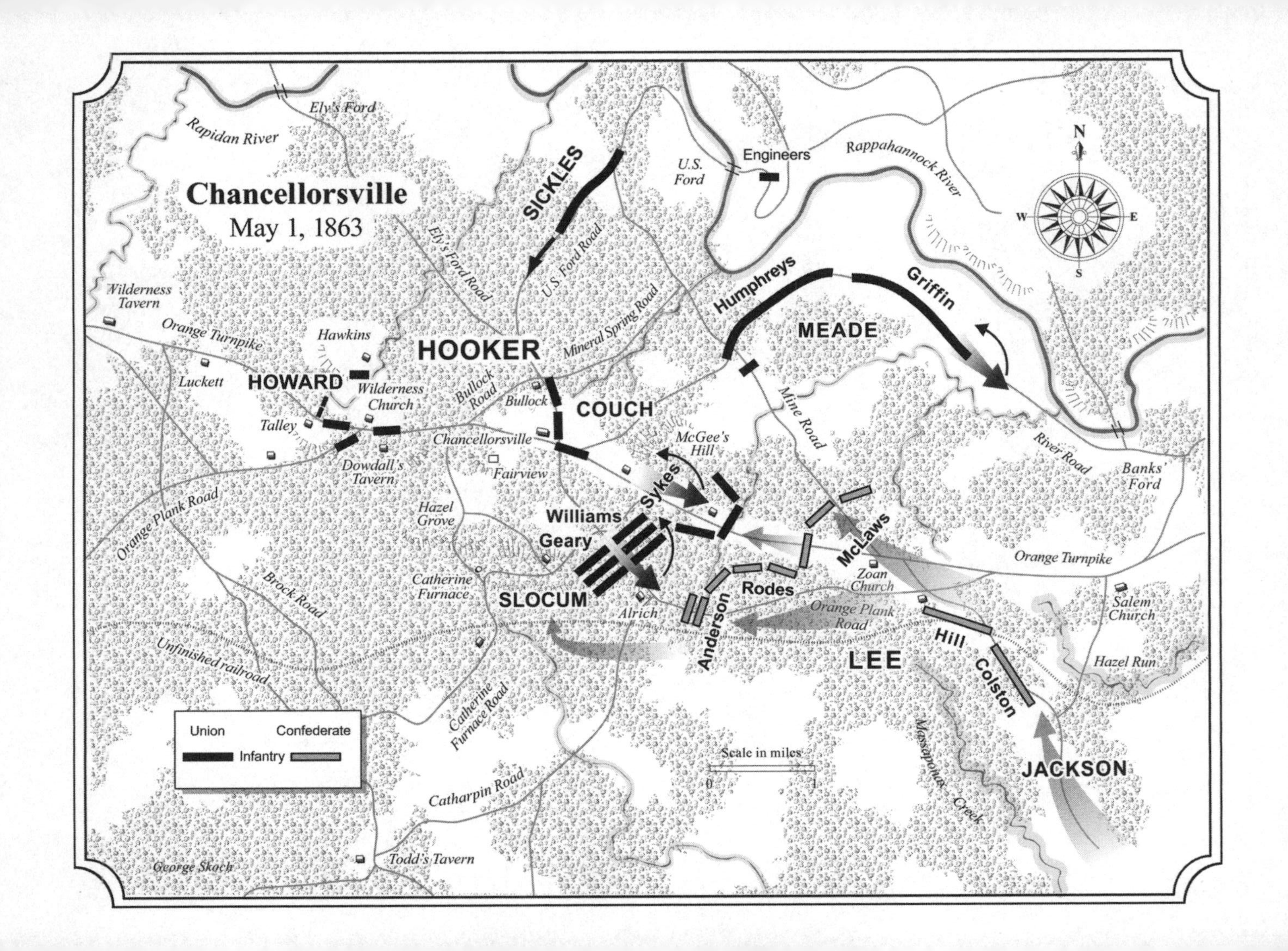
Chancellorsville
May 1, 1863
Rapidan River
Ely's Ford
SICKLES
U.S. Ford
Engineers
Rappahannock River
N
W
E
S
Ely's Ford Road
U.S. Ford Road
Wilderness Tavern
Orange Turnpike
Hawkins
HOOKER
Mineral Spring Road
Humphreys
Griffin
MEADE
Luckett
HOWARD
Wilderness Church
Bullock Road
Bullock
COUCH
Talley
Chancellorsville
Dowdall's Tavern
Fairview
McGee's Hill
Mine Road
River Road
Banks' Ford
Orange Plank Road
Hazel Grove
Williams
Sykes
Geary
McLaws
Orange Turnpike
Catherine Furnace
SLOCUM
Alrich
Zoan Church
Rodes
Anderson
Orange Plank Road
Salem Church
Brock Road
Hill
LEE
Hazel Run
Unfinished railroad
Colston
Catherine Furnace Road
Union
Confederate
Infantry
Scale in miles
0
1
Massaponax Creek
JACKSON
Catharpin Road
Todd's Tavern
George Skoch

THREE

Eight thirty a.m., May 1, 1863
Tabernacle Church, four miles east of Chancellorsville

Laff McLaws peered westward into the fog.

"I don't know," he said. Picks and spades bit wet soil to deepen entrenchments. "Nobody tells a man anything much, expect you to figure it out."

"Well, *some*body's out there," Dick Anderson, his fellow division commander, mused, "and not just a scouting party. Or Lee wouldn't have us digging, not here."

"All my boys saw yesterday was cavalry. Nuisance, not much else."

"We struck infantry. *And* cavalry. Not many, but there you are. Infantry don't scout this far from home. And there was a fuss by Todd's Tavern shy of midnight."

"Stuart, most like. At long last. Could use us some horsehumpers. Sort things out." McLaws cleared his nose on a red rag. "I just don't like not knowing."

Anderson chewed on his cheek, aching for coffee. *Yankee* coffee. Of which there was a distinct shortage in the Army of Northern Virginia. Next thing to an obsession, not just for him.

"Little Billy's cranky," Anderson said. "Won't cool down. Yank cavalry scooped up some of his men again yesterday. Twelfth Virginia, hard-luck bunch. Took maybe thirty. Now Mahone thinks the whole Union army's coming our way, and he'd like to take both fists to it." Anderson resettled his still-damp tunic: Might turn into a fine, warm day, but the morning gripped raw. "I don't see it, though. I just don't see it. If the Federals were in force, they wouldn't have stopped. Not in that godforsaken patch of no-place, not when they had free going." He lifted his face to the heavy air. "Thinning a bit."

"Not much."

Anderson removed his hat and swept back his hair. "Never expected any of this. Did we? Back at the Academy?"

Big-bearded Laff McLaws said, "Couldn't see one yard beyond graduation."

"Now this."

Both generals turned toward the west again, staring blindly along the hidden Turnpike. But the surprise came from the east, from behind their backs.

Hoofbeats. A dozen riders, at least. Both men about-faced. Staff officers tightened.

Jackson emerged from the mists, followed by a small retinue: a few aides and some couriers. No flags. Jackson had chosen his runt horse for the day.

Didn't say good morning, just:

"Both here. Good. Saves time."

McLaws and Anderson saluted. Jackson barely offered a return. Just looked down at them, hard as a Comanche, lips pursed. Pulled low, his cap's visor obscured his eyes.

"Stop that digging. Form your men." When neither division commander jumped, Jackson added, *"Now."*

McLaws just never liked the man. And here he was, the feted Stonewall, not bothering with the protocol of presenting an order putting him in charge of divisions that weren't his, that belonged to far-off James Longstreet. No, he just started in giving orders, a backwoods Napoléon.

McLaws did as told, though. Everyone did with Jackson. Since he had A. P. Hill arrested the year before. For doing his duty well but a tad too slowly.

With aides scurrying off to halt the work and assemble the men, Anderson said, not without evident trepidation, "Last orders we had from General Lee were to hold this position, sir. To defend right here."

Shoulders thrown back, Jackson said:

"Best way to defend is to attack. Best way to hold this position is to make sure the enemy doesn't come near it."

The fog was, indeed, thinning. As if Jackson had given the mists their orders, too.

Before either division commander cobbled together a response, Jackson asked:

"Who knows this ground best? Which brigades?"

"Mahone's Virginians, General. And Posey's Mississippians next, I'd say," Anderson told him. "Had their winter quarters hereabouts. Know it every inch, here to the river."

"Chancellorsville?"

"Yes, sir. Mahone, he'd know it. And the Wilderness. Well as anybody *can* know it."

Jackson nodded, almost imperceptibly. Couldn't make out his eyes at all now, but a man knew they were fierce.

"Good," Jackson decided. "Mahone leads the advance here, along the Turnpike. General McLaws, you follow with your division, commanding on this line. Posey will advance along the Plank Road. General Anderson, you'll deploy an additional brigade behind him. Position the remainder of your division to reinforce General McLaws." He paused, as if seeing all of this unfold, reading the future, then he turned that commanding nose toward McLaws. "Upon my order, you will locate and drive in the enemy's skirmishers. Advance until you strike his main line. Draw him out. Then hold him."

A horseman, half-uniformed, galloped up to Jackson, who did not look about but only said:

"Give them their maps, Hotchkiss."

As one, McLaws and Anderson stepped forward with questions. Anderson spoke first. "Will your corps be coming up, sir? If we meet heavy—"

"Follow your orders, General," Jackson said. "As I will follow mine."

Trailed by his knights and squires, Jackson vanished.

When he had gone—when he was well away—the unsettled generals, new maps in hand, stared after him.

Dick Anderson said, in a muted voice, "Wish Dutch Longstreet was here."

After a stretch of dead seconds, McLaws responded:

"Yankees don't scare me, not inordinately. But, Lord knows, that man does."

Jackson rode back to hasten on Rodes' division, possessed by an exaltation unmatched since the fight for the causeways, manning his last gun, before Mexico City. It was a boy's sensation, he knew, but the Lord had sent it, and Jackson did not resist. He could not wait to bring his divisions down upon the Federals—he literally could not wait and intended to attack before all of his men came up, to push Rodes forward and order a general advance along the Turnpike and Plank Road.

Strike first, strike hard. Never give the enemy the first grab at the stick.

He had a plan, although he had not shared it. McLaws and Anderson only needed to do their parts. As long as McLaws bit into whatever Union force appeared in front of him and held fast, the rest would go smartly. Jackson intended to flank the foe yet again, to destroy these trespassers. To slay them until there were none left to kill.

He had not wished to be rude. He never did. But words were costly to him, and fewer words meant clearer words. And he knew men such as Anderson and McLaws, had known them since West Point, even before. Things came easily to them. Until they didn't come easily anymore. And then the men accustomed to ease and used to deference made mistakes. And battles were lost.

Nothing had ever come easily to Jackson. Western Virginia had been a bare-bones land, his family a failed endeavor, his father soon gone and his mother, well-intentioned but incapable, a susceptible woman, called to the Lord thereafter. His uncle, a man of great goodness, had taken him in at the mill, and he had known a few innocent years, a boy's brief paradise, with only a sister left to him and her too soon removed (and now . . . now she was a traitor and a harlot—yes, such she was—giving herself to Yankee officers, her conduct unforgivable, his once beloved sister). Even his good uncle had failed in the end, his backcountry bamboozlements unsuited to civilization when it arrived.

He had known, beyond reason and words, that escape was necessary, and he had done all that godliness allowed to reach West Point, to gain an education beyond the near useless schoolroom where he had learned little and then taught others less. For all of his efforts, he had only gotten his place at the Academy because another boy had taken one look and turned tail the same day. Jackson had *begged*, that one time in his life. For the vacated appointment. And a congressman, amused, had pitied him.

At West Point, he had learned how little he knew, how unprepared he was, a clodhopper clutching his knife and fork in his fists, a beast of the woods who lagged in every faculty. There had been no one to teach him, no one to explain the simplest rules of society.

A target for endless gibes, he lived in dread of failure but would not quit, pulling himself up from the bottom of his class and gaining, through grit, a respectable ranking by his final years. The loneliness early on almost defeated him, but slowly other cadets accepted his presence, almost befriended him, overlooking his blunders and clumsy rudeness. He rarely could make words come right, could not retort smartly when Northern cadets argued or skin jokes like the Southrons. But if he could not debate, he could memorize; if he could not speak, he could act; and he was dutiful.

He had lived for letters from his then cherished sister.

And then he had marched proudly across the parade ground one last time.

The war against Mexico had drawn him in, with its swift campaigns against a foe sometimes brave but always inadequate.

Unexpectedly, Mexico had enchanted him. Indifferent at French at West Point, he discovered a knack for Spanish and its flourishes. The strange words and sleek intonations unlocked his tongue: He could even flirt, if timidly, with the lace-covered *señoritas* of Ciudad de México.

He'd toyed with the notion of staying on, of resigning his commission and making a new life, perhaps wedding one of those lithe girls with olive skin and flawless manners. Even the glitter of the Catholic Church had its brief allure.

But he had come home, to his country and, resolutely, to his faith. And the Army had sent him to Florida, where ruined Seminoles hid in the swamps. He found himself at a remote post, where there was little to do, serving under a commander he grew convinced was a flagrant adulterer. Jackson had pursued the matter relentlessly, unable to comprehend the disinterest of the chain of command. How could such things be winked at? Such a disgrace to the uniform, sinfulness all but lauded? The authorities barely feigned an investigation. They had seemed to think *him* unreasonable, even mad. . . .

An opening on the faculty of the Virginia Military Institute had been his earthly salvation, allowing him to resign his Army commission. He was not a natural teacher, as he soon learned, but teaching was his charge and he did his duty. He memorized the lessons he had to impart, reciting them to himself in the lonely evenings, facing a blank wall as he mouthed the words, inscribing page and paragraph numbers from textbooks onto his brain.

He knew the nicknames his cadets applied to him over the years. The insinuations cut, but he never showed it. As a Christian, he would not let anger be his master. The VMI cadets were young and did not understand that devotion and perseverance, not quick facility, made a man. He insisted on discipline, though.

Major Jackson only came to life on the Institute's drill field, teaching the proper use of field artillery.

Meanwhile, he prospered privately, rewarded by Great Jehovah, and earned a respectable place in local society. He made a fine marriage to Ellie, found happiness, and met tragedy. Maggie had been his comfort as he mourned a wife and lost child and she mourned a sister, but the church's strictures were clear: A widower could not marry his dead wife's sister. The Lord had shown him grace for his obedience, though, sending him an even greater happiness. The Lord was bountiful and good, and the fruits of the earth were lavished upon His servants.

The impending war, the war he did not want, against which he had warned and prayed, had darkened the last months in Lexington. But when war came, he pledged his troth to Virginia. He could not do otherwise. Slavery was a hideous institution, even if men could point to biblical sanctions. Twice, he had purchased slaves, at their request, to save them from being sold south, where treatment was not as mild as in Virginia. But he could not allow godless Northerners, atheists and Unitarians, to invade his home and dictate terms to his people. If the South wished to go its own way, it was tyranny to employ force to prevent it. And tyranny was an abomination, clothed in the mantle of Herod, of Caesar.

He had wept for what he knew must come, the blood, the loss, the heartbreak. He had believed—a part of him still did—that the only humane approach was to do all to force the war to a swift conclusion. He had recommended raising the black flag and granting no quarter, killing each Northern soldier without mercy, drawing his lessons of war from the book of Joshua: None could be spared until they bowed down to Israel.

He had been derided, his vision declared infamous. There had been talk of removing him from command. Again, there were whispers of madness.

Then they came to Manassas.

Nine a.m.
Chancellorsville

Damn it," Hooker responded. The morning already had brought enough frustrations. "All right then, Dickinson," he told the colonel, "reschedule the forward movement for ten thirty. But not one minute after. No more delays, make that clear."

"Yes, sir. It's . . . the roads are . . . they're hardly roads at all. The men moving up are crowding, intermingling. And that fog earlier . . ."

"Don't give me excuses. Give me results."

"Yes, sir."

The vegetation had surprised him, though. A serpent couldn't squirm through it. But that was all the more reason to hasten forward, to adhere to the timetable he and Dan had designed.

He'd slept badly. At some unholy hour, after he'd finally won his standoff with slumber, he'd awakened abruptly, sweat-soaked in terror over something vital and forgotten. Of course, it was only a dream. He could not even recall the object supposedly neglected. But the nightmare had shaken him.

Maneuvering through the staff hubbub, a sergeant brought coffee in a china cup. A delicate thing, with a hairline crack, the cup had been drafted into Union service. Generally, Hooker disapproved of looting—a mark of indiscipline—but the household's women, young and old, had been so crass and intransigent that Dickinson had confined them to one room—where they'd spent half the night screeching Rebel songs and cackling. And when he'd retired at last to the bedroom selected by his staff, Hooker had found the shit pot full and stinking.

Better day today. The weather was clearing. Professor Lowe could get his balloons aloft and check on the rumors that Longstreet had come north.

As he watched Dickinson scurry from one staff drone to the next, Hooker wished Dan Butterfield were with him. He could trust Dan, count on him. Dickinson was all right, but he lacked Butterfield's gift for anticipating his thoughts, his inspirations.

Dan was needed back in Falmouth, though, to hold things together and coordinate Sedgwick's moves on the Fredericksburg front.

Where in the hallows of Hell was the cavalry, though? Except for a small affair beyond his flank the night before—an action that apparently had gone badly—the bulk of his cavalry seemed to have disappeared. He had sent Stoneman off with firm orders to swing deep behind Lee, cut the railroad to Richmond, and block the Confederate retreat. He had to assume that Stoneman was in action, but he needed reports: All the pieces had to fit together.

Part of the problem was that damnable telegraph. It still wasn't working properly. He recalled some sort of squabble Dan had mentioned a few weeks earlier, a quarrel between the Morse operators of the U.S. Military Telegraph and the Army Signal officers. The Signal men had fielded some new device claimed to be superior. Well, progress was fine. But the buggering thing had to work.

"Dickinson!" he called.

After the colonel, eyes weary, had shouldered his way through the riot of clerks and messengers, Hooker told him, "If the march orders are out, see to the telegraph. Get my order off to Sedgwick for a demonstration. And confirm that it's gone. Or the Signal officer at the ford will find himself in the infantry this evening. At a rank greatly reduced."

"Yes, sir."

"Still no word from Stoneman, the cavalry?"

"No, sir. Nothing from the expedition. But Averell—"

"I'm not interested in Averell, at the moment."

"He's asking for orders, he's still north of the river."

"Later. And I want to see Warren as soon as he's back from his scout." Hooker grimaced and spit. "Did somebody piss in this coffee?"

"I'll speak to the mess officer, General."

Hooker splashed the contents of the cup on the Turkey carpet, speckling the toes of his boots.

"Meade still bitching? I thought he'd be happy I let him lead the advance."

"He's concerned about splitting his corps, sir. Along divergent routes."

"They only diverge initially."

"It's the lack of lateral communications in this . . . tangle. The lines of advance aren't mutually reinforcing."

"We've all read our Jomini, Dickinson. Meade just needs to obey the orders as issued. Plenty of reinforcements on hand. In the unlikely event they're needed." Wretched coffee be damned, Hooker almost smiled. "If Lee hasn't run off already, he'll have to fight me on ground that *I* choose."

"Yes, sir."

"Slocum?"

"He'll step off at ten thirty, there was just some early confusion. Everything's in order now. Meade on the River Road and Turnpike. Slocum takes the Plank Road. Simultaneous advances."

Darius Couch came in, wearing what passed for a smile. The latest corps commander to arrive, he was also next in seniority. Hooker sent Dickinson back to his endless labors.

"Joe, I thought we'd be on our way by now." Couch seemed in high spirits, though. With two of his Second Corps divisions present and Gibbon well-employed at Fredericksburg. It was indeed a mighty force, this army that he, Joseph Hooker, had rebuilt from near ruination.

"Ten thirty step-off, had to delay," Hooker told him. "Order stands, though. I expect to reach Fredericksburg this afternoon."

General Couch drew out his pocket watch. "Assuming there's no resistance . . . that's still quite a march."

"This army has to learn to respect a timetable," Hooker said. "And follow orders to the last detail."

Couch shrugged in what passed for agreement. He said:

"George is still unhappy, you know."

Hooker waved off the concern. "Meade's always unhappy. He's either glum or grouchy, take your pick."

"He . . . does have something of a point, Joe. You could have let him allocate his own corps as he saw fit. That's normally the privilege of—"

"No. I want Sykes on the Turnpike with the Regulars. I want

them to be first into Fredericksburg. In good marching order, make a proper show of it."

"That's George's weakest division, though. And with his other divisions on that mule track to the north . . ."

"If Sykes needs help, you can send him Hancock's brawlers."

"To that point . . . I thought I'd stay around headquarters for a bit. In case you *do* have orders for me."

"Glad of the company."

A sergeant delivered fresh coffee. Hooker told him to fetch a cup for Couch. And he drank, burning his lips.

The taste was as wretched as it had been before.

Hooker was about to hurl the cup against the wall, when he realized why the taste was so peculiar: There was no whiskey in it.

Couch looked at him oddly then said:

"Joe, your hand is shaking."

Eleven a.m.
The Lewis house, on the Turnpike

Cap'n, best come up here," the old woman called from the head of the stairs. "Take yourself a look."

Charlie Wickersham, 8th Pennsylvania Cavalry, leapt the steps two at a time.

"In here, in here." The woman led him into an attic bedroom that forced him to crouch low.

It was the strangest stretch of Virginia that Wickersham had encountered, where one household held to the Union, while the next was as Confederate as Jeff Davis, and everyone was blood-kin.

He bent to the low window. And yes, there they were: a broad scattering of skirmishers, a dozen of them mounted, a larger number afoot and loping forward, not a mile distant. Three ranks of infantry followed, several hundred yards to the skirmishers' rear. It looked to be a single regiment, but Wickersham knew there would be more behind them, past the farthest ridge.

The Rebs coming on were out for a scrap, not just having a look-see. He could feel the difference in the morning air.

Trying not to tumble over his spurs, he sidestepped down the stairs and hollered, "McCallum . . . Captain McCallum!" He burst onto the front porch and leapt to the yard. "McCallum!"

Only two companies, K and H, had been detailed as pickets, leaving Wickersham the senior man.

"Bricks—" McCallum rushed around the corner of the house, buckling on his sword belt and his revolver.

"Jeez, Charlie . . . a man can't even—"

"Get your men ready. But stay right here. Rebs are coming, I'm off to the forward post." He rushed for his nickering mount, held by his orderly.

"You," Wickersham told the man, "follow me." He turned. "First Sergeant, report to Captain McCallum until I get back."

"Good luck, sir."

He slapped into his saddle and jabbed his spurs, gaining the speed to leap a brush fence and ride hard. On lower ground, his forward pickets couldn't see the skirmishers, not yet, but he couldn't have risked them at a more distant position. He could see and support them where they were, but their own line of sight was limited.

They'd be a surprise to the Rebs, though.

The terrain rolled from one smoothed-off ridge down to a sopping bottom and back up, over and over. A farmhouse and ramshackle outbuildings crowned each significant crest. Even here, free of that ugly tangle of briars around Chancellorsville, only the fields along the Turnpike offered room for maneuver. On both flanks, forest walled off the tilled ground.

Excited, his horse overshot the outpost and he yanked it about. "Sergeant Keller? Where's Sergeant Keller?"

"In the brush, sir. Thought the Rebs might be up to something."

"You're Burton, right? Schuylkill County man?"

"Yes, sir."

"I want you to—"

The sergeant emerged from the bushes at a trot. Paunchy, he was more impressive on a horse than afoot. Tough, though, with fists that threatened immediate discipline.

"Sorry, sir. Thought they might be sneaking by us. Had to have a gander."

"They're coming straight on. Look."

Concealed until then, the first Reb skirmishers, the mounted dozen, loomed over a crest.

"Well, howdy-do," the sergeant said.

"More behind them," Wickersham told him. "Infantry. Slow them as long as you can, but don't overstay your welcome. When it gets too hot, mount up and come back to the house. We'll make a stand there."

"Yes, sir. We'll give them a greeting fit to start the day."

The Reb skirmishers on horseback hesitated then responded to a signal to dismount, drawing their rifles after them. The men afoot caught up and aligned with the dismounts, making the odds perhaps sixty against a dozen.

The sergeant, who knew his men, said, "Richards, if you pull that trigger before I say to pull it, I'll rip off your treasures and feed them to my horse." He glanced about. "The rest of you, take time to aim, don't waste ammunition. And touch that trigger like it's your sweetie's quim."

Wickersham left the sergeant to his business.

Bullets sought his back as he rode away.

At least they had fair weather for it. For three days they'd pestered the Johnnies, who'd pestered them in turn, in slovenly collisions in the rain.

Back at the old woman's house, he waved up McCallum and called for both first sergeants, all of them grown into hard, no-nonsense soldiers.

Wickersham pointed at the brush fence. In the distance, his outpost and the Johnnies popped away at each other, with the Rebs slowing down as they reckoned things.

"Company K to the left of the Turnpike, behind the fence. H has the road itself and the right. Just enough men in the woods on both flanks to warn us, if they get clever."

"They try to come through that undergrowth, they won't come fast."

"Slow is just as deadly, if they surprise us. And bugger the rules on horse-holders. No more than five men allotted from each company, have them herd the mounts against the tree lines. I want the maximum number of carbines on line." He met each pair of eyes in turn. "Go to it."

Restraining his own first sergeant for a moment, Wickersham added, "Pick a man who can't shoot worth a damn. I need him to carry a note to Major Keenan."

McCallum and his first sergeant strode along, bellowing orders. The men were alert and ready. Everyone sensed that this day's fight would be serious: No more fooling Rebs into surrendering, no more backcountry cat-and-mouse.

Wickersham steadied his notebook on a fence post and tongued his pencil. Writing in block letters for clarity's sake, he estimated the force before him and said he'd delay their advance as long as possible. But it would take the full regiment to hold them. With artillery.

As the first sergeant and his noncommissioned officers placed the men, Wickersham watched the fighting develop down on the lower crest. His men were making good use of their carbines, but the Johnnies kept pressing forward while curling around the flanks.

It was up to Keller now. The sergeant had to decide when the moment had come to mount up and dig in the spurs.

Wickersham checked the cylinders of his Colt.

Eleven thirty a.m.
The Turnpike

The Yankees were stubborn as mules in a temper. Same horse soldiers who'd been an affliction for days. Almost old friends, except you meant to kill them. Day before, they'd taken a passel of men from the 12th Virginia prisoner, though some had slipped off again. And that was atop the men taken back at the ford. Now, Corporal Smith reckoned, the tables were turned.

Not exactly upside down, though, those tables. The blue-bellies kept up a hellish fire with their cheater's carbines. It had taken Captain Banks and the skirmish company far too long to deal with a little outpost.

"Let's go, boys, let's go! Advance! They're ready to run."

"Hell they are," the soldier next to Smith grumbled.

Hadn't been the best stretch of days. It still downright tormented him that he'd built that bridge for the Yankees. Then the rest of the circus had followed, one fool move after another. Little Billy was hopping mad and none too pleased with the regiment.

Meant to show him, though. Just needed a fair fight on decent ground.

Almost slipped in the bottom mud. It took a few yards of climbing before his shoe leather—what there was of it—gripped again.

Yankee bullets buzzed past.

Smith's line caught up with the skirmishers and the baker's dozen of cavalrymen who'd come along. Setting up to be a real fight, it was. Smith didn't understand why Mahone didn't send up the rest of the brigade. As if he were punishing the 12th, making them pay a blood price.

If it weren't for those carbines . . .

Fool business. That brush fence ahead wasn't any kind of protection for the blue-bellies. Shoot right through it, and it didn't take a pioneer to see it. But men didn't think clearly in a fight. They only saw that they couldn't see the Yankees, while the Yankees could see them. And shoot downhill at them, even if they shot high.

Men just lined up on their own, shoulder to shoulder, not ready to renew the advance, just loading and firing up at the Yankees, hoping to hit something.

Smith looked back, "to see whence my succor cometh," as the deacon said, only to observe the third and last line of the regiment filing off into the wood line. Flanking the Yankees, surely. But that would take a painful stretch of time.

Some of the officers saw it, too, and figured things out. A beast with a mind of its own, the line halted on the slope moved forward again, even raised a cheer.

The Yankees kept popping up and firing. Good men fell.

It was enough, though. When Smith and his comrades got within fifty yards of the fence, a Yankee on horseback, an officer, rode along their line, calm as could be, bewilderingly unshot, ordering his men back.

"Shoot that-there sumbitch," a low-white voice called. But no ball struck the officer.

The 12th Virginia swarmed through the fence, scratched and nettled and cussing and howling, possessors of a small victory.

Yankees got off their wounded, though. And not one body lay sprawled around the farmhouse. Smith could see the blue-bellies rallying on the next stretch of high ground.

Noon

Reuben McGee farm, the Turnpike

Flanked on both sides again, Wickersham pulled his men from a last delaying position to rejoin the regiment, which waited, arrayed and ready, on a reverse slope. His men had been driven back a mile, but they'd cost the Johnnies an hour. And he'd brought his two companies this far with only a pair of wounded.

This would be the real fight, though. The last ridge had to be held. Behind them, there was little more ground before the tangles began, almost as bad for infantry as for cavalry.

"Go!" he shouted, as bullets hunted bluecoats. *"Ride! Re-form on the regiment!"*

They'd cut it close this time. But Wickersham made sure that he was the last man to leave the position.

As the two small companies rode pell-mell for the line of the

8th Pennsylvania, the rest of the regiment cheered them, while two fieldpieces fired over their heads to slow the Rebs.

An aide rode forward to direct Wickersham and his riders to the left. The allotted ground was poor, but secondary. The general position was good. With his men in place, Wickersham rode forward again for a better view.

The Johnnies who'd driven them back were disorganized, but their mettle was up and they were coming on again, even though they might better have waited on supports. Whoever those Rebs were, they had a grudge.

The captain calculated that he could remain exposed for one last minute. While McCallum and the first sergeants sorted things out.

When, at last, he began to turn his horse, a cavalcade broke from the line behind him, with a half-dozen flags and pennants flying.

An older fellow spurred his horse toward Wickersham. He rode close before the captain recognized General Sykes.

"Bully work, Captain," the division commander called. "Masterful, just what the damned cavalry should be. Been watching while my boys came up. Damned impressive."

Belatedly, Wickersham offered a salute. Only then did he realize how drained he felt. All he could say was, "Rebs are in a high temper, sir."

Sykes lifted his jaw. "My division will knock it out of them."

Corporal Smith's spirits soared as he saw the last line of Yankee horsemen pull back without much of a fight. Everyone felt it. A fine Rebel yell rent the day and men swarmed forward, as if they might catch them each a Yankee and drag him from his horse. Even Lieutenant Colonel Feild, down on his own two feet now, took to hollering, "That's it, boys! That's the way! For Virginia and old Petersburg! Drive on for the old Southside!"

Too thrilled to halt and fire at retreating Yankees, men ran madly, as if for a wondrous prize. Dispersed by its triumph, by having knocked the Yankees back a mile and more, the regiment grew more unwieldly with each moment, rushing for the now abandoned crest in little groups and dividing to pass a farmhouse crowning the height.

Then they stopped.

Barely a rifle shot away, the blue horsemen trotted off to reveal perfectly dressed lines of infantry, a full brigade or more.

"Oh, Lord," a soldier moaned.

"Them's the Regulators," another fellow said. "All pretty like that."

"Reg'lars," another corrected.

A gun section opened fire from the oblique. The blue lines advanced. Their bayonets shone.

"Form up, form up!" the 12th's officers shouted, Feild among them. He waved his sword and demanded, "Form on your colors, men!"

A goodly number of soldiers obeyed, but not all of them did. The regiment got off a volley, and then another. The Yankees didn't trouble to reply. They just came stepping along, stretching across the Turnpike, from tree line to tree line and beyond, ranked deep.

The 12th gave ground. Smith kept close to the colors. Men began to run, the last order broke down. Smith ran, too. It was a sensation that had grown all too familiar.

When he looked back—weary of looking over his shoulder at lucky Yankees—he witnessed the surrender of a pack of fools who'd cowered behind the farmhouse.

Down past a family graveyard and back through another bottom the survivors ran, half expecting the cavalry to pursue them with slashing sabers. But another, worried glance backward revealed only the advancing infantry. Made Smith sick, though.

And thirsty. He realized he was half fainting with thirst. The day had grown warm.

Smoke drifted, fading.

On a long shelf of ground, not yet a ridge, the officers and sergeants gathered the men again, manhandling some. No flags had been lost and not so many men, after all. The regiment still could fight.

And a blind man could see that the Yankees had their own problems. The regiments in the open fields flanking the highway were surging ahead of those thrashing through the undergrowth. Fewer to fight, if the fight developed soon.

They gave the Yankees a volley at 150 yards, but it was paltry. Closing half the distance, unusually disciplined, the blue-bellies halted, steadied their ranks, and fired.

Recoils jerked shoulders. Smoke rose. Along Smith's line, men fell.

The Yankees stretched beyond both flanks of the regiment, threatening to engulf them, to capture them all.

Men complained that they were out of cartridges. Some fled anew.

The 12th withdrew again, but in better order now. Someone said Captain Banks had been shot up badly, but Feild and the remaining officers put up a good front.

"Billy Mahone want to get us massacred?" Bart Teedlow demanded. "Ain't he got him a whole brigade to use? Or did he plain forget us?"

Detachments sent to the flanks were soon embattled, divided, and driven into the scrub pines and the brush.

They tried again to stand and failed again.

But just when all had despaired, when Lieutenant Colonel Feild's voice had quit him and the officers could barely raise their swords, as embittered men staggered back up a ridge they'd purchased with their blood an hour before, the rest of the brigade appeared on the crest, red banners leading.

The anger at Little Billy dissolved in an instant.

As the 12th withdrew and the Yankees halted behind them to make a fight of it, Mahone rode out among the hard-used men.

"Damned fine!" the brigadier general hallooed, a tiny man with a long beard, on a big horse. He took off his hat in salute. "*Damned* fine work, mighty fine!"

Word spread that Jackson was up, that the 12th Virginia had fixed the Yankees in place and bought precious time.

And all was forgiven.

Twelve thirty p.m.
River Road

With his horse tugged to the side of the trail to let his soldiers squeeze by, Meade said:

"I can*not* believe this infernal, goddamned, piss-up-a-rope buggery."

"Fucked for beans," Charlie Griffin agreed.

The soldiers slumping along were too unnerved by the general's burst of temper to be amused. They looked off into the trees or fixed their eyes on the shoulders and necks in front of them.

Meade calmed his voice to a beast's growl. In the distance, miles to the south, volleys crackled and fieldpieces blasted away. Sykes was in a fight, Meade had no doubt, and he knew nothing about it beyond what he could hear. Patrols dispatched southward had met only more tangles. He could not control the fate of his Second Division, nor tell if things were going well or badly. And no one seemed concerned enough to inform him. All he got from Hooker's headquarters were contradictory—and peremptory—orders.

His first assigned objective had been to seize the southern side of Banks' Ford, to shorten communications back to Falmouth. He met no opposition beyond the sniping of mounted scouts, and his forward element had just sighted the ford—when the order reached Meade to reverse his line of march, retrace his steps, and take the Mine Road to the southeast.

That had, at least, offered the prospect of moving closer to Sykes and reuniting the corps. So he led his two on-hand divisions of increasingly skeptical soldiers down yet another trail pretending to be a road, only to receive another order canceling the previous directive and advising him to return to his original route and objectives.

At least it wasn't raining. But the beauty of the day couldn't dent his surliness.

What on God's earth did Hooker have in mind?

His divisions countermarched again and plodded along a mud track gagged by trees, pressed between bands of undergrowth thick as mesh and dark as Hades. And George Meade, who'd been looking for a fight since the campaign began, found himself marching away from the sounds of battle, away from the unknown fate of Sykes and his detached division.

His faith in Joseph Hooker had suffered a crack the day before. Now it began to crumble.

One p.m.
The Turnpike

They'd gotten off to a bully start, but George Sykes couldn't mistake the turning tide. Nor was he happy with his apparent abandonment: He hadn't heard from George Meade and the rest of the corps on his left, and neither had he had a word from Slocum, whose corps was supposed to be active on his right. As for orders from Hooker or reinforcements, he might as well have been waging war in China.

Volleys rippled. Men shouted. Smoke shrouded the earth.

He turned to Warren, the Army of the Potomac's senior engineer and a perennial busybody who'd come out to have a look. Warren had the face of a bird of prey, but if one day he resembled a hawk, on the next he looked like a vulture with mustaches. Voice raised to be heard over nearby guns, Sykes called from saddle to saddle:

"Warren, if you please . . . go back and report the situation to Hooker. If he wants me to hold, I have to be supported. The Johnnies are piling in more men by the minute, I'm threatened on both flanks. And I'm damned well outnumbered. No excuse for it, given the force Joe has on hand. My division can't take on Lee's entire army."

"Had been going rather well, I thought."

"Well, it's not going well now. The Regulars took a whipping. It's not about tactics now, it's mathematics."

A Reb shell whistled in and struck close, stinging them with dirt.

"I can hold, if reinforced," Sykes continued. "Send in another division and we can even resume the advance, or try our damnedest. But, for God's sake, someone has to support me."

"I'll do what I can. But you know Joe, his plan."

"I *don't* know his plan, that's the worst of it. All I know is that I'm in a fight where there wasn't supposed to be a fight at all. And we're on the verge of squandering a chance to open this road." Sykes had another thought. "Listen, Warren . . . don't make it sound like we've already been whipped, that's not the message. Just tell Hooker . . . tell him we're fighting well, but we need support. That's all."

Another Rebel yell announced a charge.

One thirty p.m.
Chancellor house

Sykes has to withdraw," Joe Hooker said. That much seemed clear. Struck by another headache, he struggled to put the rest of his thoughts in order, but it was obvious that Sykes had to pull back.

Warren appeared startled. "Sir . . . if I made things sound too dire, I'm sorry. Sykes needs reinforcement, that's all. The prospects—"

"No. He *must* pull back." The racket of battle reached the porch from miles away: dull thumps, waves of muddled noise. "I've got Lee now, he's out from behind his defenses, I forced him out. But I won't let him choose the battlefield." The headache was wretched and he had no wish to explain further. But Warren was rather a gossip and needed tending. "I've had messages, Warren. From Falmouth, from Butterfield. Telegraph's working, it seems. Balloon crew detected heavy Confederate movements westward from Fredericksburg. It's all . . . everything's going according to my plan.

They're all but abandoning Fredericksburg, it should fall into Sedgwick's hands with hardly a struggle. And Lee . . . Lee has a choice. He can either fight me where *I* choose, he can fight me right here . . . or run."

Unconsciously, he laid the back of his hand over his forehead, as if reading a fever. "If he doesn't attack in force in the morning . . . if Lee loses his nerve, we'll know he's running."

Eyebrow ranging high, Warren observed, "Doesn't seem like he's running at the moment. Sykes is in a serious fight, sir. If we—"

Hooker nodded enthusiastically. "That's it, you see. Lee *had* to lash out. To protect his line of retreat. If Sharpe's correct, that's Jackson out there, force-marched from Fredericksburg. Lee must be in a panic."

Warren still looked quizzical, unsatisfied. Hooker decided he had no more time to waste on the man. He wheeled and shouted for Dickinson. Orders had to go out not just to Sykes, but to Slocum and Meade to pull back to the lines they'd held that morning. He wouldn't allow Lee to gobble his army piecemeal. Lee would have to fight them all, or none.

Dickinson appeared before the two generals, with Roebling, an engineer sort, at his shoulder.

Hooker's head made him want to lie down in a darkened room, but he refused to weaken. "Any word from Sedgwick? The Fredericksburg business?"

The colonel shook his head.

"All right," Hooker continued, "send orders to Sykes, Meade, and Slocum. Immediately." He looked at Roebling, a headquarters dogsbody. "*You* ride to Slocum, don't wait. Before he finds himself heavily engaged. I'll put it in writing later, but tell him he's to withdraw and with no delay. His corps will return to its previous position."

What was wrong with these people? With their dunce-cap expressions?

"Don't gawk, man. *Go,*" he told Roebling.

"General . . . ," Dickinson began.

Hooker held up a hand: *Silence.* "I have decided to consolidate the army. Here. Let Lee try to attack through these tangles . . . we'll trounce him, destroy him." He concentrated on Dickinson. "*All* advancing forces are to withdraw. Immediately. Can't let Lee . . ."

He lost his train of thought for a moment. His head throbbed. He closed his eyes.

"Sir"—Dickinson's voice pierced his skull—"General Couch has Hancock coming up. He's set to reinforce Sykes, if that's what's needed. Perhaps we should—"

"Hancock's to cover Sykes' withdrawal, nothing more." He remembered something. "Couch still here?"

"No, sir. He rode forward. Twenty minutes ago. He went up to coordinate Hancock's advance."

Yes. Of course. How on earth could he have forgotten that?

"Pull everyone back. Immediately. The army will prepare to defend, get the order out to all the corps. I'll force Lee to attack me. Or he can run like a coward."

Eyes aching, he met looks of doubt, of weakness almost insolent. And this was no time for weakness of any kind.

His head, his head . . .

He would have traded a first-class regiment for a glass of whiskey.

One forty-five p.m.
Alrich farm, right flank of Union advance

Wash Roebling rode for the cluster of flags. Beyond, rifles snapped by the hundreds, while a battery, freed of the road's confines, rattled into a field. Slocum had been as dilatory as his name suggested, but his corps was advancing into a fight at last. Roebling didn't understand Hooker's decision, but it wouldn't have done to argue. His expertise lay in building bridges, not in directing armies. His job was to do as told.

It did seem a bit odd, though. To quit before one got started. All blueprint and no construction.

Slocum sat in his saddle with his shoulders squared and his usual joyless expression. Roebling guided his mare through the mob of staff men.

"General Slocum! General Slocum, sir! Orders from General Hooker!"

The corps commander turned heavy eyes toward him. "What the devil does Joe want now? I'm busy, son."

"Orders, sir. You're to withdraw immediately, your entire corps. To the position you held this morning."

Slocum's mouth fell open. It didn't quite close again. He stared. *"What?"*

"You're to withdraw, sir. General Hooker's orders."

Slocum pulled his horse about, the better to face Roebling. The older man glowered.

"You're a goddamned liar."

Roebling didn't answer. He didn't know what to say.

Slocum turned to an aide and began, "Ross, you ride back and—"

He cut himself off. "No, I'll ride back myself. Get to the bottom of this nonsense. Meanwhile, press the fight." Giving Roebling a last, hard look, he told him, "If you've been lying to me, boy, I'll have you shot right here."

Two ten p.m.
The Turnpike, Union center

Missing its two front legs, a shrieking battery horse waited for someone to find the time to shoot it.

"This is madness," General Couch told Sykes after reading the order. "We can't give up this ground. We'd be locking the entire army into a prison."

Sykes looked stunned, incapable of speech.

"When I left the headquarters, Joe was full of fight," Couch added, bewildered.

Sykes found his voice. He told an orderly, "Ride to Colonel Burbank. Quickly. Tell him the Regulars are not to attack that battery, it's off. Further orders follow."

The corporal saluted and spurred his horse into the smoke, dodging a wounded man stumbling rearward and clutching his bloodied head.

Major General Darius Couch decided that there had to be a mistake. He sent his adjutant back to the army's headquarters at a gallop.

"What the hell am I supposed to do?" Sykes asked.

"Prepare to withdraw," Couch told him. "And hope."

Two twenty p.m.
River Road, Union left

George Meade read the order. Twice. Then he crumpled it, crushed it. About to hurl it to the ground, he caught himself and thrust it into his pocket. No need to make a gift of it to the Rebs.

He still heard the sounds of battle, they hadn't slackened a bit. If anything, the artillery sounded heavier. Had the day, against the odds, turned into a sudden defeat? How on earth . . .

Sykes? Had things gone badly? Had his division been beaten?

What was Hooker thinking?

Meade had left Griffin to ride with Humphreys and his division for a stretch. A fellow Philadelphian, Humph watched him now, face disciplined against any sign of emotion.

"Halt your column," Meade told him. "Then countermarch."

In his iron-hard, thirty-years-of-service voice, Humphreys simply asked, "That mud track again?"

"No. All the way back this time. To where we started."

Humphreys was too strict with himself to say it, but gray eyes asked, *Are you serious?*

Meade nodded and turned his horse.

FOUR

Five p.m., May 1
Orange Plank Road

The Yankees just plain quit. Strangest thing. Had no stick-to at all.

Up in the night before the rain gave out, the Alabama Brigade had slogged along—fellow might say "swam," just about—with old Stonewall and everybody else with braid on him in half a fit, moving men just as fast as men could go, through black fog along ankle-busting roads. As if the condition of his feet—those recalcitrant and rebellious walking utensils—wasn't plain bad enough.

Samuel Pickens could not pretend to be happy.

Half-contented, though, in a take-what-you-get way, a soldier's shrug at the world. The march seemed to be over.

The going had been cruel. That morning, the fog had burned off in the course of an unexplained pause and the day had turned fine as Alabama weather, summoning ripe, rich ghosts of verdant Umbria, of Greensboro under blue heavens. The morning had been that handsome. Uniforms and underthings dried out, if not a man's shoes.

The march had resumed, though, with his feet a misery unto him, though he spake not. Complaint was unmanly, unless it was masked in jest. They shuffled toward the rising sounds of battle, certain of their destiny that day, of a red-jawed fight impending.

Instead, they had only stopped and started and fussed, deploying into nettle-bibbed trees, a place less welcoming than a backwater swamp. Heat rose queerly, hotter in that grim forest than in the sunlight. And once they'd been thoroughly thorn-pierced, they had been summoned back to the road to march a few hundred yards farther along before spreading out into line of battle again, in growth still more forbidding. The ruckus of battle, the life sounds and death sounds, had come closer, but not close enough for stray bullets to sting.

They never did get into it. Which left men grateful and feeling let down at once. As for himself, he did fine in a fight, but he did dislike the waiting, the anticipation, the minutes and hours when a man's imagination taunted and tested him. Truth be told, times were he quivered, hoping no man noticed. Until he saw, Gospel clear, that each man trapped in those waitings turned inward and closed, wrestling his own hants and spooks. Even the officers got a jump in their voices whenever they walked a waiting line to show themselves, preaching courage and discipline and whatnot.

Now here they were, waiting still but at ease. The rattle of rifles and thump of cannon had moved away and—Pickens believed—diminished. The armies were like two boys in the schoolyard who, after puffing themselves up and jabbing timidly, decided they didn't much want to fight, after all.

Did hear the occasional Rebel yell. Clear enough to know who was being driven.

Made him miss his dogs. Whenever a scrap took on the feel of a slowed-down hunt, he missed his dogs mightily. He did hope Nestor had been looking after them. Singular Negro, Nestor, who liked dogs. Most bucks feared them, rightfully.

Auntie Delsie hated Nestor, the reason ever unclear.

Nigger business. You just had to let it run. 'Long as it didn't trouble the order of things.

Resting in the shade, the men watched as Colonel O'Neal rode past with General Rodes. Both men looked like officers were supposed to look.

Bill Price asked: "How's them feet, Sam?"

"Tolerable," Pickens lied. "Got me here."

"Those hind paws are going to get you before the Yankees do," Doc Cowin put in. "Told you to see the surgeon. But Man is an unreasonable creature."

"After the fight. I'll see to them."

Joe Grigg snorted. "Don't seem like the Yankees are in a fighting mood."

Doc Cowin's forehead was jeweled with sweat: The added years told, although old Doc was game. "Gentlemen, the majesty of the Union must not be slighted. Those boys didn't go to all this trouble just to run off again. No, we shall once more unto the breach. Or into those trees yonder."

"Can't say as I like the place," Bob Price declared. "Give a man the shivers."

"Wouldn't mind filling my canteen," good Bill Lenier said.

Price recalled the cool well water at Umbria.

Weary-eyed and serious, Joe Grigg asked Doc Cowin, "Really think they'll fight? Maybe they've already had enough."

"Might be the soldiers have had their fill. Just might be. But it's all aces their generals haven't. Can't just cross back over that river without killing lots of folks. Theirs or ours, hardly makes a difference. Just need bodies heaped up to show they tried."

Well, if they had to fight, Samuel Pickens hoped it would be nearby. He didn't want to march another step. Maybe, he thought, he ought to see the surgeon, after all. He feared taking off what remained of his shoes, afraid he'd scratch himself down to the bone, turn himself into a skeleton below the ankles.

Another cavalcade trotted by on the forest track, stirring dust where mud had been hours before. Doc Cowin said:

"Behold bold Hector, favored son of Priam."

Bill Price said, "Looks like Jackson to me."

Five thirty p.m.
North bank of the Rappahannock, Fredericksburg

"Uncle John" Sedgwick was at a loss. What the devil did Joe Hooker want him and his corps to do? He hadn't thought much of Hooker when they were classmates at West Point, and he thought less of him now.

Wouldn't say so, though.

He had more respect for Jube Early, another classmate, who waited on that ridge across the river, if the Reb deserters weren't telling tall tales.

Bugger of a thing, the way the war set men at each other. He'd served under Bob Lee, after the Army decided he'd make a better cavalry major than captain of artillery. And though it wasn't a thing to be said out loud, either, he wasn't convinced that Joe was that man's match.

John Sedgwick would do his duty, though. Always did. He'd grit his teeth and execute, the way he had carried out that affair with the Cherokees. Take a war over that shabby business any day.

The problem was that he didn't know which orders he was to follow. He'd received a telegraphic message at four o'clock directing him to shift from his demonstration to an attack, if it seemed propitious. But he'd never gotten the order to begin the demonstration until now, an hour after the attack order. And that was followed in short by another message: Hooker was suspending his advance.

What the devil did they expect him to do with one corps and scraps when Joe was pulling in his horns with over a hundred thousand men at his right hand?

Bad enough getting shot three times at Antietam—he wasn't about to get shit on by Joe Hooker.

He'd sent a message to Butterfield at Falmouth, asking for clarification. Now he wondered if he hadn't ought to ride over there himself? The telegraph was hardly reliable, with messages sent in the afternoon arriving before orders drawn up in the morning.

All he knew was that he was not going to sacrifice his soldiers' lives playing guessing games. He had thirty thousand men across that river, ready to play their role, and more in reserve. They were good men, who trusted him. Given clear orders, he'd obey, but he wasn't one to make cheap stabs at glory.

And that "demonstration" nonsense. *That* was a phony word that just shifted the blame. "Feint" he understood. And he understood "supporting attack." He even grasped "detain the enemy." But how many lives was a "demonstration" reckoned at? It sounded like a dress parade with corpses.

As for an attack against that bloodstained ridge across the river, he was not about to repeat poor Burnside's folly. Let Joe draw off more of Lee's men and he'd give it a try, if issued a clear order. But he couldn't advance without some hope of advantage.

He wasn't going to wreck his corps and become another scapegoat, if Joe failed.

Seven p.m.
Falmouth, rear headquarters of the Army of the Potomac

"Cushing, the telegraph has to be *dependable*. Do you understand me?" Dan Butterfield wasn't a shouting general, but he had to struggle to contain himself. He had issued an order that any soldier caught tampering with the telegraph lines would be shot, but it hadn't helped. "If we can't coordinate the wings of this army, the movements and actions . . ."

He stopped. Glancing about. He did not want the headquarters reinfected with defeatism. The Army of the Potomac had had enough of that.

Voice lowered to a conversational tone, he continued: "Just see to it, Captain. Make the telegraph work."

The Signal officer stood before him as if he expected the whipping to continue.

"Go and see to it," Butterfield repeated.

The captain turned to leave, caught himself, turned back, and saluted.

Butterfield ignored him. He'd had enough of the fellow's excuses. And quite enough of military inanities.

He saw now that they should have stuck with the Morse operators, the tried-and-true. He'd ordered them into action at last, and the first link was clicking away, but that was only a start, and far too many messages disappeared or made no sense.

Was the plan just too good, too complicated? He'd begun to fear it and had to bolster himself.

All had been going splendidly, but now the first stitches were popping at the seams. Nothing terribly wrong, not yet. But Butterfield had grown uneasy. Why had Joe stopped cold that afternoon? It didn't seem he'd really given battle, not if the reports that got through were accurate.

Was Joe all right? When he'd read Joe's message to the troops the night before, the swagger had left him uneasy. Every man had his faults, and Joe's—one of Joe's—was the brag he put on at times. Yes, the crossings had summed to a magnificent feat, full credit for that. Joe had leapt rivers and come down atop Lee's army, it had been a splendid coup.

But Lee wasn't beaten, not yet.

Butterfield crossed the room and bent over a map of operations.

"Bring another lamp over here," he snapped. "A man can't see a damned thing."

That was untrue. He could see a great deal. But he needed to see more.

They'd been a finely matched team, Joe as the commander and he as his deputy. But Joe did need shoring up at times, good counsel. They wanted a better connection than that blasted telegraph.

They needed to react more quickly than Lee, that was the crux of it.

What was *Lee* thinking?

Butterfield studied the map, hunting revelations and secrets. Sharpe's reports and the balloon observers alike insisted that Lee had been shifting forces westward. That had to be the bulk of Jackson's corps, since Sharpe was convinced that Longstreet had not arrived, that reports of his presence were lies planted by false deserters. That movement might portend a significant clash, or—quite possibly—Lee was retreating on Gordonsville, as foreseen. If the latter were true, a rear guard would, of course, have moved to block Joe. That could explain the day's encounter, Lee struggling for breathing room, for a safe route out of Joe's grasp.

But wouldn't it have been wiser, then, for Joe to redouble his efforts? To send in more divisions, not withdraw? Even if Lee did "ingloriously fly," Joe would have to fight him eventually. And a retreating Lee would enjoy ever shorter interior lines, if he recalled the military term. Didn't it make more sense to fight him now, when Lee had been caught off guard?

Well, Dan Butterfield told himself, I'm not one of those blasted West Pointers, am I? Joe has to know what's best, he's the man on the scene, the professional soldier.

He just wished he could sit down and talk to Joe, to get things straight.

The map was no comfort at all.

Twilight

The Plank Road at the Catherine Furnace Road

We must attack them tomorrow," Lee said.

Jackson sat on the log beside him. Waiting.

"He wants us to attack him," Lee continued. "And we shall oblige him."

"Lost his nerve today," Jackson commented.

Lee nodded. "Should that be true, we must take advantage of it."

"Wouldn't surprise me to find him back across the river come morning."

"Perhaps," Lee said. "But we must assume he will stay. And he must pay a great price for his presumption."

Jackson poked the dirt with a stick. They had no fire: A Yankee sharpshooter had been active earlier. Still, the nearby crossroads bustled with recalled detachments, shifting batteries, couriers, commissaries, and laggards trailing their regiments. In the distance, hundreds of Yankee axes felled trees to form abatis. Occasionally, a fieldpiece probed a target. But the day's fighting was done.

"How can we get at those people?" Lee asked.

"One flank, or the other," Jackson said. "They're entrenching. Ground between us is poor. No place for a frontal attack."

"No. But a limited attack might fix their attention. A supporting attack, no more. While we move on a flank."

"Right flank? Cut him off from the river? Bag them?"

Lee shook his head. His neck was stiff. And his hindquarters were sore. He was not as supple as he once had been. "I rode out there myself. The roads are few, and constricted. An attacker could not deploy, not under fire."

"Has to be the left, then." Jackson dropped his stick and took off his kepi, revealing thinning hair pasted by sweat.

"I have called for General Stuart," Lee told him. "To see what he might tell us."

Jackson fussed with the brim of the cap. Lee understood the man: Now that an attack had been agreed upon, Jackson was impatient to begin. But many, many details needed to be settled, before a plan could be devised and orders issued for the morrow. They had to be daring, while leaving little to chance. It was a difficult balance at the best of times. And these times were not the best.

The details of a flank attack, if one proved practicable, would demand their attention for most of the night. There were so many questions, so many unknowns. Lee wanted sleep but knew he would get little.

"I wish," he said, "that I knew how many men General Hooker has on the field. Here, in front of us. We know of three corps, but it could be as many as five. Or more. I still do not have an answer."

"Have to hit him, anyway. And hard."

"But where he is weakest, General, where he is least observant . . ."

Lee interrupted the exchange to wave up his waiting adjutant, Major Taylor. Even here, there were papers to sign. Jackson signaled to his young man, Pendleton, that he, too, might now see to anything pressing.

Matters always pressed.

Lee struggled with the documents in the faint light. He trusted Taylor and his staff but still preferred to know what he was signing. He was too vain, though, to ask for explanations.

Amid these skirmishes of paper and ink, Stuart rode in, his advent ever something of an uproar. After dismounting grandly, he approached the other generals in his high boots, sweeping off his hat and grinning as though he'd just done something marvelous. Lee thought, again, of how different these two men were, Jackson and Stuart, one solemn and fierce, the other jovial and, yes, a bit lax at times. Yet, in one more of the Lord's miracles, Jackson displayed a fond indulgence of the younger man and even—sometimes—laughed at his jokes with a noise approaching a bray.

Substituting a bow for a salute, Stuart declared, "Yankee cavalry seem to have gone into hiding. Unwilling to give my men the least pleasure today."

There had been reports from elsewhere of Union cavalry ranging widely. Confusing reports, from various points to the rear. But what mattered was the field before them. All else had to wait.

"General Stuart . . . what can you tell us about the left?" Lee asked.

As quick as ever, Stuart reported: "Hooker has his Eleventh Corps out there, looking lonesome. Their right runs beyond our left. Good ways past. Fitz had a brush with some of them, didn't amount to much. Scouts took a few beeves and a passel of unhappy Germans who'd lost their way."

Jackson quickened. Lee caught the sudden tension through the shadows. If those people were calling up beeves to be slaughtered, it meant they expected to remain on this side of the river, whether immobile or renewing their march.

They would not retire. They would have to be defeated.

"Have you uncovered where their line ends?" Lee asked. "Precisely? How far it's refused, how heavily?"

Stuart shrugged. "I can find out, sir. Tell you right now, it doesn't reach back to the river. They're strung out along the Turnpike, by the Plank Road run-in and beyond. Flank does seem to be in the air, but I'll make certain." He slapped his hat back on his head.

"Do so, General Stuart. Do so." Lee set a stern father's eye upon his cavalry chief. "It's of the greatest import, there must be no delay. And your men must contain them, while we decide upon matters. You *must* shield this army, prevent them from seeing us clearly."

"From seeing us at all," Jackson put in.

Nine p.m.
Union Eleventh Corps headquarters

I'm counting on you, Devens," Oliver Otis Howard told the commander of his First Division, "you've got to be my stalwart. Your fellow division commanders are, well, you know . . ."

"Germans," Devens said, in his sharp New England voice.

The two men stood on the tavern porch where Howard had fixed his headquarters. It had given him pleasure to have the orderlies empty all of the liquor onto the ground: Drunkenness was a bane, whether in an army or in private life, and he shared with his wife a deep commitment to temperance.

"Well, it's more than that, of course," Howard added, quietly. "But you understand."

Devens nodded. "Shame you can't remove at least one of them, hand Frank Barlow a division."

Howard smirked, but not in ill temper. "You Harvard men do stick together, don't you?"

Devens, more aristocratic than the aristocrats Howard had met, wasn't one to give ground. He replied, "Well, I'd say that you West Point fellows form quite the club."

"A divided club, at present. Tragically, but inevitably, divided. The Germans, though . . . between the two of us, one daren't rely on them. They're already seeing Confederate hobgoblins everywhere."

"Matter of science," Devens agreed. "Professor Agassiz' research has proven it, beyond dispute. The Teuton's inferior to the Anglo-Saxon, or to the Scot." He smirked. "You should've heard von Gilsa, he's terrified that Lee's going to leap from the darkness and holler, 'Boo!'"

Howard wondered if he might have been too frank. "One

mustn't reveal one's sentiments, of course. We do have to rub along. It's only—"

Meysenburg, the corps' adjutant general appeared in the doorway. The man was efficient, in his way, but he had been all but forced upon Howard, another relic of the Sigel era.

"Your pardon, gentlemen," the adjutant said, with the lightest of accents. He faced General Howard. "Sir . . . are you certain . . . the commissary wagons . . . is it perhaps the wisest thing to bring them up? The road is very narrow, it's hard to move as things are. We'll have even less freedom of maneuver."

It rankled Howard to have an order questioned. Always did. He sought to restrain the peevishness in his voice:

"Really, Colonel! If Lee is in retreat—as General Hooker just assured me is the case—we need to provision the men for the marches ahead."

"But earlier . . . with the beefs, the confusion . . ."

"The correct form is 'beeves,' Meysenburg. And one can't blame the cattle. The thing was poorly managed, that's human incompetence." He governed his tone again. "I expect better."

"Yes, sir."

The adjutant retreated.

Eyebrows climbing in mock despair, Howard looked at Devens.

The New Englander's face was noncommittal, but he did say, "Doesn't seem a bad sort, actually, Meysenburg."

"Fine enough clerk," Howard said. "But not the man I'd have chosen for such a position." He indulged himself in the briefest flash of temper. "All their inane sensitivities! The dreary, petty politics of it! And half of them atheists! With their tin-pot revolution, which they botched utterly. Before fleeing like mice." He grimaced, disgusted, almost outraged. "Schurz, for example. What on earth qualifies that man to command a division, even a small one? Politics, and politics alone. The blasted German vote. Oh, they're fine when it comes to small details, the Germans. Argue for hours over nothing, but, lo and behold, the belt buckles have a high shine, come inspection. Never make first-rate soldiers of them, though—"

He stopped himself short of employing the word *cowards.*

The corps commander let his thoughts pass in review and then resumed. "Really, I think the Union would do better to enlist the Negro. In generous numbers. Let him take his rightful place, show all men his mettle. Don't just free him, let him free himself. I've spoken to the president about it."

"And?"

Howard moved to fold his arms, only to realize, again, after nearly a year, that his right arm wasn't there. Habit outlasted reason.

"He said the time isn't ripe." Howard's entire body, what remained of it, tightened in earnest. "I fear they'll never think the time is ripe. Lincoln's well enough, in his way, but . . ."

He had given an arm. What had Lincoln given? That proclamation had not gone far enough, not nearly far enough.

It had not been the best of days for Otis Howard, that was the truth of it. The order had come down to ready the corps to march on Fredericksburg, and he'd made the divisions snap to it. But the lead brigade had not gone five hundred yards before a second order arrived to halt the column. Later, an order came down to reoccupy their positions of the morning and prepare for a defense. Even a German would have seen that the failure to advance was a retreat.

Joseph Hooker was an immoral man. Howard hoped he would not also prove an incompetent man, branded by the Lord and destined to fail. God's judgment could be terrible: Entire cities had perished for a ruler's sins. Didn't anyone read Joshua or Kings?

Nor was Hooker enlightened regarding the Negro.

Oliver Otis Howard had first embraced the cause of emancipation because it guaranteed him protectors in Washington and favorable mention in crucial New York papers, but over the months his calculation had become a conviction. The more he saw of the South, the more he despised it. Slavery was evil incarnate, making brutes of all, master and man. And the Negro possessed a natural virtue, a simple will to goodness, that need only be cultivated. And some of the race—particularly those of mixed blood—might raise themselves up through education. It was long past time to break the grip of the South's degenerate whites and empower freedmen.

Nor had it helped his mood that this had been one of those bad days when his lost arm haunted him, when he felt pain where there was no flesh and bone, moments when he still reached out with a right hand long since lost.

He wished his wife were present, long enough to pray together. And, perhaps, a bit longer. Under the sanction of holy matrimony.

"Good night, Devens," Howard said, abruptly. But before he took himself off to his tent to sleep, he added, "And you needn't worry—I won't forget Frank Barlow."

In a nearby field a German band struck up a foreign tune.

Ten p.m.
Hawkins' farm

Eine verdammte Schweinerei," Schimmelfennig declared. "We have throwed this day away. Away, we have throwed it. *Diese verdammten Idioten.*"

"Calm yourself, Alex. Tell me what your men found."

"Ach, the Rebels' cannons have gone away. They have no wish to fight now. But they look at us. *Es war eine Pruefung, nichts weiter.* They test our lines, they judge. My men drive them away, but they come back tomorrow, *ich wage es.* Our position is false, *verkehrt.*"

In the muted firelight, Schimmelfennig took on the look of Mephistopheles in a provincial theater. But that was merely a trick of the light: There was no devilry in the man at all.

"Well, reinforce your pickets," Schurz said. "And we'll see what the morning brings."

He took the brigade commander—his old friend—by the arm and nudged him gently toward the other officers by the fire. Staff and line had been busy this evening, and only a few old acquaintances had appeared for Schurz's *Stammtisch,* the little parliament in which old bonds trumped rank at the end of the day.

Seated on camp chairs or logs rolled close, empty pipes clenched between their teeth from habit, a mere four officers lingered. Hecker, hero and comrade of 1848; von Gilsa, who had made a surprise appearance from Devens' division next on; Peissner, a Bavarian who was both the corps' chess champion and its finest fencer; and Prince Salm-Salm, who barely concealed his resentment of Peissner's skill with saber, rapier, and foil. The prince remained an odd man out, a fervent royalist whose presence was a result of gambling debts in Germany, not a passion for freedom. But the fellow was largely accepted, since he was a distinguished soldier and, of no less import, possessed a wife of phenomenal beauty rumored to have rejected General Hooker's advances with such grace that she remained a favorite at headquarters.

Aren't we a band of gypsies, though? Schurz thought to himself. We've traveled some difficult roads, and here we are. He held back a few steps himself, arms folded, listening to the argument in his old tongue. He insisted that military affairs be conducted in English, but here, between *alte Kameraden,* German prevailed.

"But it could not be more clear," Peissner insisted. "This war is Hegel pure, the dialectic fits perfectly. The Southern thesis excites the Northern antithesis. And the war will end in a new synthesis that becomes a thesis on a higher level. This is demonstrated philosophy, active thought."

"Hegel's a bore," Prince Salm-Salm remarked. The prince was ever the gadfly and once had spent a winter's evening defending Goethe's discredited theory of optics, *die Farbenlehre.*

"I'm not convinced that philosophy moved forward one step after Kant," Hecker put in. "Anyway, in such times, I'd rather read Schiller. Or Heine. We can philosophize when the war is won."

"Without philosophy, we are animals."

"My horse does seem to get on fine without Hegel," Prince Salm-Salm noted.

"And you"—Peissner went on the attack—"you will admit, I think, that you are a man who seeks recognition? Isn't that true?"

"All men seek recognition," the prince allowed.

Peissner clapped his hands. "There you have it! Hegel pure again!

His theory of *Anerkennung*. Hegel was the great world thinker of this century! Schopenhauer is a feather, an after-comer."

"To a Bavarian."

It would go on like this until Schurz shooed them off, and he was on the verge of doing so when von Gilsa rose from his log and stepped toward him. The man, who had remained silent, had something on his mind. Tactfully—for once—Schimmelfennig stepped away.

"What is it, Leo?" Schurz asked, drawing the colonel deeper into the shadows.

Another former officer who had gone over to the revolution, the Prussian looked at the ground, at the darkness, at nothing.

"My brigade," he began. "General Devens has us on the flank, there is nothing beyond us."

"Someone has to be on the flank."

"But not in such a way. There is no cavalry. The flank is not refused properly, only two regiments. This is not the way. And General Devens mocks me, I think. He believes I am frightened."

"*I* know you're not frightened," Schurz said. "We all know that."

Von Gilsa waved that away. "But you are not my division commander." His breath sounded like panting in the darkness. "*I* am not frightened. Yet, I have fear. For my men. This is not how things must be done."

"Double your pickets. You can do that much."

"No. Even there, I am restrained."

Schurz understood the problem all too well and he shared the Prussian's concerns. But he was not von Gilsa's superior officer. Military discipline—military courtesy—had to be observed.

He wondered, though, if he might not have a quiet word with Devens.

"Well, Leo, if we march tomorrow, it should all come right. General Devens has to get to know you. And you have to get to know him. In time—"

"Carl," von Gilsa said, voice earnest, "I think that I already know him, this is the problem." The colonel's eyes caught the firelight. "I worry, Carl, that things have gone wrong already."

When Schurz did not reply, von Gilsa repeated:

"I worry."

Three thirty a.m., May 2
The Plank Road at the Catherine Furnace Road

So shall we come upon him in some place where he shall be found, and we will light upon him as the dew falleth on the ground; and of him and of all the men that *are* with him there shall not be left so much as one."

The verse haunted Jackson this night, 2 Samuel 17:12. It wasn't perfectly fitting, given the fate of Absalom, but it did express his sentiments: "there shall not be left so much as one." He would kill them all, if he could. And then they would make peace.

"Show us," he said.

Jed Hotchkiss placed a cracker box between the two generals and spread out the map in the lantern's cast. Jackson left his own seat to kneel on the earth for a closer look. Lee remained still.

"Chaplain Lacy was correct, sir. The Wellfords know a way. Happens the old colonel recently opened a logging road, not on the map. Couldn't be better placed to solve the problem, makes just the connection we need to keep out of sight."

Jackson made a deep-throated sound of approval. There had been a scare, when the first route planned for the flank march had been found to lie partly inside the Union picket lines. His promise to Lee to march at four a.m. had, of necessity, fallen through. Frantic rides through the darkness had brought this answer, though.

"Continue," Jackson said.

Hotchkiss, who seemed to love maps more than the world they described, pointed out the route, increment by increment, with named roads and nameless trails. There were twists and multiple changes of direction, taking them south only to turn north again. But the route did appear to be concealed and would bring them out beyond the Union flank. *If* Stuart's midnight reporting was accurate.

"It's convoluted, sir. Forest tracks, hardly roads at all. And it's long. But it can be done."

"How long?"

Hotchkiss hesitated. "Ten miles, General. Maybe eleven."

That was long, indeed. With a battle to be fought at the end of it. But there was no alternative.

"Can it pass artillery?"

"I'm led to believe so, General. Though not without an effort."

The near silence of a great army in its slumber held them close. Lanterns flickered, as if the flames had grown drowsy.

At last, Lee said, "General Jackson, what do you propose to do?"

Jackson swept a finger along the route Hotchkiss had traced. "Go around here. As Captain Hotchkiss described it."

"And . . . what do you propose to make this movement with?"

"With my whole corps," Jackson said.

"And . . . what does that leave me?"

Jackson looked at his commander in surprise. Lee knew exactly what would be left to him. Only after a moment did Jackson grasp the vision Lee was sharing with him: The rump of the army left here, with Lee, would be the only barrier between the Union troops and the direct road to Richmond. And that barrier would prove slight, should Hooker find the courage to strike in force.

"Only the divisions of Anderson and McLaws," Jackson answered bluntly, belatedly. Yes, he was asking Lee to take an enormous risk. But this attack could not be half-hearted or weak, it had to succeed. If it were to be done at all, it had to be done with the might of avenging angels.

Still . . . with Early's Division and a brigade already peeled away at Fredericksburg, he was asking Lee to part with two-thirds of the army remaining to him, to take that great a risk. It was a terrible thing, he understood.

Lee tormented the stub of a pencil with unsteady fingers. It was the clearest symptom of doubt he had ever seen in the man.

Lee looked at him. "Well, go on. And Godspeed."

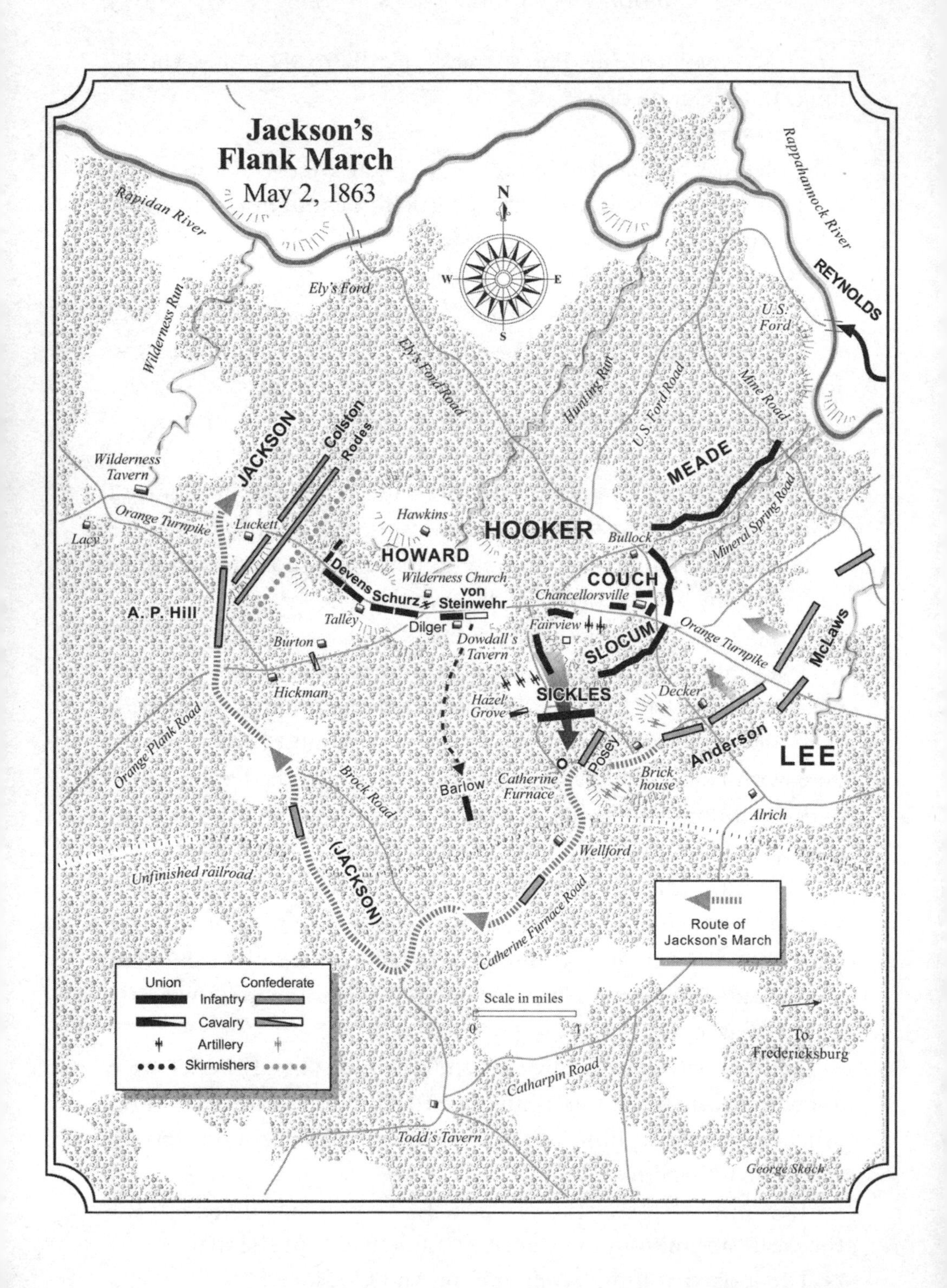

Jackson's Flank March
May 2, 1863
Rapidan River
Rappahannock River
REYNOLDS
U.S. Ford
Ely's Ford
Wilderness Run
Ely's Ford Road
Hunting Run
U.S. Ford Road
Mine Road
MEADE
Mineral Spring Road
JACKSON
Colston
Rodes
Wilderness Tavern
Orange Turnpike
Lacy
Luckett
Hawkins
HOOKER
Bullock
HOWARD
Devens
Schurz
von Steinwehr
Wilderness Church
COUCH
Chancellorsville
A. P. Hill
Talley
Dilger
Dowdall's Tavern
Fairview
SLOCUM
Orange Turnpike
McLaws
Burton
Hickman
SICKLES
Hazel Grove
Decker
Orange Plank Road
Brock Road
Posey
Anderson
LEE
Barlow
Catherine Furnace
Brick house
Alrich
Wellford
(JACKSON)
Unfinished railroad
Catherine Furnace Road
Route of Jackson's March
Union
Confederate
Infantry
Cavalry
Artillery
Skirmishers
Scale in miles
0
1
To Fredericksburg
Catharpin Road
Todd's Tavern
George Skoch

FIVE

Nine a.m.
The march

A tribulation it was. Lordy. Hardly one hour of marching and his feet burned like he was setting them down on skillets, step after step. He had been an unruly youth and had not been mindful when brimstone preachers inveighed against the corruption of the body, warning of its loathsomeness, but now he understood. His feet were surely corrupted.

A pause. In the slant-shade cool of morning. A sharing of last crackers. No rations had caught up with them, no manna had fallen from Heaven, and deepest damnation to the man who had started the cruel, infernal, and demonic lie that commissary wagons would serve them before they set out.

Great deeds were in the air, though, stirring a man's pulse. When Old Jack rode by close, it gave Sam Pickens his first true, near-up sight of that man, a fellow finely assembled, though showing a bald spot when he lifted his hat. His comrades had cheered wildly for the black-bearded man on the runt horse. Then, not fifteen minutes later, word had come back down the column that there must be no more cheering, that silence was vital from that moment on.

There had been some confusion to start. Used to marching early, the men, all of them, had been astonished to find the daylight already upon them when they were awakened not by grunting sergeants but by an artillery duel, a petty scrap between redlegs. Then there had been uncustomary dawdling, Pickens had even had time for a wash in a creek. The cold water soothed his feet, but only for as long as he stood in it. After that, commands cracked out and, where there had been lassitude, there was haste: They must march, although no one knew where.

Certain to be a fight at the end of it, though.

Pickens prayed the march would be short and the fight near, an inversion of his usual sentiment.

As the going resumed—a misery unto him—he tried to bully his mind onto goodly things: the promise of a handsome day, and the faint, remaining softness of the forest roads, a last hint of damp that refused to give way to dust. A man could breathe, at least.

Didn't help.

They marched, four abreast, no gabbing, not yet, morning stiff. He tried to think on his home, on the goodness of Umbria, but, again, he only conjured Auntie Delsie, this time her declaration after Romulus got his leg taken off and he rigged himself up a hobble-on, fit for light work by harvest: Cinnamon-fleshed and upright, fragrant and oracular, she had declared, "Rom ain't minded to be the less, he got pride."

And *he* would not be the less, he would bear this trial.

A misery, though, a misery.

Delsie. Why did she command his memories? It was disloyal to his mother and kin, to whom his thoughts should cling.

Avoiding a hot pile of horse droppings left by the cavalry gone ahead, he sidestepped into Bob Price, who shoved him off with a minor imprecation: It was all business now, all war again. Which made him recall the perfectly reasonable explanation of the war's necessity that Lieutenant Borden offered to all who were of half a mind to listen. They had not taken up arms to preserve slavery, Borden insisted. They were fighting to protect the *right* to hold slaves, same as the right of a man to own his own house or hold title to land. The niggers themselves hardly figured. It was all about a man's *rights,* about Southern manhood's virile resistance to sanctimonious tyranny. Let one right be stripped away, and the others would soon be taken.

Where would that leave even the poorest man?
With tormented feet, Sam Pickens reckoned.

Nine thirty a.m.
Chancellor house

Holding out a dispatch he'd drafted personally, Joe Hooker said, "Get this off to General Howard immediately."

Brigadier General Van Alen had arrived to provide relief to crumbling Dickinson, who'd been worked beyond his capacity. He took the message and stepped off sharply.

Hooker stretched, feeling his good muscles. Still give a younger man a time of it. Or, preferably, a young woman. He rubbed his eyes, wary of a return of his headaches, and allowed himself a moment's sit-down before plowing through the latest reports and dispatches.

The morning had been mixed, but largely positive. His ride along the army's lines had drawn extravagant cheers: The men remained in good spirits. And with the telegraph functioning again, Butterfield had sent confirmation that Longstreet was still at Suffolk in southern Virginia, depriving Lee of two of his finest divisions. Best of all, treetop observers reported glimpsing movement in Lee's lines, infantry and artillery—and they seemed to be marching westward and then southward. If the movement continued, it meant that Lee was, indeed, retreating on Gordonsville. Ingloriously flying.

There had been some delay in field reports reaching him, since he'd been off on his tour for almost two hours, but Dan Sickles now had approval to push artillery forward and shell the Rebs. To help them along.

If only he truly had Lee on the run, it would count as the victory that changed the course of the war. Let Grant succeed or fail on the Mississippi, this would be the turning point men remembered.

Even those Rebel witches had volunteered to nurse the wounded soldiers, in blue or gray, in the rooms turned into wards. Perhaps there was hope for the world.

After the war, should he stay in New York and grow wealthy? Or return triumphantly to California? The choice was delicious.

Concerns remained, though, and he intended to see to them. It wasn't a time to let down one's guard, no time for foolish errors. John Reynolds had not received the first set of orders sent to get his First Corps on the march to Chancellorsville. Then Confederate shelling had delayed him. Reynolds was marching hard now, on the north side of the river, but he was unlikely to arrive before evening or even night, leaving the army's right flank hanging open.

And Otis Howard, annoyingly lackadaisical, had not acted upon his order of the previous day to refuse his flank and prepare west-facing defenses. Yes, it appeared that Lee was quitting the field. But Hooker did not trust Lee or Jackson one bit. One had to be prepared for unwelcome surprises, even now.

And Howard had remained unconcerned during their ride along the Eleventh Corps lines. Hooker had even overheard him telling the army's chief engineer that no attacker could make it through the undergrowth on his flank. Hooker had refrained from upbraiding the corps commander and embarrassing him in front of his subordinates, but now he regretted the courtesy. By the time he had returned to his headquarters, his concern had swelled to the bursting point. So he'd sent Howard a directive to be prepared to resist not only a possible frontal attack but a flanking movement as well.

He hoped Lee wouldn't try to bring off some stunt, that he'd leave without fighting. It really was the best solution for all.

Flaring again, he decided that the message just sent to Howard had not been firm enough. Horace Greeley's favorite one-armed Christian abolitionist had seemed lethargic, at best, and needed the spurs applied. The man had looked exhausted, true—but weren't they all bone weary? His own headaches, his queer spells, were formidable, but he mastered them. Everyone just had to stand up on his hind legs and do his duty.

He would have welcomed a glass of whiskey, though.

"Van Alen!" he called. "To me."

The brigadier general quick-marched through the crowd of staff men and hangers-on.

"Take this down," Hooker told him. "Additional message to Howard."

"Yes, sir." Van Alen drew out a notebook and a pencil.

"General Howard . . . the right of your line . . . does not appear to be strong enough."

Van Alen scribbled and looked up again, ready.

"No artificial defenses worth naming have been thrown up . . . and there appears to be a scarcity of troops at that point . . ."

"Yes, sir."

". . . and not, in the commanding general's opinion . . . as favorably posted as might be." Hooker paused, wondering what remained unsaid, undone.

"That all, sir?"

Hooker's head abruptly began to throb again. Why must he bear this? He'd expected the fresh air of his inspection tour to have bought him more peace.

"Add that the enemy is moving to our right. And that Howard's corps has to keep a heavy reserve."

Van Alen raised an eyebrow. "Sir . . . I thought it had been decided that Lee was retreating?"

Hooker nodded curtly. "He *is* retreating, damn it. But I want goddamned Howard to pay attention. I can't trust anyone, anything. . . ."

He dipped his head and pressed his hands to his temples.

"Just get the message off, will you?"

Ten a.m.
The March

Press on, press on!" Jackson called as he rode forward. "No straggling, keep up. Press on."

He longed to drive them harder but knew he dared not. His

soldiers had to arrive with the strength left to fight. So the march had to be kept to a pace of two miles per hour, with pauses. It grated on him to do the mathematics and realize how little of the day would be left him to slay God's enemies.

As Jackson regained the head of the infantry column, with Rodes, mounted, at the front of his division, he neglected to so much as nod. He respected Rodes, who fought well and earned his promotions without politics. Tall, broad of shoulder, and lean, Rodes even looked the part of the ideal warrior. But there was too much on Jackson's mind for niceties.

The lithe tongue was the foe of the flaming sword.

He reviewed each detail of the march, with Fitz Lee clearing the path ahead, while Stuart deployed the rest of the cavalry on the flank of the march, pushing out troopers to block each road and trail that might let the Yankees stumble upon the column. He'd placed Rodes' division first in the order of march, since Rodes exacted discipline and would permit no delays. Raleigh Colston came next, in temporary command, while Powell Hill brought up the rear. Chastised and chastened, Hill would not dally today; still, it irked Jackson that Hill was next in seniority.

As for artillery support, each division had its batteries, but the only wagons permitted to clutter the march were ammunition carriers and ambulances.

Even with all things superfluous pared away, Jackson calculated that the tail of the column would just be beginning its march as the head neared its attack position. Based on the latest returns, he led thirty-three thousand men of all arms, while Lee had been left to face Hooker's might with fewer than fifteen thousand.

But Thomas Jackson had faith that the Lord, the God of Battles, would see justice done.

He refused to think of his wife, his flawless *esposa*. When she entered his mind, he expelled her. There was no time. Not even for the child.

War demanded all of a man, and he had no patience with anyone who gave less.

The mounted party of generals and colonels had fallen silent at Jackson's arrival. Rodes smoothed his mustaches and stared ahead. Crutchfield's eyes narrowed, expression as grim as his guns. The others of lesser rank strove to look severe. But they were Southern gentlemen all and could not go long without talk. Tom Munford, trailing his cavalrymen, announced that, by his calculation, almost two dozen faculty members or graduates of VMI would be in this attack.

Jackson snapped his head up and threw back his shoulders. Yes, he himself, Rodes, Colston, Crutchfield, Munford, so many others. Turning to Munford, he said:

"Colonel, the Institute will be heard from today."

With that, the silence was broken and a mood of goodwill and confidence swept the party. Relieved of his calculations for the moment, Jackson added:

"If I had one more division, we would destroy them utterly. We would humble them as Jericho was humbled."

"I suspect we'll do well enough, sir," Bob Rodes offered.

But Jackson had been taken by his vision. There were never enough men, not ever. He added:

"Our problem . . . this army's problem . . . is that we never have enough men to keep a reserve. We have to put everybody in and there's no reserve when needed, no men left to finish things. And they escape us."

"Won't many escape us today," Tom Munford said. He still possessed the confidence of youth.

Jackson grew silent again.

Ten fifteen a.m.

Dowdall's Tavern, Eleventh Corps headquarters

Carl Schurz held in his hand a message he hoped would bring Howard to his senses.

It had been a disheartening morning. Enraptured by the cheers of the troops as he rode the lines, Hooker had not challenged

Howard regarding the neglected flank and the corps commander's obvious disobedience. Hooker had seemed to take the matter lightly.

This message, just delivered, corrected the oversight.

Schurz stood on the tavern's porch, waiting for the orderly to wake Howard. With reports streaming in from pickets who'd sighted Confederates on the march, he'd ridden off to the high ground on Talley's farm to see for himself. And there they had been, unmistakable, in a dirty-gray column glimpsed through a break in the trees, not two miles distant. They were moving across the corps' front, not to the south.

Meanwhile, artillery fire had erupted to the southeast, echoing the fight of the previous day. That would be a distraction. The Confederates were attempting an envelopment. It could not have been any clearer.

Was that Jackson out there?

He'd galloped back to the tavern, pausing only to order young Dilger to seek out west-facing positions for his guns. And he'd found Howard grumpy and haggard, skeptical of every word.

Instead of showing alarm, the corps commander had told him:

"Schurz, I'm blown. Tried to get some sleep last night, but they gave me no quarter, woke me every half hour until I gave up. Look here. You're my number two, I want you to stay here while I nap. Read any messages, deal with the nonsense, but *don't* take any action. And don't let anyone roust me unless it's important." Before he retired, he added, "*Truly* important."

This message was truly important.

The half hour prior to its arrival had been a torment for Schurz, left powerless while Howard took to his cot. He'd stood, arms folded, watching supply wagons and even a sutler crowd the single road that served the corps.

The morning was gorgeous, ironically so. Its azure and golden grace called to mind the Rheinland and, for a moment, he'd felt an unaccustomed surge of homesickness, of *Heimweh,* along with his hopelessness. But soon enough he remembered that *this* was his home, this land of immense freedoms, and a finer one than ever he had known.

This was mankind's chance. In Europe, the counterrevolution had prevailed, leaving the people chained as never before. Now the Confederates fought to uphold their own ancien régime, a lingering aristocracy based not only on slavery but on serfdom—call the latter what you might, it was feudalism pure. The forces of reaction must not prevail, not here. Freedom, the wondrous freedom of here and now, in these United States . . . it was worth dying for, if need be.

But no good man should die without necessity because of the sour mood of a man who had been unwisely empowered.

Bravery on the field of battle was easy, Schurz had learned. A man simply got caught up in it. Harder by far were the challenges in between, the need to subdue oneself and serve a common good, to accommodate men you not only disliked but even despised, for a higher purpose. He recalled all too clearly how the Frankfurt parliament had frittered freedom away, as personalities and programs clashed, as petty jealousies undid great dreams and *Freiheit* bled to death amid endless squabbling.

And so he had struggled to get along with Howard, to show forbearance, and to keep his officers in line and loyal. They *had* to find common ground, to remember their shared cause. At least Howard was committed to ending slavery, to preserving the Union, to human liberty. And he was a brave man, if pigheaded.

If only . . .

Schurz did not believe in God, but he found himself praying to the vastness that Howard would see sense.

What was taking the fellow so long? Was his slumber that profound?

Howard appeared from around the corner, awkwardly fitting his sword belt over his coat with the one hand left him.

"What on earth is it now?" he demanded.

Schurz held out the message. "It's best if you read it yourself, sir."

Howard snapped the message from Schurz's fingers. As he read it, his face grew sullen. Schurz almost expected him to ball it up, but instead the corps commander handed it back.

"Have it logged."

Schurz hesitated. "Orders, sir? Should we tighten the lines? Refuse the flank in depth?"

Howard looked genuinely surprised. "Don't be absurd."

"But the message . . . it's an order. . . ."

"For Heaven's sake, don't be such a . . . such a *German*. Spare me the lessons and lectures, would you? You haven't any military background, none to speak of." Howard looked into the distance, past a teamsters' quarrel out on the road. "Joe's just got the jumps. All the responsibility on his shoulders. Natural enough to have moments of weakness. Yesterday, for instance. If Butterfield were here, he'd buck him up." He fussed with the fit of his sword belt. "One thing that man's good for."

Working his way through the jumble on the road, another courier made haste toward the tavern. He slipped from his horse a mere yard from the porch. Saluting and sweating, he offered his message to Howard.

The corps commander smirked at Schurz. "Marching orders, I suspect. Get after Lee." He glanced eastward. "That artillery. Their rear guard, no doubt."

But after Howard had opened the message and read it, his look turned cutting.

He passed the paper to Schurz. "You'll delight in this."

It was another directive from Hooker, restating his last order still more forcefully: Howard was to prepare to defend his flank.

Schurz raised his eyes to Howard.

The corps commander waved his one hand dismissively. "Oh, I'll see to it, do something or other. Never expected Joe to be such an old hen."

"It says we're to form a strong reserve," Schurz noted. "If we shortened the line and Devens refused the flank . . . my division could—"

"That's Frank Barlow's job, his brigade's the largest in the corps. I should think that's reserve enough."

From the direction of Chancellorsville, rifle fire joined the artillery shelling.

"Hear that?" Howard asked. "If there *is* a proper scrap today, we're unlikely to get near it. The fact is this corps isn't needed. Lee's whipped, and he knows it."

"General Howard . . ."

"Go back to your division, Schurz. I'm wide-awake now. And try not to frighten your soldiers with ghosts and goblins."

Twelve thirty p.m.
Catherine Furnace Road

General Posey, you *must* blunt their advance," Lee said, striving to conceal the alarm he felt.

"We'll do it, sir," Posey, a Mississippian of intense dignity, promised. "By God, we'll do it!"

His men double-quicked forward, raising their hats in salute at the sight of Lee.

Lee disciplined the muscles of his face: The men must see confidence.

It was as he had feared: With Jackson well on his way, the Federals had shown curiosity then spunk, and a fight for the furnace had begun to develop, threatening to further divide the army. Colonel Best had returned from the field with the flag of his Georgians but not with the Georgians themselves: The regiment had been captured. A give-and-take of skirmishers had exploded into a crisis.

Ahead, the firing intensified. Federal cheers met Rebel yells. More Union guns joined the fray.

They just had to hold now, to keep those people at bay, until Jackson could strike.

Nor was the situation entirely disadvantageous. If Hooker's

attention could be held here, if he could be mesmerized by the fight under way, Jackson would have an even greater chance at achieving surprise.

He waved up his chief of staff: Posey's Brigade would not be sufficient. Judging by the roar of the Union batteries, at least another brigade would be required. He would have to thin his lines elsewhere and take the risk. Then wait.

The fate of the South, of their world, lay with Jackson now.

Pulling off his riding gloves, Lee discovered a tick on the back of his hand. He pinched it off and crushed it between his fingers.

"Hooker," he muttered.

Two p.m.
Hazel Grove

By damn, that's how you do it," Sickles cried.

His forward artillery positively *pounded* the Rebs. His corps had driven them back a mile since the first shots were exchanged, and he'd bagged four hundred prisoners—including three hundred bedraggled Georgians from a single regiment.

The damned West Pointers could eat their words: He was winning this battle for them, while the rest of the army did nothing.

Somebody had to fight. He could not believe the sloth and confusion around him. Or, for that matter, the cowardice.

Joe had done a fine job, to a point—Christ, if he and Butterfield weren't the perfect companions for a carouse, though. But Joe had turned yellow the day before, no other way to put it. Now it was time for Sickles himself to land his fist on Lee's nose and draw the claret.

"Excellent gunnery, Randolph!" he told his chief of artillery. "Splendid! Guns to the front, that's the ticket." He reached into his tunic and drew out his cigar case. "Captain, you deserve a smoke."

Randolph's eyes grew avaricious at the sight of the famed Habanas, which delighted Sickles. He liked to win men over with little treats. You'd get more gratitude for a well-timed swig from a silver flask than for a no-interest loan of ten thousand dollars. As for the cigars, they followed him faithfully, courtesy of a pal in the New York Customs House. Even Dan Butterfield, for all his deep pockets, couldn't get finer smokes.

Cigar plugged in between his chops, he watched Whipple's boys join Birney's in the donnybrook.

"Mighty fine cigar, sir," Randolph said over the guns.

"Damned right, young man. Nothing like it." Sickles turned his politician's smile toward the captain. "I always say, if you can't have a woman, have yourself a smoke."

"Yes, sir."

War was a grand business, really. The great redeemer of reputations. Joe's. His own. Shot that whoreson Key down like a dog and did not regret it. Plumping his wife while his back was turned, the bugger had it coming. Trial had been a spectacle, and he'd needed to deal gingerly with Teresa, but this war was bound to launch him back into office. And Ed Stanton had been a member of his defense team, a sharp one behind the scenes. Now Ed was the secretary of war.

It was just the way Dan Butterfield liked to put it: Life was about erections and connections.

He'd even made things up with Mary Lincoln, who had the distinction of being even less favored by nature than her simian husband. Now she called him "Dan" and took his part.

Sickles raised his field glasses again.

Unmistakable. Lee *was* retreating, had been all the damned day. Just watch 'em go. While their rear guard struggled to stave off destruction.

He'd nudged Hooker to come forward and see the show for himself. Better than a line of dancing girls sans undergarments. But other than his morning ride round the lines, Joe seemed downright afraid to leave his headquarters. Tied to that damnable telegraph. Which Butterfield had buggered up indescribably.

He turned to the captain, who had done good work and stank of powder, despite the cigars' perfume.

"Randolph, I want you to ride back to General Hooker with a message. Oh, your guns will do fine without you for half an hour, don't make faces. I'll write it up in a moment, but I want a *fighting* man to carry it back, someone who knows what's what and can answer questions. Not another damned clerk." Sickles tossed the rump of the cigar into trampled grass. "If he asks for your opinion, you tell him the Rebs are running faster than whores with the shits. And whether he asks you or not, you repeat what I'm going to write, that if he can just send one more brigade to come up on my right, I'll finish these peckerwoods. We'll run Lee down like Five Points ratcatchers."

Just one more brigade. Surely that do-nothing Howard on his flank could spare a few men.

Two thirty p.m.
The March

Jackson felt his confidence grow by the minute. Rodes had marched his men crisply, nearing the end of the route and the line of attack. Colston was coming along, as was Hill, although Hill had needed to face two brigades about to parry a probe. And the cavalry had screened the flank with skill, turning back all Federal scouts and patrols.

He would crush them, these Moabites, these Philistines, these Egyptians.

In the heat of the afternoon, he turned toward Rodes and said, "Good. Good."

Rodes understood that Jackson did not mean to invite conversation. He nodded toward Jackson, and the party of horsemen continued in renewed silence.

The men would be tired, Jackson knew, and thirsty. But he counted on their fervor when faced with battle. They would do their duty. Because they must.

Ever instantly recognizable, Fitz Lee galloped back toward the generals.

Jackson quickened. Something had to be wrong. Lee's urgency pierced.

Reining up, the younger man didn't bother with a salute, which was unusual.

"General Jackson . . . sir . . . please . . ." Lee gasped for breath. "If you'll ride with me, I'll show you the enemy's right. It's not where we thought."

Jackson pulled his horse about.

"Just bring one courier," Lee told him. "Yankees will be able to see us, they need to take us for a couple of scouts. And halt the column, sir. You'll see the reason."

Jackson nodded to Rodes, who understood the order and raised his hand.

The little party rode forward, with Lee's horse spattering foam from its mouth. The cavalryman turned them onto a track and slowed as they broke into open ground by a hillock.

Topping the rise, Jackson needed no warning to rein up. Before him stretched a long, thin band of blue—well to the rear of where Stuart had reported them at midnight. Were the attack to go forward as planned . . . it wouldn't turn their flank but strike their front at an oblique angle.

For a moment, Jackson's heart sank. To get around the flank of those men, to shock and overwhelm them, his soldiers would have to march on.

He looked up at the sun. Time was their master now. The Lord had stopped the sun for Israel, but he could not expect such a miracle. He had been given as much as a man could ask.

Lee chattered a bit. Jackson ignored him. Peering at the Federals through his binoculars.

They were at ease, unprepared. There were abatis in their front, but their line was thin, the soldiers at their leisure, with arms stacked and blouses removed. Wagons crowded the few open spaces, and beeves had been hung for butchering. The position forbade a rapid change of front.

He would have to push on, to get well past them. But the Lord had blessed him truly. The Federals could not have been more vulnerable.

He would have to act swiftly now. With the swiftness of the angels.

He turned to Lee. "Can you get us behind them? Without delay?"

"Quick as I can, sir. Just a matter of going a lick farther. Same roads, mostly."

That "lick" would consume an hour and more, Jackson reckoned.

He turned to the courier. "Ride back to General Rodes. Tell him to continue across the Plank Road and halt when he reaches the Turnpike. I'll meet him there."

The man didn't wait for further encouragement.

Jackson looked at the sun again. Its descent was unmistakable.

He would have to change his plan: He could not wait for all of his men to close up, for the divisions to be deployed properly, side by side, in deep echelons. He saw what he would have to do instead: Spread each division out in a long line, one behind the other, advancing as soon as the first two were in position.

Three thin lines, division behind division. It was the same unsound arrangement Johnston had used at Shiloh. Now his soldiers would have to make it work. Surprise and valor would have to carry the day.

What was left of the day.

Still in sight of the Yankees, he removed his hat and bowed his head in prayer, repenting his sins and asking forgiveness for his struggling nation.

Then he rode back at a merciless pace, unsparing of Little Sorrel or himself.

Time, it was all about time.

Two forty p.m.
Dowdall's Tavern, Eleventh Corps headquarters

Schurz abandoned his last attempt to be calm and accommodating. He rode up to the tavern as if pursued—and he was, by a sense of fate.

Dismounting, he caught his boot in a stirrup and danced a clumsy jig to free himself. Loitering staff men found it entertaining.

Schurz didn't care. He strode toward the porch just as Meysenburg emerged.

"Theo, I have to see Howard right now."

"What's wrong?"

"Barlow. His brigade, the corps reserve. It's marching away. I have to see General Howard."

"You can't. He's with Barlow."

"What . . ."

Meysenburg shrugged. "Orders. From Hooker. Barlow's to support Sickles. A pursuit or suchlike."

"Pursuit? We're going to be *attacked*. You've heard the reports, the sightings."

"The general doesn't believe a word of it. Hooker told him, personally, that Lee's retreating." The chief of staff nodded toward the on-and-off fight in the middle distance and well out of sight. "General Howard believed he'd be of greater use with Barlow." He shrugged again. "Curiosity, I think."

"Damn it, Theo! You know what's going on. The only man in Devens' division who doesn't think we're about to be attacked is Devens himself. And my pickets have—"

"What do you want me to do? General Howard thinks you're all wrong. His orders are to remain here and reprovision."

"What do *you* think?"

"What I think doesn't matter. I follow orders."

Schurz rode the short distance back to his division headquarters. He'd had the tents near the farmhouse taken down to clear fields of fire. Earlier, on his own authority, he'd pulled his two largest regiments from the line and faced them west, one north of the farmhouse and one south of it, on the only defensible ground granted to his division. He'd cleared off as many wagons as he could and, later, he'd drawn back a third regiment, positioning it in echelon, willing to risk a reprimand or worse. And young Dilger had repositioned his battery. It wasn't much, not if they attacked in strength, and it wasn't going to save Devens' division, but it was all he could do.

Poor von Gilsa, he thought, poor Leo. He hasn't a chance. And damn Devens right along with Howard.

Searching out Krzyzanowski, his Second Brigade commander, he found him conferring with Jacobs of the 26th Wisconsin, the division's largest regiment but one untested in battle.

Dismounting—with more care this time—he warned himself not to appear or sound pessimistic. Somehow, these men had to be given confidence.

It was hard.

The two colonels saluted. Krzyzanowski was a Pole, a fellow revolutionary, and phenomenally brave. To Schurz he seemed almost a caricature of his country's *szlachta* although Kriz only sprang from the minor gentry: Dashing and high-spirited one day, sunk in Slavic gloom the next, he was as Polish as beet soup.

Now Kriz's brows were low and his face was grim.

Schurz knew the dilemma the Pole had faced. Just as the shots were fired at Fort Sumter, another Polish revolution against the Russians had erupted. Kriz had been torn over which fight to join. Finally, as Schurz himself had done long since, Kriz had chosen this new land.

Jacobs, too, was an immigrant.

They all knew how much was at stake.

"Is it true?" Kriz asked. "Have they pulled off the corps reserve?"

"Only temporarily," Schurz said. He had to believe that.

The Pole looked aside, mustaches quivering. He said nothing. There was nothing to say. Schurz turned to Jacobs:

"Willie, your boys will have to give a good account of themselves."

"They'll fight. You'll see."

"Well, keep them well in hand. Devil of an introduction to combat."

Jacobs smiled. "They wait for their chance to fight. *Sind ja gute Kerle.*"

"Well, they're going to get that chance."

Kriz turned about, facing the two men equally. "How can they not listen? The reports . . . all day . . . a madman could see it, only a fool could not."

Schurz resisted replying that there lay the difference between the mad and the foolish. He concentrated on Jacobs.

"Skirmishers out?"

"My best men." He pointed. "In those trees. Across the field there."

"Good." He considered both subordinates: two men of great decency, captivated by a dream of freedom passing all borders.

He said, "*This* is your ground, your place. I need you to hold it. This is Poland, Kriz. This is Germany, Willie."

Jacobs smiled. "Don't forget Wisconsin."

Dilger, the young artilleryman, found them. He looked uncharacteristically unsettled. Hubert Dilger was known almost as much for his coolness as for his exemplary gunnery skills—and for his uniform, with which he took liberties. Handsome to break hearts on successive continents, he always looked more like a hussar flirting with opera girls than he did like a smoke-tarred gunmaster.

He didn't look a bit romantic today. Picturesque still, but too fierce for soft hearts. Nor did he dismount. The young man clearly had more work on his mind.

He saluted handsomely, though.

"General Schurz, sir. Colonels." He drew off his shako and swept a sleeve across his forehead. "I just rode over to the First

Division. General Devens is the only man there who doesn't believe the Johnnies will attack, it's not just the Germans now. McLean, Richardson, Rice, Lee, Reilly . . . they've all tried to convince him, but Devens won't be moved, he won't let them reposition a single regiment. Poor Dieckmann's beside himself, he's got two guns pointing west but no fields of fire beyond the road."

Dilger paused to drink from his canteen. Usually possessed of flawless manners, today he slopped water over his chin and neck. Finished drinking, he gasped.

Schurz knew his men. He asked:

"That's not all, is it, Captain? You rode outside the lines to have your own look. Didn't you?"

Nonplussed, Dilger said, "Sir . . . I just wanted to . . ."

Schurz smiled, if faintly. "Well, tell us what you saw."

Dilger opened his mouth, but no words passed his fine white teeth. At last, he said:

"They're everywhere. I blundered into them. I barely made it back."

Krzyzanowski raised his eyes back to Schurz. The Pole was about to speak, but Dilger got in first, addressing the division commander.

"Sir . . . I took another liberty."

"And what was that?"

"I tried to convince General Devens myself. It did no good."

"No."

"Then . . . I rode to General Hooker's headquarters, sir. To tell him what I saw. What I saw with my own eyes."

"And what did General Hooker say?"

Dilger looked as forlorn as ever Schurz had seen the man. The captain said:

"I didn't see him, sir. They wouldn't let me in. A major stopped me." Dilger took a profound breath. "When I told him what I saw, he called me a coward."

As Schurz moved on to encourage Schimmelfennig and his brigade, he attempted to take a shortcut through the tangles. But a man on horseback couldn't pass and he had to turn around, laboriously. As he re-emerged into the glare of the afternoon sun, it struck him that he'd encountered such a dense and forbidding forest long before, when he'd read the fairy tales of the Brothers Grimm.

Four p.m.
Chancellorsville, headquarters of the Army of the Potomac

Joseph Hooker's physical headaches granted him an interval of relief, but headaches of a different sort assailed him. Wagons had cut the ground-laid telegraph wires again and he had no idea how Sedgwick was doing at Fredericksburg. But that was a minor irritant compared to the silence from the cavalry. Stoneman still had not been heard from, not for four full days.

He found himself wishing he'd held back more of the cavalry, that he had not given Stoneman so much freedom. He'd felt the need of more cavalry all day, with the Rebs parrying every attempt his outnumbered horsemen made to penetrate their screen and confirm, beyond doubt, that Lee was retreating. Gathered together, the horsemen he had present barely numbered enough for a nipping pursuit.

Of course, he wasn't certain how aggressively Lee should be pushed. Dan Sickles, bless him, had shown grit, chewing into the Reb rear guard and making a fine catch of prisoners—and mass surrenders were always a sign of demoralization.

Still, a man had to be certain. He'd allowed Sickles one additional brigade—from the Eleventh Corps, which stood idle—but that was as much as he intended to do. Sickles thought the entire left wing should advance to crush the Rebs, but he could not bring himself to give the order.

Even George Meade, on a visit to headquarters, had argued that they should attack in force immediately. A rigorous Philadelphia snot who took no joy in life, Meade always knew what other people should do.

Better to let Lee escape, for now. That would count as victory enough. It made no sense to give Lee an opening for some escapade that the press and his rivals could use against him. Let Lee get free of this jungle. Then he would follow. And fight him at some better time.

Perhaps it wouldn't even be necessary to fight? Perhaps Lee and Davis would see the futility of dragging out what was clearly a hopeless cause. Might they not surrender, given the reality they faced? Spare further bloodshed, on both sides? If the South would see reason, that would be best for all.

But if they had to fight, if he had to fight . . . another day would be better.

Major General "Fighting Joe" Hooker just wanted Robert E. Lee to leave him alone.

Four thirty p.m.

The Wilderness, one half mile west of the Union flank

His feet were bleeding. He didn't need to remove his shoes and stockings to see it. A man could tell the difference between sweat and blood without looking.

Didn't think he'd ever been so miserable in his life. Not since he'd begged Auntie Delsie to let him finish churning the butter, only to climb up on that chair and find he wasn't strong enough to drive down the stick. But that had been a different kind of misery: his first shaming.

Now this. Pushing through briars worse than a crown of thorns and thick as a woven basket. Wasn't only his feet that were scourged, but the backs of his hands, those rifle-clutching hands, were streaked red as well. The scratches itched like a hundred bedbug bites. On his face, too.

He struggled to keep the thorns out of his eyes. Those cap-grabbing, deviling thorns.

Hushed by officers, they'd filed off the road, doing their best to keep silent but crashing through the brush like a herd of spooked cows. Surely if there were Yankees out there, they heard them coming. Wouldn't be no surprise, or not much of one.

His canteen was empty.

Heart set to bound from his chest.

The terrible waiting.

They stretched out Indian file then stopped and faced to the right in a queer formation, as if they were darkies lined up to flush game.

Every man in the 5th Alabama knew there was trouble ahead.

Fears came sneaking. Scratching at a man's courage the way those long thorns scratched his flesh. A man's breath roared like a hurricane. Heart thundering. He quivered in secret.

Lieutenant Borden thrashed by, telling them all to lie down, rest, and be quiet.

When they did so, they heard Yankee voices.

Five p.m.
Right (western) flank of the Eleventh Corps

Standing in front of two of Dieckmann's guns, Colonel Leopold von Gilsa heard Southern accents.

Five p.m.
Abandoned railroad line, south of Chancellorsville

This," Francis Channing Barlow said, "is a grotesque absurdity. It's a wild-goose chase missing the goose."

Beside him, Major General Oliver Otis Howard didn't reply. Barlow's tone was insolent, but that was Barlow. Best family, right sort. Harvard, and top his class, if Devens could be trusted. Howard wondered how his own life might have been had he gone to Harvard rather than West Point.

"There's not a Johnny anywhere in this godforsaken morass," Barlow went on. "If there were any, they're damned well gone."

"Retreating," Howard said. "Faster than we could advance."

The ghost of his right arm haunted him for a few unsettling seconds. Would that never cease?

To the left and a bit to the rear, perhaps a half mile distant, fighting continued in front of Sickles' corps, but not at a level to cause anyone alarm. The day's little squabble was already winding down, and the flanking movement by Barlow's brigade had barely seen a skirmisher.

"Lee must have gotten off," Howard said. "We'll be after him in the morning, though. Joe won't waste time now."

"My men will have to retrieve their knapsacks and bedrolls. Rather wish we hadn't left them behind. No point lightening up for battle when there isn't a battle." Barlow smirked. "Much ado about nothing. Again. Cat-and-mouse without the mouse."

"I'll have Meysenburg see to the baggage. Bring it all up in commissary wagons, now they've been emptied." He considered the situation again: Unlikely that Joe would have the Eleventh Corps lead a pursuit. "You may well be recalled in plenty of time."

Barlow glanced about, all but ignoring his superior officer.

"Thought we'd have a fight," he said. "Hoped we would. Wretched place though it is." He snorted. "Wouldn't give you a broken stick for a hundred acres of it."

Howard agreed with the sentiment, but didn't reply. Barlow could be a bit much, but he'd proven himself quite the soldier, the sort you wanted where the fighting was heaviest. Already wounded badly—twice—the brigadier general didn't show a trace of damage; rather, he still resembled an undergraduate, quite a handsome fellow, in his superior, highbred way. Until he smiled and showed that crooked tooth.

His brigade was the pride of the corps, the backbone.

"All right, Frank," Howard told him, "you're on your own. I need to go back and see to things. Report to General Sickles in the meantime."

"Not a gentleman, Sickles," Barlow said.

Again, Howard agreed, but he decided he'd best not say it.

Sickles could stroll into the President's House anytime he liked, he had Mary Lincoln's ear. Never did do to make powerful enemies.

"I'd best be off, then. It's miles back to our bunch. And rough going."

"Don't get lost," Barlow told him.

Howard couldn't tell whether the younger man was casually wishing him well or insulting him.

He waved up his escort. It really was rough going. He'd be lucky as the devil to make it back to his headquarters in half an hour's hard riding.

As Howard tugged his horse about, Barlow muttered:

"I must say I feel rather wasted."

Five thirty p.m.
The Turnpike, at the Luckett house

With two divisions spread out in the woods—overlapping the Union flank by nearly a mile each way—Jackson decided his instincts had been right: He could not wait for Hill to complete a third line. Hill could continue deploying his men while the attack went forward, then he could follow.

The sun would set in just over an hour.

He sat in silence, horse stilled, beside Rodes. Waiting only for young Blackford to return and confirm that the skirmishers had been deployed. Alabama sharpshooters. Good, hard men.

Rodes didn't speak. There was nothing left to say.

Around them, artillery batteries waited to roll forward the moment the road had been cleared. Scouts loitered, their work done. Beyond a few remarks made in low voices, beyond the mild chinking of gun chains, beyond the occasional snort or tap of a mount, the world had hushed. Miles away, guns sounded, where Lee was fighting off an untold number of Federal divisions. Here, Jackson heard birdsong: not the morning calls or the birds that sang at eventide, but day birds, their calls sharp and businesslike.

He loved birds, flowers, plants.

How dearly he longed for an end to this. War enticed him, succumbing was a sin. He fought well, by the Lord's grace, but feared he was too fond of it.

Lee, too, was wary of that sin, he'd remarked on it back at Fredericksburg, during the slaughter.

After this war, after this terrible necessity, he would make his dream come true. Nothing would stop him, short of the hand of the Lord. He would have his farm in the Valley. His family would grow, with the Lord's consent, and they would build their Eden, a blessed place and safe, a good and godly place.

At the sudden caw of a crow, he recalled how the big, black birds would gather on the roof of his uncle's mill. And then he remembered the wondrous days, when he was still too young to know misery's depths—in his memory, it was always summer—and he would have hours of freedom, lazy hours. Alone, or perhaps with a rare friend, he would wade across the river's shallows to the sheltering grove then sprawl and drowse and dream with a child's purity. He remembered lying on the moss, at peace, for hours. Resting, before he had this dreadful, grown-man's need of rest.

He would like to rest again.

Perhaps, he thought, those were the best days of all. Before he knew sin. Before he knew this world. Before he had lifted his hand against another.

Once he had met a copperhead snake there and killed it. His uncle said every paradise had its serpents.

And there were frogs. And raspberries at the end of June.

He reminded himself how blessed he had been in his later life. His wives, the child. Yet the memory of that fragrant glade across the river remained a comfort.

His paradise.

Major Blackford returned.

"The skirmish line's posted, sir. Four hundred yards to the front. Give or take."

Jackson cocked back his head and peered at the eager young man. A smile touched his lips and he said:

"Today, Major, we shall take, but not give."

He turned. "Are you ready, General Rodes?"

The last near silence. That memory of flowing water, of the glade.

"Yes, sir," Rodes told him.

"You may go forward then."

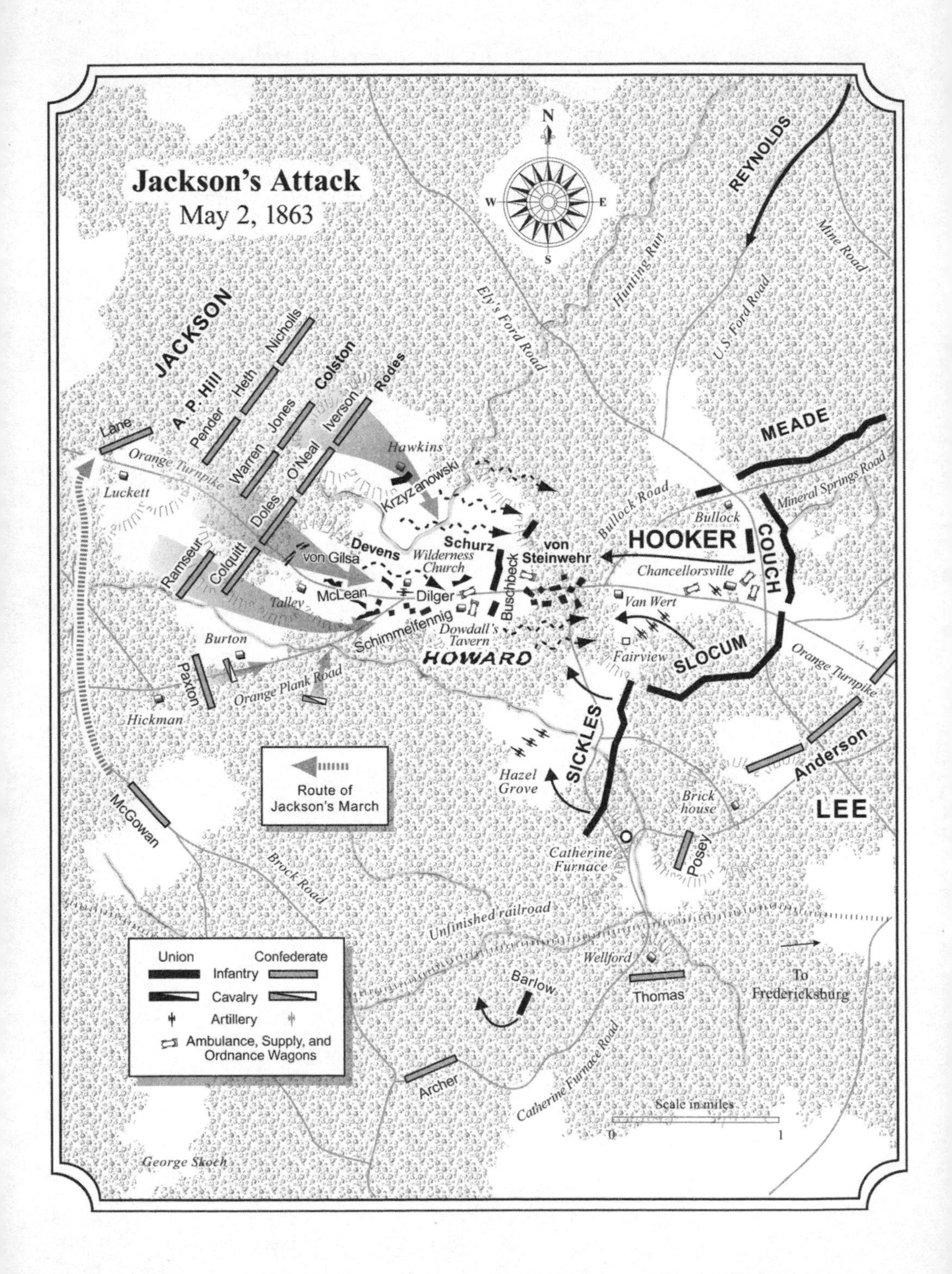
Jackson's Attack
May 2, 1863
N
W
E
S
JACKSON
A. P. Hill
Lane
Pender
Heth
Nicholls
Colston
Warren
Jones
Iverson
Rodes
O'Neal
Doles
Colquitt
Ramseur
Orange Turnpike
Luckett
Hawkins
Krzyzanowski
Devens
von Gilsa
McLean
Talley
Schimmelfennig
Dilger
Wilderness Church
Schurz
Buschbeck
von Steinwehr
Dowdall's Tavern
HOWARD
Burton
Paxton
Orange Plank Road
Hickman
Route of Jackson's March
McGowan
Brock Road
Ely's Ford Road
Hunting Run
REYNOLDS
Mine Road
U.S. Ford Road
MEADE
Mineral Springs Road
Bullock Road
Bullock
HOOKER
COUCH
Chancellorsville
Van Wert
Fairview
SLOCUM
Orange Turnpike
SICKLES
Hazel Grove
Anderson
LEE
Brick house
Catherine Furnace
Posey
Unfinished railroad
Wellford
Thomas
To Fredericksburg
Barlow
Archer
Catherine Furnace Road
Scale in miles
0
1
Union
Confederate
Infantry
Cavalry
Artillery
Ambulance, Supply, and Ordnance Wagons
George Skoch

SIX

Five fifty p.m.
Eleventh Corps' right flank

All God's greenery gripped, grabbed, tugged, scraped, and just plain tried to trip up Sam Pickens, but on he went, busting his way through the undergrowth. Ahead, the skirmishers were having it out with the Yanks and the stump-a-fellow strangeness was that a blue-belly band just kept on playing, "The Girl I Left Behind Me." Couldn't yet smell gunpowder, but the perfume of Yank beef and frying bacon reached into the woods to lure on hungry men, to torment them body and soul.

"Keep moving, keep going," Captain Williams shouted, barely heard above the thrashing and crashing of who knew how many thousand men going forward. All of the officers were hollering.

Pickens burst through a veil of blackflies, spitting them out and freeing a hand from his rifle to wipe his eyes.

More firing now, forward and to the right. A pair of cannon opened up.

The band's music withered to a last few honks.

Somebody yelled, "Yankees!"

Men stopped, lifted their rifles, and fired into the brush. Then more of them fired. Peering forward, Pickens did believe that—maybe—he saw a blue line ahead.

He planted his feet and fired, shoulder bucking.

"Stop firing, cease firing! There's nothing out there. Cease firing! Reload, men, reload at a walk!"

They went forward again, thrusting their carcasses through the dense, green nothingness into which they'd aimed their volleys.

There were no Yankees. Not yet.

Gobble some of that bacon, oh, Lord Jesus. Smelled like Christmas twice over.

The smell was everywhere but the bacon nowhere.

A deer shot from a hide. Pickens crouched, startled.

Infernal place. A man couldn't see at all.

"Double-quick, *march*!" Lieutenant Colonel Hobson's voice. Junior officers repeated the command.

Pickens didn't see how they could go any faster through that Hell-sprouted undergrowth, but they did. They started screaming and howling.

Fright the Yankees *and* wake the dead.

No true line of battle left, just a scatter of souls by the dozens, hundreds, thousands.

In the thrill, he forgot the misery of his feet.

They broke through a wall of briars and found madness. In an open patch, men in gray and blue ran every which way, some just scooting off, others clinging to ranks and leveling volleys, the hardiest swinging rifles at each other, butts and barrels, smashing skulls. Men cursed and threatened or grunted ugly nothings. Pickens heard heavy speech he reckoned was German.

He swore he wouldn't fire again without a plain target. Stepping over a blood-puling Yank who clutched a shiny horn, he just kept moving. The Yank had terrified, otherworldly eyes and graying hair.

Another Yank, confused or crazy, marched toward them at carry arms, as if on parade. Someone shot him. He twirled and fell. Then he got up, laid his rifle against a bloodied shoulder, and came forward again and got shot again.

Some fellows did get carried away, killing blue-bellies trying to surrender. Lieutenant Colonel Hobson saved one Yank himself and sent him rearward.

Smoke spread at shoulder level.

Yanks off to the right got up a match, but nothing much stood in the way of the 5th Alabama. Just bad ground and fools.

Everybody wanted somebody to fight, but they just weren't

there. They'd spilled so far around the Federal flank, it seemed, that they had all but free going.

Bullets zipped past, a flurry of them. Coming from behind.

Shot in the back, astonished, a man toppled.

In a rage, Hobson wheeled about, screaming and waving his sword.

"You're shooting your own men! Cease fire, *cease fire*!"

Pickens realized that he'd outrun every last man he knew except the lieutenant colonel. He decided to stick with Hobson.

Where did everyone go? Plenty of yelling, gone-crazy soldiers crowded around, but not a one he recognized.

A second line overtook them, mingling.

"Forward! Forward!" unknown officers shouted.

A Yankee sergeant sat against an overturned wagon that had tried to run through the brush. The Yank just shook his head, staring down at the crimson-streaked slop of guts he held in his hands.

"Oh, my," he said. "Oh, my . . ."

A line of blue-bellies tried to make a stand, maybe two companies. A longer line of Rebs formed, triple their number, to answer the challenge. They traded volleys, cutting the Yankee enterprise by half.

A wounded Union officer tried to pull his men back in fighting order, but Rebs swarmed all around them.

A Yank gun section let loose. *Canister.* Those who were not struck threw themselves to the ground.

By the time Pickens dared to raise his head, the guns had been captured, the horses of their limbers and caissons shot down.

He stopped a mad-eyed boy from firing into the melee, knocking the barrel of his rifle skyward.

"Don't you shoot till you got something clear to shoot at, hear?"

The boy looked at him as though he understood nothing.

He briefly lost sight of Hobson amid the wild gray mass. So he just went on, yelling when everyone else yelled.

At the base of a tree, a beauty of a Newfoundland dog, shot through its belly, stared up at him.

* * *

His wound from Cross Keys had picked this day of all days to revisit him, but Colonel Leopold von Gilsa ignored the pain.

Riding along his crumbling lines, bellowing commands and trailed by a dwindling retinue, he cursed Heaven and earth, Devens and Howard. They had been warned, again and again.

Now they were all in the shit.

"Du Feigling, kehr um!" he told a fleeing man.

He slapped the fellow with the flat of his sword, but it did no good. The fellow ducked and cursed and called, "I ain't none of your goddamned Dutchmen."

There was pride, though, too. Good men stood their ground or gave it up grudgingly. The 153rd Pennsylvania stood like heroes.

But too many men grasped the odds they faced. Lines buckled and broke.

And the damned wagons. Those that had teams at hand clogged up the road, preventing the effective movement of troops. Dieckmann's gun section on the Turnpike had been shot down or captured, unable to escape. The damned Rebels were everywhere, swarming, their lines extending as far as a man could see.

He'd had to watch from a hopeless distance as the Johnnies took Charlie Glanz, the colonel commanding the 153rd, prisoner in a fistfight. But Major Rice managed to re-form the regiment—what remained of it—a hundred yards to the rear.

The 54th New York was all but surrounded.

It galled him, but the only choice was to withdraw or lose his entire brigade.

He rode through his shattered regiments, unable to give the order. Until he heard another wave of triumphant Rebel yells.

He'd be blamed, of course. The "Germans," the "Dutchmen," would be faulted for this debacle. But he could live with shame. After the revolution had failed, the renegade Prussian officer had survived in exile by playing the piano and singing in Bowery bars. Yes, he could endure shame, even humiliation. But he could not kill brave men when there was no hope, when no good would come of it.

The 153rd Pennsylvania was the most exposed, their position had become a salient.

The Johnnies screamed that unearthly howl of theirs.

Von Gilsa turned to one of his two remaining aides.

"Captain Blau, trag mal mein Befehl an Major Rice. Er soll—nein, er muss—schnell retirieren."

Order Major Rice to withdraw his men. He should—no, he must—do it quickly.

"Zu Befehl, Herr Oberst." The young man spurred his horse.

The captain dropped from the saddle, hands clutched to his breast, before he had gone fifty yards.

Von Gilsa looked to his remaining aide, Ludwig Bisky.

Bisky nodded: *Verstanden.* I understand.

Spurring his mount into the smoke, the captain launched himself forward. In seconds, his head splashed blood and brains and bone.

"Scheisskerl."

Feeling the weight of his years and wounds, von Gilsa thrust his saber into its scabbard and drew out his pistols.

Guiding his horse with his knees *à la Russe,* he charged into the maelstrom, cursing and firing to left and right. Not caring a damn whether his flag or any man followed.

Amazed, he reached the shrunken Pennsylvanian line, where Rice was manhandling any soldier who tried to run away.

"*Gottverdammt, was willst Du, Rice?* To send these boys to Hell? Withdraw now, save your regiment. Form on the next line."

Blood splashed from von Gilsa's neck.

He saw the horrified look on Rice's face before he felt the pain.

Von Gilsa calmly holstered one pistol and probed the wound with his fingers. He wiped the blood on his trousers.

"*Ist doch nichts.* It is nothing. Withdraw your regiment, *Herr Major.*"

Rice began shouting orders. Faces blackened by powder, the Pennsylvanians inched back, struggling to keep their order. One man shouted:

"Let them other sonsofbitches run, we don't skedaddle."

Still capable of booming a response, von Gilsa wiped away more blood and told him:

"You obey orders, *ja*?"

As he turned to ride to another threatened spot, his horse reared, spurting blood from an artery, shrieking and writhing.

It fell on top of him.

The shock was enormous, stunning.

Rice and a handful of soldiers wrestled the quaking horse off the colonel, drenching themselves in gore.

Covered in blood himself, von Gilsa stood up. Astonishing his rescuers.

"Don't just stand there," the old Prussian told them. "Catch me another damned horse."

General, don't you think you're too close?" Sandie Pendleton—not without trepidation—asked of Jackson. Stray rounds fizzed past, teasing a man's ear.

"I can't *see*," Jackson snapped. "I can't see what's happening." He kept on riding forward.

Indeed, Pendleton thought. Already hard to make sense of the pieces. But the vital thing was that they were moving forward, and rapidly. Disarmed Yankees streamed toward the rear. Most were hushed and high-nerved, but some abused each other in English and German. As if soldiers in gray weren't even present.

But present they were. Raleigh Colston's line had just passed forward, headed into the fray. The division commander rode over when he saw Jackson. Pendleton eased his horse aside to make way.

A double punch of cannon sounded ahead.

Jackson called to a soldier headed the wrong way: "You turn around and do your duty. Where's your rifle?" His voice was of iron and scorn.

Confused, the soldier, a young one, held up a tied-off stump where a forearm had been. Flies circled the clotting blood.

Jackson made no apology but rode on.

"Look at this," Colston said as he came abreast.

Around them, the wreckage of Union camps displayed the wealth of Babylon—a Babylon now broken in the dust. Smoke wreathed the trees and the landscape stank of powder, shit, and bacon.

The air was alive with the means of death. Spent bullets pelted the earth like a storm's first raindrops. On the ground, the wounded quivered beside the dead. But the stilled bodies in gray were few, vastly fewer than the number of Federal prisoners. It had all gone too fast for much killing to be done.

Just ahead, Colston's lines were already threatened with disorder, ruptured by the landscape before they'd fired a shot.

"See to your men, General," Jackson said. "By the grace of God, they must carry us to the end. See to their order."

"Just moving so quick, all of it," Colston said. He braved a smile. "It's a triumph, General."

Another Rebel yell rose.

"Not yet," Jackson told him.

A runaway ambulance nearly felled both Howard and his horse. Turning into the brush, he lost his hat and a sharp branch scratched his face.

The Turnpike was a doomsday pageant of ditched wagons and overturned caissons. Artillery sections attempted to set up in the roadway, the only spot that promised fields of fire, only to find crowds of fleeing soldiers blocking their discharges. Then the Rebs flowed over them.

Major General Oliver Otis Howard, followed by a fraction of his staff, rode in among the soldiers who had gone quits.

"Don't shame me, men! Don't embarrass me!" Then he added, "Don't shame yourselves, boys!"

A few men heeded him. Others paused then went on. Those infected with panic just ran gaping.

"I'll have you all shot!" Howard shouted, but his voice had frayed. In quieter tones, he said, "I'm ruined, I'm ruined. . . ."

Devens' division was all but gone. Exchanges of volleys, unseen, promised that lone regiments resisted, but those who attempted to form on the road were rapidly swept away.

Howard had barely returned from Barlow's brigade when the world exploded. He'd ridden, promptly, toward the sound of the guns, leaving Schurz to change his front in haste.

The thought of the know-it-all Germans having been right was too much to bear.

Would Washington and the newspapers blame *him*? Yes, those reeking Germans had warned him of an attack, but Hooker was the one truly at fault. It was Hooker who had insisted that Lee was retreating. Wasn't it? The view had been forced upon him. *He* was only responding to higher headquarters, a martyr to the errors of other men. . . .

Howard tried to recall if he had put any dismissive remarks in writing. He didn't think so.

Could he trust Meysenburg to destroy anything embarrassing? Or would the man stick with his Germans? Better to ask Assmussen, who knew what was good for him.

All this was *their* fault, actually. The Germans. Yes, they'd warned him. But had they *done* anything? They could have acted on their own. But the Germans hadn't lifted a finger, had they? And Joe Hooker, robbing him of Barlow's brigade, his reserve . . .

How could he be blamed for any of this?

Would Greeley stand by him?

A regiment broke apart before his eyes. While some men stood, bitter and fierce, most ran. The Rebs surged almost to touching distance.

Howard seized the national colors from a fleeing bearer. He heaved the pole across his saddle and tucked it under the stump of his missing arm.

"Stop, boys!" he cried. "Rally on me! *Rally!*"

His horse reared and hurled him to the ground.

Orderlies dismounted and rushed to his aid. One of them fell with a cry, shot through the knee.

This was war. The fellow didn't matter.

"Help me up," Howard demanded. *"Help me."*

Pickens almost shot the Yank in the belly. The fool had leapt out of the brush right in front of him, throwing down his rifle. Startled, Pickens came within a shaved second of pulling the trigger.

Instead, he commanded, "Give me that canteen, Yank. Hurry up."

Slinging the canteen over his neck—it had the good weight of water in it—Pickens ignored the blue-belly and trotted on, catching up with the raggedy, broke-back pretense of a line. He continued to stick close to Lieutenant Colonel Hobson, and the colors rejoined them. Ed Hutchinson and Doc Cowin came up, too. Moving forward, they crested a mild slope and poured down the other side amid a gray torrent. There were ever longer intervals between the pauses required to drive off Yankees.

It seemed like they'd gotten well behind them. Unless all the Yanks had run off. No, that couldn't be so. Organized volleys still tossed the pepper back and forth on the right, down toward that road.

Didn't hear no Yankee cheering, though. They'd feel this whupping for a goodly time.

The light softened a touch. Excitement wrestled exhaustion.

"Fifth Alabama!" Hobson called. "To your colors, Fifth!"

Dutifully, Williams waved the battle flag. But other flags encroached, with other voices. Splintered off among strangers, Pickens' chaw of the regiment seemed barely the size of a ration detail.

Beside him, a stranger clutched his thigh and fell headlong. The Yankees were still out there, after all.

Untended but handsomely saddled, a fine horse grazed amid pines.

"Get that horse!" the colonel cried. "Grab on to that-there horse!"

He scooted off toward it, yelling he had first claim.

Distracted, Pickens tripped over a played-out Yank, dropping across the man's legs to slam the ground. His rifle didn't go off, but it smashed his knuckles.

The blue-belly groaned. Then he whispered, "Help me, Johnny. Give me a swig, some water." In the shadows, Pickens read a lieutenant's rank. Barefaced but for small mustaches and young, the Yank was in a bad way, lung-shot and bubbling blood.

"Don't know as it's wise," Pickens told him.

"Water. Please."

From whence my succor cometh, Pickens thought. He took to his knees and helped the Yank to drink. The Yank tried to swallow, choked, and gasped. Blood foamed pink from his torn uniform. But the boy insisted on drinking again. His eyes gathered fading light.

When he could speak again, the lieutenant asked:

"What's your name and regiment, Johnny? I'll be ever mindful of you."

"Sam Pickens, Fifth Alabama."

"Can you help me? I need a surgeon. I'm bad."

"Ain't none here. Can't even help my own kind."

Sam Pickens decided he'd tarried long enough. The helplessness of it, his own and the Yank's, unsettled him. He left his enemy and—feet still forgotten—ran puffing to rejoin his brethren.

There was a fight ahead.

It's our turn next," Schurz told the Polish colonel. "Alex is doing the best he can on the road, but you . . . your regiments are all this army has for a flank now, Kriz. We've got to buy time for von Steinwehr, let him realign his division."

Krzyzanowski remained imperturbable. Schurz could imagine the man in full *Husaria* armor, facing down the Turks before Vienna. The odds weren't much better here.

In a calm voice, the Pole responded, "I understand."

The Rebel yells sounded closer.

* * *

Lee felt a vast relief. The nagging probes of his overstretched lines had ceased, those people had other worries.

The sounds of battle from the west were music.

Jackson's music.

As defeated soldiers streamed across the Chancellor house clearing, Joseph Hooker asked, "What happened?"

Amid his enemy's devastation, Jackson found Robert Rodes attempting to impose order on his division.

Rodes had done well. But the critical hour lay ahead, the twilight hour, when they must turn a Federal calamity into a catastrophe, when they must inflict the Lord's fulminous wrath upon heathen transgressors.

If Rodes expected congratulations, he was to be disappointed.

"The attack is slowing. It cannot be permitted to slow down," Jackson told him.

"Sir . . . the regiments, the brigades . . . they're intermingled. Even the divisions, it's beyond description. And the men . . ."

Jackson understood that Rodes—an excellent officer—was trying. But he needed to try harder.

"Excuses don't win battles. We must press them, General Rodes. *You* must press them."

The Federals would be struggling to build a defense. It must not be permitted.

"Drive them," Jackson ordered. "Shoot any man who runs. We must finish them now."

"Yes, sir. I'll see to it."

"Show them no mercy," Jackson ordered.

The Lord's will raged within him.

What the devil was going on? Frank Barlow wondered. For over an hour he'd heard the sounds of battle from the northwest, about where he judged the Eleventh Corps to be. Yet he'd heard nothing from Howard, and his last notice from Sickles, sent hours before, had been to remain where he was and await orders.

Actually, he wasn't sure quite where he was. He'd been given no map, and contact with Sickles' corps did seem a bit tenuous. He'd begun to feel rather isolated.

A proper racket back there. It sounded like a rough match, with guns in play. He would have liked to get into it.

Of course, if he were needed, they would have recalled him.

Robert Rodes bullied bits and pieces of his division back into the semblance of a line. And he sent the men forward again, overtaking clots of soldiers splashed from a stew of regiments. Broken companies fought their own lesser battles in the brush, while more and more men, wearied, had gone to ground, waiting to be called to account by authority. Stray officers seemed to do more shouting than leading.

It was grand, though, despite all. They'd smashed into the Yankees, overwhelming them. By Rodes' calculation, they'd advanced over a mile from the first contact.

And they would go farther. Jackson wanted it, he wanted it. It was essential to continue to overwhelm the Federals, to keep them off balance, to push beyond any resistance, to flood around their flanks, to complete the victory.

But what did Jackson have in mind for tomorrow? Or even for the next hour? With twilight nigh, how much farther should they go? Judged by the prisoners taken, they'd only encountered a single Union corps. At some point, a reorganization would be essential, before night descended and they themselves became vulnerable to the Yankees, before the odds reversed themselves.

Around him, officers and men shouted out the letters and numbers of companies and regiments, lost sheep all.

In blue or gray or patchwork brown, wounded men staggered about.

Cannon boomed close by, but he could not see their flashes.

Obedient and ever inspired by battle, he drove his men forward. He just wished that Jackson weren't so infernally close-mouthed, that he'd share some expectation of what came next and outline a plan.

Meanwhile, there was plenty of work to do.

He saw ghosts. Phantoms. Out there in the deep brush, deeper still than the tangles that clutched his uniform.

Lieutenant Karl Doerflinger, of the 26th Wisconsin, waited for his first sight of the elephant: Were those Johnnies? Or did he just have the jumps?

Commanding the center of the skirmish line, he hesitated to give the order to fire. He couldn't tell if those darting forms—they seemed real now—were his own kind in flight or actual Rebs.

He peered into the premature dusk of the woods.

This was it, then. This was what it was like.

Late in the afternoon, Colonel Krzyzanowski and Colonel Jacobs had gathered in the officers of the 26th Wisconsin and of the 58th New York, which stood on their flank. The brigade commander had explained that they, a mere two regiments, formed the deep right flank of the entire corps. If the Rebs attacked, they would have to hold the high ground by the farmhouse, the only open terrain their division had, or the Johnnies would sweep into the rear and cut off the corps from the army.

For almost an hour, they'd heard the war, but they could not see it. The only physical evidence of combat came from fugitives, crazed men straying left and right, one crying that "a million" Rebs were upon them.

Hadn't seen one Reb.

Until now. Perhaps. Those shadows.

Men, all right.

Rebs? Skedaddlers?

"Should we fire, Lieutenant?"

Doerflinger felt reluctant. He did not want to kill comrades.

The isolated phantoms swelled into a thrashing line of battle. They began to wail, unnerving.

"Aim and fire!" the lieutenant called. Hoping, even now, that he was right.

One rifle, two, dozens fired into the woods.

The advancing line halted. Voices foreign to Doerflinger's ears barked orders.

A terrible volley slashed through the vegetation.

"Fire! Fire!" He could not remember another command.

The Rebs rushed forward again, screaming that wild witches' cry, their *Hexengeschrei.*

"Gott im Himmel," a soldier near him called out as he fell.

But no man ran. They stood by him. Expecting him to do things correctly.

A sergeant found him amid the brambles.

"Captain Pizzala . . . dead . . . brains come right out of his head . . ."

He was in command now. And the skirmish line's fire seemed paltry, the Rebs a multitude.

"Fall back!" he shouted. "Fall back on the forward companies. Fall back!" He ran along his line as fast as the brush allowed, striving to ensure that every man heard him.

The Rebs were so close he could see their faces clearly, even in poor light. One man's eyes met his. Hating eyes.

The Johnny raised his rifle.

Saber useless in his fist, Doerflinger dodged and followed his men.

Dutifully, his soldiers aligned with two companies posted forward, at the wood's edge. They reloaded with speed.

All of that endless drilling had served a purpose.

With the last skirmishers cleared—barely in time—the companies let go a volley. The Rebs wavered, but only for a moment. There were so many, so many. . . .

The companies fired again. This time, the Rebs paused for a proper volley.

Directly to Doerflinger's front, a soldier's tunic tore open, spraying blood at shoulder level.

Others fell, too.

Doerflinger and his handful of men realized they'd been left behind, their comrades had already fallen back on the regiment.

The Rebs were nearly on top of them.

"Run!" Doerflinger ordered. *"Run for the regiment! Run!"*

He and his small flock of soldiers dashed across the open ground, cheered on by the blue line atop a slope. Doerflinger saw that he'd gotten mixed up in the woods: He was in front of the 58th New York, not his Wisconsin brethren. But he hadn't time to correct his course and he aimed for the New Yorkers' color guard, running as fast as he'd ever run in his life.

Something knocked him down, with a clang. When he leapt back to his feet, he saw that his sword's sheath was bent at a useless angle.

No time to feel for a wound. He ran on and felt a tug on his haversack, felt it slipping away. Still running madly, he clutched the bag against him. The strap had been shot through.

"Come on, come on!" the New Yorkers hollered.

He finally grasped that they needed to shoot and didn't want to hit him.

With a leap, he thrust himself through a gap they made for him.

Behind him, the Johnnies howled.

The New Yorkers fired.

By God, they stood the fire! Colonel Willie Jacobs was proud of his men, proud beyond words. As he sat on his mount directly behind them, he didn't have a thought left for himself. Only for them, his boys, his *Burschen*.

"Give it to them!" he barked, in a voice that would have shocked him had he heard it raised in his bank back in Milwaukee. He had always insisted upon decorum, and the Second Ward Bank had been an island of civility, of order and financial chastity, in the city's lively, grab-a-dollar streets.

He had never dreamed of going to war. But war had come to claim him. Now men who had trusted him with their savings trusted him with their lives.

"That's it, boys! Knock 'em down. Knock 'em down like pins. *Gib Feuer!*"

Not a hundred yards away, Rebs massed in ragged lines took turns spitting flames from their rifle muzzles. In the softening light, the flashes appeared to be hundreds of giant fireflies.

Deadly fireflies. Hugo Carstangen, Jacobs' sergeant major, crumpled. The senselessness of his posture, the odd sprawl of his limbs, announced his death.

The noise was painful. No drill field could prepare you for the noise.

Smoke thickened over the crest.

Jacobs' horse quivered beneath him, as if gripped by a fever. Before Jacobs knew what was happening, the creature collapsed on its forelegs and he tumbled past its neck.

The animal shook its head and its mane flared, as if sweeping off flies. It struggled back to its feet and collapsed again. Jacobs rolled out of the way with a second to spare.

"You all right, sir?" Major Baetz asked. Men nearby had stopped firing, staring in concern.

Aching and raging, Jacobs got to his feet. "*Zum Teufel,* what are you looking at? Look at the Chonnies, not me. *An die Arbeit!*"

A miracle. The Rebs, greater in number, began to withdraw.

Krzyzanowski pierced the smoke, a broad-shouldered, somber man on a great black horse.

"They'll be back," he cautioned. "Fine work, but they'll be back." Above cutting cheekbones, his eyes were grave. "They'll move around your flank. Refuse it by a company. Two, if you want. But hold as long as you can."

Stung, the Rebs re-formed by the tree line. Within a minute, they sent out a well-controlled volley.

Krzyzanowski sat calmly in his saddle, leaning forward, as was his habit. But his eyes registered the losses all around him.

"We'll hold," Jacobs told him.

The Pole nodded but said nothing. He turned his horse to the left, toward the New Yorkers holding out on the other side of the farmhouse.

More of Jacobs' soldiers dropped. And still more.

No man ran away.

Captain Winkler and his horse toppled together. Back from his duty on the skirmish line, Lieutenant Doerflinger shouted encouragement to the men, clutching his sword in one hand and, oddly, holding his haversack in the other. The young fellow managed to look both heroic and comical.

As Jacobs watched, Doerflinger's leg buckled. Forgoing the sword and sack, the lieutenant clutched his thigh, bellowing in pain, rocking back and forth. Two of his soldiers dragged him behind the farmhouse then dashed back to the line.

Good men, such good men. The best men in Milwaukee's German community.

They began to take fire from the flank, as Krzyzanowski had predicted.

He just didn't have enough soldiers. He couldn't pull more from the line.

How long had they been fighting? Fifteen minutes? Twenty? It seemed like hours and yet no more than an instant.

"Stand, boys, stand! Make your families proud! Stand for Wisconsin!"

Krzyzanowski reappeared. His face had been spattered with blood.

"Withdraw your regiment fifty paces. Re-form on the reverse slope."

Jacobs gave the order. The company officers still on their feet repeated it.

Before he faded back into the maelstrom, the Pole told Jacobs, "I've sent to Schurz, I've told him we need reinforcements."

"What's happening?" Jacobs asked. "Everywhere else?"

Krzyzanowski opened his mouth to speak. Then he closed it again. Pondering. At last, he said:

"What matters is what happens here."

The regiment stepped backward in good order, pausing to fire and bringing along as many of its wounded as could be carried. Many, too many, could not be moved.

The Rebs followed after. Shouting curses and threats. But they were more cautious now.

The back-and-forth volleys and loose firing resumed, reducing the regiment by the minute. The reverse slope helped little, it merely shortened the range. Looking over at the Johnnies, peering through the smoke, Jacobs understood that if the Rebs made one determined rush, his regiment would be overthrown in a blink.

His regiment. Never before in battle. And here the men stood. As unwilling to move as he was himself. No one would ever dare mock Germans again.

Back on his feet, Captain Winkler reported:

"Sir, we're under fire from the rear, they've gotten behind us."

"How many?"

"Some. Not many. Yet."

What order could he give now? To refuse the refused flank? Was there such a command?

Krzyzanowski returned, at a gallop this time.

"I've ordered the Fifty-eighth to fall back. A fighting withdrawal. You need to pull back, too. We're all but surrounded."

"But . . . the reinforcements?"

"There are none. Not for us. They're being held back with von Steinwehr. What few there are."

"Where's the rest of the army?"

The Pole shrugged. "Wherever they are, they're not here. You need to pull back now, Willie."

To his embarrassment, Jacobs felt tears crowd his eyes. His men . . . they'd fought for this ground. They were still fighting for it.

"I can't. We can't withdraw. I can't leave all my wounded. There are too many. . . ."

Krzyzanowski's expression didn't change. He might as well have worn a mask.

"You will obey orders. Immediately." His voice softened a degree. "Willie, you either pull back now, or you'll all be captured. Those who aren't killed outright. Your duty now is to save what remains of the regiment."

The tears broke free.

"I can't."

In a voice trimmed by agonized centuries spent fighting off Poland's enemies, Krzyzanowski told him:

"You will give the order this instant. Or I will relieve you from command."

Jacobs did as bidden. As his men began to pull back, loading and firing as they went, the Pole sat fiercely upon his horse, as if bullets had best avoid him.

As the long spring twilight deepened, Jackson's anger grew. It wasn't enough to destroy a Union corps, or even two. His plan had been to split Hooker's army apart, to drive past Chancellorsville and reunite with Lee, to devour half of the Army of the Potomac.

He meant to reach the Chancellorsville crossroads, at least, before halting for the night. Tired they might be, but the men did not need to sleep. Or eat. They only needed to rejoin their regiments and brigades and refill their cartridge pouches. In the first predawn light, they would renew the attack and connect with Lee's right flank.

They had not gone far enough, not yet. He judged that another mile had to be covered before dark. Or after dark, if need be. They must not stop. The Federals must not be given one moment to breathe.

He rode from flank to flank, from general to colonel and on to the next general, always insisting that they continue the advance without the least pause, hastening batteries along, clearing ambulances out of the way for ammunition wagons to pass, ignoring the prisoners plodding rearward like sheep . . . if his men were disorganized, the Yankees were demoralized. They had been defeated. Now they had to be crushed.

His soldiers could do it. Men did not understand what they could achieve until you taught them. And Thomas Jonathan Jackson would see that they learned.

Joseph Hooker issued a flurry of orders. Swinging between interludes of near despair and bursts of confidence, he had directed Sickles to hurry Berry's division back to bolster Howard; ordered Van Alen to prepare to contract the lines; established a provost marshal's line to intercept runaway soldiers; alerted Slocum to be prepared to support; and called up the artillery reserve.

When the chief of staff approached him with another report, he concealed his quivering hands inside his pockets.

He was all right, though. His mind was clear.

The artillery was an especial challenge. He saw now that he had erred by taking away authority from Hunt. The damned self-righteous artilleryman had seen it all along: the guns needed a central figure in control, no matter how the corps and divisions complained. Now, on the field of battle, his artillery was all captains and no colonels.

It was always the one thing you took for granted that bit you, a snake coiled in the outhouse. The way he had assumed that barley and wheat would prosper on his ranch in Sonoma.

Brushing off the latest report of disaster, he called for his horse. It was time, at last, to see matters firsthand.

They surged forward again, weary men walking at a steady pace, flushing terrified Yankees from their hiding places just by putting one foot in front of the other.

"Got himself wounded," Bill Lenier said. "Not to a muchness, though."

Sam Pickens was sorry to hear that: He and Bob Price had shared many a blanket. He hoped that, indeed, Bob wasn't too badly off.

In a small miracle, a number of the Greensboro Guards and more men from the 5th Alabama had found their various ways back to one another. Lieutenant Colonel Hobson had been wounded, too, but lightly. Colonel Hall didn't quite have himself a regiment, but he had a respectable company's worth of men again.

General Rodes came and went, all but flaying any man who lagged. The entire attack seemed to have regained its ambition.

Worn, though. They were worn. Ed Hutchinson was cursing to kill a deacon, angry as ever he'd been after tumbling, corporal's stripes and all, into what he was convinced was a poison ivy patch.

"Hate this place," he said. "Just *hate* it."

Somehow they'd gotten rightward of the road, about the distance of a full company front, with men from the brigade gathered on both flanks and Colonel O'Neal in every bit as whipping a mood as Rodes.

"Old Jack lit a fire under those boys," Joe Grigg put in. "Bet you gold dollars."

"You ain't got no gold dollars," Ed Hutchinson told him, cranky.

Joe cackled. "Got me two Yankee watches, though. And looking for a third."

Doc Cowin, recently reunited with his camp mates, said:

"Ah, the spoils of Troy. . . ."

They entered an open space marred by Yankee debris. It was a tad brighter, once out of the woods, with the field and sky about the same half-night paleness. They were even closer to the road now. A double line of strangers advanced ahead of them.

Rifle fire crackled here and there, and the occasional gun thumped in the distance, but they seemed to be through the worst of it.

"Think the Yanks went quits?" Joe Grigg asked.

His answer came immediately.

One right after the other, artillery pieces thundered to their front. The shadowed line ahead of theirs burst apart: men flew or fell, while some dissolved in a blur.

A severed head bounced toward them.

"Canister!" a man shouted. Others took up the cry. But few men went to ground. Instead, ranks closed and thrust forward.

A second turn of canister slowed them.

"Where are they?" a voice demanded.

"In the road. Ahead there, in the road."

"Going to kill those blue-belly sonsofbitches."

Again and again, Battery I of the 1st Ohio Light Artillery had been forced back—not by the Johnnies alone, but by the endless fugitives corrupting their already limited fields of fire. By the time the skedaddlers cleared the muzzles, the Rebs were all but atop them. Each Napoléon got off one round before the battery had to pull back and repeat the cycle.

Now it was different. Captain Hubert Dilger's six guns faced a rough-made battle line of Rebs crossing a clearing. His artillerymen blasted them, reloading with practiced speed. It was the first time that day that Dilger felt he'd served a purpose.

The Rebs kept coming, regardless, their losses made good by ever more arrivals. His men kept firing. Gun crewmen jerked suddenly and collapsed, but the savvier Rebs aimed at the limber and caisson horses.

General Schurz appeared in the roadway.

"Dilger," he called. "Hold as long as you can. We're forming a new line."

"Yes, sir."

"Wiedrich's lost half his guns. He's in a bad way. I'm counting on you."

Dilger wasn't certain he heard much hope in Schurz's voice.

He thought again of that dismissive cavalry major lounging at Hooker's headquarters, the bastard who'd called him a coward when he tried to report that the Rebs weren't retreating at all.

Where was that lout now?

Remnants of broken regiments rallied briefly by his guns, but as the Rebs closed the distance they melted away.

"One more round of canister each," he shouted, riding his gun line. "Then *move*. Five hundred yards to the rear and unlimber again."

Six muzzle blasts in succession sent Confederates flying to Hell. His men scrambled as Reb sharpshooters paused to aim at the horses.

Neighs, shrieks, chaos.

Three guns got off quickly, followed by a fourth then the fifth. The last gun had three horses down out of four. Still, its crew tried to cut the traces and drag off the gun. The Johnnies shot them down, one after another.

"Leave it," Dilger told the survivors. "Get out of here, leave it."

The gun was lost, he didn't want to lose good men as well.

He turned his horse to follow his battery.

Johnnies screamed behind him, cursing him.

The horse buckled and fell, pinning him beneath its flank. As the animal convulsed, Dilger yanked the right rein as hard as he could, desperate. And the mount twisted up just far enough for the captain to free his leg.

He got up. Fast. Hurt like the devil. He almost lost his footing.

Bullets stung the air. Southern voices cried: "Give up, Yank. Give up, you murdering sumbitch."

He ran, hobbling.

Not enough time.

The Rebs.

Hate to be shot in the back. . . .

His orderly rode back toward him through a blue cloud of fleeing infantrymen. Dilger ran stiff-legged toward him, aching at each second step. Inexplicably, his mind filled with the phrase *the world as will and idea*. He repeated it like a prayer, willing his survival.

Young and gun-crew brawny, the orderly barely halted his mount as he helped Dilger swing up behind his saddle.

Then they rode headlong.

His artillerymen cheered when they saw him. Their guns were ready to do their work again.

* * *

Schurz's last attempt to form a division line consisted of the remains of five regiments. The men stood well, until a flood of Confederates flowed past their flanks, threatening to engulf them. The surviving field officers struggled to hold their commands together as the line broke.

Schurz tried to rally them, too. Several times he persuaded a number of soldiers to stop and face about. But as soon as the gigantic swarm of Rebs approached, they ran again.

There were just too many of them. The Johnnies were wild and disordered, but they came on in multitudes, smelling blood.

This wasn't a contest of armies any longer. It was a battle between mobs.

He galloped back to Buschbeck's line, where Schimmelfennig and Krzyzanowski were rallying their survivors to stand with von Steinwehr's men by a country church. Even in the dying light, Schurz could see from one end of the blue line to the other. And there just weren't enough men.

While they waited for the shrieking Rebs to appear through the brush or across the scant open ground, the soldiers dug frantically at their shallow entrenchments, wielding bayonets, tin plates, or naked hands.

Even the regiments that had held together smelled of defeat. They'd fight. For a time. But no man could say for how long.

Why hadn't Hooker rushed up reinforcements? Why hadn't Barlow's brigade returned?

Before Schurz could reach his brigade commanders, Howard intercepted him. He'd glimpsed Howard often, right at the front lines—to the extent one could speak of lines—and no one could accuse the man of cowardice. Of folly, yes. But not of cowardice.

The corps commander had regained a degree of composure.

"Krzyzanowski," he began, mispronouncing the Pole's name as he always did, "was magnificent. At that farmhouse. My compliments."

"You should tell him yourself, sir."

Howard's features weakened. "I tried." After a painful interval, he added, "He was busy. He was too busy. . . ."

Schurz said nothing.

"I'm ruined, you know," Howard said, with remarkable calmness.

Schurz almost exploded, a human round of canister. Howard wasn't ruined. He never would be. Schurz knew the politics of it better than any man on the field. Many another might be ruined over this debacle. But not Howard.

"I need to see to my men," Schurz excused himself.

Buschbeck's line collapsed and with it went the hope that von Steinwehr's division might redeem the corps. Outflanked yet again, the surviving regiments withdrew in relative order this time, simply unable to withstand the onslaught, their ranks infected with a soldier's sense that they had been hopelessly beaten and could do no more. Generals and colonels rode back and forth in the deepening darkness, attempting to maintain discipline and rally the soldiers on the brigades rushing forward from other corps.

An unidentified officer galloped about, shouting an order to the last holdouts to join the withdrawal.

But Hubert Dilger did not want to abandon his position. So he didn't. He kept his five remaining guns in battery, covering the collapse.

The Rebs were at once triumphant and angry, converging on him in the gloaming, roiling shadows under the sky's faint paleness, spooks from a child's nightmare.

He had one stroke of luck. The last blue-coated men to retire along the road were Ohio boys, from the 61st. Dilger hailed an officer he recognized, but when the captain didn't respond he spoke right to the men:

"Don't abandon Ohio's guns, Sixty-first! Stand with us, cover our flanks."

Men slowed, but didn't stop. The few officers seemed doubtful.

"Damn it, Ohio!" Dilger snapped. "*We're* staying. *Some*body's got to put up a fight."

"By God," a man called from the ranks, "that Dutchman's right."

At first a few, then dozens of the Ohio infantrymen spread out by the guns.

For a handsome moment, they stopped the Rebel advance, with the foot soldiers firing and shouting, "Ohio! Ohio!" while Dilger's crews worked their fieldpieces. The artillerymen were black as minstrels now and wreathed with smoke, darker than the new night.

Dilger had no time to revel in his small victory. His turned his attention back to directing fire at the most urgent targets, the lunging shadows in the open stretch.

"Converging fires, midfield! Number two gun, drop a quarter turn. *Re*port!"

"Number one ready!"

"Number three . . ."

The Rebs were undeterred, and they were a multitude. Man by man, then in small groups, the Ohio infantrymen faded into the shadows until only a hard-minded dozen or so remained.

Dilger had taken his orderly's horse. He dismounted and returned it. His men were deafened and he had to grasp Lieutenant Dammaert by the sleeve to command his attention. He shouted in the man's ear:

"Withdraw every piece but Allen's, he's got the last intact crew. Take them back to wherever the next line's forming and go into battery. Listen to me: Leapfrog the caissons as you go, dump charges and all the canister that's left by the side of the road, pile it every hundred and fifty yards, all the way back. Jump to it!"

"You—"

"Just go, Bill. Save the guns. *Go!*"

He strode over to Corporal Allen's fieldpiece and told the men, "Rope her up and wheel her into the center of the road. Then load double canister. Don't fire until I tell you."

Turning to a last cluster of infantrymen, he announced:

"We're staying. One gun. Glad of any support you choose to give." And he turned his back, leaving them to their consciences.

With hard-practiced agility, the gun crews limbered up. Dead horses were cut from their harnesses and whips cracked.

And they were gone.

An artilleryman with a swab in hand fell bleeding.

The Rebs howled and rushed forward again.

Dilger let them come.

An infantryman, a man who had made the fateful decision to stay, dropped beside him and lay there with stilled eyes.

"Let them get closer."

"Sir, for—"

"Closer!"

Und wenn die Welt voll Teufel waere . . . Yes, the world *was* full of devils, packed with them.

"Now!"

The doubled canister shredded man-meat four rows deep and ten yards in breadth.

"Haul her back, let's go." He looked to the remaining infantry soldiers, still a solid dozen. "Grab the ropes, half of you. Help us."

Their fellow Ohioans pitched in. Chased by bullets and taunts, they dragged the cannon along the road at a dog's trot, with Dilger limping beside them. The infantrymen who had not found a grip on the guide ropes returned fire.

The night was alive with blinks of light and brief glares. There was just enough last paleness along the road for Dilger to spot the piled ammunition.

"Halt. Load single canister. Then double it. Corporal Allen, fire when ready."

An unexpected volley from a wood line swept the gun crew, leaving only the corporal and one man standing.

Dilger pitched in, putting his shoulder into the wheel to turn the loaded gun toward the wood before the Rebels had time to reload.

Infantrymen rushed to help.

"Drop trail. Now. Back!"

Corporal Allen yanked the lanyard.

The fieldpiece bucked and spit fire.

"Re-center, *re-center.*"

As they wheeled the gun back to face down the road, an infantry sergeant told Dilger, "We can crew ye up, Cap'n. For we've seen it done time enough."

And they did. They gave the Rebs another double load of canister then manhandled the piece back another stretch.

The darkness was their last friend.

Thrice more, the lone gun and its guardians made a stand. Corporal Allen was wounded, as were men whose names remained unknown to Dilger. At last, out of ammunition and all but surrounded, Dilger ordered his tiny command to abandon the piece and save themselves.

Without a word spoken, the infantry soldiers chose to save the gun.

When they were safely behind a thickening Union line, with fresh troops pouring in, the infantry sergeant dropped the gun rope and told Dilger:

"Couldn't leave her, yer honor, sir. For we'd formed us a fond attachment."

The sin of pride was a danger unto him. He knew it and he resisted. He would not revel in what his men had done. Nor would he accept this verdict of weariness. The work was not yet accomplished, the last and sweetest grapes had not been gathered.

Sensing Hill's presence in the smoke-addled darkness, Jackson said:

"We cannot stop. Not now. You must drive your men forward."

"General Jackson, I can hardly *find* my men. We need to reorganize. Hooker still has entire corps uncommitted. . . ."

Jackson knew that Hill resented—perhaps hated—him. But it mattered not. Hill was a loathsome sinner, visited by the Lord's enduring punishment.

Hill had been weak and derelict, at West Point and at Cedar Mountain, and here there could be no weakness.

"You will go forward."

They were so close. Another half mile, perhaps less.

Cut them down, cut them in two. Smite them, drive them from Israel, from Judah, and then from Canaan.

They were close, tantalizingly close, to shattering Hooker's pagan army by midnight, before the Lord's day began.

Yes, there would be fighting on the morrow, whatever happened tonight. But less, less.

Cannon still thundered. Union guns. Their defense had begun to show character. This labor had to be made complete, Pharaoh's chariots must be overturned, their masters drowned not in the Red Sea, but in a sea of their unholy blood.

One last, hard push.

He closed his eyes in prayer and beheld a pale horse.

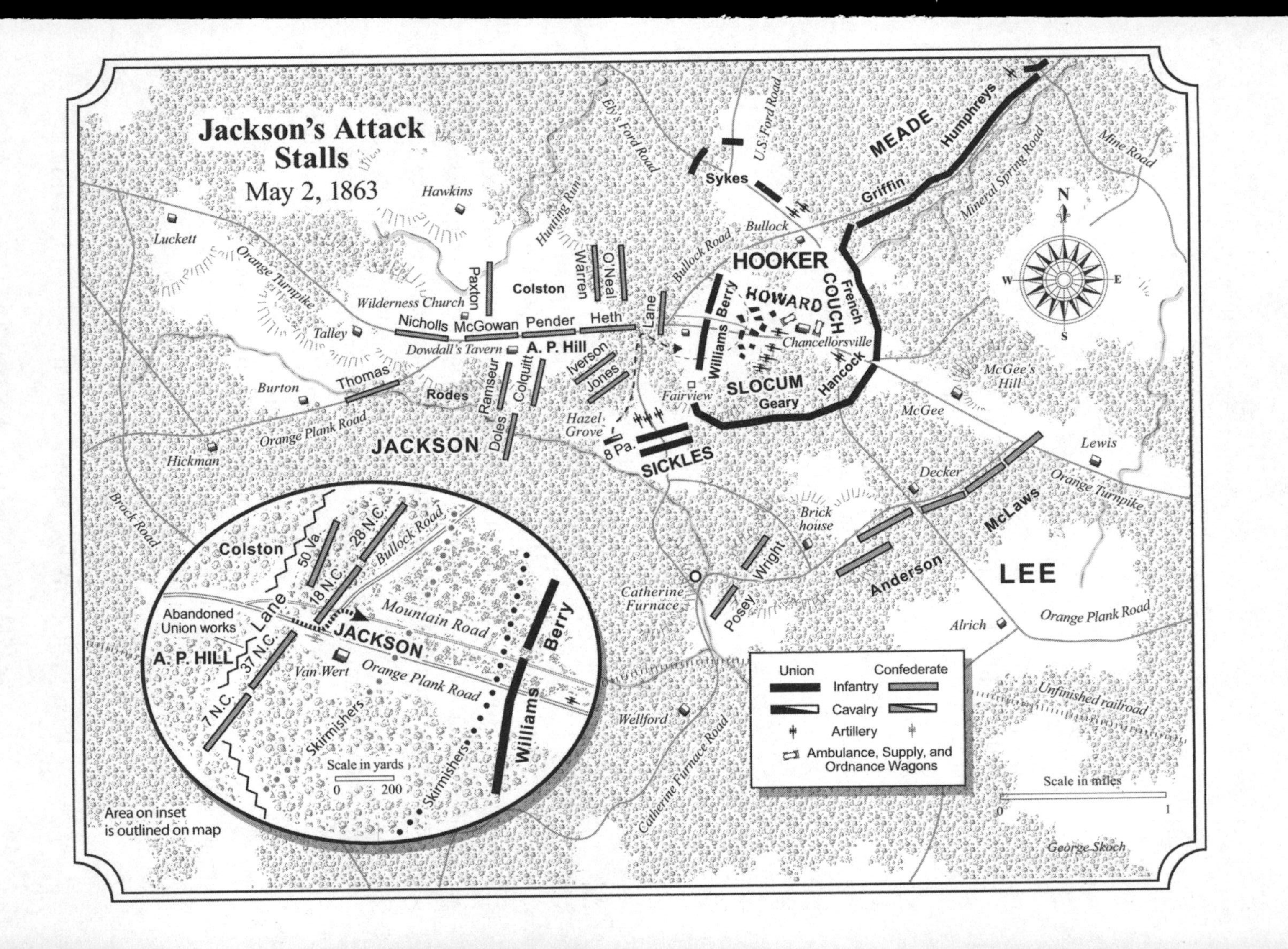

Jackson's Attack Stalls
May 2, 1863
Hawkins
Luckett
Orange Turnpike
Talley
Wilderness Church
Paxton
Colston
Hunting Run
Warren
O'Neal
Ely's Ford Road
Sykes
U.S. Ford Road
MEADE
Humphreys
Griffin
Mineral Spring Road
Mine Road
Bullock Road
Bullock
HOOKER
HOWARD
COUCH
French
Chancellorsville
Hancock
SLOCUM
Geary
Williams
Berry
Nicholls
McGowan
Pender
Heth
Lane
Dowdall's Tavern
A. P. Hill
Iverson
Jones
Ramseur
Colquitt
Doles
Thomas
Rodes
Burton
Orange Plank Road
Hickman
JACKSON
Hazel Grove
8 Pa.
SICKLES
Fairview
McGee's Hill
McGee
Lewis
Decker
Orange Turnpike
McLaws
Brick house
Wright
Posey
Anderson
LEE
Catherine Furnace
Alrich
Orange Plank Road
Wellford
Catherine Furnace Road
Brock Road
Unfinished railroad
Union
Confederate
Infantry
Cavalry
Artillery
Ambulance, Supply, and Ordnance Wagons
Scale in miles
0
1
George Skoch
Colston
50 Va.
28 N.C.
18 N.C.
Bullock Road
Lane
Abandoned Union works
Mountain Road
JACKSON
A. P. HILL
37 N.C.
7 N.C.
Van Wert
Orange Plank Road
Skirmishers
Skirmishers
Scale in yards
0
200
Williams
Berry
Area on inset is outlined on map

SEVEN

May 2, early night
Hazel Grove, Union lines

Charlie Wickersham watched his fellow officers gamble. The rising moon was so full and grand that the campfire's light was frivolous: The earth glowed and the tattered playing cards shone. Pete Keenan was winning, as usual, emptying the pockets of Haze Haddock and Chas Arrowsmith.

Leaning against a tree, Wickersham fended off intermittent gibes from Keenan, a major and chum. Wickersham had sworn off cards for the war's duration, maybe forever. He suspected that a man had only so much luck in his account, and he didn't want to squander his playing poker. The teasing was endless, though: A cavalryman who didn't lay down bets was akin to one who feared horses.

He'd had his share of luck the day before, though, when his skirmishers from the 8th Pennsylvania Cavalry had sparred with the Rebs out on the Fredericksburg road. Today had been a different, duller story, with General Pleasanton—a braggart not much liked—issuing frequent and contradictory orders for a pursuit that never happened. The men were tired, annoyed, and still waiting to be told, at last, to stand down.

"Sure you don't want to have yourself a seat? Just one quick round?" Keenan asked him.

"Reckon not."

Keenan grinned and told the other players and spectators, "Captain Wickersham's going to go for a Quaker after the war. Or maybe he'll be one of those tightfisted deacons, kind who starve preachers to death. Possibly even a regular man of the cloth, given all that sobriety of his. Amen."

"Only cloth I'll want after all this," Wickersham told him, "is a good wool suit that doesn't stink of me."

Another eruption of artillery caught the men's attention.

"*Something's* going on up there," Haddock, the adjutant, said.

"Well, let them settle it."

"Sounds closer."

"This afternoon they were at it down the other way," Keenan responded. He shrugged. "Not enough guns for a real to-do. You going to draw, or not?"

Haddock brought his cards closer to his face, pondering them.

"Cripes, Haze . . . we're playing poker, not chess. Shit, or get off the pot."

"I fold."

Keenan looked over at Arrowsmith and the low fire lent him a devilish look. "How about you, Charlie? Up the stakes a little?"

Arrowsmith made a disgusted face. "I'm out." He threw down his cards.

Keenan cackled. "Whipped by a pair of nines, in case you're curious. God bless you boys. I was thinking about investing in a little farm back home, but now I'm considering taking up one of these plantations I keep hearing about and not seeing. Reckon they'll go cheap, by the time we're done with 'em." Shuffling the cards, he looked around at the idlers who'd been following the game. "Anybody else care to try his luck?"

"Not with 'Golden Pete,'" a lieutenant joshed.

"That's '*Major* Golden Pete,' Lieutenant.'" Keenan laughed. He was a merry companion even on the rare occasions when the cards ran against him. Tonight, he was almost elated, despite the day's frustrations. He said, "Lord, here comes Pen. Who, I believe, has suffered a visit from the distinctly unpleasant Mr. Pleasanton. No rest for a man's tired bones. . . ."

Major Pennock Huey, commanding, came up at a sharp pace.

Before he could speak, Keenan asked, "Now, why do I feel that you're about to break up some fine entertainment, Pen?"

Straight backed, stern, and tired-eyed, Huey said, "Boots and saddles, gentlemen. Howard's got himself in some sort of fix and he needs cavalry."

"Nothing but brush between here and the Eleventh Corps, sir," the adjutant said. "About the same beyond. Cavalry isn't much use in this—"

"Adjutants are supposed to *draft* orders, not question them," Huey told him. He looked around. "Oh, I don't know what the devil it's all about. But it's an order. On your feet, gentlemen."

Rising and growing serious, Keenan nodded toward the combat sounds in the middle distance. "Rare for them to keep scrapping after dark. I'm with Haze, though. Cavalry won't be much good in those woods. Nighttime, too."

"This isn't a town hall meeting, Pete." Huey wasn't in the best of moods. "Let's go. Everybody." To Keenan, Wickersham, and Joe Wistar, he said, "March by battalion, numerical order. Column of twos."

"Delighted to share your company," Keenan told him.

Mounts had not yet been unsaddled and the regiment set off quickly, with barely kindled cooking fires tramped out and half-warmed rations gobbled or stowed again. The greatest delay stemmed from the need to file into the forest trail two by two, with flags furled and clutched low to avoid the branches.

In the tangles, the moonlight deserted them, trailing a sickly paleness above the treetops. Riding at the head of the second battalion, Wickersham heard another flare-up of musketry. It was closer now, but not near enough to be dangerous. Still, he warned himself to stay alert and not let his mind wander: He'd been thinking of home all day.

He'd come to hate the war, though he hid his sentiments. The excitement of battle captivated him, as it did every man, but, win or lose, the carnage left him with doubts he could not put into words. The only thing he liked about military life was the camaraderie, the community, the warm, unmasked humanity around the campfire.

Smiling wryly, he wondered if Pete Keenan might not be on to something: Maybe he should give the Quakers a try.

He knew he wouldn't, of course. He was too fond of life's lesser delights.

In the stagnant darkness, he smelled horses and men, ripe growth and gunpowder. Sheaths caught spurs and chinked, saddles creaked, and reins slapped easily, but the men behind him remained unusually quiet. They didn't like the confines of the grove, it made them feel trapped and vulnerable. As it did Wickersham.

Cavalrymen liked open spaces, rolling hills, firm fields.

Just get through it. Get through the wood and maybe things would make sense. Had to be a purpose. Same as with the war. Just get on through it. And trust it would make some sense, once all the smoke cleared.

After covering less than a mile at a stop-and-start pace, Wickersham heard a shot that sounded close.

A sprinkling of shots followed, a few hundred yards ahead. Then full volleys ripped out, dazzling through the trees.

He heard the shrieks of horses, heard men shouting.

The order came down the column: *"Sabers! Charge!"*

It was madness, impossible. But Wickersham drew his saber and repeated the command.

The pace of the horses ahead of him—Pete Keenan's battalion—increased, but fitfully. His own stretch of the column never achieved a trot, let alone a gallop.

Mounts collided in the dark and men blasphemed. The firing ahead intensified. Men shouted, their words indistinct.

It would have been impossible to reverse the column. And no trails branched off. They might as well have been swallowed by a cave. Apparently, Huey had decided to charge right through whatever he had encountered. With no other choice.

A branch caught Wickersham's saber, nearly jerking him from the saddle. His pennant-bearer's horse bumped hard against his.

The firing—maddened and just ahead—smothered any complaints.

The horses in front of him picked up speed. Wickersham increased his battalion's pace.

The trail broadened into a compact field. Smoke veiled the moonlight, but muzzle flashes revealed pandemonium: riderless horses, sabers slashing, bayonets jabbing, and men brawling on foot.

To his surprise, a Reb at his mount's foreleg raised his hands and cried, "I surrender," even as Northern voices begged, "Don't shoot me, Johnny."

Wickersham held back his mount, letting the first of his men fill in around him, sabers ready and, for the moment, useless. It was all but impossible to tell friend from enemy, until it was too late.

Another volley crackled and flashed, cutting down soldiers from both sides, though the horses suffered most. Only then did Wickersham realize that volleys were coming from multiple directions, indiscriminate. He spurred his horse rightward, where Union troops might be, and called to them:

"Don't shoot, cease fire! We're Union, *we're Union!*"

"Up your shithole, Yank."

Bullets hissed past, fired by men he'd thought must wear blue coats. But the Johnnies seemed as confused as anyone, firing at Yankees, phantoms, and each other.

The way ahead was utterly clogged, his battalion was penned, with another pressing behind it. In the nightmare flashes, he glimpsed a pack of Rebs bayoneting a horse and its rider, as if assaulting a centaur.

Rising in his stirrups, he hollered:

"Second Battalion, by the right flank . . . *charge!* Cut through them, cut through."

It was a forlorn hope, at best: attacking not just the Rebs but nature itself, this Virginia jungle.

Forgoing his saber, he drew his Colt and kicked his horse to full life. Plunging into a confusion of Rebs, thorns, and muzzle flames close enough to blind.

"Charge!" he cried again, mindlessly, reduced to a beast fighting for his survival and that of his pack.

His bugler, thought lost, blared out the call but broke off halfway through it.

Tangles ripped him, stealing his kepi and clawing his face. His mount complained and shied. He spurred it to bleeding.

Just in time, he chest-shot a Rebel swinging a rifle butt.

"Second Battalion! Ride for our lines! Keep going!"

An immense thrashing of horses underlay the sharp report of rifles. Men shouted, cursed, and died.

Wickersham yelled to rip out his throat, unsure if anyone heard him, let alone whether they would follow his orders.

What had just happened?

His horse didn't want to go on. He punished it, digging in the spurs like blades. Torturing a creature he all but loved. He jammed the spurs deeper. The mount cried and reared slightly. But it bashed on.

The shots were fewer now and not so close. Other riders struggled through the brush, he could hear them. It sounded like a vast number, but Wickersham knew better.

A shot flashed ahead. He heard, almost felt, the round.

Taking a chance, trying to think, to locate himself, he shouted, "Eighth Pennsylvania! Eighth Pennsylvania Cavalry, don't shoot! Don't shoot!"

Miraculously, the men ahead held their fire.

When he emerged from the brambles, he saw a long gun line in silhouette and dark rows of massed troops. The skirmishers let him through, and he waited, in a nether-realm, for any of his men who might rejoin him. Several did. Then ten, maybe twenty. Out of a battalion.

A few more troopers emerged from the brush on foot. And that was the end.

Men panted and cursed, a few wept. Horses bled sweat and shivered. In anguish, a sergeant reported, "Major Keenan's dead, sir, I saw them finish him."

Wickersham didn't respond. He thought of that last round of cards.

Afterward, he lingered on in the hope that more of his troopers would appear, and he found himself shaking almost uncontrollably.

A skirmish-line officer stepped up by his boot. The flood of moonlight revealed a fellow captain. The fellow asked:

"What the hell was cavalry doing out there?"

Nothing," Pickens said in disgust.

"Same thing over here," Joe Grigg responded, dropping another Yankee haversack. "Just ain't right."

"Seek justice not upon this earth," Doc Cowin told them. But his voice, too, was fraught with hunger and weariness. "Something for you, though, Sam. Nice pair of stockings."

"That's a kindness, Doc," Pickens said. But it only reminded him of his suffering feet.

In their belated efforts to sift through the wealth abandoned by fleeing Yankees, they'd met with grave disappointment. The men who had followed them in the attack had picked this portion of the battlefield clean. The moonlight, a force unto itself, revealed only looted packs, strewn letters, and, once, a pack of vile pictures of women that made Pickens sick to puking, confirming the infinite virtues of bachelorhood.

He still smelled that bacon, he swore he could smell it. The bacon he never even got a look at.

More Yankee artillery joined the fireworks show. Mad as hornets, the blue-bellies were. Ashamed of themselves, most like. Hadn't they been turned upside down and spanked? Hadn't they just? They had so many guns in action now that they must have been lined up wheel to wheel ahead, just to say, *We ain't done, Johnny, don't you go thinking we're finished.*

Hill's men were taking over up there, waiting to advance. Well, more power to them. The 5th Alabama had done its part and Pickens was glad to be out of it—those batteries didn't sound welcoming. No, the Greensboro Guards had done their share. And the wondrous thing was that only five men in the company had been wounded, none gravely, and none had been killed. Fumbling reunions had triggered an hour of handshakes.

Those damned Yankee guns just would not quit, but rare was the shell that landed sufficiently rearward to be a bother. Still, the feel of a terrible anger awakened made Pickens think: What would the morning bring?

"Best get back to the regiment," Ed Hutchinson, the voice of authority, told them. He was still riled over that poison ivy patch. "Be calling roll again."

And back they traipsed. What bodies they passed or kicked up against were almost exclusively Yankees, clustered where they'd tried to make their stands. Didn't stink yet, not of decay. Just the usual reek of filth and shot-open guts. Nothing to spoil an appetite.

Lieutenant Borden surprised them in the darkness. He'd come to gather in the foraging parties.

"Ill met by moonlight," Doc Cowin said.

Borden had heard rumors of Yankee cavalry moving behind their lines. There'd already been a clash, according to some reports. He told them everyone needed to watch out.

"Horse jockey wanted to ketch me," Charlie Hefner said, "he'd have to see me first. And I reckon I'd hear him long before he did."

"Worry not, ye faithless!" Doc Cowin declared. "Old Ned's Ironsides shall be opposed by our very own Prince Rupert."

Sometimes a body just had no idea what Doc was talking about.

The Yankee barrage on the front line grew heavier still. Sounded like they'd called up every last gun from every state in the unlamented Union.

Didn't envy Hill's men when they did step out. Which had to be soon or never.

Wouldn't be a great surprise to the Yankees, either. With officers hollering at their men in the dark, making their intentions plain as could be.

Again, he thought of what might be asked of his regiment in the morning. The prospect would not give him any peace.

All those Yankee guns. . . .

Life wasn't only a sorrow, though: A happy surprise awaited him and his messmates. When they reached the regiment's rallying point, sergeants were divvying up the wealth from *two* commandeered Yankee commissary wagons. There was ham, tinned cheese, crackers to fill up haversacks for an entire marching season, sugar, and *coffee,* good Yankee coffee, its scent already calling out to the men like a scarlet woman late on a Saturday night.

Still no sign of that bacon, though.

Oh, we had a few bad moments," Hooker told the newly arrived John Reynolds. He steadied his hands by gripping the edge of his saddle. "Livened things up for a time."

Reynolds was late, but his First Corps was welcome. There had been still more telegraph problems, but all would come right. It had to.

Dan Butterfield had met face-to-face with Sedgwick to straighten things out on that flank. The Sixth Corps should be marching west from Fredericksburg already, to close the vise on Lee. The morrow might see a complete reversal of fortunes. After all, only one of his corps had been beaten—and that one the least reliable.

Surely there was reason to hope, the campaign was far from over.

"Rebs played a little trick on us," Hooker continued, forcing confidence into his voice. "There was some roughhousing, I won't kid you. The Germans panicked, simply ran away. Howard tried to restrain them, but they're incorrigible. It's all right now, though."

The two generals sat their mounts in front of a gun line in the Chancellor field. To the immediate west and south, artillery hammered away, man-made thunder and lightning.

He added: "Dan Sickles is itching to go at them. May let him do it, too."

Reynolds spoke at last. "I saw the runaways. Meade's men were halting them at bayonet point." He didn't smile. "George was livid. He takes every setback personally." After a moment's hesitation, he added, "Every bit as angry as he was back in December."

"Speaking of Fredericksburg . . . Sedgwick's on his way. The Confederates abandoned the town, I have good information. I expect Uncle John by morning, he'll strike Lee in the rear. Teach that old dog a lesson."

"That would be . . . refreshing," Reynolds said.

Hooker leaned from his saddle, as if to confide a great secret. "The truth is . . . the truth is Lee's gambit backfired. Prisoners we took claim that Jackson hit us with his entire corps. Which means Lee's hopelessly thin on the other flank, only two divisions left to hand. And Early appears discomfited, unable to come to his aid." He nodded, as much to himself as to Reynolds. "We just need to hold off Jackson. Until Sedgwick can come up."

"Well, you've got six corps present, even Jackson's handsomely outmatched." Reynolds paused, as if reviewing too broad a selection of words. "He's a trickster, of course. This affair tonight . . . you have to respect the man, if not the cause. Give him that." He gestured westward, toward the tireless guns, toward an enemy weary, perhaps, but snarling. "The fellow does bear watching."

Hooker didn't need to be reminded. He rather resented it. But, yes, *Jackson* . . .

Considered objectively, though, what had the old fanatic really done? Pulled off a grand surprise, but how much damage had been done? Nothing irreparable. Once Sedgwick came up . . .

He almost began to expound again on the worthlessness of the Germans—before recalling that Reynolds was a Lancaster man and might take a somewhat more generous view of the Dutchmen. Always had to weigh the politics. Better to simply show a good front.

Hooker sat up straight and said:

"Tomorrow will be a glorious day for the Union, John. The fact is Lee hasn't a chance, he's blown his powder."

A few seconds passed in silence then Reynolds said, "I'd best see to my corps, then."

As Reynolds and his escort rode off, Major General Joseph Hooker regretted his last brag. Why couldn't he ever control himself? Why couldn't he keep his mouth shut? Lee, he feared, had more than just a chance. And Jackson, damn the man . . .

Have to fight him tomorrow. Both of them.

But Reynolds was right, of course. About the odds. If Sedgwick didn't make a complete hash of things . . . perhaps he might just . . .

Major General Joseph Hooker felt as unsteady as his hands. For hours now he'd passed from exhaustion to bursts of energy and back again, from discouragement, to hope renewed, and back to unspeakable fears.

Nor would the old craving spare him, the need almost physically painful. . . .

Just make it through tomorrow. It wouldn't take a miracle. Just a decent turn of luck, the right hand at cards for once. Everything could still be turned around. He'd been embarrassed, not beaten. Nothing had been decided, really.

Damn Howard, though. It *wasn't* just the Germans. But Howard was . . . unassailable. And someone had to be blamed.

Tomorrow. The prospect weighed on his shoulders like a cadet's full marching kit.

In the morning, the men would need to see the Hooker they adored, the man with the will of iron. The old Joe Hooker.

Good old Joe Hooker. "Fighting Joe." He'd long disliked the moniker, but now he wished he might find that man within him.

Tomorrow.

Major General John Reynolds trotted back to emplace his division, passing yet more stragglers and wondering how much of his own blustering Joe Hooker believed.

General . . . don't you think this is the wrong place for you?" Sandie Pendleton asked. "It's too far forward."

"Danger's over," Jackson snapped. He knew his aide meant well, but the boy's endless admonitions were annoying. It was impossible to lead from the rear at a time like this. "Federals are whipped," he continued. "Only worry now is our case of the slows." He twisted in the saddle, the better to observe Pendleton's large silhouette. "Go on back and tell General Hill he needs to attack immediately."

From the brush by the side of the road, a voice inquired, "General Hill?" That was Jim Lane's voice, Jackson believed.

He sidled his horse closer. "What do you need of General Hill?"

Startled by Jackson's presence, the brigadier general said, "Sir, I've got my brigade in line, North Carolina's ready. Had some confusion, thanks to that Yankee gunnery a time back, but we're ready now. Just need General Hill's permission to step off."

"Push right ahead, Lane. The instant General Hill gives the command. Smite them."

Not a minute later, Hill and his party clopped up the road. Jackson rode to meet him.

"You are much delayed, General."

"Yes, sir. I know it."

"When will you advance? Time runs against us."

"Soon as I finish relieving Rodes' men. All the confusion. Then the artillery fuss."

"Lane's Brigade is ready."

"Don't want to attack piecemeal, sir. The others will be up soon."

Jackson controlled his impulse to upbraid Hill, subduing his deep distaste for the man. It wouldn't help to reopen the wound here and in front of their staffs. But the Federal line was stiffening, he could feel it. They needed to press on *now*.

His burning ire brought him an inspiration and recharged his confidence: Extend a goal and men would stretch to achieve it.

And Hill must not get off lightly.

"General Hill, when you attack—and I trust it will be soon—do not pause at the Chancellorsville crossroads. I want you to continue on to United States Ford."

Features polished to ivory by the moonlight, Hill looked astonished.

"It is a long way," Jackson allowed. "But your men are capable."

It had struck him that it was not enough to reunite with Lee and trap half of the Union army. They needed to seize the ford and trap them all. It could be done—he knew it with the force of revelation.

Hill appeared doubtful but did not argue.

"Do you know the road?" Jackson asked. "From the crossroads to the ford? This is your country, I believe."

Recovering his composure, Hill told him, "Haven't passed that way for years."

Jackson turned. "Captain Boswell, report to General Hill. You will guide him."

"Yes, sir."

There would be no more excuses.

More staff men joined Jackson, returning from various tasks to swell his party. Hill took leave and rode over to Lane, to issue the new instructions. Jackson remained on horseback in the road, a few yards ahead of Lane's waiting battle line.

Sounds of skirmishing lingered off to the right, but here, at the point he judged crucial, the Federals had gone quiet, apparently content to go unmolested.

Or had they already decided to pull back? Was their new resistance genuine, or was it a demonstration to mask a withdrawal? How far would Lane and the other brigade commanders need to advance to reach them? Each hundred yards would matter under artillery fire. How strong were the Federals gathered in front of Hill?

Time burned.

Jackson nudged Little Sorrel forward, away from the waiting regiments and toward Lane's skirmish line. Pendleton had not returned to badger him and he intended to inspect the field himself, to examine Joseph Hooker's embarrassed legions, to smell them out.

He rode through a realm of uncanny silence, following a rustic track that branched off from the main road, leading his staff northward and, gently, eastward, behind the skirmishers. He was not incautious and paused where the byway forked. Turning in the saddle, he called softly, "Private Kyle? Where are you, son?"

The young cavalryman was near. Jackson had kidnapped him earlier in the day, the instant he learned that the lad had grown up on this ground.

"Tell me where these roads lead."

Still shy of the general, the private spoke slowly. "That there'un . . ." He pointed to the right trail. "That'un sort of doubles on the Plank Road. Finishes up a ways below Chancellorsville. Runs straight toward the Yankees, pretty much." He nodded toward the other track. "This'un edges rightwards, too, but on a ways. Slow like, not straight off. Folks call it 'Mountain Road,' though there ain't no mountain."

"Lead us that way," Jackson said. And he followed the cavalryman, with his retinue strung out behind him. He opened his senses to his surroundings, the way he always did. It was not a trick he'd learned or a conscious decision, just the way he always had been, for as long as he could recall: in tune with everything but his fellow humans. He saw and sensed and knew things others didn't, although he had learned not to speak of it to others. It was yet another of the Lord's abundant gifts, akin to his ability to know, immediately, what to do on a battlefield, even as others doubted and dithered. The Lord's bounty was endless unto His servants.

Again, he ordered himself to beware the mortal sin of pride. He sensed himself growing vain about this day, about the accomplishment still unfinished. It was already as complete a victory as he'd known. But it needed to be forced to a conclusion. With the help of the Lord, whose blessings exacted humility.

He came abreast of the guide and halted him.

And he listened. Yes. The sound of axes, the calling of Union voices. They were not leaving, not quitting. They were preparing defenses and extending their flank.

They had come very close to the Federals. Too close, in truth. Pendleton would have been beside himself.

Jackson smiled, slightly and briefly, at the thought of his ever-worried aide, a tall, solid man who at times seemed almost womanish.

They had not even breached Lane's skirmish line. The enemy was close, then. The North Carolinians would not have far to go.

But they must go soon.

He turned his horse and rode back past the various staff men. Signal officers and couriers nudged their mounts aside to let him pass.

He did not need to tell them to be quiet. They had ears.

Toward the rear of his party, he paused again and whispered to Captain Randolph, who oversaw the couriers:

"Who's that behind us?"

"General Hill, sir. He decided to accompany us, I suppose."

In a flash of pique, Jackson said, "He should be organizing his attack, the fool. Too long, too long." Then he mastered himself and told Randolph, "Ride back and tell him to turn around, to clear the way." He hesitated. "Randolph? My remark just now . . . was unguarded."

"Yes, sir."

As they eased back toward the Plank Road, with Hill's party leading now, Jackson began to seethe almost uncontrollably. He deplored Hill's repeated tardiness. It was Cedar Mountain again, but with far more at stake.

What would it take to make the man attack? Oh, Powell Hill was fine in a fight. But he had to be dragged into it. In his building anger, Jackson told himself that he'd never encountered an officer so laggard in his duties. He knew he was exaggerating, knew he was being unfair. He understood that their long-standing grudge had become personal and his own behavior un-Christian . . . but he could not help himself, this deep rage was a weakness, a temptation against which he had to struggle time and again.

He felt the greatest opportunity of the war—a chance to *end* the war—slipping away.

At times, the wrath coiled deep within him, the gnawing fury locked in its cage of flesh, the venomous ire aimed not merely at Hill but at all of sin-ridden mankind . . . it made him fear he'd been possessed by Satan and cast off by the Lord. Then he would walk in the darkness, praying feverishly, longing for release from the madness that gripped him.

He was being tested, he knew. As those God loved were tested. The path to salvation was sharp with stones and men must walk it barefoot. The flesh must bleed.

Yet on other, better, blessed days, he took delight in the very air, in birdsong and the miracle of blossoms, in his wife, his child . . . elated by a world absolved of sin by Jesus Christ, overcome with merciful tenderness toward his fellow man.

He resolved not to speak in temper on this exalted day. He would chide Hill, but not chastise him, when they returned to the line.

And if Hill failed again, he would bring new charges.

The moon had taken on a crimson cast.

With a start, Jackson saw they had already reached the Plank Road, just in front of Lane's still-waiting regiments. He had let his mind wander unforgivably, slighting his duty.

He heard the report of a rifle nearby, but he could not read the direction.

A flurry of shots followed.

A volley exploded from Lane's front. Ambrose Powell Hill realized at once what was happening. He leapt from his horse and rushed toward the North Carolinians, shouting, "Confederates! We're Confederates! Don't shoot!"

To his right another voice, unfamiliar, screamed, "Cease firing! You're firing at your own men! Cease firing!"

The firing broke off.

* * *

Who gave that order?" Major John D. Barry demanded, voice hoarse and furious. Around him, soldiers of the 18th North Carolina reloaded with veteran speed, while those with rifles ready held their fire, uncertain. "Who gave the order to cease firing?"

No one answered him.

"It's a lie!" Barry told his men. "That's Yankee cavalry. Pour it into them, boys, give them all you've got."

EIGHT

Night, May 2/3

Pain. *Pain.* First the blazing light, red and yellow. Then the noise, and the shock of being struck. Once, twice. A third time?

Instantly, the wild confusion of pain.

His horse bolted, crazed. He tried to master the reins. His left arm was useless, utterly disobedient and gripped by phenomenal pain. His right hand, too, refused to follow orders.

Still in the saddle. Barely. Maddened, Little Sorrel careened against the brush along the path.

He had never imagined such pain, had reckoned wounded men weak when they cried out.

A branch lashed his face, sweeping him backward, clawing. He almost tumbled from the horse's back.

Forcing his wounded right hand to follow his orders, he gripped the reins to the extent he could. Unable to close his fingers into a proper fist.

Why had they fired at him? His men, *his* men. . . .

He believed that he pulled up the horse himself, but was unsure. Perhaps others did. It didn't matter. There were voices. Close. And furious shouts in the distance. Admonitions.

The pain.

"Hold the horse while I see to him." Was that Wilbourn, the Signal officer?

His left arm felt deadened, yet flesh and bone screamed within. He felt blood wetting his face.

"My own men, my own men," he muttered. "Why?"

"Are you badly hurt, General?" Wilbourn, indeed. His voice. "Are you hit bad?"

Gasping, Jackson opened his eyes. The moon through the branches shone of bloodstained ivory.

"Where are you hurt, sir?" Another voice. Unknown. Young.

"I . . . fear my arm is broken. And my hand . . ."

"Which arm?"

"Left arm . . . right hand . . . broken."

The pain urged Jackson to clutch himself, but he could not.

The Lord had left him helpless. Why?

What sins . . . what shortcomings in his devotion . . .

"Try to move your fingers. The right hand."

"I . . . cannot."

"General, what . . ."

"I wish you . . . would you . . . see if I'm bleeding? My arm. I fear I am bleeding very much."

He could not see clearly. He could only feel the pain, the conquering pain.

A hand explored his left arm. Tenderly. Almost as if the hand belonged to a woman.

His *esposa*? She . . . no . . . impossible . . .

Abruptly, the hand pulled away.

"Will they fire again?" Jackson asked timidly.

"I . . . no, I don't think so. I don't know."

"Help me down," Jackson requested. He could not put strength in his voice.

He felt hands upon him. Another wave of pain, sudden. Tangled bodies, an apology, something about an old wound. He had no old wounds. *Take your feet out of the stirrups.* A command he could not obey.

Other hands searched for purchase, touching him cautiously. Slowly, strong arms lowered him from the right side of his horse.

That was wrong. You always dismounted on the left. Why . . .

Pain, too much pain. How could he bear it? *Had* to bear it.

A voice called: "Hold the horse, grab the reins."

The sound of galloping, followed by complaint.

He lay on the ground, bewildered.

Wilbourn said, "It's remarkable, sir, that any of us escaped."

"Providential," Jackson told him. "The Lord's hand." His mind seemed clearer now. He felt himself being shifted and leaned against a tree.

"You're bleeding. There's more blood."

"Blood."

"I have to cut away your sleeve, sir. To get at the wound, tie it up. It . . . may be troublesome."

"Yes."

"I don't have much of a knife."

"Do . . . go ahead, go ahead."

More voices now. Morrison. Brother-in-law. Think of her, his darling. No. Must not. Attack. They must *attack.*

Was that Hill? Hill had to lead the attack.

"General Jackson . . . I'm so sorry to see you wounded, so sorry. I hope you're not hurt much."

Yes, Hill. It was Hill. His voice was kind and true.

"My arm is broken."

"Is it painful, sir?"

"Very painful," Jackson said, before he could stop himself.

"Anywhere else?"

"Right hand. Fingers broken."

He felt Hill gently removing his riding glove. New pain jolted him. He bit it back.

Wilbourn's voice again: "I have to cut away the entire sleeve."

"Cut away everything."

He clenched his teeth, ground them, fighting to conceal the tyrannical pain from those around him.

It had been the sin of pride, he was sure. The Lord had punished him. The Lord knew best, His ways must not be questioned.

Firm hands tied a knot on his upper arm and drew it tight. Nearby, there was a fuss he did not understand. Someone whispered, "Yankees." Another voice asked, "Where is he?"

"Dr. Barr is here," Hill said, hush-voiced. "From Pender's Brigade."

Jackson felt a bolt of fear. "Is . . . is he a skillful surgeon?"

"I don't know him, not personally. But the soldiers like him." Then Hill added, "He's not going to do anything much. Just help you back to the rear, he just needs to look at you. Until we find Dr. McGuire."

"Good, good."

The pain made him want to weep like a child, but he would not.

Suddenly, Jackson said, "You must take command, General Hill. It's yours now, the corps is yours. You must attack."

"Yes, sir. I'm only sorry that—"

"You *must* attack."

"I . . . I'll try to keep it from the men. Your wounding."

"Thank you. But . . ."

Then Hill was gone. In his place, Morrison's voice, gone urgent, said, "Yankees are placing a battery in the road. Not a hundred yards off. Ambulance would never make it."

"I can walk," Jackson said, unsure whether it was true.

Shells struck nearby, introduced from yet another direction.

"Just get him back behind the lines," someone said. "And, for God's sake, don't tell anyone who it is."

"Must not . . . take the Lord's name . . ."

The pain . . . what if a man were condemned to such pain for all eternity? What if that was Hell? What if he had failed the Lord his God, somehow betrayed Him?

Aided by good men, he stumbled along, fighting back the pain, unwilling to show weakness even now.

A voice challenged them. "Who's going on along there? You speak up."

"Friend got himself wounded." Wilbourn's voice again.

But soldiers crowded up.

"Good God, that's Old Jack!"

"Hush your mouth and move off. You shut your mouth."

More soldiers approached. A litter team. They eased him onto the canvas and hoisted the stretcher onto their shoulders.

"Stay on the road, don't jar him."

A shell tore the air. It burst nearby.

"Damn the Yankees."

Another shell screamed in.

"Get off the road," some shouted. Too late.

A blast. Close. Jackson felt the litter sag.

He fell to the ground.

When he struck the road the pain was of an immensity he never could have imagined. Perhaps this was, indeed, what sinners were destined to endure for eternity.

He groaned.

A Union barrage swept the road and the nearby brush. Men cried out in pain that was all their own.

Jackson felt a body press against him as shells burst on every side. Someone was shielding him, he understood. He feared he was sobbing because of the pain. Whimpering.

When would it stop? All of it.

The Union artillery shifted onto targets in greater depth. Soldiers hurried from ditches, re-forming, moving on.

Someone asked for volunteers to help with the litter.

Soldiers jeered. One said, "Some goddamned fancy boy, that one, I bet. Why don't you sissy-boys tell his mama to fetch him."

"For God's sake, you have to tell them who he is," a voice whispered.

"He . . . we're not supposed to."

"You want him to die right here?"

Another voice called, "You men there. Help us. That's General Jackson lying there."

In moments, eager hands raised the litter again. Competing to help, the soldiers carried him into the woods, in case the Union artillery dropped its range again.

A soldier tripped and Jackson fell from shoulder height again. He landed squarely on his ruined arm.

He cried out. Helplessly.

Apologies, accusations, embarrassment.

Pain.

For the first time in his life, Jackson begged for whiskey.

There was none to be had.

They bore him back to the road then, deeming it the lesser danger. Hoofbeats approached, several riders.

The litter bearers halted.

A voice. Dorsey Pender. Unmistakable. How odd it seemed of a sudden, this God-given individualization of all men.

"General Jackson, I hope you're not seriously wounded."

"General Pender . . ."

"I have to retire my brigade," Pender told him. "To re-form them. Yankee artillery busted things up right awful."

Jackson discovered unexpected strength. "You will not retire an inch, sir! You must hold your ground!"

The effort was too much. He sensed less of the world around him. Drained, swooning. Time grew elastic. Only the pain was constant.

He wondered if he would die.

Anguished, Jim Lane could not bear to see to his duty. Not yet. He needed to lie to the officers and men of the 18th North Carolina, to console them that their terrible mistake was only that: a mistake that could hardly be helped. It could have been any regiment on the line that fired those volleys. He needed to tell them that, to buck them up and avoid crushing out what still remained of their spirit. But he could not do it, not yet.

He hoped to God that Jackson would be all right. He knew it was selfish, but he, too, did not want the opprobrium, a lifelong reputation as the man whose soldiers had shot, perhaps killed, Stonewall Jackson. Nor could the army afford to lose that man, that unexpected genius of the battlefield.

Unexpected, because he had known Jackson well enough before the war, first as a cadet at VMI, where Jackson had been a hapless, if stern, professor. Later, he had known Tom Jackson as a colleague, during his own stint on the faculty. There had always been something to the man, he thought now, but his peculiarities had obscured it. Only war had brought Jackson to his flowering.

It wasn't right, this dreadful luck. His brigade was as good as any in the army, and the 18th was made up of stalwart Yankee killers. Now what would men think?

He didn't imagine for a moment that all this would be forgotten, even if Jackson made a full recovery. It was the sort of thing that stuck to a man.

Brigadier General James Henry Lane was not of great physical stature. All of his life, he'd had to fight to make his way past bigger men. In the war, he'd proven himself on the battlefield, and he'd tithed his own blood to the Confederacy, the dull pain of his wounds a dreary companion that never quit him.

Now this.

Powell Hill was down, too. But the Yankees had done that. In their last cannonade.

Better that the attack had been delayed. He did not know how the men would behave just now. In the morning, though . . . in the morning they'd be out to prove their mettle, to redeem themselves.

If ever they could be redeemed.

Before he could muster the will to do his duty, to rouse men plunged into the deepest despair, the Yankees attacked on his right flank. It was a relief to rush over and see to it, to have something to distract him. But the Yankees let him down. After a sharp encounter, they reeled back and seemed to be firing into their own ranks, cutting down their comrades in the darkness. Their attack soon petered out.

Warning his adjutant to keep everyone away for a few minutes, Jim Lane sat down on a stump and cried.

* * *

George Meade had no patience with anyone that night. Moving his division from the left flank to the right-center in the moonlight, he tyrannized officers who showed the least bit of slackness and arrested any teamsters or stragglers who dared get in his men's way.

His language grew indelicate. Margaret would not have approved.

The behavior of Howard's corps had appalled him, but Hooker's sheer inattention and belated response infuriated him the more. He even grew short with Charlie Griffin, telling him: "Move those men sharply, Griffin, or I'll find a man who can."

The one encouraging aspect of it all was that the morning would find his corps poised to join the fight. After all the marching, delays, and follies, his men would have a chance to show their grit.

If Joe Hooker didn't fold his hand again.

He knew what the chills he felt meant: He had lost much blood. Dr. McGuire sat by his bedside, silhouetted by the lantern fixed to the tent pole. Now and again, the surgeon took his pulse. Jackson understood that, too: McGuire needed signs of strength from his damaged body before he could wield knife and saw.

At times the world seemed acutely clear, then he drifted off again. The whiskey-and-morphine tincture he'd been given helped a little. Still, the ambulance ride had been an ordeal. He had learned so much about pain in so little time. The Lord had instructed him in his ignorance, and he felt a novel mildness toward the countless wounded men whose pains he had discounted.

"More," he said.

"What?"

"The whiskey. Please."

McGuire and an orderly braced him up and helped him sip.

"I . . . do not care for the taste," Jackson told them.

"Lucky for you, General," the surgeon said. "Many a man's found the taste a sight too appealing."

He did not like the taste, but he valued the effect in this hard night. Once and only once, celebrant upon graduating from West Point, he had indulged with comrades in a Washington hotel room. He had enjoyed himself immensely, dancing barefoot until he collapsed, but when next he woke, a crumpled being, he had vowed he would never touch liquor again. And he had kept that promise. Until now.

For a time, he had thought he was dying. The pain had been so immense, his weakness so all-encompassing. But McGuire had assured him that he would survive, it was all but certain. Still, the doctor's voice was not untroubled.

McGuire had hinted that the left arm might be lost to him. He had expected no less. He only hoped that the Lord would allow him to live. There was so much yet undone. . . .

He drowsed, but did not sleep. Tides of pain swept over him, though without the fury he had endured earlier. To his shock, he thought of his wife with abrupt carnality. His first wife, dead a decade, not his *esposa*. And that was wrong.

He asked the Lord's forgiveness.

He had wet himself. He believed it had happened when he fell from the litter the second time. But he was uncertain. A matter that once would have embarrassed him terribly seemed a small thing now.

If the Lord allowed him to live, he would subdue his pride and learn humility.

McGuire felt his pulse again. Then Jackson sensed him leaving. Had Hill resumed the advance? Hill . . . had something happened to Hill? Had he heard someone say that Hill had been wounded as well? But Hill had comforted him, it couldn't be. Hill was attacking. Why couldn't he hear the guns?

He believed that he smelled cloves.

Pain gripped him anew. He thought to ask for still more of the whiskey, mixed again with morphine, but decided against it. The Lord had sent this suffering unto him, and he must not flee His judgment.

Why had the Lord done this to him? And why now? His pride, yes. But there had to be something more. Had he done wrong, had he somehow warred against the Lord, against the divine will? What was the Lord telling him?

Lane needed to go forward. Why wasn't Lane going forward?

He saw the flash again, felt the awful impacts, recalled the panic and chaos with a start.

He wished to go home. Perhaps he would need to visit Lexington for a time, to convalesce. He would see his *esposa* and the child, their house a mighty fortress against the world's cruelties.

The canvas above him swirled.

He sensed men crowding into the tent. McGuire's voice cut through the veil of dreams:

"General . . . I've brought along Doctors Black, Walls, and Coleman. For their opinions and, if need be, their assistance."

Jackson felt fingertips upon his wrist.

"Good," the surgeon told him. "Strong enough for us to have a proper look at that arm, General." When Jackson didn't respond, he continued, "We'll want to put you under chloroform. To subdue the pain."

Jackson nodded his assent. Or believed he did. His head seemed clear now. Brutally clear.

With reluctance in his voice, McGuire added, "If we all agree . . . if all our opinions find amputation to be necessary . . ."

"Do what you think right," Jackson said.

The joke ran that John Sedgwick's New England family had been there before the Indians. They'd been a steady bunch, by and large, his ancestors, though siring a naughty woman every second or third generation. Nothing to prove, with routine ideals of service, perfunctory religion, and, for most, money enough to avoid the old-blood curse of "genteel poverty." Sedgwick men controlled their tempers in public, and "Uncle John" didn't have the high mercury in him that George Meade or Andy Humphreys did. Nonetheless, this night was a test of his capacity to resist outrage.

For the first time since one bad morning as a lieutenant, he cursed himself for going to West Point all those years ago. He wished he'd stayed home in the Berkshires and grown apples.

Hooker was unbalanced, he had to be. His expectations were nothing short of mad. Even had all gone perfectly, his Sixth Corps could not have reached Chancellorsville—or Lee's rear—by dawn. And things had not gone perfectly.

That evening, he'd ridden back to Falmouth himself to straighten things out with Butterfield. The telegraph system continued to deliver messages out of sequence or jumbled up—or failed to transmit them at all. Butterfield had assured him that, yes, Joe wanted him to move on Fredericksburg immediately then march a further ten miles to strike Lee's rear. Dan had sworn that he had perfect intelligence and the Rebs had abandoned the defenses facing the Sixth Corps. Sedgwick just had to get his troops on the road.

But the Rebs had *not* disappeared. When his lead elements stepped off in the dark, they had been fired upon almost immediately. And no one knew the size of the Rebel force now, whether or not he was marching into a trap. Meanwhile, Gibbon's division, upriver, had orders to cross directly into Fredericksburg and seize the infamous heights, "cooperating with the Sixth Corps." But Gibbon's pontoon bridge had been removed and no one knew why—it would have to be retrieved and could not be laid again until morning. *If* the bridge sections had returned by then.

Now there were rumors—only God knew where they came from—that Joe had faced a nasty scrap upriver and it had not gone at all well.

Major General John Sedgwick, artilleryman, cavalryman, Indian fighter, and veteran of Mexico, would obey his orders as best he could. But not much would get done before first light.

Damn Joe, though. When they'd been classmates at West Point, Hooker had been a bigger talker than he ever was a doer. It looked like the man hadn't changed.

* * *

When Captain Wilbourn had gone, trailing shock at the sorrowful news he'd delivered, Lee's adjutant returned to the general's tent.

"He'll lose his left arm," young Taylor said. "It sounds all but certain."

"And I . . . shall lose my right hand," Lee told him. "Better it had been me, better for the army. To lose him now, at this juncture."

"If it's only the arm, he'll recover," the aide went on.

Still, that meant months, at least, with Jackson lost to the army.

"To lose him for a day is hard to bear. And General Hill . . ."

"His wounds are not severe, sir."

"But incapacitating."

"Only for a time, sir. His legs . . . it's not . . ."

Lee recognized that the major wished to console him. But it was not so easily done. Better that the attack had not gone forward, better that they had withdrawn without a fight.

What was he to do?

Hill had called up Stuart to take command. That was correct, the best thing that could be done. Rodes, who would have been next in line to lead the corps, was a splendid officer but new to division command. He could not be entrusted with a corps. No, Stuart was the only choice, with Longstreet still south of the James. Stuart had never commanded infantry in large numbers, but the men knew him and trusted him. And they would need to have faith in whoever led them.

Early, too, would need to detain the Union Sixth Corps as long as possible. Each day, Lee had feared its descent from Fredericksburg upon his rear. He could not understand why Hooker had left Sedgwick so idle.

Indeed, the day before had brought brief terrors, when garbled orders had led Early to withdraw from his entrenchments. The profane Virginian had needed to countermarch in haste, rushing back to the defenses beyond the town.

There was always so much to be done, too much to master. In

cynical moments—interludes he concealed from all around him—Lee suspected that wars were won not by the most competent army, but by the least incompetent.

On his better days he believed he led the finest troops in the world.

Denied sleep again, Lee yawned. As a cadet and junior officer, he dutifully had read about Napoléon's clever campaigns and the genius of Frederick the Great, but none of those books, in which the confusion of war was greatly simplified, had told him that battles were fought by exhausted men, that the fateful decisions, wise or catastrophic, were made by leaders who had not slept for days.

He thought, again, that he was too old for war. But he knew—he always knew—that he would not quit.

Jackson. It was the oddest thing: He had never considered that Jackson might be a casualty. He had assumed that Jackson would always be there. The evening's success had come at a terrible cost.

Now they would have to attack again in the morning, to deny Hooker the initiative, should that man have the fortitude left to seize it. It was too late to withdraw, the army could not escape—the poor roads that had undone those people would be his undoing, too.

They would be fighting for the army's survival. It would be grim.

"You might sleep for a few hours, Major," Lee told the younger man. "I must sit for a while and ponder things."

Carl Schurz was drained but could not sleep. For want of his captured tent, he reclined against a tree trunk. Around him, soldiers groaned in their slumbers or snored. Once in a while, a man called a woman's name. Those, like him, who were unable to sleep licked their wounds alone or spoke in whispers.

They had been humiliated. And they were bound to pay an unfair price. Schurz long had thought that the day Rastatt capitulated had been the worst of his life. Now he wasn't so sure.

Krzyzanowski found him amid the disorder and darkness. "My

men have been resupplied with ammunition," the colonel reported. But Schurz understood the Pole just wanted to talk.

"Join me in my salon, Kriz."

The light of a declining moon showed where he might sit.

"What do you think?" he asked Schurz.

"I think . . . that our trials aren't over."

The Pole misunderstood him. "You think we'll be sent back in? Have you heard something? We can still fight, we'd show them. If they let us."

"No. They've put us where they think there is no danger. We'll be the last troops called upon." He sighed. "We weren't trusted before, and we're trusted less now."

"But you saw my men. . . ."

"It's unjust, terribly so." Schurz was about to commiserate when he felt pure anger grip him. *No.* He *refused* to be discouraged. He would not be made small by anyone. He had come too far. They all had.

Krzyzanowski was about to speak again, but Schurz spoke first:

"We're hurt. We'll feel it, for a time. Perhaps for a long time. But we must take an even longer view. This struggle, all of this . . . it's part of something greater, Kriz. As vast as this war seems, it's only one incident. This struggle . . . this sublime struggle for human freedom, for liberty, for lives of simple decency . . . we play our parts, you and I, and others will play their parts after us. It won't end soon. It may never end. But the fight will continue." He leaned toward his subordinate, as earnest as ever he'd been. "This is the greatest cause in all of history, from the Rhine to the Mississippi, from Poland . . . I don't know . . . to China, perhaps. And history is on our side. Look at the Two Sicilies, the most backward bit of Europe, what Garibaldi achieved. Or the South Americans before that. The Greeks. And here *we* are, fighting not just to end slavery, but to finish off the old ways, the ancient belief that one man, by virtue of birth or wealth, is better than the other."

"Some will always be better born or richer," the Pole said, still glum.

"Yes, but they will be equal before the law. That is what these Americans mean—*we* Americans—by 'All men are created equal.' Equal before the law, Kriz. Equal in chances, if not in gifts. Unable to hold another man in bondage for any reason, whether the Negro in South Carolina or a serf in Russia, a peasant in Poland . . ." He waved a cramped hand. "I refuse to be defeated. Say what they will, *we* know what happened and why. The point is . . . the point is not to be damaged inside, even when we're damaged on the outside . . . to believe not because, but despite."

"And if this war is lost?"

"Then there will be another war. Somewhere. The struggle goes on. But this war *won't* be lost. It can't be. We'll win because we must win." He shook his head. "Show me another country, anywhere, that has fought a civil war to free its own slaves—and men of a different race, at that. There is no such country. Only here." Despite his fervor, a hint of bitterness reclaimed his voice. "These Americans, these people we have joined. The 'native-born.' They have been given so much, and they're ungrateful. They have no idea of their miraculous fortune."

A voice called from the darkness: "Would you two fellows be quiet?"

Sandie, I can't wake him now. Not even for this," Dr. McGuire said. "His life—his *life,* mind you—depends on him resting for as long as possible." The surgeon shook his head. "He's had a fearful ordeal."

Pendleton rubbed the back of his skull. Quite a lump. When he'd learned of Jackson's wounding, he had fainted and dropped from his horse. No great harm done, though. Pendletons were a hardheaded bunch, so his mother always said.

And Bossie Boswell was dead, killed in the same fusillade that had struck the general. Kate would be terribly done in by the news. But there was no time to mourn, not now.

"Mac," Pendleton tried again, "you're the authority, I'm not contesting that. Your decision . . . I suppose your decision stands. But

I'm telling you, I *need* to speak with him. We need to know his plan, what he meant to do next. Hill's been wounded, too, he's handed things over to Stuart. But Stuart's at a loss. He needs the general's advice. The fate of the army, our entire cause, depends on it."

McGuire dead-eyed him. "My first responsibility . . ." He didn't finish the sentence, didn't need to.

"I know, Mac, I know. But thousands of lives, the country . . ." Bearing down again, he asked, "What do you think he'd say himself, if the choice were up to him?"

The surgeon's expression weakened from stubborn to merely exasperated. McGuire did look weary. They all were blown.

"Wait outside the tent. Or stand in the entrance, if you like, but don't follow me in. Wait until I call for you." He added, "And I might not."

At the surgeon's approach, a guard lifted the tent's flap.

Pendleton halted at the borderline drawn by McGuire, half in the night's last grip but with his face caressed by lamplight. He watched as the doctor pulled up a stool and began his inspection. When McGuire shifted his shoulders, Pendleton glimpsed the general's face for the first time: It was scratched and torn. Severely. Above the cuts, Jackson's thinning hair had matted to strands. Not forty, he looked ancient.

Pendleton was so shaken by Jackson's appearance that it took him a moment to realize McGuire was beckoning to him.

At the aide's approach, Jackson's eyes opened. In a surprisingly normal voice, he said, "Major, I'm glad to see you. Very glad. When you didn't report back, I feared you'd been killed."

"Not me, sir. Yankees don't figure I'm half worth the bother."

McGuire rose and gestured for Pendleton to take his place by the bedside.

"Don't tire him," the surgeon said.

Pendleton bent toward the ravaged face. Jackson's eyes were very clear. Pure.

"Sir . . . I regret to say that General Hill has been wounded, just after—"

Jackson's eyes tensed. "Is it serious? Will he be all right?"

"The wound isn't severe. It's not, that is to say, he's not in danger, sir. But he's not capable of command, not at present. General Stuart has replaced him, but he needs your guidance. General Stuart's asking what he should do."

Those deep, clear eyes took fire. Torn skin grew taut. Jackson's head rose from the rolled blanket. His lips parted to speak.

"Yes, sir?"

Jackson quivered briefly and went slack. His eyes turned away from Pendleton's.

"I don't know," he said, in a voice much weakened. "I can't tell. General Stuart must do what he thinks best."

Bleary, Hooker sat on the porch of the Chancellor house, awaiting the dawn. He wore his overcoat unbuttoned. It was still too warm, but without it he was too cold.

Few campfires burned: Those too close to the battle lines drew artillery fire, and those farther away had burned themselves out. Despite the occasional shots, the night had grown quiet. Even the screams called up by the surgeons' saws had ceased for now.

They'd start up again soon enough, he knew.

He could not sleep. After sparing him almost all the evening and into the night, the headaches had returned with renewed savagery, a merciless enemy resupplied and rested.

Nor had it helped when a fumbling courier delivered a telegraphic message received at United States Ford: Sedgwick would *not* be up by dawn. He wouldn't even be truly on his way.

Sedgwick had let him down. Unforgivably. Where was the man's vigor? Why did he keep delaying?

Now he'd have to face Lee without his Sixth Corps, at least through much of this day. In the small hours, his hopes had soared that he might crush Lee while fending off Jackson. Now . . . now he'd have both of those rabid dogs coming after him at first light.

Well, hadn't he wanted Lee to attack him, after all? His lines were better drawn now than they'd been before the last evening's debacle and he intended to tighten them further. Wherever his opponents attacked, they'd find him ready this time.

He *still* could defeat them, couldn't he? He had the strength. Unless . . . what if the reports that Longstreet was still detained below the James proved inaccurate? What if Longstreet was nearby or already on hand?

He rued his dispatch of Stoneman with most of the cavalry. He still had not had a proper report of his actions or location; meanwhile, the army was fighting blind. Was Stoneman astride the Richmond road and the rail line, as envisioned? Was that part of the plan working, at least? It was as if Virginia had swallowed the Cavalry Corps.

And the mounted regiments he'd retained had proved of little worth. The 8th Pennsylvania had made an infernal mess of things, and someone would have to pretty up the report.

Why didn't he ever get any comforting news?

He was tempted to simply disappear and find a crock of whiskey, to sit in a corner and drink it down to the bottom.

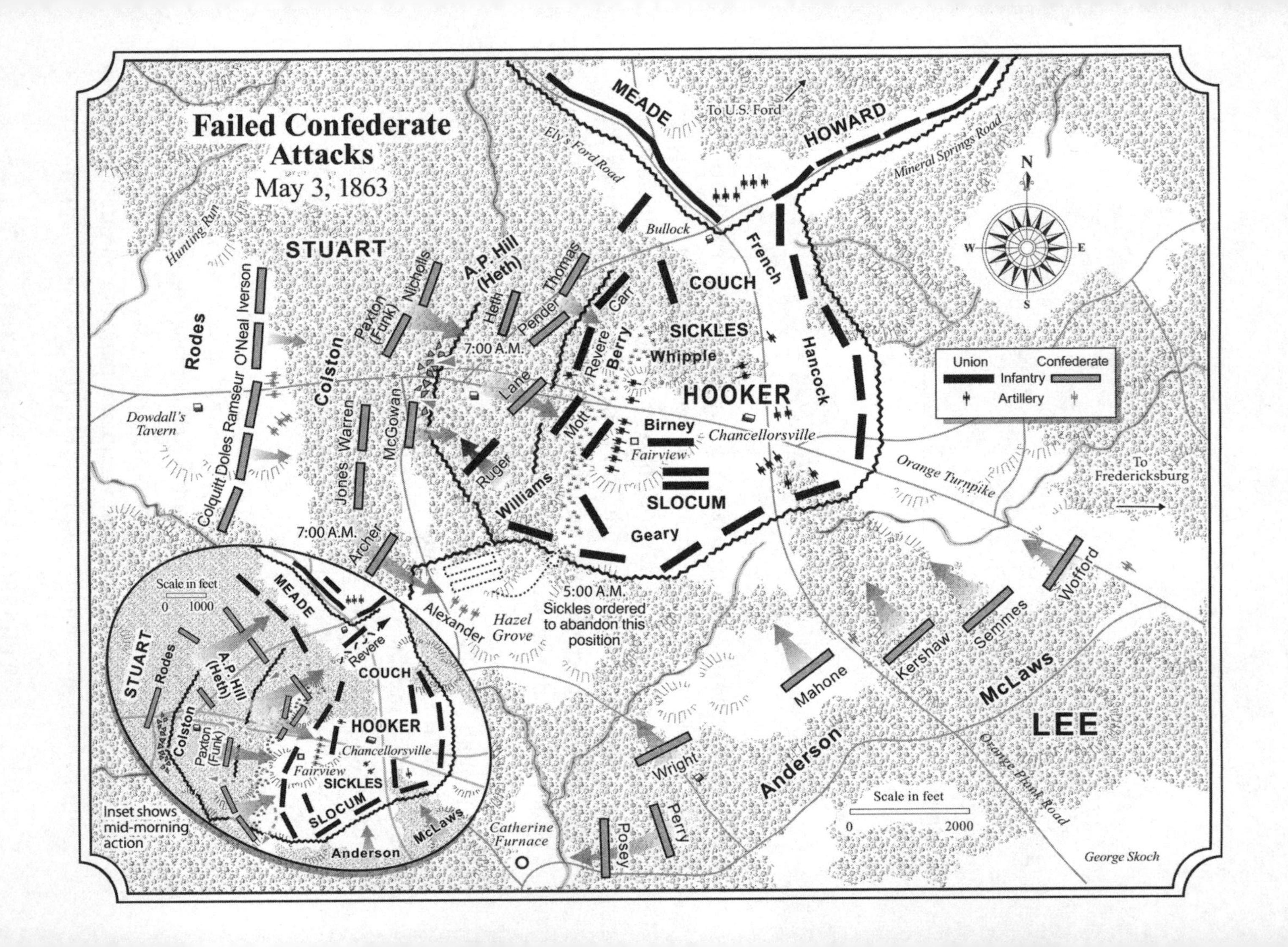
Failed Confederate Attacks
May 3, 1863
MEADE
To U.S. Ford
HOWARD
Ely's Ford Road
Mineral Springs Road
Bullock
N
W
E
S
Hunting Run
STUART
Rodes
Colquitt Doles Ramseur O'Neal Iverson
Colston
Paxton (Funk)
Nicholls
A.P. Hill (Heth)
Heth
Pender
Thomas
7:00 A.M.
COUCH
French
Hancock
SICKLES
Whipple
Carr
Revere
Berry
HOOKER
Lane
Mott
Birney
Chancellorsville
Fairview
Dowdall's Tavern
Jones
Warren
McGowan
Ruger
Williams
SLOCUM
Geary
Union
Confederate
Infantry
Artillery
Orange Turnpike
To Fredericksburg
7:00 A.M.
Archer
Alexander
Hazel Grove
5:00 A.M.
Sickles ordered to abandon this position
Scale in feet
0
1000
Inset shows mid-morning action
Catherine Furnace
Posey
Perry
Wright
Anderson
Mahone
Kershaw
Semmes
Wofford
McLaws
LEE
Orange Plank Road
2000
George Skoch

NINE

Morning, May 3

The moon was down but the sky hinted at paleness.

"He says you have to do what you think best," Pendleton told him.

Jeb Stuart had almost expected and dreaded such an answer, but he refused to show any sign of discouragement. The first rule he had learned about leadership was that the men had to have faith in the man commanding them. The second rule was that lying was fine as long as it got results.

"Well," the general said, "I do expect we'll do handsomely. This army will never fail us, just have to point the boys in the right direction, turn them loose, and get out of the way. General Jackson left us in an excellent position—a strong position, indeed."

His first statement expressed hope; the second veered into the realm of untruth; and the third was doubtful: Jackson had whipped the Yankees, all right, but the resulting confusion in his corps was still a good ways from being straightened out. Stuart had arrived intending to continue the attack, only to be mortified by the chaos at every level. Nor did he know the ground in detail, and he couldn't see worth a lick. Still, the men would have to go forward on the gray side of sunrise.

Surrounding Stuart and Pendleton, couriers waited to be tasked and dismounted staff men busied themselves by demanding reports from units that could not be found. Brushing the ears of hard-used mounts, flags drooped, darker than the darkness. Caissons and ammunition wagons creaked along the road, their progress slow and rights-of-way contested. Sergeants called to their men to replenish their cartridges, while soldiers still astray bleated the names of missing friends and vanished regiments.

Well, forward they'd go, ready or not. The single message Stuart had gotten from Lee made two things clear. First, he was to resume the attack with vigor. Second, he had to push toward the wing Lee commanded directly, to reunite the army.

Stuart turned to an aide. "Sidney, lead the way to General Heth. We need to powwow. Nigh on time to let his hound dogs loose."

Yes, Heth. A scrapper. With Hill carried off, Harry had been thrust into command, and he'd have to make a success of it. His men were freshest, they'd been the least engaged. Colston's division would follow right behind, with Rodes held in reserve to complete the work. That much fell out naturally.

And after that?

He did wish he'd paid more attention to infantry tactics. Not his specialty. Raids and scouts and lightning saber fights were the skills he'd mastered. Never had been one to trudge along loaded down like a mule then line up and offer the enemy a target. Have to trust the division commanders to know their business, to solve the problems in front of them. Not much he could do but cheer them on.

He prayed the Yankees were every bit as muddled.

And he thought again of Rodes, who by report had done fine work the past eve. Bobby had a noble soul, a man had to give him that. By right of seniority within the corps, Rodes should have gotten command after Hill went down. But Rodes had not protested at Stuart's assumption of command, despite his lack of infantry expertise. Bobby had accepted their roles as sensible, even remarking, "The men know you, General Stuart. Not all of them know me."

Given a few more men of such high character, they might just win this pig race.

Somehow, Porter Alexander—as fine a cannon-stuffer as ever was blackened by powder—found him amid the turmoil and the gloom.

"Well, Porter? Where do you intend to put our guns?"

Breathless, the artilleryman drew closer. "General, there's the Lord's own heavenly beauty of an artillery position over on the right. Can't say with absolute certainty, but I reckon guns atop it could sweep the field."

"Well, occupy it."

"Problem is the Federals are on it. Honestly, sir, if we could clear it and stack batteries up there . . ."

"This Matterhorn have a name?"

"Hazel Grove, I believe."

Stuart smiled mightily. Unlikely that men could see the grin, but he always figured they could feel it, somehow.

"I do believe we'll go there, this fine morning. Come along, we'll share your precious discovery with General Heth, give him a purpose."

Confidence. That was the thing. Morale. Soldiers who believed things would go right made them go right.

Thrice as worn as he'd been after his ride around McClellan, Jeb Stuart began to sing, belting out his own lyrics to the tune of "The Old Gray Mare":

"Old Joe Hooker, won't you come out of the Wilderness, come out of the Wilderness, come out of the Wilderness . . ."

Laughing, staff men and couriers joined in. Stuart regretted leaving behind his banjo picker.

Finding Harry Heth did take some doing. Stuart's fellow Virginian had rambled into the brush in yet another effort to organize his brigades and regiments. Runners went to fetch him.

Meanwhile, another aide located Stuart.

"Got it, General. Some fool tucked it down at the bottom of your wagon."

"Now I know the day's going to be a fine one," Stuart said. Addressing all, he declared, "You know, boys, my West Point nickname was 'Beauty,' and on this glorious day I mean to live up to it. Resplendent, I shall be, as radiant as the sun on the shields of Attica."

He laughed merrily, a laugh he could produce as dependably as a plantation belle summoned unfelt tears, and he turned back to the aide. "Red sash, too?"

"Yes, sir."

"Well, I surmise that this spot here will do for a gentleman's dressing room."

Jeb Stuart dismounted, patted his horse, and handed it off. His aide unpacked the carefully rolled new uniform.

Couldn't appreciate the colors yet, it was still too dark, but Stuart knew the new coat, with its country mile of braid, was a touch too blue for a proper CSA uniform. He'd always felt the shade had a dash to it, though. As for the sash, he normally draped his waist in cavalry yellow, but he did think wearing artillery red would be a nice gesture toward that noisiest element of his new command.

As light from beyond the horizon diluted the darkness, Harry Heth thrashed his way back to the scene, cursing like a cheating gambler cheated.

When he made out Stuart among the men and horses, he stopped and stared.

"God almighty," the infantryman said, "this a battle, or a whorehouse wedding?"

Stunned, Dan Sickles managed to say, "Joe . . . don't do this. I beg you, don't do it. Retract the order."

In the broadcloth gray before dawn, Sickles and his wartime carousing companion sat their mounts on the high ground. Batteries on both sides of their party stood to, ready for what the next minutes would bring. Below and behind them, infantry sergeants dressed their lines and checked cartridge pouches while their officers huddled.

"Military necessity," Hooker said. "We have to tighten the lines, reduce our front."

"But Joe . . . this is the finest high ground on the battlefield. Only competition's that rise toward the Chancellor place."

"Fairview," Hooker said. "That one's called Fairview."

"Well, whatever it's called—and whatever this-here bump's called—"

"Hazel Grove," Hooker told him.

"Hazel Grove, Molly Grove, Annie Grove, whatever you call it, this is the key position. My artillery . . ."

Hooker's smile, indulgent and smug, was already visible in the quitting night. "Dan, I admire your spirit, you've studied up on military affairs. But I think I know what I'm doing. After all"—he brushed the almost-morning with his sleeve, as if he might sweep away the lingering darkness—"this *has* been my profession."

Dan Sickles was, for the first time, tempted to ask Hooker what his profession had been in California, but he feared an irreparable breach. No, he wasn't at all sure his friend and drinking companion knew what he was doing. He'd been losing confidence in Joe for two full days. He'd begun to feel the way he often felt about West Point men, that the country had not made the wisest investment with its public funds when it sent the lot of them for a free education.

Sickles tried one last time: "If we give up this position to the Rebs, we're going to regret it."

Hooker renewed his smile, although—Sickles believed—with a ghost of doubt. Then the big, bluff voice rang out as usual.

"Dan, if the Rebs drag any guns up here, we'll blow them all to Hell. Settled and done. Withdraw your men and fortify the new line. We're wasting time." Hooker shook his head, as if trying to clear it. "If I don't withdraw you now, your entire corps could be cut off and trapped."

Sickles felt the impulse to protest again. He recognized the risk of being severed from the army well enough. But the Rebs already were severed from one another, and he believed his Third Corps could give as good as it got. Slocum's blackguards could do their part on the flank, too. He didn't pretend to be a martial genius, but Dan Sickles did believe he recognized a perfect artillery position when he stood on one.

He knew Joe Hooker, though. When Joe truly convinced

himself of something, it became impossible to move him. Stubbornness had its place in war, to be sure: The Rebs were stubborn as priests. But he wished Joe would be stiffer with the Rebs and less so with subordinates.

The prospect of giving up the high ground sickened him, almost literally: He felt his stomach churn, as if he were coming down with a dose of the camp trots.

Wasn't that, though. It was plain, old-fashioned disgust.

What the devil was wrong with Joe?

As a single cannon sounded and the first rifle fire snapped over on the right, Hooker led his retinue toward the next command. Flags snapped and hoofbeats drummed.

It was, Dan Sickles suspected, going to be an interesting morning.

In faint light, Hooker reached his old division. When the men recognized him, they cheered. *They* believed in him. Still.

His headache had faded. He sat taller in the saddle.

Hiram Berry, the division's present commander, was, like Dan, a self-taught soldier, but deadly serious. And he was brave. For a New Englander, Berry was affable, if not much of a tippler or petticoat-lifter, and for a politician he wasn't flamboyant. Really, there was no color to the man. Likable and capable, he lacked a sense of drama, any flair. Berry would do his duty, but he'd never replace Joe Hooker in soldiers' hearts.

Hooker had viewed him as the perfect choice to take his division.

"Morning, sir," Berry called, saluting.

"Hiram." Hooker touched the rim of his hat. "Ready for 'em?"

"Boys are always ready."

"Dan's going to be realigning. He'll need you to hold fast, give him time to move."

"We'll hold."

Berry wasn't one for lengthy speeches.

It was essential to secure the right, to give Sickles time to withdraw to the new defensive lines. It was vital to shun mistakes. He'd welcome a victory, of course, and perhaps Sedgwick would appear behind Lee before the Second Coming, but the critical thing was to avoid defeat. That meant limiting risk and fighting defensively, giving Lee no openings, forcing the Johnnies to smash themselves against successive entrenchments. An outright win would be grand, but a battle fought to a draw on Lee's own ground would count as success, given the past record of the Army of the Potomac.

Lincoln and Stanton would have no cause to relieve him.

"Well, you boys don't need me," he announced to Berry and his gathered staff. "Still the best division in the army, give the Rebs the devil!"

As he turned his horse, he spoke to Berry in a quieter voice:

"I'm counting on you, Hiram."

Rosy-fingered dawn," Doc Cowin announced.

The instant he closed his mouth, a cannon fired.

"Wish everybody with rank on their collars would keep their fingers off me. Rosy, or otherwise," Joe Grigg said, with more edge than usual. "Ain't right, if they send us back in."

"We must endure our going hence, even as our coming hither," Doc Cowin told him.

"Just as soon not go anywhere myself," Sam Pickens seconded. "Let Hill's boys take their turn. We did our part."

He did hope Hill's men—whoever had charge of them now—would do the trick against the Yankees. Even if they needed help from the poor lot under Colston, that would be fine. Just let Rodes' division be for once. Particularly the 5th Alabama.

Hoped it wasn't true about Old Jack. They all did. If a man had to fight, it was preferable to win.

Claimed it was just his arm. Grant it be so. A man could spare one arm, if it came to that.

Hill had gone down with a wound of his own, they said, but his was a scraper.

Couldn't say who was up and in charge, if anybody.

Pickens stood a few steps apart from his comrades as the grove brightened. He'd been teased enough. When he'd finally dared take off his shoes, or the remnants thereof, to put on those new Yankee stockings, the stench had sickened even him. Normally pleasant as peaches, Bill Lenier had commented, "Lord, Sam, you're the first living man I've smelt who stunk worse than a corpse left in the sun. Them feet."

"Send him into battle barefoot, Yankees would run off like driven hogs," Jim Arrington, usually quiet, added. "Wouldn't even need to swim that river on their way home, they'd jump right over it."

Sam had not answered. He had drawn on those stockings—an act that gave him five seconds of comfort—to avoid the monstrous temptation to scratch himself down to the bone.

Now he stood, alone, and listened.

Volleys shattered the calm and Rebel yells rose.

The North Carolinians of Jim Lane's brigade went forward with a ferocity that burned the air around them. Preceded by a heavy line of skirmishers, they howled as if they would eat their enemy's flesh. Shoving their way through the underbrush, pausing at nothing, men felt a power almost supernatural course through them.

Lane rode with them, calling encouragement. Some men barked, "Remember Jackson!" but Lane chose other words. He did not want to remember. He wanted to forget.

And he never would. No man among them would.

His horse balked at a thorn patch and Lane punished the gelding with his spurs. It would have been more practical to go forward on foot, but Jackson had been shot on horseback and Lane would not dismount and seem a coward.

"Forward!"

He couldn't yet see the enemy, but his skirmishers were at them. He could hear that much.

An aide rode up, an earnest boy.

"Sir, we're losing contact with General McGowan."

"His responsibility, Captain. We're the guide brigade, road on our left. South Carolina will have to cling to North Carolina today."

"He's going awful wide, sir."

"And we're going straight ahead."

Hard enough to control his own brigade. Sam McGowan would have to see to his.

The firing was close now, but he still could not see. The undergrowth was a second enemy.

His men bullied their way forward.

Another wave of Rebel yells, raised in triumph this time, not in anger. Lane spurred his horse ahead of his seething ranks.

Great Jesus, his skirmishers, unsupported, had swept over the first Yankee entrenchments, a defensive work of stacked logs, formidable. They should have been shot down before they'd gotten within twenty yards.

Had the Yankees lost heart?

The main body of his troops rushed ahead, raising a cry that might have been heard in Wilmington. They clambered over the entrenchments like pirates seizing a ship.

Lane looked for, and found, a low section of the barricade where he could jump his horse. The spot was close to his ill-fated 18th.

He had done his best to invigorate the men, to cajole them past their shame, but he needed to watch the men of the 18th North Carolina closely. Couldn't say whether they'd fight all the harder because of what they'd done, or just go quits. Purdie would have to keep a tight grip on his regiment.

Waving their swords, his officers bellowed at the men to re-form in a hurry. The usual, almost nauseating, confusion required sorting. Lane rode along his misshapen lines, calling:

"Dress ranks, men, dress ranks. We have work to do."

"By damn, we'll do it, too!" a hill-folk voice responded.

Those hills, those mountains. Where loyalties had diverged, with families sundered and cousins ambushed on back trails.

Not all of the Yankees had disappeared. Skirmishers and sharpshooters began to take a toll. Back to the enemy as he reordered his ranks, a captain barked a last command before his face exploded, hurling blood and teeth at his gathering soldiers.

They moved forward again. A line of Yankees seemed to rise from the earth, a double line.

A massed volley cut into Lane's ranks, scything. His horse bled from the neck, but seemed unaware of it.

"Don't stop, men! They won't stand!" he shouted. "Tar Heels, at the double-quick . . ." He waited for his command to echo then roared, *"March!"*

He was wrong about the Yankees. They stood their ground. At seventy yards, his brigade stopped of its own, the veterans sensing the work that was required. Slower to react than the men, officers hastened to give the orders that would authorize volleys.

Lane's senior flag-bearer fell. Another man seized the staff.

From the left, hidden Federal guns raked his flank. A round shot tore through a gray rank just behind Lane, sending men and body parts flying, streaking the air crimson.

They had to be firing from the road. Lane had been so concerned about the 18th he'd neglected his left. He turned his horse and spurred it, riding just behind his busied ranks, the men loading and firing at the enemy to the front.

"Shoot down the crewmen," he shouted in anticipation, long before he gained his flank. But the men on his left already knew what to do.

He saw the Federal battery now, two of its guns turned toward them. He watched as bullets ripped into the gun crews, while maddened horses warred against their harnesses. Federal artillerymen crumpled as if gone boneless, limp as dollies.

His men swept forward, only to be halted—slaughtered—by canister.

More men took their places.

"Shoot the damned officers," a man shouted.

Smoke clotted the air. The morning had already been poisoned by powder.

Confident that his men would finish up with the battery, Lane rode back toward his center. Only to find himself amid the hottest fires he had ever experienced.

A courier afoot reported, "Colonel Purdie's dead, sir. Shot him right through the head."

"Lieutenant Colonel George took over command?"

"Yes, sir."

"All right."

But it wasn't all right. Damn fool, Purdie. Had he been trying to get himself killed? Wash off the shame of shooting down Jackson, wash it off with his blood? Well, he'd succeeded in the first part, the damned idiot.

With a cold shock, Lane realized that he'd fairly described himself. Sitting atop a horse in this antechamber of Hell. Atop a bleeding horse. Was *he* trying to get himself killed?

No, he was trying to kill Yankees. The Yankees who were still standing there, beyond the veil of smoke, standing their ground even if half their number lay motionless or crawled rearward, unaided by comrades intent on fighting.

Lane's own dead and wounded lay about in shocking numbers.

He cantered from regiment to regiment, telling their colonels or whoever stood in command to prepare to charge. When he reached the 18th again, Forney George had been carried off with a wound and Major Barry had taken command.

Barry, the man who had given the order that would cost Jackson an arm. The major's eyes were crazed, his mouth aquiver.

"Barry, when you charge, you don't stop. You go right through them. Don't even stop for prisoners." He rose from his saddle and raised his voice. "Eighteenth North Carolina, when you go forward, I want you to rip the shit-packed guts right out of those nigger-lovers, hear?"

The soldiers, yearning for absolution, roared.

And Lane's Brigade charged forward. Even then, not all of the Yankees broke. A startling number had to be clubbed to the ground with rifle butts or shot point-blank. Already drenched in blood, a blue-coated sergeant came at them with his fists. Muzzles rammed into his torso just as soldiers pulled their triggers. The Yankee's life ended in quick jerks and he lay sprawled, the front of his uniform smoldering.

"Don't stop, don't stop!"

Lane's horse gave way under him. He had just time enough to throw himself free. Hard earth shook his bones and his sword flew.

Men helped him up, returning the blade. Artillery found their range.

"Keep going forward! Forward, men!" His voice came weaker, the wind had been knocked from his lungs. And his knee hurt. He pressed on afoot, fighting a limp, separated from the last members of his staff.

The remnants of his brigade plunged ahead, obedient and ferocious. They tore through another belt of brush and slopped through a stretch of moor. Lane judged they had covered a half mile since stepping off.

Another line of Yankee entrenchments loomed. Muzzles blazed from raw battlements. Artillery tore through the brambles and swept the open stretches.

His soldiers didn't pause. Reason had no purchase. Blood-drunk, they sensed the end of the hunt. They didn't yell, they screamed. Turned to animals.

Massive sounds of battle surrounded them.

Lane seemed to see more of his men fall than remained on their feet. But those still up on two legs led the way, officers an irrelevance.

Astonishing Lane, his soldiers hurled themselves over the Yankee barricades and dropped into the trenches behind them, swinging their rifles like war clubs.

They took the second defensive line. Just like that.

Again, officers rushed to reassemble companies and regiments. Almost simultaneously, couriers from both flanks warned that the brigade had outdistanced the rest of the attack, there was no one out there, left or right, but Yankees.

Where was Archer? Where was McGowan? Harry Heth? And where were Colston's legions?

As his men—so few remaining—gathered around their officers, tribesmen around their chieftains, a soldier shrieked:

"Here they come!"

A wall of Yankees, a long, blue wall aglitter with bayonets, surged over a low rise, realigning on the march as they left the tangles behind. Drums beat the pace. To Lane, it seemed a death march.

The situation was impossible. The numbers were too skewed. Fantastically so.

But his men formed up. They did not shout anymore. Faces gone grim, they shoved down ramrods with urgent paws.

A lone voice called, "Remember Jackson!" No one took up the cry.

The Yankees didn't cheer but just came on. Nor did they stop at regulation distance to trade volleys.

One after the other, Lane's officers ordered their men to fire and rifles bit shoulders. Some Yankees dropped, but the gaps they left were swiftly filled by men from the second rank.

At fifty yards, the Yankees finally halted and leveled their rifles. As smoothly as if on a drill field.

The volley was devastating.

Then they charged.

Yankees thrust in from the flanks as well.

A few of Lane's men just plain ran. Orders had become superfluous and every soldier who still could walk withdrew. At first, most halted now and again to shoot back toward the pursuing Yankees or just to shake a fist. As they passed back through their own dead and wounded, the disabled pleaded to be taken along. Some were aided by familiar hands, but many went ignored by men in a growing hurry.

Christians cursed like souls in deepest Hell.

Jim Lane felt their rage. Because it was his rage. They'd come so far, done so much. And where was the rest of the army? Why hadn't Colston's men been sent forward as promised? Would the bastards remember this? Or would they only recall the wounding of Jackson?

There was no precise moment when it happened. The moral collapse was gradual at first but soon accelerated. Even the best men began to race rearward, fleeing the Yankees and their drums in panic.

By the time they got back to the first line of Yankee entrenchments, Sam Lowe of the 28th was the only regimental colonel not killed or wounded. Surviving officers in all of the regiments struggled to rally their men at the captured defenses, determined to hold their one remaining prize. But soldiers—veteran soldiers—threw down their rifles, suddenly deaf to their officers, blind to all but the Yankees, bewildered as if betrayed. Men who had fought bravely cowered behind piled timbers, shivering. Others were surly toward their own superiors, not the enemy. Some realized for the first time that they'd been wounded.

One man, bewildered to find his chest ripped open, died at the sight of his still-beating heart.

Soldiers from other failed brigades ran through them or mingled to hide from their officers.

Then the Yankees came at them, a hard bunch, hitting them from the front while swinging around both flanks.

A few men stood and fought. Inspired, or just bred to habit, other soldiers, broken a moment before, rose to fight again. But the number of all who resisted was negligible and the Yankees arrived in a host. As the slight defense collapsed, blue-bellies perched atop the logs and fired down into the disordered mass.

"Like what ya git? Like what ya gittin' now?" a Yankee voice, distinct and western, demanded.

The brigade dissolved. Men ran like boys spooked by hants.

Lane emptied his pistol at the nearest men in blue. He didn't care if they killed him. But they just wouldn't.

Only the 28th North Carolina kept together and held its ground. Joining them—drawn to them—Lane ordered the regiment back, unwilling to sacrifice the remaining soldiers for nothing.

His runaways only stopped when they found themselves behind Colston's do-nothing regiments, which still had not received orders to go forward. Catching up with the survivors, their remaining officers found them docile now and embarrassed. Lane pitched in to gather his soldiers and rally them, but he reached a point where he had to turn away.

He could have wept at the injustice and folly. If only his men had been supported, if only . . .

Instead of bawling his eyes out, he unbuttoned his trousers and pissed against a tree.

Hooker felt a marvelous surge of confidence. After some initial success, the Rebs had been repelled all along the line, at every point that mattered. And they'd paid dearly.

Better still, every prisoner taken had been from Jackson's command. That meant that he, Joe Hooker, had just beat Stonewall Jackson.

Whipped that hymn-howling sonofabitch like a dog that soiled the carpet.

As he led his party through the drifting smoke, veering behind busy batteries, Joseph Hooker believed that the tide had turned.

Plaudits were due all around, but Ruger's brigade had been utterly savage in its repulse of two brigades of Carolinians, North and South. Ruger had been so successful and had advanced so far that he had to be recalled before the Rebs realized how exposed he was.

And Sickles was almost consolidated on his new line, although his rear guard had gotten mauled and some guns had been lost.

All in all, a very propitious morning. And it was just seven thirty.

Let them come on again, let them launch another clumsy attack straight into his guns.

Just as he reached the edge of the Chancellor clearing, he spotted a pack of officers carrying off a casualty in a blanket.

Had to be someone with rank to merit such company.

Hooker turned his horse, pulling up only when nearly on top of the detail. No time to waste this morning.

Still clutching their burden, the officers halted. Only one tried to salute. Two wept.

"Who is it? Who's been hit?"

"General Berry, sir. It's General Berry. He's dead, sir."

Hooker slipped from his horse. "Put him on the ground. Let me see."

"I tried to warn him, sir. I tried to warn him not to cross that road."

Hooker didn't listen. He bent over a face already changed, lifeless, with one cheek powder-smudged.

The strength of his emotions almost unmanned him, the depth of the sentiment unexpected. He leaned now like a worshipping Mohammedan and kissed Berry on the forehead.

"My God, Berry, why did this have to happen? Why you? I relied on you. . . ."

His headache returned with the force of a clubbed musket.

Colonel Edward Porter Alexander could not believe his good fortune and half suspected the Yankees had set a trap. Surely no foe in the history of gunpowder and cannon had willingly abandoned such a commanding position for artillery. It just plain made no sense.

Nonetheless, a prisoner, hastily questioned, had insisted that it was so, that his regiment and everyone else had been ordered off the hill. Had those in gray waited ten minutes, they could have had the elevation without the minor resistance they had faced.

Glory hallelujah! In all of his nigh on twenty-eight years, Alexander had never been given such a gift.

As he rode about guiding batteries to their positions, Stuart trotted up with his entourage. Alexander had encountered him most everywhere he'd gone since the early hours, the cavalryman was a wizard of sheer presence, colorful as a one-man medicine show. Today, he looked half Reb, a quarter Yankee, and one-eighth high-seas commodore, with a leftover portion of minstrel.

Stuart always was a sight to see.

Wearing his familiar smile, the cavalier declared, "Why, this here ain't no hill, Porter. Hardly a pimple on the backside of our fair Virginia."

"Best artillery position I've had in this war. Just look."

As the men turned their heads, the first guns in battery spoke. Alexander and Stuart watched black dots course through the sky. The shells landed just short of a Yankee gun line readying for action on a hill not a mile to the north.

"Take that one, too, sir," Alexander said, "and the Yankees are finished, far as their present ground goes."

"All in good time, Porter, all in good time. Our Yankee brethren have been teasing us something wicked this morning. Almost seems they've got on their fighting manners." He reinforced his smile. "We'll see to that, of course." He gestured toward the guns and men nearby. "With the help of these brazen fellows of yours."

A second battery rushed into action. Gun carriages recoiled and strong men rushed to return them to their positions. Swabs went to work. Sergeants shouted.

The Federal guns on the other hill sought their range, their interest fixed by the lengthening line of fieldpieces and Stuart's bevy of flags. Surely, Alexander thought, they're already regretting the depth of their folly, Lord help them.

It hadn't been a Yankee artilleryman who'd made the decision to limber up and leave. That much was certain.

A shell sailed overhead and struck trees to the rear, shattering branches and sending a discomfited artilleryman stumbling out of the brush with his trousers down.

"Might be best if you moved on, General," Alexander said. "Hot work ahead."

"Just the kind of work I like. But I shall retire, knowing this Olympus, this Vesuvius, is in good hands."

Alexander couldn't help adding, "Sure would like to stack a dozen batteries on that other hill."

"All in good time," Stuart repeated. About to ride on, he paused and said, "Word on General Jackson is that he's like to recover just fine. Lost an arm, but not that hard head of his."

He gee-upped his mount, and the medicine show moved along.

Each minute, more Yankee guns answered Alexander's batteries. He respected his redleg opponents. Even yesterday, getting themselves a whipping, the Yankee artillery had been full of spleen and a hazard.

He watched as a well-aimed shell struck a Yankee caisson, sending rubbish and men into the sky.

Didn't even have to offer encouragement to these boys. The section chiefs and gun crews knew their business and worked with relish.

Steadying his mount, Alexander judged distances. He reckoned that with the proper elevation applied, the rifled guns could even range the Chancellor house, which prisoners insisted played host to the Yankee headquarters. Didn't have an ideal line of sight, but instincts counted. He hated the prospect of damaging Southern property, but war didn't whisper requests, it shouted demands.

Wouldn't it be handsome doings to send that Yankee libertine a greeting?

Colonel John Funk of the 5th Virginia, Stonewall Brigade, just could not believe it. Never had he dreamed of, let alone seen, such a spectacle: hundreds upon hundreds of his fellow Confederates cowering on the near side of a line of Yankee entrenchments. Most lay belly-flat on the ground, trying to sink into it.

"South Carolinians," one disdainful Virginian remarked. He spit and added, "Trash."

Funk led his brigade right over them, insisting his men dress their lines and step on whoever lay there in their way.

Couldn't believe it. He kicked a bareheaded, shaking captain hugging the earth like a drunkard atop a hoor.

"Get up, you coward."

The captain did not rise. Funk kicked him again, harder, and moved on. Many another disgusted Virginian gave voice to their contempt. The men were riled enough over Jackson's wounding—thanks to a lawless pack of *North* Carolinians, men who at least had some fight in them now and then. Before promotion had taken Jackson from them, the veterans striding forward had served under Old Jack like unto forever, right back to the miseries of western Virginia in winter—coldest nights a man had ever felt and days as bad.

Insulted and shamed, a voice rose from the mass of men who'd quit: "You Ginny-boys going to learn, just wait. Be back faster than you done gone, you'll see."

An irate Virginia voice answered, "South Carolina started this-here war. Seems better men have to fight it for you."

Funk's first line climbed over the entrenchments and re-formed. The men didn't need orders. They were the Stonewall Brigade.

Bodies lay about, a tithe from both sides. In blue or gray, the wounded went untended. Those who could muster the strength propelled themselves along at an agonized crawl, dragging ruined limbs. Groaning, bleating.

A boy whose eyes had been shot from his head complained that he could not see.

Through all of it, General Paxton strode forward proudly, marching between the brigade's regiments, an inspiration to every man who saw him. The brigade commander had been other than himself earlier that morning, unusually somber, but now he looked fine and fit.

The morning had been a trial, with Raleigh Colston gallivanting from brigade to brigade, dispensing orders that ranged from the uncertain to the impracticable. The Stonewall Brigade had been ready to go forward, but others weren't. And time had fled.

From the ranks, a soldier called, *"Jackson!"* Other voices took up the name, chanting. Funk joined in, guiding the regiment onward with his sword.

His skirmishers had disappeared, gobbled by the undergrowth. Funk's boots plopped into mud. The first line staggered as a hidden marsh grabbed shoes and the worst thickets yet defied efforts to go forward.

The calls of "Jackson!" faded as men cursed unexpected aggravations, angrier at having their feet mud-slopped than they were at the heathen Yankees.

"Come on, boys!" Funk called. "Keep going. Just get on through it. It's just a little ways now."

He had no idea whether it would, indeed, be "a little ways." But he didn't know what else to say.

Miserable place. The bog made him think of snakes, creatures he did not care for. But there were far more dangerous animals waiting, up on two legs.

The regiment had not progressed a hundred yards from the entrenchments when a streak of blinding light filled the low horizon. The volley's roar followed instantly.

Men cried out or dropped with a splash. Nearby soldiers looked to Funk.

"Keep on, keep on," he ordered. "Get through this, don't stop now."

Natural enough to want to halt and shoot back, but it wouldn't do. Couldn't even see any Yankees to shoot at.

His men bashed at the undergrowth with rifle butts. Some of nature's lattices were so thick they stopped men cold.

"Keep going! Forward!"

Another volley thudded into his lines, the cost terrible.

"Don't stop, boys! Come on!"

The Yankees were firing at will now, picking their targets, while Funk's men remained stymied by nature itself.

Funk could see them now, though, the blue-bellies. Heads, shoulders, rifles.

The regiment kept going. As best as Funk could sense matters, the entire brigade continued to advance.

Infernal place.

And the Yankees . . . he couldn't remember facing such a concentrated fire. Men kept falling, draping themselves over briars.

At last, Funk reached dry ground. A wounded Yankee had crawled atop it to avoid drowning in a few inches of marsh water. His eyes were huge with terror.

Rough ranks parted and stepped to both sides of the Federal.

A line of entrenchments, uneven but effective. Cocked blue caps, indistinct faces, here and there a torso exposed as the Yankees steadied their rifles atop the works. Plenty of them, too, thick as prunes in a stew pot.

Without an order, his soldiers paused on the solid earth, firing at their antagonists. There was a sense, an instinct, in play, the sudden conviction that going one step further meant certain death. Yet there was no inclination to retreat: They were where they were, and this was the fighting ground.

Stink of powder. Biting smoke.

It wouldn't do. His men were too exposed, while the Yankees had the cover. They had to charge or quit.

About to demand that his soldiers plunge ahead, Funk was delayed by the splashing of Lieutenant Barton, General Paxton's man, coming from the rear.

"Colonel!" he called. "Colonel Funk!" His words were barely audible through the racket.

Funk expected an order to advance. Then he saw that Barton glistened with tears.

"The general's dead, he's dead!" the lieutenant shouted, as if deafened. "You're in command, you have the brigade! General Paxton's dead, he had a presentiment. He's dead, you—"

Funk gripped the lieutenant's arm and shook him. "Stop this, Barton. *Think*, man. What can you tell me? How's the brigade faring, overall?"

Barton was unmanned. Still, he reported: "Colonel Edmondson's down, too. Arm all but shot away. And the Fourth . . . the Fourth Virginia's been shot all to pieces. In that swamp."

"You go on back now. Find General Colston. Or speak right to General Stuart, if you see him. Tell him where we stand and ask for orders. Tell him we need support, the Yankees are thick as termites on a stump."

The lieutenant gathered himself and left.

Funk collected soldiers he knew and trusted, sending them right and left to sister regiments, ordering his fellow colonels to prepare for an assault on the entrenchments. Then, in an irresistible fury, he led his own men forward twenty yards and steadied the line. The storm of musket fire was fit to stun, but he thanked the stars the Yankees had no cannon along this line.

Sounded as though their guns were busy elsewhere.

A passel of Yankees climbed out of their ditch and attempted a countercharge. The Virginians shot them down with hardmouthed glee.

They stood there, his men, firing and reloading, waiting for an order that would take them in one direction or the other. Stalwart.

What should he do?

As his couriers filtered back, the consensus was that the Yankees were too strongly posted, that a charge would only add casualties. But Funk could not bear the prospect that his first order as the head of the Stonewall Brigade should be to withdraw.

He walked his line, still doing the work of a regimental commander, calling out encouragement. It was evident from the jarring gaps that his casualties had been severe as well.

Suddenly, Northern cheers rose, close at hand and powerful. New flags appeared behind the Union barricades.

His men read the future. The first to quit splashed back into the moor.

The Yankees were about to attack with those fresh troops, it was punishingly clear. And his men could not withstand it, not here, not now. With the marsh at their back, they were like to be captured, gobbled up entire.

Runners from other regiments reported desperate conditions.

More of his men drifted back from the firing line. The best fell where they stood.

Hating every syllable he spoke, Funk ordered his soldiers back. After turning over the regiment to his lieutenant colonel, he hurried to extricate the bloodied brigade.

He did not make it all the way to the flank. The brigade collapsed too quickly. Men fled, running as they had never done before. The Yankees didn't bother to pursue them but stopped and cheered.

The blue-bellies knew that bog was there, they'd learned the hard way.

Why hadn't he been warned?

Off to the flank, on dry ground, a thicket had ignited, adding its own smoke to the fog of volleys.

As he clambered back over the first Union entrenchments, crusted with mud to the crotch and among the last of his soldiers to return, he heard a delighted, infinitely spiteful South Carolina voice crow:

"Looks like those high-toned Virginians come back for a visit. Somebody boil up tea."

If there were better soldiers on the battlefield than his, Tom Ruger was going to need convincing. He'd never been prouder of any men he'd commanded. Earlier, the 27th Indiana alone had taken on the better part of a Reb brigade and sent the Johnnies flying. All of his regiments had been as savage as Visigoths. He wasn't sure his minister father would approve of the epithets that had graced the morning, but no man could ever criticize the results.

The men needed ammunition, though. He'd called for resupply again and again. And not a single cartridge had arrived. Even men who'd marched with eighty rounds were running out.

And the diabolical Reb artillery: Who had allowed the Johnnies control of that hill? When they weren't dueling gun against gun, they pounded every Union line they could range, and his brigade had become a popular target.

Wasn't anyone thinking? Who the devil was in charge? Anyone?

Where were the cartridges?

Where was the artillery ammunition? Did they expect his men to walk back to Trenton and petition the governor to fill their caissons?

Jud Clark was outraged, livid. His guns had done good service. All of the Third Corps batteries had done splendidly. But they had yet to discourage the ever-increasing number of Confederate guns gathered on that hill. And he'd just had to see off the New Jersey Lights under Bobby Sims: Their caissons and limbers were empty.

The remaining batteries were low on every type of round but canister—grand, if they had to deter Confederate infantry, but useless in a long-range artillery duel.

Why on earth had they given that hill to the Rebs?

He'd ridden back as far as general headquarters, only to be dismissed as a minor figure amid the commotion. Inside the house, he'd found staff men at work amid discarded bandages, trails of blood, and the screams of soldiers under the surgeon's knife. General Hooker had been surrounded by an impenetrable cordon of colonels and officious majors, and the only intelligible answer Clark had received was useless: "Go see Sickles, he's your corps commander, ain't he?"

He'd already gone to Sickles. The general had cursed to shame a barkeep but had no help to offer.

Clark missed Henry Hunt, as hard a taskmaster as the old fellow could be. General Hunt would never have let this happen, there would have been ammunition to spare and reserve batteries ready to serve as replacements. But Hooker had some peculiar grudge against the man, or at least against his concept of artillery support, and had left the old gunner behind. Some artillery officers had rejoiced at the prospect of being out from under Hunt's thumb, but those fellows were learning their lesson now.

Nobody was in charge, and no one felt responsible, except the men who were busy actually fighting. From what he had seen of the rear, chaos prevailed.

"Sir, the lieutenant's been wounded, he's bad," a red-striped sergeant reported. "And Captain . . . we need ammunition, we're down to one shell per gun. Maybe two for the slower crews."

A Reb shell struck near a horse team, producing damage and panic in equal amounts.

"Well, make those last shells count," Clark told him.

* * *

He had thirty-six guns in action and three fresh batteries waiting to take their turn. Meanwhile, the Yankee fires had slowed, a sign that they were low on ammunition.

"Keep pounding them," he called as he walked his upper gun line. "Make them use up every round they've got. Keep at them, men."

When he reached the battery atop the highest ground, he told its commander, "Shift your fires to the Chancellor grounds. Don't worry about identifying targets or sparing the house. Just stir things up back there, make them think twice about bringing ammunition or reinforcements through that gauntlet. Make it a challenge no mule skinner will accept."

If only, Alexander thought, the infantry would take that other hill. . . .

Hooker was sick to death of being pestered. Despite losses—not least, poor Berry—and errors, even outright cowardice, the morning had been a prodigious success, with the Rebs paying a blood price they'd never forget. *And* the vaunted Jackson had been humiliated, his gains of the night before revealed as worthless.

Now everyone claimed an urgent need, filling the headquarters with complaints and clamor. Units wailed for ammunition, both small arms and artillery, but it wasn't *his* responsibility, that was the affair of the corps and divisions. Even those commanders faring well whined for reinforcements. Which they were not going to get. He was not going to thin his lines and render them vulnerable elsewhere.

Then there was Meade. In clear contravention of his orders, Meade had sent forward a brigade, insisting that he'd seen a crisis developing. But the "crisis" would have passed without his meddling. Meade was a malcontent, temperamental and disloyal. Conceited. Superior. Rebellious. The Philadelphian had to be made to see that he was not the commander of the Army of the Potomac.

And Revere. Descendant of Paul Revere or not, the man would

never again hold a command, he'd see to that. On Berry's death, the swine had assumed command—an authority to which he had not been entitled—and marched half the division to the rear, damned near to United States Ford, leaving a gap in the line a more astute foe could have used to rupture the army's defense. It was the most barefaced example of cowardice Hooker had ever seen from a general officer.

And yet things had gone well. *His* generalship, *his* decisions, appeared wiser than many a jealous heart had wished. Jackson and Lee had run into a wall.

Hooker stepped out onto the porch of the fetid house, hoping fresh air would ease his latest headache. He leaned against a pillar atop the steps. Reb artillery had begun to range the surrounding fields and patch fires burned. Fighting units waiting nearby kept their discipline, but disorder ruled among the supporting elements.

Nature of war. Couldn't expect perfection.

After this campaign, though, he intended a further reorganization. His reforms had not gone far enough, particularly when it came to ordnance matters and supply. And heads were going to roll among the Signal boys.

The army needed discipline, from its generals on down.

He'd made a mistake about Henry Hunt, though. And he intended to do the manly thing and admit it—not publicly, of course, but privately—as soon as the campaign ended.

He did wish Hunt were on hand. The old bugger had been right. The guns had to answer to a central authority.

Live and learn. Spilt milk.

What mattered was that the Rebel yells had ceased. Those boys had taken a licking. Repulsed on all fronts, repeatedly. He'd ridden over their dead and liked the sensation.

The headlines would be glorious, canceling out the previous evening's embarrassment: HOOKER DEFEATS LEE, REPULSES JACKSON.

He'd be the hero the Union had been waiting for.

If only Sedgwick would do his duty at last. Van Alen had just sent off a peremptory order: Sedgwick was to advance and attack *at once.* No more excuses, no tall tales of resistance. The fellow had to come up in Lee's rear *today.* The Rebels had been weakened, they'd lost their drive. Bled out. It was time to crush them, and Sedgwick was the press.

Hooker scratched a bug bite on his cheek.

If Sedgwick dallied, any failures ascribed to this campaign would rest at his feet. Beloved Uncle John would pay a price.

He heard an abrupt round of firing. Not from the right this time, from the center-left. Where the two divisions left under Lee had been behaving themselves.

An act of desperation? A forlorn hope?

If only Sedgwick would appear. The timing could not be better.

Two Confederate shells dropped near the yard. One of them gutted an unattended mule.

Might be time to shift the headquarters, move it out of range. Unable to do more, the Rebs were spewing artillery like bile.

Darius Couch appeared around the corner of the house, returning from whatever fuss he'd been making or avoiding. His corps, too, had done handsomely when engaged, but now his face bore a look of consternation: Couch was the sort who was born to a bad digestion.

Obedient, though. And that counted.

Before his senior corps commander reached him, Hooker spotted Major Tremaine, Hooker's factotum, coming back from the battle lines at a gallop.

Hooker shifted his weight from the pillar back to his feet. His head throbbed and he felt a rush of dizziness. He leaned forward, gripping the porch rail.

Tremaine didn't look as though he bore good news.

In the instant before it struck, Major General Joseph Hooker saw the solid shot sailing toward him. It was the queerest thing, to see it coming.

Then there was darkness.

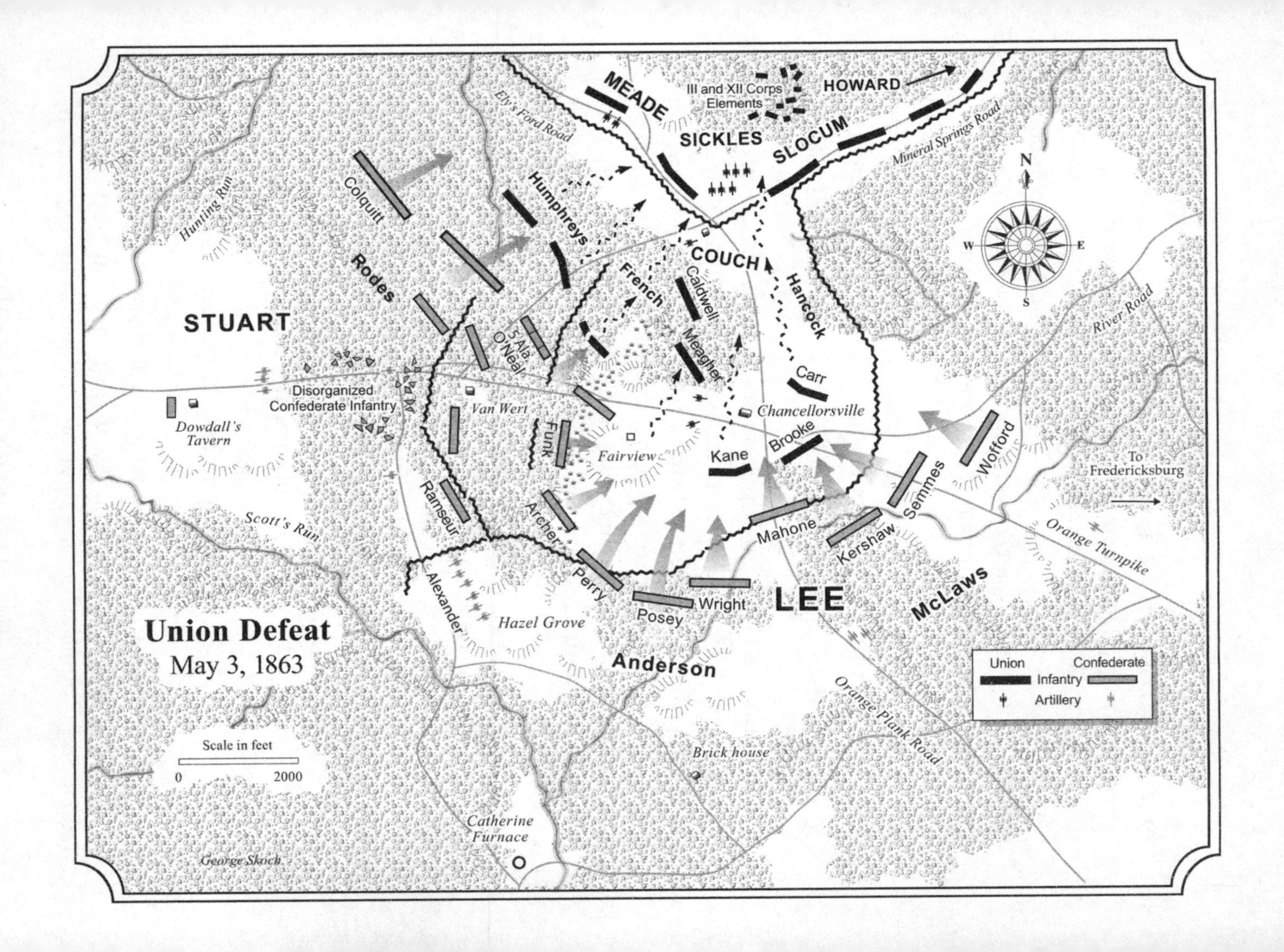
Union Defeat
May 3, 1863
MEADE
III and XII Corps
Elements
HOWARD
SICKLES
SLOCUM
Ely's Ford Road
Mineral Springs Road
Colquitt
Humphreys
Hunting Run
COUCH
French
Caldwell
Hancock
Rodes
STUART
5 Ala.
O'Neal
Meagher
Carr
Disorganized
Confederate Infantry
Chancellorsville
Van Wert
Dowdall's
Tavern
Funk
Fairview
Kane
Brooke
Wofford
Semmes
To
Fredericksburg
Ramseur
Archer
Mahone
Kershaw
Scott's Run
Orange Turnpike
Alexander
Perry
Wright
Posey
LEE
McLaws
Hazel Grove
Anderson
River Road
N
W
E
S
Union
Confederate
Infantry
Artillery
Orange Plank Road
Brick house
Scale in feet
0
2000
Catherine
Furnace
George Skoch

TEN

Midmorning, May 3

The boys were cranky. All of them. Even Doc Cowin, who mostly had an easy way of letting the world go by.

Nobody wanted to go back into that fight. Runaways from the other divisions had been as common as ticks on a hound in August, gone-eyed men skedaddling until apprehended or until tired legs and worn-out souls just quit and they sat down shaking. They came back wailing of disaster, as if they'd just witnessed the opening of the Book with Seven Seals and didn't much care for the contents.

Which meant, Sam Pickens did not doubt, that the 5th Alabama would be called on for more Yankee killing. Which led, inevitably, to killing the other way around.

Alabama always seemed to follow the mule's hind end.

Nor was he feeling his best down-belly and lower. Many a man had feasted too freely the night before, gobbling with abandon, grab-handed in the dark, stuffing himself to a ruin with Yankee delicacies. More squatting than standing now, a passel of Greensboro boys rued their greed this morning.

Mean, too, these wartime brethren of his. Uncharacteristically nasty. The teasing of Ed Hutchinson had been merciless, downright un-Christian, after Joe Grigg had stepped back into the brush to find a private spot not soiled to gagging and, of all things, discovered the corporal petting the pony, right there in broad daylight, poison ivy forgotten.

Everybody did it, of course. But that a man would feel that base desire at such a time fell on the far side of strange. Just who would do a thing like that, just then?

Even good Doc Cowin, normally as pleasant as well-made whiskey, had declared that from then on, Hutchinson must be addressed as "Corporal Onan."

Just sour, every man. This waiting to know for sure what you already knew for certain was a mean thing.

Hadn't had any more word on Bob Price, either. Pickens hoped it was true that his wound wasn't bad. Then he wondered if Bob had been the lucky one, to be out of this.

Don't think like that. Don't do it.

Still, he'd made up his mind to stop his younger brothers from joining up, no matter how long the war lasted. They weren't especially close, the Pickens boys—theirs was not a hugging, kissing family—but there was more than sufficient brotherly amity to want to deter them from the downright folly of thinking there was anything good at all about wearing a uniform.

Fool fellows thought women liked it, but women just liked bawling over corpses.

Plenty more corpses to cry over today.

His feet burned like the fires of Hell in high summer.

A man could even *smell* the fighting, the stink of degradation, sniff it raw right where the regiment waited, suspended in this stretch of high-nerved indolence before hearing the fateful verdict of men empowered. Like waiting on a doc to yank a tooth that, all of a sudden, didn't seem such a bother compared to those pliers.

Of a sudden, Doc Cowin recited: "'Now, if these men do not die well, it will be a black matter for the king that led them to it . . .'"

And Bill Lenier, pleasant Bill, said hard: "You planning to die, Doc? I ain't."

Lieutenant Borden put a quick stop to matters by saying: "Shut your mouth, Doc. And keep it shut."

Sam Pickens had never quite seen the like of it: friends just waiting to turn their fists on each other, ready at a feather's touch to cast off the newly oppressive chains of civility and go at it like field hands lit by corn liquor.

Strike a match, and the whole place might explode.

Up front, artillery pounded. But Pickens didn't hear volleys suggesting that others were doing their part.

Captain Williams came over and tore into Lieutenant Borden because the men weren't standing right, then Lieutenant Borden made everybody stand up and play pretend. Pickens would not have been astonished had someone shot the lieutenant for no reason. And Borden was as good as lieutenants got.

"The poet erred abominably," Doc Cowin announced, "when he deemed waiting 'delectable.'"

Everyone else ignored Doc, but Pickens figured he had it about right.

Where the devil was Tremaine? Sickles had sent him back to remonstrate with Joe forty minutes ago. His corps had to have its ammunition replenished—damn Joe and Butterfield for their strictures against "excessive" trains—but even a downpour of cartridges might not suffice. Just as the attacks on the right had lulled, bled to a weakness, the Rebs leashed up on the left had been let loose. Advancing up the Plank Road and the Turnpike from south and east, they were biting into Slocum's positions and snarling at Win Hancock's, the only protection left for Sickles' rear.

The threat of encirclement pressed. The corps had to withdraw beyond the crossroads, and swiftly. And his men would have to do it under the worst artillery fire of the war, thanks to Joe's folly in handing that bare-back hill over to the Rebs.

Now the Johnnies were gnawing at the last high ground he held, an ugly piece of nowhere mislabeled "Fairview," where one of his batteries after another had been forced to pull out with emptied caissons.

It was a reverse just waiting to be a catastrophe.

Shells tore into his lines, butchering men who had done fine work that morning. For all the West Pointers' malarkey about "cold steel," his corps wasn't going to stop the Reb onslaught with bayonets.

Dan Sickles vowed that if he survived this day, he would never again let the enemy have the best ground for artillery: He'd grab it and keep it.

He lit another cigar and waited for orders.

His eyes snapped open to a blinding light and Hooker saw another shot hurtling toward him. He jerked—awkwardly, painfully—to avoid it.

But there was no shot, no shell, descending now. Artillery thumped from the fields nearby, answering the Reb guns, but all Hooker saw as his vision cleared were concerned faces above him.

He heard a voice, distinct, cry, "General Hooker's been killed! The general's been killed!"

"I'm all right," he muttered. At least, he thought he did. Then he spoke with more clarity:

"Not dead. Not . . . what happened?"

"You're alive, sir. That's what matters."

Hooker tried to sit up. He hurt. Head to toe.

"What happened?" he demanded. He thought he knew: a black dot plunging toward him. But matters were confused. His brain had grown disobedient. And it hurt like ten headaches at once.

"Solid shot hit the pillar right beside you." That was Couch. "Half of it split off and struck you."

"Where?" He struggled to think, to feel with coherence, to inventory his body.

"On the porch. You were up on the porch."

"No. Where . . . where did it get me?"

Hesitation. "Your head, I think. Shoulder, chest. It was quick. You know how it is."

"Am I . . ."

"You should be all right, you look fine." Couch again. "You're not even bleeding. Just a good knocking, you're going to have quite a lump."

Rocks pounded his skull. He struggled to think clearly. Abruptly, he said:

"Help me up."

"He should rest," a voice said.

"Not damned well here," Couch said. "Rebs have us ranged."

"My horse," Hooker said.

"We'll take care of you, sir." That was Van Alen. "There's no need—"

"My *horse,* damn you." He did grasp one thing clearly. "The men have to see me . . . know I'm alive. No panic . . ."

"He's right," Couch told whoever was listening. "Bring up his horse."

"Help me up."

Once on his feet, he felt the world swirl and reached out for invisible grips. His back hurt, his shoulder, his hip. His left arm malingered, reluctant to take commands, numbed.

"Hold him upright."

"I'm fine."

Shells crashed down around them. One exploded just beside the house, showering all with dirt and laying a soldier low. Wood cracked hugely, splintering. Brickwork growled and collapsed.

Steadying himself, shutting his eyes then opening them again, Hooker said, "The wounded . . . have to get them out . . ."

"What, sir?"

"Wounded. Have to . . . get them out of the house. Shelling . . ."

"Yes, sir. It's already being done. Reb prisoners are helping clear them out."

Couch gripped his arm and said, "Your horse, Joe. Are you sure you can ride?"

In answer, Hooker turned and attempted to mount, to inspire confidence. When his effort faltered, unbidden hands gave assistance.

"Men have to see me."

But he allowed his horse to be guided rearward with him atop it. Brightness pierced his eyes, despite the smoke. He felt as though his skull had been cracked like an eggshell.

After riding a short stretch up the ford road, he stopped abruptly: The burst of pain had been overwhelming, extravagant.

"Down," he said. "Have to . . ."

Quickly, hands gripped and guided him.

"Lay out a blanket. Unstrap mine. Put it over there. Hurry, damn it." Couch. Good man. Couch would see to things.

No. He had to retain command. Not trust anyone.

He closed his eyes as others gripped his weakened arms and guided him onto the blanket. Lying flat helped and didn't help. He felt nauseated.

"Get a surgeon," Couch said. "For God's sake, get someone to see to him."

"They're all busy, General. There's so many—"

"Get a surgeon, damn you."

Whirling, swirling.

"It's Major Tremaine, sir. Can you hear me?"

"Of course I hear you." He tried to nod.

"It's General Sickles. His men are out of ammunition, every kind."

"Not now . . ."

"Don't pester him, Tremaine."

"Sir, General Sickles needs to pull back. Twelfth Corps, too. They're almost—"

"Pull back," Hooker said. "Defend . . . defend . . ."

"Yes, sir."

"Tremaine, he doesn't know what you're saying. Let him be, for God's sake."

"You heard him. He said General Sickles can withdraw."

"Tremaine, I'll have you arrested." Then Couch added, "Yes, Dan can withdraw. Coordinate with Slocum. Now get out of here."

"Withdraw . . ."

More hands braced him up. He met the fiery scent of brandy, shoved right under his nose.

"No."

They poured it into his mouth and he swallowed it. Then more.

A lucifer match ignited in his body. A bright, splendid match.

He knocked the flask away. "*No*. Nobody able to say . . ."

"For Christ's sake, Joe."

"Never say I was drunk . . ."

But the slugs of brandy were magic. He felt as though he'd been shocked awake by one of those electrical devices, wired to one of those telegraph batteries.

"All right," he said. "Just help me up. Need . . . need to reestablish headquarters. Need to . . ."

"Bring his horse over here. Help him. Joe, can you ride?"

"I'm all right."

Shelling. Screams. Smoke.

In the saddle again, he found his eyes in better focus. He felt . . . alert.

As the party began to ride northward again, amid retreating soldiers, a shell whizzed down behind them. It struck the blanket upon which he had lain.

Colonel Joseph Dickinson climbed through splintered wood and over a corpse to get to the cellar door. He had to pry it open.

The stairs were still intact. One small blessing.

It was his second descent within the hour. The first had been to flush out skedaddlers who'd found their way inside, crowding where the Chancellor women huddled. Now he had another purpose, one too long delayed.

Dust rode shafts of sunlight where the wall above had been shot through and the floor had collapsed. The women kept to a murky corner. Two sobbed, but the rest maintained fragile looks of defiance.

"I'm sorry," Dickinson told them, amid the racket, "for all this."

Nothing.

"Come with me," he told them. "You need to get out of here now."

One, whom he had come to know as the strongest, though not the eldest, got to her feet.

"This is our home. *You* need to get out."

Her lips quivered and her hands, balled into fists, were unsteady.

"I'm getting out, all right. And so are you. The upper floor's on fire. I'm sorry."

"*Our* people will be here. Soon."

"Not soon enough, missy."

An explosive shell struck above their heads. More of the floors above them collapsed, crashing down. One of the women screamed. Another jumped up, maddened. Above them, soldiers groaned and pleaded and cursed.

"You . . . you intend to thrust us out among your . . . out with your blue beasts? We'd rather . . . rather . . ."

Brushing dust and debris from his hair and beard, Dickinson said:

"You don't have a choice." Another shell landed close. The building's remains trembled. "You're not going to stay here and die."

He moved toward them. The spokeswoman winced and stepped back.

"Look, I'm sorry," he continued. "I'm sorry for everything. I'm . . . I'm sorry for locking you in that room the first night." He scanned them, their blood-ruined dresses, sacrificed to the filthy work of helping wounded men—not the romantic labor some women imagined. "No one will interfere with you, you'll be safe."

"You say."

He smelled burning. There was no more time.

"Yes, *I* say. Because I'm going to escort you." Then, in a quieter voice, he said, "It's the one worthwhile thing I'll do today."

Brusque again, he added:

"Hurry up."

Another unwelcome visitor. Hooker grimaced. Who was it this time? His brain was a torn muscle, it hurt to think, and the endless decisions demanded of him blurred. Couldn't they leave him alone for a few minutes?

A tall man, Meade ducked under the tent's flap, nodded to Couch, and asked, "You all right, Joe? I just heard . . ."

And salivated at the thought, Hooker suspected.

"What is it, George?" He struggled to focus.

Meade removed his spectacles and applied a dirty handkerchief to the lenses. "Well, I'm glad, if you're all right."

Hooker forced himself to sit up on the cot, rejecting Couch's help. "Of course I'm all right. See any blood? Now . . . what is it? Get it over with, whatever you've come for."

"Reynolds and I . . . we could sweep down on their left, they're in utter turmoil. We could roll up their entire flank, turn things around." Meade towered over the cot. "Joe, we could destroy them, this is our chance."

"No."

"Joe, would you just listen—"

"*No.* Remain on the defense. That's my decision. Hasn't changed." He shut his eyes, tightly, just for a moment. His head, his head.

"Joe, they've taken frightful losses. Now their flank's wide open, worse than ours was yesterday. Barely half of this army's been engaged. My corps, Reynolds' corps . . . even Howard could put in a brigade, he wants to fight."

"No!" Hooker was not about to be tricked in a moment of weakness, not by George Meade. "My decision . . . as commander of this army . . . is that we will defend." Struggling with his thoughts, he added, "Sedgwick's on his way. He'll take Lee in the rear."

"All the more reason for us to attack their left. Strike Lee on both flanks. John and I agree that—"

Hooker exploded. "That's it, isn't it? You and Reynolds? Conspiring against me, the two of you." He made a fist, as if about to rise from the cot and strike Meade. "You think *you* should command this army."

Meade stepped closer. "I wouldn't *want* command of this army. Not with . . . with cowardly drunkards in it. I'd shun it."

Couch stepped between them. "Jesus Christ, we're supposed to be fighting the Rebs. . . ."

But Meade had been aroused. He leaned a long, severe face toward Hooker.

"I can smell the liquor on your breath."

Hooker felt himself go pale. His shoulders sagged. His head . . .

"George, that was unworthy of you," Couch said. "And insubordinate. We gave him a sip of brandy when he collapsed. He tried to refuse it."

"Get out of here," Hooker muttered. "Just get out. Advance one skirmisher, and I'll see you court-martialed. For mutiny."

When Meade had gone striding off, Hooker sat with his face in his hands.

"You're at fault, too, you know," Couch told him. "They're not 'conspiring' against you, Joe. Everyone's doing his best."

Hooker looked up. "And you think I'm not?"

"I didn't say that."

"Call in Van Alen, would you?"

Couch did as asked. When the field chief of staff appeared, Hooker addressed Couch in his presence:

"Couch, I turn over command of this army to you. Until I'm better able to . . . until . . . until I'm ready to resume command. You will withdraw this army and place it in the position designated on Van Alen's map, it's all been detailed . . . our new line of defense. . . ."

After a silence framed by the sounds of battle, Couch said, "Joe, you're not giving me command. You're giving me an order, you're tying my hands. What if—"

"Do as you're told."

Damned hemorrhoids. The enemy within. And under. Jeb Stuart reckoned that if a surgeon cut them out, they'd be Yankee blue, every one.

And the spells of grogginess.

The morning had been a disaster up to that moment, with two grand attacks shattered and soldiers cowering in a shameful spectacle. Now the Yankees had two fresh corps poised on his flank, a nightmare prospect. If they attacked his left, he had no doubt that the entire wing of the army would collapse: The men were already demoralized.

He had . . . failed.

He had a single division left, Rodes' men, and he did not know what else to do but to send Rodes in as he'd sent in Heth and Colston, hoping that this time he'd break the Yankees before they roused themselves and broke him first. The order had already been issued, Rodes' men were moving up. Rodes hadn't said much, just got down to work.

Stuart waited. Fearing that he was squandering all that Jackson had achieved.

Couldn't show it, though. Just dared not show it. Men had to *believe.*

The latest message from Lee made it clear that he was expected to gain the Chancellorsville crossroads, and promptly. Lee was attacking in force now, from the south and east. And Stuart just did not know how to do what others did instinctively, didn't know the magic tricks that Jackson kept hidden in his uniform's pockets.

The only bright spot was the artillery. Alexander had been right. Trusted, he'd seen to it that his guns not only held the Yankees at bay but pressed them back. To Stuart's surprise, those batteries had done what the infantry could not, and he was resolved, in this next, last gasp of an attack, to be certain that Alexander got that other hill, too. He'd made it clear to Dod Ramseur, Rodes' choice for the task, that Fairview had to be taken at any cost.

Let Alexander stack his guns up there and see what came of it.

He was glad he'd chosen to wear a red sash this day.

What if, even now, the Yankees beat him to the punch and attacked his flank as Rodes was going forward?

No choice. He had to take that chance.

His rump grew just plain miserable. Wished he could reach a paw back into his drawers and scratch out some peace.

Couldn't even sneak off and do that.

Rodes men began to appear along the road, flags up, and more emerged from the slashed and battered undergrowth. He didn't see much pleasure shining off them. Word had gotten around of the morning's debacles.

Last chance, last hope.

Just ahead, thousands of men still cowered along those no-good-now entrenchments, a humiliation to all.

Something had to be done.

As Bobby Rodes led his men up, silent and grim, Stuart spurred his horse back to life and rode ahead of the advancing lines. Turning his mount parallel to the human flotsam washed up behind the entrenchments, he rose in his stirrups and began to speak, to announce a confidence he didn't feel:

"Why, look, boys! Here comes Rodes! Set to finish the splendid work you've done."

No one seemed to pay the least attention, but Stuart would not be deterred. He continued:

"Yankees are already quitting. Can't stand up to our guns, let alone you boys. Finest attacks I ever did see, what you done this morning. Bravery folks back home would never believe, just couldn't believe it." He paused for breath, still waiting for men to stir. "Get up now, men. Every man needs to go forward, rally on Rodes, line up with General Rodes."

The mass did not stir.

Rodes men reached them, stepped through them, on them.

And still the soldiers cowered.

There was some rough treatment, a bit too much hard mockery from Rodes' boys.

They did look determined, though. Say that much, and bully for Rodes.

A weight on his heart and an itch back in his rump. Not his loveliest hour.

Near despair, he rode along behind the survivors of the Stonewall Brigade and gave it one last try:

"Damn it, men . . . Jackson just gave his arm for the Cause. And he didn't so much as blink. Is there any man here, right here in the Stonewall Brigade, who wouldn't give as much as Jackson himself?"

Rodes men swept on. Alone.

"Jackson would be here with you, if he could. Missing an arm, boys, he'd still be here to lead you. But he can't. Not today. You've got to do it for him, got to get up on your hind legs and finish his work."

Did one man rise? Two?

"Can't let Old Jack down, men, we just can't do it. Can't report to him this evening that we failed him, after all he did for us. Don't shame yourselves, men. Don't shame Stonewall Jackson. Go forward and make the Yankees shame themselves." As more men rose, he took a deep breath and continued: "They haven't got your hearts, your plain, old guts. Nor other parts to match. Come *on,* men, get up and do your duty by Tom Jackson. . . ."

Miraculously, they did.

Captain Hubert Dilger wanted to fight. He still had five guns left, and his caissons had been refilled, the losses to his crews made good by infantry volunteers. He listened to the artillery duel, which increasingly sounded one-sided, and could not understand why he wasn't called forward. He didn't mind the insults on the lips of the rest of the army: He minded being forced to do nothing at all.

They all wanted to fight, their informal council that morning had been unanimous in favor of going forward, of redeeming reputations unfairly maligned. Schurz, Krzyzanowski, von Steinwehr, Schimmelfennig, even the battered, livid, and limping von Gilsa. And Schurz had told them that Devens and Howard wanted to do their bit, too.

They went ignored.

The corps would fight like beasts now, every officer believed it. Their losses the night before had been terrible, true. By dawn, though, more men had rallied than were expected. The Eleventh Corps was still a fighting concern.

Hubert Dilger limped along his gun line. The muzzles aimed at nothing. He held his teams in harness, ready to respond at once to a summons.

It never came.

* * *

Porter Alexander watched through his glasses as the first red banner climbed the crucial hill. The infantry had found its footing, at last.

He turned to the next-ranking officer on Hazel Grove and told him to shift his guns forward the instant he saw the first Confederate battery go into action atop Fairview. Meanwhile, he would himself guide up the batteries held back for this moment.

He raised the field glasses for a final look. Here and there, scrub forest burned, and the high flames by the crossroads suggested that the Chancellor house was ablaze.

None of that mattered. What mattered was that the Yankee batteries at work were ever fewer.

At West Point, military history had not been his dearest interest, but now he recalled the "Cannonade of Valmy," where an outnumbered French revolutionary army, by the artful use of artillery alone, had convinced the Prussians and their invading allies to abandon the field before one foot soldier advanced.

The fight under way might not be the first battle in history decided by artillery, but Alexander was determined to run those Frenchmen a near second.

He rode forward at a gallop to lead up his guns.

Hadn't gone but a few steps past that ditch and all the quitters before Pickens took him a notion as to why they were reluctant to step off again. The litter of bodies was grayer than most times, grayer by a sight, but the worst was the mass of crawling or plain-stuck wounded who went ignored. That just wasn't how things were meant to be done, just letting them lie like that.

And it got worse. Before one Yankee leveled his rifle toward the 5th Alabama, Pickens reached the first island of flames. Shot-up fellows from both sides struggled frantically to evade the spreading fire, helping each other, blue or gray, if they could. But that wasn't the stick-with-a-man part: It was the shrieks of men burning alive, just screams like you never heard. Some fellows paused, shaken, to try to help, but officers with pistols drawn ordered them to keep moving.

Would've liked to shut his eyes, to be just any place else.

Passing a second flame-licked stretch, he heard more cries for help, and a man couldn't help but look, bad as he might want to look away. One fellow Johnny, leg-ruined and trapped, too terrified even to scream, swatted the encroaching flames with bare hands, slapping at the fire, and there wasn't a way to reach him, unless a man plunged into the flames himself. So Pickens turned his eyes away and moved along, past a sooty patch, with bodies part scorched but still human-looking, clothes burned off most, and it startled him when a tar-black body wasn't dead at all, but weeping and whimpering in some immeasurable anguish as his selfish body took its time to die.

Then the Yankees started shooting at them.

In that unholy instant, Pickens wondered what the world had come to when the lives of white men, the sanctity of their bodies, counted for less than those of the Children of Ham. Where was the fairness in that, when white men burning alive—less than pennies to a wealthy man—didn't merit saving?

His mother was strict about whippings. Not one of her niggers ever got put to discipline unless he deserved and needed it. Even then the manager took care not to damage the property: A slave was worth gold dollars and just wanted chastisement, not ruination.

How was that fair?

The reflection passed, leaving only rage redoubled. He stood there, careless of life, aiming at the Yankees and pulling the trigger, feeling the buck then lowering the butt and fingering up a fresh cartridge, biting the sour, resistant paper and suddenly tasting the tongue-stinging powder, working the ramrod smoothly, not with the awkward jerks of a new recruit—all done so fast that before he knew it, the rifle was up again, with the butt back against his shoulder, hunting Yankees through the smoke.

They rushed forward again, charging, and the Yankees gave way—except for the fools who had to be beaten down.

"Forward!"

Not a man needed that order now. The company, the regiment, shared one desire, begat by bloodlust luxuriant, inspired by a gorgeous, barbaric longing to deal out pain, to prove the master, to be done with civilization and its fussing.

Previous assaults had beaten paths through the brush, so things went quicker. The Alabamians skirted the burning stretches and stepped over the bodies, and Pickens found himself delighted, captivated, to be part of it, running on past Yankees fallen or surrendered and let be, their bewildered, bearded faces fit for remembrance. One Federal who thought too highly of himself was beaten down by half a dozen men who took exception. Wasn't getting up again, that fellow.

Onward.

Volleys.

Halt. Re-form the line.

"On my command . . ."

Just standing there and firing, actions repetitious as a mechanical doll he'd seen one time in a shop window in Montgomery.

Shells screamed overhead, their destination some unlucky place behind the Yankee line. Reb yells swelled like a tide, drowning the fewer and fewer Yankee cheers. The volleys, the lone shots, the cries, the hoarse-throated orders, the smoke . . . were immeasurably intoxicating, better than smuggled rum.

"Forward!"

They monkey-climbed their way over another Yankee barricade, hooting and bragging to all the world with noises, not words, unstoppable.

A lone Yankee fieldpiece let go a burst of canister. It struck just at the edge of the Greensboro Guards. And someone cried:

"Doc's hit!"

Pickens could not help himself: He turned from a muddled firing line and scanned the tortured landscape for Doc Cowin.

Got to him just as Bill Lenier did, too.

Doc's eyes were wondrous and his legs were gone. Bright blood pumped from what remained of a thigh. Leaned against a tree, Doc declared:

"I'm gone, boys, I'm gone. I'm done."

Then he almost smiled and told them:

"'Ask for me tomorrow and you shall find me a grave man.'"

"Doc, you got a message for anybody? Anything?" Bill Lenier asked.

They didn't get an answer. Captain Williams stood over them with his Colt pointed first at Pickens then at Lenier.

"You boys get up and get back in that line."

Doc seemed to deflate as the blood spurted out of him.

"No need for that," Bill Lenier told the captain. "We're going."

"Now. Or I'll blow your head off."

They got up, saying quick goodbyes to Doc, already moving. And Doc, in a ghastly, tormented voice, called after them:

"'I am dying, Egypt, dying . . .'"

Bill Lenier just said, "I'll miss old Doc," and they went back to killing.

Advancing again, coughing through layers of smoke, they broke into a great open space and saw they were not alone: Other Confederates had reached it even before them, swarming and overrunning everything Yankee. Bricks sizzling, a house burned away. Dead mules and horses dotted the field like boulders defying the plow. At the far edge, by a road off to the right, bands of Yankees fought on, but a fellow sensed that the work was nearly done.

"Come on, men! Forward, Alabama! Ain't nobody going to claim we lagged behind. . . ."

Elation! Exaltation! The thrill of winning subdued bad feet and even the body's hunger to survive. They crossed that field and its wastage at a half-run, weariness forgotten. Nobody would outdistance Alabama.

The paltry resistance the Yankees put up was no more than the nip of a granny's pet dog. The blue-bellies were finished and Alabama was going to make damned sure of it.

They crashed into more undergrowth, a realm less trampled, without wounded men or corpses: They'd passed beyond the battlefield, plunging like a gray dagger into the heart of the Yankee army. No man paused for even a moment as they crossed a clearing where a Federal commissary wagon had overturned, spilling its treasures.

"Alabama!"

Not so many answering voices now. Pickens looked around. Just a handful of men left, familiar faces that had come this far, Greensboro men. Flag was still with them, though. He met Bill Lenier's eyes. Didn't need words, they understood each other's unspoken question:

We alone out here?

The Yankees answered the question for them. Firing at them from what seemed to be every direction. Men took to their knees and replied, but there wasn't much to the answer.

"You Johnnies give up," a voice recommended when the shooting lulled. "Don't want to kill you boys, if we don't have to. You give up now, you just gone too far."

The dozen men left kept to their knees, seething and ready but pondering. One fool fired into the brush. A sight more Yankees fired back.

A Northern voice, the officer sort, called, "Cease firing, men! Cease fire!" Then: "You Rebs are surrounded, have yourselves a look. And be sensible."

Fellow from another company stripped the regiment's flag from its pole, balled it, and tossed it deep into the briars. The blue-bellies were going to have to work to get it.

Another Yankee asked, "You Johnnies done your mathematics yet?"

One man after another rose slowly, holding his rifle high in the air, butt heavenward, in a gesture of surrender.

* * *

With a fine horse dead and a nag stuffed under him now, Major General Winfield Scott Hancock steered through the chaos, imperturbable, bracing up his brigades as they held open the gauntlet north of the Chancellor fields. Avoiding another withdrawing regiment, he cantered up to Tommy Meagher, whose Irish Brigade held the most exposed position.

"I see your green rag's waving," Hancock said.

"And wave it shall. We'll not be troubled to lower it."

"That's the spirit, Tommy."

The Reb bombardment shifted again, tormenting their position where it spilled from field to grove. It was the fiercest gunnery work that Hancock had ever endured, slaughtering the already slaughtered and making it impossible to drag the wounded from the burning woods.

"Not the prettiest ball I've ever attended," Meagher noted.

"Goddamned fucking shambles," Hancock said.

"A man might put it that way, Win." Meagher grinned and added, "If he had your poet's heart."

Hancock firmed up his jaw again. "Tommy, they'll come back at you. Soon. They've got their piss up."

"And we'll knock the last drop out of them."

A shell's impact hurled dirt at their faces, their eyes. Hancock forced his expression to remain stoic, but he couldn't recall being in so grim a position, with his brigades fighting nearly back-to-back, taking fire from three sides and threatened by the mass of Lee's gathered army, gripping a narrow strip of earth to allow the last of Slocum's men to escape the trap the Rebs were closing on them.

"You know, Win," Meagher said, reading his mood, "whenever the doings are fit to discommode me, I tell meself, 'Oh, 'tisn't as bad as Fredericksburg.'" The Irishman smiled again, his teeth imperfect. "Although there's novelty enough, with a burning house to one side and Jesus knows what on the other."

"Just hold on," Hancock told him. "Fifteen more minutes, Tommy, then I can pull you back."

Meagher saluted with a light touch and said, "You know, Win, time's the queerest thing of all. A Christian man ponders eternity for decades, only to find it's fifteen minutes long."

Funk doubted he'd ever forget the burned men, their limbs curled skyward, as if they'd died fending off a last attacker.

He supposed they had: the flames.

If he had to die, let it not be thus.

The Stonewall Brigade—what remained of it—followed him eagerly now. The change was unaccountable, but welcome. Infused with spirit again, made all but fearless, they ignored their losses as they followed orders barked and bellowed, one tendril of a massive gray leviathan. They had closed with one breaking Yankee line, man to man, and the melee had become a contest of fists and even teeth.

Victors with blood on their faces laughed like madmen.

Funk led them forward again and again, through smoldering tangles and over uprooted trees, with bodies scattered everywhere and the worst of the wounded begging to be shot.

"Virginia! Remember Jackson!"

But war cries weren't even needed. The men were drunk with bloodlust. In that inexplicable way soldiers grasped the uncanny, they sensed that they were winning and would not be stopped. Exhausted and filthy, canteens empty, bleeding and unaware of it, his men—how easily they had become *his* men, in the strangeness of war, the grand unfairness—were literally racing with the brigades on their flanks to reach the crossroads. And every Yankee attempt at holding them back seemed frailer and doomed.

They swept over a Federal artillery position already cleared. The Yankees had dragged off their precious guns, but the field was strewn with horrors. Disemboweled horses and caissons blown to pieces thickened the wastage, but here the gun crews had had the worst of the luck. Torsos sprawled fifteen feet from hips, with guts laced in between. Heads had been torn away, leaving spikes of bone with crimson scarves. One man, still bubbling blood, had a beard but no face. His hand jerked and fell, jerked and fell. A sergeant had been cut through from shoulder to belly, the sides of his body opened out like the petals on a flower. Bowels curled on the earth, sausages scorned by the butcher. A boy missing an arm, a leg, and an eye dragged himself along.

But the worst of it remained those burned alive.

The sputtering Yankee artillery found his men, but they kept going.

After thrusting forward nearly a mile, as Funk judged the distance, the bled-thin brigade burst into a broad field, joining a vast confusion of other Confederates pressing forward, converging from multiple sides on a burning house and Yankee scraps.

Bone-weary men ran like boys. Funk had difficulty keeping up.

Thousands of voices cheered. Red flags waved by the dozen.

Lord, Funk thought, if the Yankees had a gun line ready now, wouldn't we be in for it?

But the Yankees had no batteries up. Old Hooker appeared to have ceded his ground.

Funk shouted himself hoarse, willing his command to reassemble. Short-tempered with his officers, he found it a marvel that men—amid all this—would actually heed him.

Rounded upon by their lieutenants and captains—those officers still on their feet—soldiers returned to their flags, boys summoned by the dinner bell. Others snatched Yankee loot from pack or haversack before rallying.

The re-formed brigade was hardly the size of one regiment, but somehow, in that moment, staring at those blackened faces, admiring the sweat and stink and elation and weariness, it didn't matter. It only mattered that they had not failed.

Up past the crackling house, a Yankee line emerged from the woods and halted. Funk advanced his men to meet the threat, but the Yankees melted back into the trees.

"Reckon some lieutenant took a wrong turn," a soldier commented.

"What do we do now, sir?" a major asked.

"Load back up on cartridges."

Blasted day. Blasted, blasted, *blasted*.

As his lips dueled with a tin cup of mud coffee, Sickles hoped the Rebs would attack one more time. Arrayed in its new position, his corps was ready, the entire army was. They had a solid defensive position now, with entrenchments that improved as the minutes passed, and the river shielded both of the army's flanks. Someone even appeared to have taken charge of the artillery. If they tried just one more rush, the graybacks would not have the advantages—or his boys the disadvantages—of the morning.

True as all that was, it did not help. They had been defeated. Severely. It was just difficult to face it. Whether the Rebs attacked again or not, the campaign was lost, and it didn't take a West Point man to see it. The question was how long things would drag on.

Damn Joe, though. Damn all his hollow vainglory.

Informed that Joe had taken a knock on the head, Sickles had been too busy fighting, withdrawing, and repositioning his battle-bitten troops to look in on his friend and ally, but he hoped the blow had knocked sense into him.

Joe had made a hash of it. There was no excuse for his cascade of mistakes, although, of course, excuses would be found—Sickles already knew that his outrage would pass. He'd stick up for his friend, should congressional meddlers require testimony. His butter was all on that side of the bread, and he didn't intend to ever go hungry again.

That part of the business would be all right. An iron law of politics held that someone else could always be given the blame. The Germans would do, for a start, as long as the charges didn't spread to all foreigners: The Irish were valuable Tammany constituents.

Nonetheless, the campaign had been costly. Victory had been handed to Robert E. Lee. A little shame would touch everyone involved. It was time to stay in the shadows and not play the peacock. Joe had to demonstrate that much common sense.

Filthy mess, all of it. And needless. Sickles felt things he knew he would never say.

He was proud of his soldiers, though. His Third Corps had fought ferociously. As had Slocum's men, to be fair. Ruger had been astonishing, a lion. And Hancock, Couch's trump card, had just withdrawn his last brigade in good order. . . . Win deserved a corps as soon as one opened up.

A grand-looking fellow popular with the troops, Hancock could have a winning future in politics after the war. The party needed men from Pennsylvania, and Win seemed to lean Democrat. . . .

All that had to be kept mum, of course. Until Lincoln blessed any new appointment and brought along the Stevens Republicans.

And a corps command for Win might appease the army's Pennsylvania faction. Meade would be out for blood, but Reynolds was circumspect and Gibbon didn't count, at least not yet. They needed to keep an eye on Andy Humphreys, though: There was nothing more corrosive in politics than a man of integrity.

Army scheming made Tammany seem genteel.

As ambulances and ammunition wagons contested the trail that pioneers had cut, Sickles' thoughts returned again to his soldiers. He'd never thought he would feel such affection for them—at first, he'd seen the men of his Excelsior Brigade only as postwar votes up on two legs, saloon suckers to be bribed with beer and city jobs for the ward boys. But as he'd risen in command and led men from other states, too, they'd fought so hard and so well, time and again, that he'd come to respect them as men and even as citizens. And today they'd bled severely. . . .

How could courage be so utterly useless? Wasn't that a fundamental question? The grating truth was that the sacrifices of the day had not mattered. None of the dying and bleeding had done any good. Joe had been getting things wrong for days, and he wouldn't listen, and men with unknown names had paid the price, men of flesh and blood, with families, decent men who trusted those above them. . . .

Don't be an ass, he warned himself. Sentiment was the enemy of judgment. Always. The dead were dead, and mawkishness helped no one. Save it for campaign speeches.

He held out the tin cup. "More coffee," he told an aide. "And put something in it."

In the splendid early days, when the war had been nothing more than a rush to the tailor shop, Sickles had envisioned easy glory. Even now, he expected his service to revive his career in Washington or, at least, in New York. He'd learned a great deal in camps and on the battlefields, not least that heroism was no cure for folly, and a hundred lesser successes could not make up for one crucial mistake.

Of course, life had already instructed him on that last point. He'd just been slow to learn.

Beyond the smoldering trees to Sickles' front, waves of Rebel cheering rose from the fields his men had lost.

He reached for a cigar but had none left.

The men cheered him as he had never been cheered before. As Robert E. Lee rode northward, trailed by his staff, his soldiers in their thousands opened a lane for him to pass. Men by the roadside threw their hats in the air or raised them on the muzzles of their rifles, pumping them skyward. The boldest soldiers reached out to touch not Lee but the flank of his horse. Faces grimed with power, men wept ecstatically.

They chanted: "Lee, Lee, *Lee*!"

He took off his hat and slackened the reins, letting Traveller take him forward.

These men knew how grim their own struggles had been. They knew the price paid by their companies and regiments. But did they grasp the magnificence of their victory? The fearful odds they'd faced? The desperation?

He suspected they did. They might not express it in refined

words or even in cruder language, but in their souls, in a sanctum of the spirit, they understood.

He raised his hat above his head, holding it up as though it were their trophy.

"It is good," he said. "You have done well. It is good."

The crowds of soldiers grew thicker still as men broke from reformed ranks to join the multitude. As he approached the vital crossroads, charred brick walls and lingering flames drew his eyes. Yes, war was terrible for the innocent. And many a home had been lost, his own property seized and his wife dispossessed, his nephew's fine house victim to sanctioned arson, so much ruination, such waste. But it could not be helped.

The press of soldiers spared him the sight of the nearest dead, of another army's wreckage, but he already sensed the terrible cost of this day. He did not need to wait for the casualty lists.

The price had had to be paid and must not be regretted. To think too much of losses courted defeat.

He did rue the loss of Jackson, though, for even the briefest period. As the man who had breathed life into a plan any other general would have resisted, Thomas Jackson had a right to be here, riding beside him.

Again, Lee felt the odd twinge in his heart, one more concern.

He must not be despondent, not on this day, not amid this clearing smoke with a good May sun above, and not before these men. The Lord might permit him to indulge his pride, just for this hour.

Soldiers laid captured flags beside his path.

The work was unfinished, the fight must be renewed, Hooker had to be pushed into the river, it had to be done, and soon.

But this moment was of spun gold. Lee's mind already had passed far beyond his humbled opponent. With this army, with these men . . . so much more might be possible.

He fixed his gaze northward, Caesar eyeing Gaul.

Amid the magnificent tumult, a rider from the rear forced his way through the crowd. Alerted, Lee turned and saw Marshall intercept the man, a lieutenant.

He let himself bask in the cheers again. By God's grace, this day had seen a miracle. David had brought low Goliath.

Was there anything these men could not do?

Jackson would return soon, would not let him down, wouldn't dally a moment. Then they would drive this war to its conclusion.

The press of reeking humanity became so great that Traveller could not go forward. The cheers had the force of artillery. Red flags waved at the brink of madness.

He was about to chide the men to let him pass, when Marshall forced his way forward, rough-handing soldiers when necessary.

"You must hear this, sir," the military secretary called, leaning from his horse. "Lieutenant Pitzer just came from Fredericksburg. He claims General Early's been driven south and Sedgwick's advancing toward Chancellorsville."

Lee's face remained impassive as he said:

"There is still more work to be done."

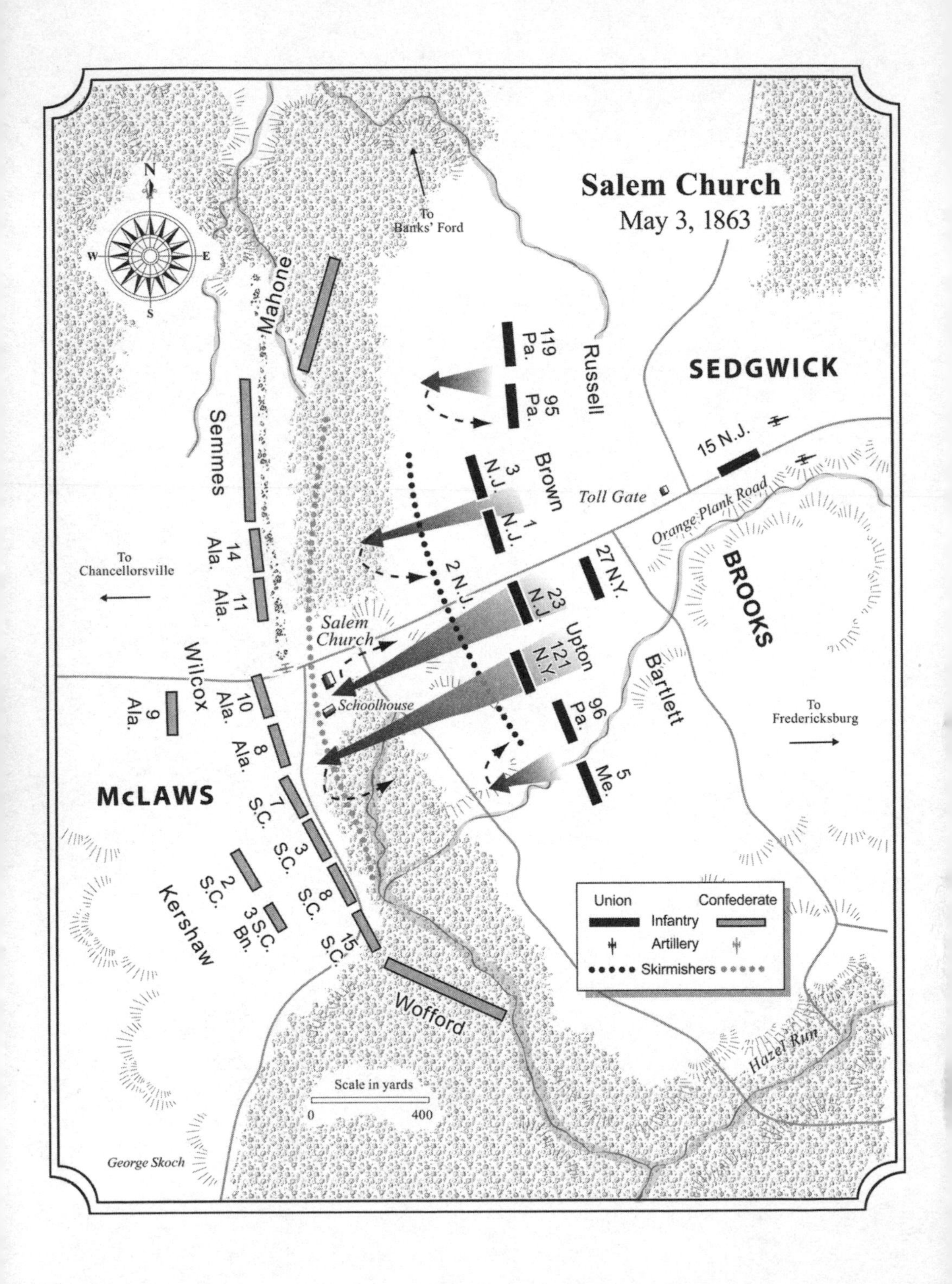
Salem Church
May 3, 1863
To Banks' Ford
Mahone
Semmes
14 Ala.
11 Ala.
To Chancellorsville
Wilcox
9 Ala.
10 Ala.
8 Ala.
McLAWS
7 S.C.
3 S.C.
2 S.C.
Kershaw
3 S.C. Bn.
8 S.C.
15 S.C.
Wofford
119 Pa.
95 Pa.
Russell
SEDGWICK
3 N.J.
Brown
1 N.J.
2 N.J.
15 N.J.
Toll Gate
Orange Plank Road
27 N.Y.
23 N.J.
BROOKS
Salem Church
Schoolhouse
Upton
121 N.Y.
Bartlett
96 Pa.
5 Me.
To Fredericksburg
Union
Confederate
Infantry
Artillery
Skirmishers
Hazel Run
Scale in yards
0
400
George Skoch

ELEVEN

Afternoon, May 3
Between Fredericksburg and Chancellorsville

Cad Wilcox tugged his gelding aside to let a gun section pass. Straw hat pushed back on his head and hickory switch in hand, he'd been mounting a delaying action since noon, shaking out skirmishers, putting up brief resistance at key points, and constantly shifting the handful of cavalry troopers he'd pressed into service—all to slow the Yankee Sixth Corps, a behemoth compared to his Alabama Brigade.

He'd been cut off from Early's Division when the Yankees swarmed over the heights at Fredericksburg. Now his men were all that remained between the Federals and Lee's rear at Chancellorsville.

He welcomed the challenge.

It was the first time in the war that he'd been entirely his own man, able to implement infantry tactics precisely as he'd taught them to the cadets:

Put up the pretense of a fixed defense, forcing the enemy to deploy into battle lines, then withdraw to the next position under artillery cover. Alternate heavy skirmish lines with Jaeger bands to "amuse" the enemy. Use the strength of the foe's formations against him, forcing him to unfold his column and then re-form again. Inflict delays, not necessarily casualties. When necessary, fight.

Fighting—real fighting—would soon be necessary.

Wilcox did wish he had one particular witness to his performance: his friend Tom Jackson, who lay severely wounded. For that matter, he wouldn't have minded having Sam Grant, long his dearest friend, observing him, too.

His mind deserted the battlefield for a moment, flying to Grant's wedding out in Missouri, when they served at Jefferson Barracks in better times. He'd been Sam's best man. Julia had looked lovely, her father dubious. Sam had appeared high-nerved and immeasurably happy, disbelieving his good fortune. Of course, Grant shouldered his share of hard times afterward, nor did he seem to be prospering on the Mississippi this spring: Vicksburg was a harder nut than Donelson.

Gone into battery on the road and in the yard of the tollhouse, the section of Napoléons he'd placed teased the oncoming Yankees, lofting shells over blue skirmishers to annoy the robust columns marching westward.

When might he hear from Lee? Or Early, who had disappeared down the Telegraph Road? Wilcox knew the ground from a shivering winter: He'd have to make his real stand at Salem Church and that schoolhouse, hardly an artillery shot away. That's where military art would break down into a death match, where all the books on tactics would avail little, where Yankee numbers would tell. He'd already sent back two regiments, with instructions as to how they should position themselves, but he wouldn't be able to hold very long against an entire corps without reinforcements. He had expected support to arrive by now.

Meanwhile, every small advantage mattered.

The afternoon grew hotter as the sun declined, hard on men who'd been on their feet since dawn. His soldiers were game, enjoying this agile fraud, but empty canteens and double-quick dashes wore on them. You could only ask so much of an honest soldier.

Tom Jackson would disagree, of course, demanding that the soldiers bend to his will. Strange Tom, so awkwardly kind to intimates, so brutal in a fight. If the running rumors were accurate, Tom should recover just fine, but you never really knew about wounds until the fickle body made its decisions. He was just getting over a visitation of dysentery himself—so much for the charms of war.

To his front, the blue-clad skirmishers advanced gingerly, determined but wary, pressing across fields that marked the last respectable cultivation—the last civilization—before the primeval Wilderness began. This was indeed a battle*field*, and the church just to his rear marked its hind end.

Turning a churchyard into a butcher's shop, and on a Sunday. Tom would not have approved, and yet he would have done it himself, if necessary. Then he would have prayed over his sin, begging forgiveness.

Wilcox had always liked Jackson, from their time as West Point classmates, when Tom had been stiff as an oak tree and just as rustic, and during the thrilling hazards of Mexico, right up to this fateful day. Yet he couldn't have explained exactly why he was so fond of the man, other than his own conviviality. Jackson was the most unlikable likable man he knew.

Maybe it was the innocence. Tom had always seemed the most innocent of men, even amid slaughter.

Wilcox prayed he'd be all right. The army needed Tom.

"Hurry on there, hurry along, boys!" Wilcox called to his retiring skirmishers, sweat-drenched, soot-faced men striding rearward to reorganize and resume their task anew. In the road just to his front, an artillery lieutenant barked orders to switch to spherical case. Wouldn't let the Federals get close enough to need canister. Not here.

Back at the church, though.

Sedgwick had not been a fireball as he advanced, and that was a blessing. His corps was coming on more steadily now, but still didn't seem in a hurry. Methodical Uncle John, another likable fellow from the old Army. Well, let him advance as slowly as he liked. . . .

During his teaching days at the Point, Wilcox had stressed alacrity and speed. Now he wanted everything to slow down.

A Yankee battery went into action a thousand yards away, replying to his carefully husbanded guns. Almost time to pull them off. Daren't lose a piece, not yet.

He did enjoy it all, though. Just had to admit it. Applying the rules he knew so well, issuing confident orders, making the system work without interference. And, thus far, he'd kept his casualties to a minimum. Never did relish bleeding his own men.

Judge the time, judge it perfectly. Stretch the leathers until they're about to snap. Then move sharply.

The foremost Yankee skirmishers paused to fire, waiting for their leading brigade to unfold again.

Four more minutes, Wilcox judged, and then he'd leapfrog back. The regimental commanders present glanced in his direction, nerves alight and waiting on a command. Wilcox offered a smile in return.

Time it just right. Then skedaddle. Back to the church and that first fringe of forest. And one last surprise for the Yankees.

Riding a surge of confidence, of pride, Wilcox pondered Jackson again and granted himself a last interlude of reverie, recalling that night of mild dissipation in Brown's Hotel in Washington, on furlough after graduating West Point. As nobodies, they'd been consigned to a sweatbox of a room on the top floor, four of them packed together—in a cholera summer—and Tom had gotten drunk unto singing and dancing in his unmentionables, inflamed by the bottle for, perhaps, the only time in his life. The next day, Jackson's desolation had been so morbid it made his more experienced classmates laugh.

Hard not to be a touch jealous of Tom's success, of course. On the eve of war, folks would have bet on him, Cadmus Marcellus Wilcox, to rise rapidly, while no one had thought much of Tom, but Wilcox languished atop a brigade, dutiful but undistinguished, while Jackson had risen like a Congreve rocket.

He didn't want to be jealous, didn't believe in it. But it was hard sometimes.

Today was his day, though.

He tapped his mount with his switch and rode his line.

* * *

General Bartlett rode up in a mood so black he seemed to darken the sun. Campbell did his best to turn invisible amid the clinging dust and sudden bustle. They were in for it now, he suspected.

The brigade commander reined up beside his favorite regimental colonel, Campbell's superior.

"Upton," Bartlett began, "this is going too slow. Might as well crawl along on our hands and knees." The general swallowed the cloud that his arrival had created, cleared his throat, and spit. "I want *you* to take the lead, push ahead while Edwards re-forms. Move fast and get your teeth into the Johnnies."

"They're ready to make a stand, sir," the boy-faced colonel said.

The colonel's certainty annoyed the brigadier. "How do you know that, Upton? They haven't dared fight us yet. They just make us dance like monkeys then stop the music." The general grunted. "I wish they *would* make a goddamned stand, we'd maul the sons-ofbitches."

As Campbell expected, his colonel winced at the mild profanity. Emory Upton did not smoke, drink, curse, or play cards, and there was always a Bible on his field desk.

"I'll see to them, sir," the colonel said.

"You do that. Catch 'em and pitch into 'em. The rest of the brigade will be behind you, if I have to horsewhip every man into the fight." Bartlett grunted again. "Go on. Get moving."

Campbell didn't wait for the general's party to ride off or even for an order from his colonel. He began shouting back to his fellow officers to get their idling men back on the road and do it quickly.

When Campbell turned again, Upton just nodded.

Wiry, abruptly terrifying, and twenty-three years old, Colonel Emory Upton was an officer his soldiers would never love. But, Campbell knew, they had learned to admire and trust him. When Upton took command of the 121st New York, the regiment had been an untrained shambles, with drunken officers disappearing from camp and lassitude the rule for everyone else, its ranks drained by the worst sick lists in the army. Upton had enforced stern sanitation, improved the men's diet, drilled them to exhaustion, and worked his officers so hard that the political men and debauchees resigned. The soldiers had cursed him to the nether regions, and neighboring regiments had mocked the endlessly parading New Yorkers as "Upton's Regulars."

Ever so gradually, the men had come to embrace that name with pride.

If Upton proved right, as he usually did, and they were about to fight, it would be their trial by fire. At Fredericksburg, in December, they'd merely looked on behind a screen of skirmishers. Even that morning, their brigade had marched from the rear of the corps, unmolested.

Now here they were. With hooting, shooting, flesh-and-blood Rebs to their front.

Polite and savage, Upton led the men forward, straight up the road. Jutting cheekbones gave the colonel the look of a youthful Mongol.

Campbell watched the last Rebs—tiny figures—pull off the crest ahead, flitting away before the New Yorkers' sister regiment could move forward and catch them.

Upton's expression remained that of a Christian who feared no hellfire.

A stone-cut Methodist, the colonel came from the burned-over district of western New York, a realm of religious revivals, curiosities, and fanaticism, and the rural New Yorkers he led found him no phenomenon. For Campbell, though, his colonel was passing strange: A rigid abolitionist, Upton conversed with Negroes as normally and respectfully as if he were chatting with white men, his voice and choice of words the same as if passing the time with a neighbor or a cousin, without distaste or the slightest condescension.

Once, Campbell had alluded to Upton's treatment of the Negroes they encountered and the colonel had appeared genuinely surprised.

"Why, Campbell," he'd said, "they're the same as you and I."

Upton did not impose his beliefs on his soldiers, other than disdaining vulgar speech, but Campbell had come to know him well enough to realize he would never know him well, grasping only that Emory Upton was a crusader.

Erect in the saddle, the colonel gained the crest the Rebs had abandoned. Halting the regiment, he called back, "Skirmishers forward. Double-quick!"

As the designated companies trotted briskly to the fore, Upton turned to Campbell and pointed at a building in the distance.

"That church," Upton said. "That's where they're going to fight."

Major General John Sedgwick was frustrated enough to kick a mule and see what happened. From the porch of the house where his staff had stopped to attempt to speed the march to Chancellorsville, the hastening columns of his corps looked potent enough. But he worried that he'd made one fateful mistake.

Following Hooker's orders—clear orders at last—he had advanced. But the heights that trumped the army back in December had been judged, from a distant headquarters, to be only lightly defended and easily seized. Instead, the morning had been a bloody mess, with punishing losses before they took the ridge and a bundle of captured Rebs no consolation. At last, he could have destroyed Early's Division, eating it whole, but his orders forbade him from following Early south. Obedient, he had turned the Sixth Corps west toward Chancellorsville, but his lead divisions had been so disarranged by the morning fight that he'd felt the need to call up Bully Brooks, whose men had gone unscathed. Their march from rear to fore had cost him two hours. Now, with the afternoon on the wane, he wasn't halfway to a union with the rest of the army.

Worse, the battle noise off to the west had all but stopped. And it did not indicate a Union victory, or there would have been Reb fugitives on the roads. John Sedgwick felt his confidence slipping.

He should have driven on immediately, letting his battered brigades lick their wounds on the march. If he had a weakness, he knew, it was his reluctance to waste his soldiers' lives. And he'd squandered enough that morning.

On top of it all, Southern captives taken from Early insisted that Longstreet was marching to their rescue with two more divisions. Sharpe dismissed the reports, but the colonel in charge of spying was back at headquarters and bore no responsibility for tens of thousands of soldiers.

Sedgwick turned to Marty McMahon, his chief of staff and a good man who still felt the loss of a brother. "Bring the horses around, I can't stomach this nonsense. I'm going forward to prod Bully Brooks with a pitchfork."

No," Wilcox told his regimental commanders, "we're not going to hold the tree line. That's what the Yankees expect."

He gestured to right and left of the church and the schoolhouse, beyond the interval of cleared ground to the arms of forest reaching toward the road, with trees and brush a few hundred yards in depth.

"Williams, Sanders, you've seen the ditch. And the rifle pits from last winter. Guide your brother colonels to their positions."

"That ditch, it's inside the woods, sir. And toward the rear, at that."

Wilcox offered his usual, friendly smile. Behind him, his rallied guns went into action, harassing the Yankees.

"You're thinking just the way the Yankees will," Wilcox continued. "When they realize we're not in the tree line, waiting, they'll come sauntering through the undergrowth, full of confidence. And the brush will break up their formations. Then, when they catch the sun-dazzle from the far side, when they're blind and expecting nothing, you'll give them a volley then keep pouring fire into them."

"Hard part's going to be holding the center, General. Even with that church there and the rifle pits, it's wide open, no meat on that bone. And the Yankees got plenty of fat to throw in the pan."

"Just hold the shoulders, gentlemen. Any Yankees push through that gap, we'll close in behind 'em once the others run off." He smiled again and looked around at faces that shone with sweat. "Unless you object to taking a herd of prisoners."

"No, sir. Never did have no objection to that."

Wilcox released his colonels to see to their men. He was confident he could give the Yankees a time of it. But he knew he couldn't hold forever, not once the Yankees cottoned to the trick and brought up more men.

It was all about that gay deceiver, time.

His life had not been a bad one. More fair things than foul. But he never had witnessed a miracle. Until that minute.

A small party of horsemen cantered up from the rear, banners trailing. As they closed on the hillock that hosted the church and his guns, Wilcox spotted the bearded bulk of McLaws. He waved to show his position.

A big man fond of his vittles, McLaws swung his bulk from his horse to punish the earth. Sweat-sheathed and grinning, he tugged off his riding gloves and whewed at the heat.

"Now what the devil you been up to, Cadmus? I hear you been having yourself a party and didn't send me an invite. So I came anyway."

"Invitation must have gone astray. How far back are your men, sir?"

McLaws gestured rearward. "See 'em any minute."

"If I may ask a favor, sir . . . do what you can to keep them out of sight, hold them back of the woods. Extend the flanks on both sides, but lay low and no flags up. Let the Yankees run into a fine surprise." Wilcox caught himself: McLaws outranked him, it was his fight now. "Not trying to tell you how to suck eggs, General," he added. "I'm under your orders."

McLaws reinforced a grin that had welcomed many a chicken and ham in its time. "Good old Cadmus . . . no, brother Cad, this is *your* fight, you know the ground. Consider me under your orders. And let's whip us some blue-bellies."

* * *

Thought it was over. Thought it was dogged out and done. Thought it was all wrapped up with a bow atop it.

Now this. Sweating like a pig in an overcoat. Rushing back over all-too-familiar fields because there wasn't enough road to go around, not just marching but nigh on to running, with General McLaws shouting orders to Little Billy, and Mahone, all sass and lightning, passing them on to Lieutenant Colonel Feild and the jump-to-it others.

Cannon pounded up ahead. Not many, but enough.

Only a few hours earlier they'd been cheering Robert E. Lee and victory, certain the 12th Virginia and its neighbors had earned a respite after the morning's fuss. Now Bill Smith and his messmates knew plain as day and dark as night that their troubles weren't over.

At least his comrades were too heat-burdened to resume their teasing that all of this was his fault, that if he hadn't built a bridge just for the Yankees, they wouldn't have come calling this-away. It wasn't true, every man knew it. But it stung.

Just ate at him like termites under the porch, knowing that his work served filthy Yankees.

Heat had him on the verge of the dizzies, too, but he would not falter.

Little Billy himself came trotting along, the biggest little man in Confederate gray, with a beard fit to tickle the ground when he took him a squat.

"I don't want any cheering," Little Billy called, voice bigger than his chest. "I want *doing*, not hollering. Y'all move right along and go where you're told, you step out now. Don't want to hear any jabbering. Let your rifles talk. Now you step out."

He rode on to the next regiment.

"Don't mean it in an insulting way," John Wagoner said, "but that man is the downright meanest underfed rat-terrier I ever saw."

"You ain't seen his wife," a voice declared.

"Go for them, Upton!" General Bartlett ordered. "I can't wait for the others to form, the Rebs are already running, their artillery's pulling off. Guide left of the road, left of that church, clear them out of the trees. I'll send these slow-bottomed sonsofbitches forward as soon as I can, you'll be supported."

Emory Upton's 121st New York had all but finished deploying into line, its well-drilled movements precise and, to the colonel, beautiful.

"Yes, sir," was all he said. His salute was practiced and perfect.

He felt unleashed. Before Bartlett could add another word, the colonel bellowed:

"Regimennnt!"

Company captains repeated the command.

"Fowarrrrd . . ."

Another echo.

"March!"

He ordered his staff to dismount but remained in the saddle himself and drew his sword.

Upton had left West Point as an artilleryman, and he'd found gunnery enjoyable, the admixture of mathematics and inspiration. But nothing rivaled the thrill of men by the hundreds responding at once to his voice. And promotions were far swifter in the infantry—he'd leapt from captain to colonel at one stroke. Upton intended to end the war as a major general.

He guided his mount to the center of the regiment's first line, calling:

"Officers, guide your companies on me."

He fixed his attention ahead, on his probing skirmishers, as they covered the last open stretch to the wood line. Another hundred paces and those men would face a volley, he was certain.

Just to his left, the regiment's colors sagged in motionless air. But the blue lines that stretched out to the flanks were as polished in their movements as if on parade. Their uniforms were dusty, but his men bore themselves as *soldiers.*

He was glad of Bartlett's order to advance straight on and to do it without delay. For troops who'd never seen the elephant, simplicity was best.

The boldest skirmishers passed the mark where Upton had expected the first volley. The Reb's own skirmishers had long since disappeared.

Were they running?

Don't assume.

Be ready.

The foremost skirmishers had almost reached the wood line.

He *still* expected a volley.

None came.

Upton sensed the high nerves of the skirmishers as they eased into the brush, slowing like watches running down. Delaying. Wary. Eager for the regiment to close the distance between them, to offer a fictive safety.

Upton glanced back over his horse's rump. To his right rear, the 23rd New Jersey appeared ready to step off.

A few shots cracked through the trees. Just enough firing, Upton realized, to slow his skirmishers further. He was tempted to gallop forward and order them to drive hard into the woods. But he had a regiment to lead, he had to maintain control. And all discipline began with self-discipline.

He did not pray. Not now. But he had prayed mightily the night before and again in the morning. Now the day's result was up to the Lord, whose reasons were beyond men's comprehension.

If he were to fall—he did not believe he would—his soul was clean and his cause had been noble and just.

Surely the Lord wished all men who might heed the call of Christ to be free of bondage, no matter their color. When he had studied at Oberlin College, preparing himself for West Point, had there been any difference between the white students and the Negroes who read and worked problems beside them? Only, perhaps, that the coloreds took greater pains to be neatly dressed, even when threadbare, and to sit upright and demonstrate good manners. Were *they* meant to live in shackles? Men and even women versed in Latin and trigonometry? How could an entire race, in all its mortal variety, be subjected to slavery by Christians?

His front rank neared the tree line, the bafflingly innocent grove.

"Colorrrrs . . . trail," he ordered. He wanted only rifles to the fore.

The skirmishers had barely penetrated fifty yards into the trees, their jagged line detectable despite the foliage.

Upton's horse neighed and balked. He applied the spurs and the beast plunged into the thickets.

As his men battled briars and low-hanging limbs, officers and sergeants urged them forward, touching backs with the flats of swords or using a well-judged fist when necessary. The noise of their progress, of man against nature, warned all Creation: The regiment sounded like cows spooked in the canebrake.

Upton peered ahead, into the tree gloom. Thorns cut the oiled leather of his boots and vines snaked over his stirrups. The air stank of condensed heat.

"Forward . . . steady the lines . . . forward . . ."

He glimpsed the end of the grove ahead, a golden glow. Jacob's ladders of sunlight dusted the greenery.

The shock of the Reb volley, the blaze, made the forest quiver. Men cried out. Upton's horse revolted, squirting blood.

He jumped clear. Thumping against the trunk of a tree, he felt a bolt of pain. His horse collapsed at his feet. Ordering a private to save his saddle, he collected his sword and drew out his revolver.

"Fix bayonets!"

His men obeyed. Steel grated on steel.

"At the double-quick . . . forward . . . *charge!*"

Sword in his right hand, Colt in the left, Upton led the way, undaunted by a second volley unleashed almost in his face. With a hurrah, his men dashed for the Rebs, their bravery heedless, surprising. It was hard to keep up.

"Officers . . . forward, *forward!*"

He heard cheers—Union cheers—to his right. That would be the fight for the church, he figured. The New Jersey line had not been slowed by undergrowth, they'd faced open ground and had all but overtaken him.

But they were *not* going to overtake him.

As he emerged from the trees, face stinging, dozens of his men were out ahead of him, pursuing fleeing Confederates.

Well-trained, his company officers forced the men back into ranks and chased the Rebels with volleys.

"Re-form! Colors up! *Re*-form!"

It had not been three full minutes since that first volley in the woods. That quickly, things turned again.

From the right he heard a rising Rebel yell. Seconds later, a powerful volley tore into his men from the left. Instinctively, the soldiers drew together into packs, only making them into easier targets.

Untroubled by the bullets ripping and striking, Upton strode among his confused soldiers.

"Officers . . . form your companies, *form your companies* . . ."

To their credit, his officers tried. But his men were falling, spurting blood, clutching heads, shoulders, thighs, bending double, shedding scraps of blue cloth, bone, and red meat.

As another volley struck from the left, a swarm of Rebs, demonic, appeared on the right, charging into his flank.

Bullets dropped his soldiers so quickly the sight briefly paralyzed Upton.

Breakaway New Jersey men fled before the gray swarm, unnerved, undone and screaming at Upton's soldiers, "Run, you damned fools!"

His soldiers wavered. Officers looked toward him.

He saw the soon-to-be-inevitable.

"Withdraw. By company. Withdraw!"

Men bolted back into the woods before their officers could obstruct them. Following after, Upton found soldiers standing dumbfounded amid the undergrowth.

Bullets tore off leaves and smacked into tree trunks. Rebs screamed like harpies, touching close.

"Go! Just go! Get through the trees, re-form on the other side!"

He pushed ahead himself, intending to intercept his men in

the open, to rally them. But soldiers accustomed to marching were swifter than a man used to riding a horse.

The Rebs continued to fire into their backs.

When Upton's men regained the shape of a regiment, the 121st had lost over half its 450 officers and men. In seven minutes.

Emory Upton wasn't the sort to weep. But the trained artilleryman did resolve that he would never again lead a frontal attack in regimental lines, nor would he heed advice from "veteran" officers, the sort of men who had assured him that this was how things were done.

As he wiped his sweat and other men's blood from his forehead, Emory Upton made the drastic decision to think for himself.

Corporal Bill Smith knew he should give thanks, but he couldn't help feeling resentment. All that step-out marching had gotten them to the fight five minutes ahead of a bushel of nothing. Whipped with a big gray strap over by the road, the Yankees hardly fussed with the 12th Virginia—except for stray rounds and one timid advance swiftly reversed, a fellow might not have known blue-bellies were present. Smith and his comrades just waited in a ditch behind a hedge, doing their best to avoid the poison ivy extending its tentacles. It put everyone in mind of a sergeant of theirs who'd been able to roll up poison ivy leaves and eat them, but he'd been killed a time back by the typhoid.

If one thing didn't do a man in, another something lurked. Smith knew soldiers who'd decided that they were as good as dead and acted accordingly, light-stepping past the troubles of the day and sleeping soundly. But Smith had taken a liking to being alive.

Billy Mahone came along on foot, the size of a boy still years from his first shave, dispensing orders to colonels and cursing like a bargeman run aground.

Beyond the preacher-curdling epithets, Smith heard only "should have" and "tomorrow."

* * *

What now?"

"Pardon, sir?"

Sedgwick grumped his face and said, "Nothing. Just muttering like some old fool."

"The orders are out," his chief of staff continued. "Can't defend the penmanship, but it's legible and the meaning's clear enough."

Sedgwick hardly listened. The day had been nothing but a succession of damned-fool mistakes by everyone in a blue uniform, with himself atop the list of malefactors. First, he'd delayed to bring up Brooks' division. Then he'd encouraged Brooks to drive forward, to strike the Rebs and not wait for the other divisions to come on line. Then Brooks had sent his own brigades in piecemeal, with the brigade commanders only making things worse. It was as if every officer in the corps had taken laudanum. Or gotten stone drunk. It was an excellent corps, but today its performance had been abysmal, if brave.

Hooker wasn't guiltless, either. Not by a country mile. Joe certainly hadn't kept Lee occupied, let alone come to the Sixth Corps' support. His men hadn't faced Reb scraps at that church, but ready divisions.

All Joe's grand planning and bluster, all the marching and jockeying, had left Lee with interior lines and the Sixth Corps isolated from the army.

Uncle John Sedgwick had no doubt as to what Lee would do in the morning. He'd "entertain" Joe while bringing a crushing weight to bear on the Sixth Corps, bent on destroying it entirely.

So much for grinding Lee between two millstones.

The sole bright spot—and there wasn't much shine to it—was that Banks' Ford was open to him now. Should he be forced to withdraw, he would not have to pull back to Fredericksburg first.

He had sent successive messages to Joe, asking for further orders. In the meantime, with Lee breathing death in his face, his immediate priorities were clear: Prepare the corps to repel the next day's inevitable attack, and hold on to Banks' Ford at any cost.

Turning to his waiting chief of staff, Sedgwick said:

"I feel like I've been shit on by a sick dog."

* * *

Tomorrow. He would destroy them tomorrow, annihilate their Sixth Corps. He would strike them with Early's regathered division, with McLaws and Anderson. His men would cut them off from Fredericksburg then from the local fords, trapping them in their thousands and their pride. Sedgwick could take his choice: surrender or perish.

An entire Union corps erased at one stroke. It would not be a poor result, but a fair consolation for this day's disappointment, for his inability to renew the attack north of the crossroads and drive Hooker's legions back into the river, to complete his task and, perhaps, finish the war.

And should he fail to recross the Rappahannock with good speed, Joseph Hooker himself, a barking scoundrel, would not go unchastised. After concluding the business with Sedgwick, he would turn back to a reckoning with Hooker, a whoremonger and drunkard. Surely the Lord would overthrow such a man.

Robert E. Lee only wished Jackson were with him.

He dreamed as if under opium, pressed into the blanket by cascading visions, by impossible combinations of people and places, by time ruptured and disordered.

He wished to awaken, to rise. But inner flames, white flames, scourged and scorched his skull. His brain felt too big for the encompassing bone, throbbing to burst through its shell.

Joseph Hooker plunged back toward the darkness.

"No!" he cried, warding off a bygone menace. "Don't! *No!*"

A hand gripped his shoulder.

"What is it, Joe? What's wrong?"

He couldn't answer. He did not know what was wrong. He must get up. The cot was a trap, a witch's cauldron in which he was drowning. He had to save the army.

Time bent again. He lay on a blanket in the open air. They brought him brandy.

"No!"

He fell back into taunting fantasies. The woman. So beautiful. *Her.* Turning away. Exquisite. . . .

His eyelids had the weight of marble slabs.

Scarlet flowers. His mother, mute. A torchlight parade. A bell. His farm, the withered crops. Hounding bankers. Eager whores. A trumpet.

"Water."

His army.

No," Couch said. "I can't assume *full* command, that would be mutiny. He just needs rest, you heard the surgeon yourself. He was perfectly lucid an hour ago, on his feet much of the day."

That was an exaggeration. Both men knew it. But Couch did not want responsibility for the army, not now.

Van Alen's lamp-lit face was too worn for emotion.

"The one thing he made perfectly clear," Couch went on, "is that we are not to attack."

"And General Sedgwick?"

Couch crossed his arms. On the cot, the army's commander began to snore.

"Sedgwick will have to fend for himself for a while."

The surgeon found Jackson in higher spirits and better condition than he would have predicted. Exhausted himself, he sat on a stool beside his patient's cot, clothing mottled by the blood of the hundred other men he'd treated that day.

"And the pain in your side? It's gone?"

"The Lord is kind," Jackson told him. "I have no pain. Not there. And little elsewhere."

The surgeon was confounded. Perhaps, he thought, there's something to all those prayers. Jackson did seem favored.

"Well, rest is the important thing. Long journey tomorrow. You mustn't strain yourself."

"Dr. McGuire, I am in the hands of our Lord. But . . . you do think the journey wise?"

"General Lee thinks it's necessary."

On his mound of pillows—gathered from eager donors in the neighborhood—Jackson nodded. "Yes. He fears I might be captured. Union cavalry."

"That's right."

Jackson's eyes moved elsewhere. "I would not fear it, of course. I have ever treated their wounded well. They would not misuse me."

"But General Lee doesn't want to *lose* you, sir. He's eager for your return."

"Yes."

"And Guiney Station's the railhead now, in case . . ."

"Yes. The Chandlers are a Christian family, I know them. They are generous, Fairview will grant me a welcome." He spoke as if reciting prepared lines.

"But?"

A change passed over Jackson's face, as if willed. The surgeon reminded himself to have an orderly clean Jackson's beard.

"Tell me more of the day," Jackson insisted. "Lieutenant Smith shared what he knew . . . but I should like to hear more."

"Well . . . it was a . . . I should say a remarkable day, sir. The fighting was difficult at first."

Jackson nodded. Signaling that he knew as much, that he wished McGuire to move on.

The surgeon understood.

"The Stonewall Brigade . . . the morning's fight was savage, but they weathered it. In the final charge, they led the way. 'Passing brave,' as they say. They were the heroes of the hour."

It was an exaggeration, if not quite a lie, but the surgeon believed it justifiable.

"They went into battle shouting, 'Remember Stonewall!'" McGuire added.

Jackson's eyes grew moist. "Just like them. Good. Good."

The general made a queer movement with his torso, one that only a doctor might recognize: an attempt to reach out with an arm gone missing.

Stymied, Jackson eased back into his pillows and said, "You know, Dr. McGuire, the name 'Stonewall' belongs to the brigade, not to me. I have no right to it, it's theirs." His eyes searched a private distance again. "One day . . . the time will come when those men will be proud to say to their children, 'I fought with the Stonewall Brigade.'"

The surgeon feared that Jackson might weep and looked away.

"You must rest, General. It's the best medicine on offer. Sleep now, try to sleep."

But Jackson seemed reluctant to let him go.

"How long? Before I can see to my duties again?"

McGuire shook his head. "Impossible to say, it's much too early. Oh, you've come through admirably so far . . . but I can't yet judge the length of your recovery. There are numerous factors . . ." Alarmed by an intuition, the surgeon added, "You mustn't hurry yourself. That would be . . . a dereliction, General." He smiled an official smile. "The Confederacy needs you whole and hale and hearty."

Jackson smiled, bemused.

"I fear, Dr. McGuire, that I shall never be entirely whole. Unless I can grow a new arm. But my soul . . . I believe that is complete. And in good hands."

"Well, rest. Tomorrow will be a long day."

As the surgeon turned to leave the tent, Jackson said, "I have never been more at peace. All this . . . all has been done according to His holy will. My Heavenly Father designed this affliction for my good, Dr. McGuire, all for my good."

The surgeon heard a tone of doubt and fear.

Jackson told himself that he wished, above all things, to do his duty, to serve first the Lord then his country. He insisted to himself that he desired nothing more upon this earth than to return to the battlefield.

But his thoughts betrayed him, fleeing to his *esposa*. He wished to feel her hand upon his forehead, to sink into her comfort, to feel her warmth and her light breath upon him. He had agreed to the transfer to Guiney Station not only because Lee wished it but because once Hooker had been driven off, his wife might be able to reach him there.

He needed her. He had to keep up the appearance of strength for the others. But he needed her.

His traitorous desires even lured him to dream of weeks at home in Lexington, perhaps a full month with his wife and child.

Such wishes were undutiful, he knew, but he could not help himself.

There were times when he felt so alone he feared he would die of it.

He missed Doc Cowin. Poor Doc. Would've liked to hear what high words and poesy he'd apply to this Babylonian Captivity.

Their guards—not quick-witted sorts—ordered them to the side of the road again. More wagons passed, high springed in the gloaming, emptied of treasures. The blue-bellies did have a wealth of everything.

Then they were put back to marching again, and Pickens' feet were a downright atrocity committed by the body against itself. He had half a mind to return to the university after the war—to take the doings seriously this time—and study up on medicine. So he could always fix himself, if he ever had to go through this again.

Wouldn't his mother be proud, at last, if he took a degree in anything?

Well, he'd been young, after all.

Auntie Delsie had been the only one who had not chided him outright, just hum-humming over her stove and—maybe—pleased to have him home again.

When would he be home again? Not soon. Even if promptly exchanged, the men with gold fuss on their collars were not about to send him to Alabama to take his ease.

Might get a few days in Richmond, though, while the clerks sorted things out. Other fellows had.

Where would the Yankees put him up in the meantime?

Hadn't been bad keepers so far, the blue-bellies. Some cursing, sure, but not set to wound, not deeply. One guard asked about Stonewall Jackson—a prisoner had told him that Jackson was wounded or dead. Pickens, who didn't know much and was inclined to say even less, just answered:

"Seen old Stonewall myself, healthy as a bear, not fifteen minutes before y'all laid hands on me."

Wasn't it odd, though, what a pleasure it was to lie sometimes? Made him think that women must be happier than they let on, since they didn't do much but tell lies all day long.

Once he and his parade of fellow prisoners had plodded over the Yankee pontoon bridge, they'd even been given two crackers each and a chance to fill their canteens. Pickens had tested his teeth on the hard goods while watching a battery pass—it seemed to him to be going the wrong way. Like Doc always said: The ways of the Yankees were unknowable.

Crying shame about Doc, it truly was. It would have been a heathen delight to hear what he had to say about all this.

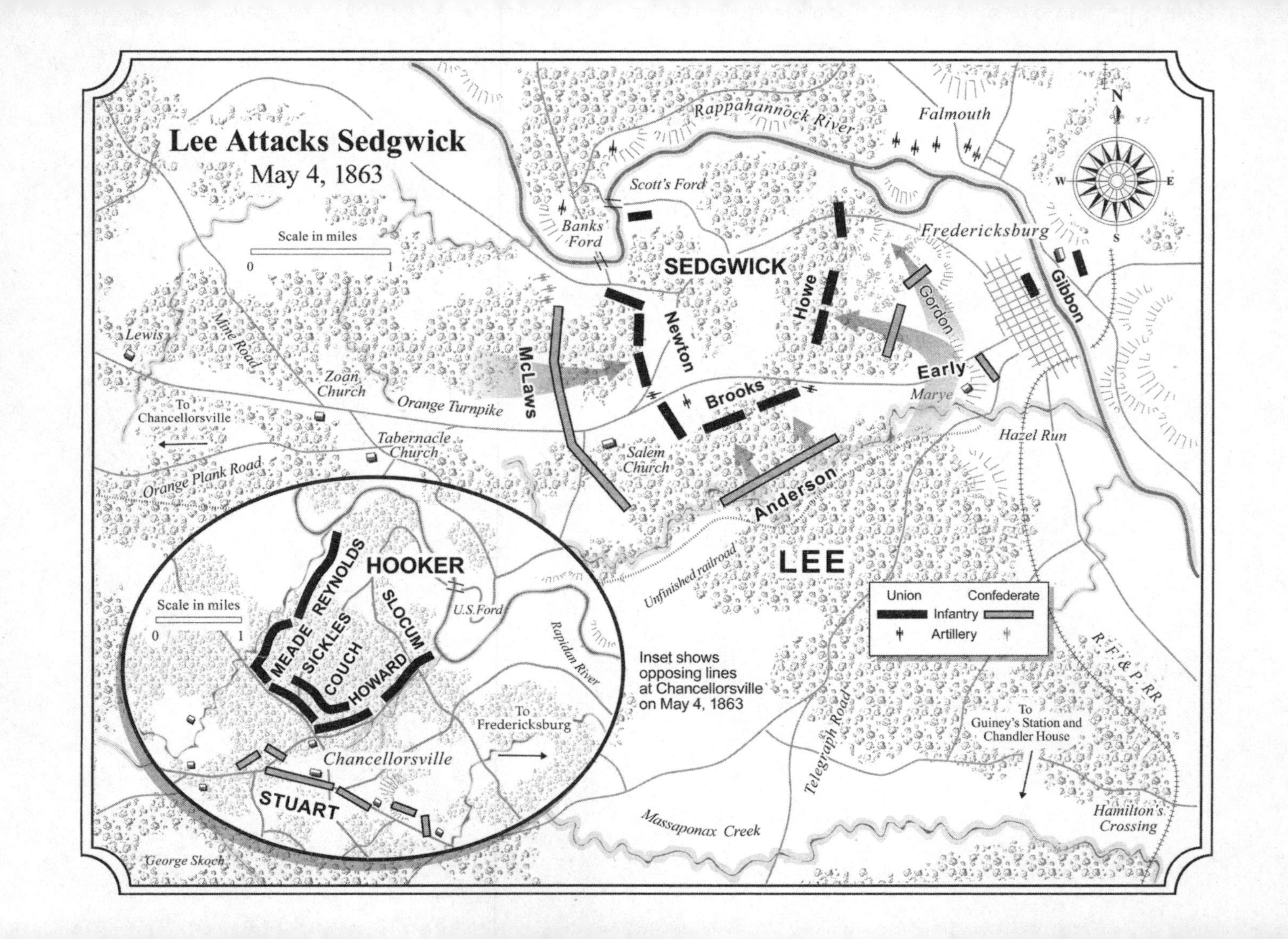
Lee Attacks Sedgwick
May 4, 1863
Scale in miles
0
1
Rappahannock River
Falmouth
N
W
E
S
Scott's Ford
Banks Ford
Fredericksburg
SEDGWICK
Howe
Gordon
Gibbon
Newton
Lewis
Mine Road
McLaws
Early
Zoan Church
Orange Turnpike
Brooks
Marye
To Chancellorsville
Tabernacle Church
Salem Church
Hazel Run
Orange Plank Road
Anderson
HOOKER
REYNOLDS
MEADE
SICKLES
COUCH
HOWARD
SLOCUM
U.S.Ford
Unfinished railroad
LEE
Union
Confederate
Infantry
Artillery
Rapidan River
Inset shows opposing lines at Chancellorsville on May 4, 1863
R F & P RR
To Fredericksburg
Chancellorsville
STUART
Telegraph Road
To Guiney's Station and Chandler House
Massaponax Creek
Hamilton's Crossing
George Skoch

TWELVE

May 4
Fredericksburg to Chancellorsville

Chewing remained a trial for John Brown Gordon, with the left side of his face reluctant to heal, more than seven months after Antietam. He could not commend getting shot in the jaw, with the ball exiting the opposite cheek in the company of four teeth. His jaw was no longer wired shut, but the natural act of mastication remained an infernal ordeal, an argument for soups and meat ground fine.

But John Brown Gordon could talk. He could speak with volume and clarity, his enunciation perfect, in a cadenced voice aped from his reverend father, a man whose accounts with the Lord were not untroubled and whose accounts with his fellow man were in chronic arrears. And Gordon loved to speak to multitudes; the very act of opening his mouth evoked Ulysses, his ideal, and Achilles, bronze-helmed on the plains of Troy, his idols both, worshipped in classrooms until his father's self-wrought tribulations cut short the son's university career, necessitating a hasty retreat to northwestern Georgia, where Alabama impinged and Tennessee loomed—all of that prelude to this Virginia morning, with his men already sweated from a quick march meant to outrace the division's other brigades.

Richmond had been recalcitrant in awarding him a brigadier generalship, leaving Gordon a colonel, although commanding a brigade, so he had chosen to interpret his orders from Early to advantage, stepping out ahead of his peers to accomplish the morning's mission on his own. Gordon reckoned success would be worth a star. And he did not contemplate failure.

Now, with his men approaching the ridge that demanded retaking—the pivotal heights behind Fredericksburg—he halted his brigade in a fallow field, drawing the regiments into a compact mass.

Well aware of the splendid figure he cut, with eyes set deep beneath an aggressive brow, his forehead high, and the family nose sculpted by Scotland's gales—Fanny was fond of that nose—he rose in his stirrups in the brilliant light and stiffened his never-less-than-immaculate posture.

"Men of Georgia!" he began. "*Heroes* of Georgia! The hour is dire, the need is terrible. Will you . . . the glorious sons of our peerless state . . . take back the crucial ground Mississippi lost? Will you go forward, no matter the cost, and plant your banners where now invaders transgress? Will you show them stalwart hearts and bayonets? Will you save your country?"

He waited for the soldiers to realize they should cheer. And cheer him they did.

"Noble sons of Georgia," he resumed, "inheritors of freedoms dearly purchased . . . Myrmidons of the Confederacy . . . I ask you to go no step beyond the ground my own boots tread. The fight may be grim, the price of victory dear, but what man among us doubts that Georgia's sons will pay it gladly?"

He waited for, and received, another cheer.

"I want to see every man who's with me raise his hat. Come on, men!"

Thousands of hats in a hundred styles rose skyward.

"Forward, then, let us go forward, but go in silence, as guardians of this new domain of freedom. Let not a cry escape your lips as you cross the deadly fields and scale the heights. But when you near the crest, when the Yankees already dread annihilation . . . it's then that I want you to howl to be heard in Augusta, in Macon, Savannah, Atlanta . . . are you with me, men?"

The cheering seemed fuel enough to propel the brigade to wondrous deeds.

Gordon drew his saber, letting the early sun gild polished steel. Before calling out the orders to deploy into line and advance, he bellowed:

"Georgia does not follow. Georgia *leads!*"

Alone against what was surely a deadly foe, the brigade went forward, with sergeants brusque and muscled correcting the lines. Red banners, torn by battle, lofted in rhythm with their bearers' steps. Fortunate soldiers tramped along the road, while others labored through fields and over fences, their formations parting to flow around houses and barns, faces growing more earnest with every yard, all the world suffused with the brushing of trouser legs through infant crops, with the slosh of canteens still full and the useless admonitions of nervous officers.

He had deployed the brigade into line too early and the men had to exert themselves marching cross-lots, but that speech to a command he had not yet led in battle had been essential.

Georgia was going to hear from him. As was his Fanny, the most delicious woman ever produced by a sprawling continent, sugar candy that left a taste of pepper.

John Brown Gordon was ambitious. And he had realized at a blink that the men who made reputations in the war would lead the people afterward, brushing aside the politicians, the parlor champions, who chose to stay at home and pass resolutions. The future would belong to the war's survivors.

He did wish Fanny could see him this fine morning. Sweep that woman right up across his saddle and ride off to someplace private.

He saw the rump of the hill and the sprawling ridge now, elevations high enough to invite a proper slaughter. He didn't really care to be shot again, given his druthers, but life was about taking chances when others faltered.

Now and again, a soldier tried to raise a Rebel yell, conditioned to it, but he was soon hushed.

Every man had his eyes set on those heights.

The Yankees had made good use of their day of possession, digging in, hiding their guns with exasperating skill. Even their flags were concealed. They knew full well how essential that terrain was to both sides, key to control of Fredericksburg and its crossings. He had still been abed back in December, but he'd heard that the carnage on the ridge's far side had been gruesome.

He waited for the Union guns to speak.

But the Yankees waited, allowing him to come on. Daring him. Luring him. He felt their eyes upon him, their numbers legion. Sharpshooters were surely taking aim.

He corrected his perfect posture again and pointed the way with his sword. Well-bred, his dapple gray pranced.

He hoped they wouldn't shoot the goddamned horse. The beast had cost him plenty.

The ground began to rise. Ever so slightly. Hinting at the steeper slope to come.

Gordon felt every man in his lines go tense. Waiting for the eruption of death and butchery, each man selfish now, hoping that those to either side would fall and not him—yet selfless, too, willing to die for those same men, for a country hardly formed.

What were the Yankees waiting for?

Lying low. The bastards. Waiting. Merciless.

They reached the foot of the hill near the run of the ridge.

No sense in waiting: The dammed-up spunk would burst free on its own.

"Now! Now, boys! Charge!"

The brigade sent up a howl to shiver Lucifer. Men dashed up the leg-searing slope, determined to kill Yankees.

Gordon spurred his horse.

Still, the Yankees held their fire, waiting for Gordon's men to reach point-blank range.

"Charge!" Gordon cried again. Beyond that, he was at a loss for words. Panting.

As his mount neared the crest, he raised his saber, ready to slash it down on threatening Yankees. He spurred the horse again, viciously now. The animal leapt to the top.

The Georgia Brigade faced a dozen astonished women who had come out to search for yesterday's overlooked wounded.

The Yankees were gone.

Farther along, a pair of gray-clad cavalry scouts took their leisure.

"Why, good morning, ladies!" Gordon exclaimed, removing his hat and smiling.

Hooker felt almost entirely recovered. Best he'd felt in a week, in fact. A surgeon's reexamination had found one pupil dilated, and he did have a ghost in one eye, but the frightful headaches he'd endured for days had disappeared, leaving only fleeting spells of uncertainty.

If taking a blow to the noggin was the price of ridding himself of those monstrous headaches, it was worth it.

He didn't even feel a craving for drink.

The fresh air pleased as he rode along his lines on his morning inspection. The field fortifications his men had erected were masterful, complete with firing apertures and head-logs. Nor were the engineers and soldiers finished: Successive lines were being developed in depth, with interlocking fields of fire and carefully calculated artillery fans. If Lee succumbed to his pride and attacked him today, the result would be a massacre of all the wailing tribes of the Confederacy.

As he passed into the Fifth Corps lines, the density of soldiers and their evident readiness continued to lift his spirits. Had to admit that Meade kept his corps in good order. There was no malingering, and even the stench of men packed tight seemed milder.

The lines teemed with soldiers ready to fight, even as thousands more labored. When they recognized Hooker's party, they gave him a cheer.

The men still believed in him. As they always had.

Mounted and alert, Meade saluted as Hooker rode up to his headquarters. Hooker seemed to remember a tiff with Meade the previous day, but the memory was unclear. Anyway, Meade appeared cordial. If hard words had passed between them, Meade was contrite.

"My kind of morning," Hooker said by way of greeting. "Couldn't ask for better Reb-killing weather, the sonsofbitches."

"I'm all in favor of killing Rebs," Meade told him, adding, "How are you feeling, Joe?"

"Ready to eat raw meat and chaw the bones. Just needed a little sleep."

"Glad to hear it."

"You always claimed I was hardheaded, George. It's not without its advantages, it seems."

"Virtues of our vices," Meade observed.

Hooker wasn't certain how to take that. He nodded and forged on. "Just let Lee attack. Let the old devil try it."

Before they could turn to inspect Meade's lines together, Otis Howard appeared along an artillery trail, followed by two riders and no flags.

"Oh, Christ," Hooker said to Meade. "I've already had my fill of Howard this morning."

Meade said nothing.

Howard reined in his mount, his pinned sleeve flapping. "Morning, George," he said, getting the greeting out of the way before swinging to Hooker.

"Joe . . . I've been thinking . . ."

Hooker looked at Meade. "Here's trouble: Otis is thinking again." He did find it hard to forgive Howard's negligence, his outright neglect of orders. And he did not intend to pamper the man: Let him eat his shame cold. But he could not afford a political enemy, either.

He did his best to contain a surge of temper.

"I'd like your permission to push out one brigade. Toward Sedgwick. Test Lee's intentions. Barlow's brigade hasn't even—"

"No," Hooker said, "I've already told you."

"But if the Sixth Corps were cut off, Lee might—"

"All Sedgwick has to do is hold his fords. Since he seems reluctant to play any other role." Hooker's lips narrowed. "I want every man in position when Lee attacks."

A regiment of flies attacked the generals and their horses.

"You know, Joe," Meade interfered, waving at the swarm, "Otis and I have had our disagreements, but a limited advance to feel out Lee . . ." He hesitated. "Doesn't it make sense for Lee to strike Sedgwick first? While keeping the rest of us waiting at the altar?"

Hooker's head began to throb again. "*No.* For God's sake, Lee's after more than just one corps. He's a slave to ambition, that man. His blood's up, he's going to come at us. Today. And then he'll see what I'm—what this army's made of."

Howard seemed bent on impertinence. "Joe, my men need a chance to redeem themselves. In the eyes of the rest of the army. If it *should* become necessary to support Uncle John, my corps is well-positioned to lead the way. We could—"

"If you're looking for redemption, find a chaplain," Hooker snapped.

"The Germans—"

"Your Germans need their beer barrels shoved up their asses." Hooker snorted. "Just try to keep them from running away again."

"Joe, that's uncalled for," Meade said.

"'Uncalled for'? That's rich. I'll damned well tell you what's uncalled for. Disobeying orders. Endangering this army. Jeopardizing this entire campaign. Giving Lee a chance to humiliate—"

He stopped himself and shut his eyes for a moment. When he eased the eyelids again—with his left eye not quite focused—he changed his demeanor by an act of will.

"Listen to us," Hooker said, forcing a smile. "Just listen to us. At each other's throats. It's wrong, all wrong. We need to fight the Johnnies, not each other."

"Well, I agree with that," Meade said.

Howard nodded. "Of course, Joe. I was only trying—"

"No harm done," Hooker allowed. "Decisive day ahead. Plenty of work." He refreshed his smile and threw back his manly shoulders. "I'd best be off, make sure Reynolds hasn't got up to some mischief. No need to join me, George—your corps looks fine."

As he rode away, the lack of confidence just encountered nagged him. Why *wouldn't* Lee attack him? When *didn't* Lee attack? Well, let him try it today and Lincoln himself wouldn't quibble about the result.

Lincoln. A dullard given charge of a torn country. Democracy was a doubtful enterprise. McClellan had been right that the country needed a stronger hand, a leader empowered.

But Lincoln remained in authority, occupying the President's House. His uninformed caprices decided careers.

What would Lincoln do, if . . .

Joseph Hooker wanted to keep his command. That was the shrunken extent of his ambition: to retain command until he could show success. There had been times, before the army moved, in the days of dress parades and soaring morale, when he'd imagined himself elected president in the subsequent year's election, the hero who'd won the war.

Now, though . . .

With his escort strung out behind him, Hooker followed another cut trail, all white stumps and reeking of sap, and he forced himself to think on brighter prospects. Dan Butterfield was coming out from Falmouth to take charge of the staff and set things straight. First Dickinson, then Van Alen, had failed him. Just as his fellow generals had failed him. No one had supported his plan with a will, no one had given him the support he needed.

Dan would put things right. Whether Lee attacked or not. Dan would save things. And Dan would be his witness that the avalanche of errors had not been his fault.

They all believed he was finished. He could tell. Vultures, all of them. Their jealousy was palpable, thick as mud.

In a clearing just ahead, he spotted John Reynolds. The First Corps commander stood waiting in front of a tent and a pair of flags. A handsome man and capable, but a sneak, Reynolds was another one not to be trusted, another slave to ambition, another man who wished to seize the crown.

Joe Hooker felt the world conspiring against him.

When Hooker had gone, Meade said to Howard, "Joe would be a great general, if the enemy followed his orders."

Clement Evans couldn't deny his men a pair of minutes to loot the wagons. Wouldn't let his regiment run wild, but the 31st Georgia had earned the right to stuff its haversacks with Yankeedom's endless bounty.

Tempted, but unwilling to appear grasping, Evans watched a soldier attempt to stuff a sack of coffee beans into a knapsack many sizes too small.

Like the loaves and the fishes in reverse, Evans decided. He did look forward to the war's conclusion—let it come soon—when he could return to his cherished dream of becoming a Methodist minister, preaching the Lord God's majesty and mercy. And when he could rejoin Allie and the little ones—but, above all, Allie. Men were not meant to worship living creatures, but he did approach idolatry with his darling, a Christian woman whose faith allowed for smiles.

A good woman was not least among the miracles wrought by the Lord.

Far away, though, Allie was far away. Sometimes, at night, he didn't know how to endure it, the thought of her pushed him to the verge of folly, to deeds unthinkable. He could smell her in the darkness, feel her hair beneath his cheek. . . .

In their excitement, some of his men cast unwanted goods on the ground. It was time to put a stop to things. Waste was un-Christian. Others had needs, too.

He turned to his acting adjutant. "All right, Creighton. Get the boys back in line, time to push on. Detail a dozen men to watch over the wagons and guard the prisoners."

A mile back and barely visible, the rest of Gordon's Brigade trailed Evans' men, who had been advanced as skirmishers and pursued the mission with vigor. It was dangerous work, but not without rewards: There had been cries of exaltation when his men crossed a ridge and spotted the Yankee wagons stopped by a creek, protected by no more than a handful of soldiers—blue-bellies who hadn't felt much inclined to challenge a screeching host of ravenous Georgians.

Gordon would be pleased, of course, at the capture. But Evans felt inspired to do more. The Yankees were out there somewhere and needed finding.

John Brown Gordon. If there was a man, short of Robert E. Lee, worth serving in the Army of Northern Virginia, it was Gordon. The man was—what was the word?—"irrepressible." You couldn't keep that hound dog under the porch. The men adored him, hanging on his words, even when they had not the faintest notion what Gordon was going on about. The man was . . . an enchanter.

Clem Evans reckoned his future ministry could profit from Gordon's uncanny knack for rhetoric.

And Gordon had dash. After his morning speech on rivers of blood and impending sacrifice, the regiment had stormed that ridge, only to delight a passel of belles. Any other man would have been embarrassed to the core, but Gordon had passed it off by declaring, in that stirring voice, "Now look at that, boys! The Yankees ran off at the first hint you were coming! Isn't that fine?"

The women had flocked to Gordon in a manner almost unseemly.

Gordon was not that sort of man, of course. A flirt, perhaps, but surely no betrayer. Gordon professed a devotion to his wife that echoed Evans' adoration of Allie.

It was only Gordon's commitment to Jesus Christ that wanted praying over. He said the right words, always, but there were glint-eyed moments when Evans feared that his superior merely found the Lord useful.

With his regiment spread out in a doubled skirmish line again, Evans waved the men forward and joined them on foot. Horses had grown scarce for mere regimental commanders—his last mount had died of nothing much in the winter and he was not a wealthy man, possessed of neither land nor slaves to work it. If he couldn't catch a Yankee horse on the battlefield, colonel or not he was going to wear down some shoe leather.

In the distance, off to the west, shots pierced the morning, but all seemed sweetly peaceable where the Georgians trod, with the petals and leaves of May adorning Creation.

Couldn't figure out those Yankee wagons. Unprotected, off by themselves, and not even paying attention. As if they were safe as children under a quilt. Had they just gotten lost?

Well, he wasn't about to lodge a complaint with Lincoln. And his men surely wouldn't protest.

"Stay alert," he called to his nearest officers. He'd said it as much for himself as for his soldiers: Enveloped by the glory of God's bounty, a fellow's mind tended to wander. Even his shadow seemed beauteous and a wonder, stretching before him as he strode through new barley.

He'd come to relish fighting, a sin he often prayed over. Surely the Lord would be merciful to those who went to war to uphold the Bible—why couldn't He make Northerners understand the wisdom of His injunctions? Colored folk could no more look after themselves than could a milk cow. Slavery was ordained, it was necessary, and had only to be regulated with justice. The Negro wasn't merely the white man's servant, but his responsibility, a burden to be borne with Christian rectitude. The Yankees would simply turn the Negro out of his home, leaving him helpless, bereft, and prey to sin.

Insects rose from trampled grass. The sun climbed and shadows shortened. Evans began to sweat properly. Trailing the scent of coffee beans, his soldiers brushed along, any remarks they made pointed and brief.

Might have been a hunt back home, a hunt with no game flushed.

Then there they were: Yankee skirmishers, waiting idly down a reverse slope, off on their own, with no other Federals anywhere to be seen.

Evans felt an urge to run right at them and scoop them up. The Yankees hadn't the numbers and he doubted they had the grit to stand their ground. But he didn't want to exhaust his men or slip into disorder. Gordon's charm masked a fierce belief in discipline, and Clement Evans would not be found lacking.

So his soldiers just continued to advance, crossing through one budding crop after another, eyeing the waiting Yankees as the details of faces and uniforms grew sharper.

Evans reckoned those Federals would exchange two shots before running. Yankees had their deficiencies, but they could count.

Instead, the blue-bellies let off one round each and then turned high-tail, not just falling back but running as if chased by Satan with his fiery pitchfork.

Before Evans could voice an order, his Georgians hallooed, as if at home driving their hounds. The entire regiment gave chase, having themselves a fine time.

To the rear, cheers—what he took for cheers—rose from the rest of Gordon's Brigade, far back on higher ground. It looked as though another of Early's brigades was moving up to fill in the left as well.

Big fight coming, all right. Once they uncovered the Yankees.

Missing his late horse at least as much as he would have mourned a cousin, Evans sprinted ahead of his colors, determined to hold his regiment short of anarchy. The Yanks just plain skedaddled, fleeing over another of the crests that scalloped the landscape.

When Evans' men topped the low ridge themselves, every man stopped on his own. A mighty line of men in blue stood before them, well within range, and unleashed a volley to deafen the high heavens. Evans threw himself to the ground, with his color-bearers going flat behind him.

The mathematics were running the wrong way.

The Yankees cheered and reloaded. Evans rose and ran along his line, crouching and ordering his soldiers back behind the crest.

They'd come upon at least a brigade, if not a full division.

Evans liked an honest scrap, but he didn't enjoy finding himself on the wrong end of a target shoot.

His men scrambled back to a parlous safety, encouraged in their flight by Yankee bullets and chased by jeers.

Shielded by a swell of ground no higher than a wave, Evans drew his regiment into a tighter formation, one that might allow for a brief defense if the Yankees advanced. And then there was nothing to do but wait, either for Gordon's Brigade and its new neighbor to join the soiree or for an order to withdraw. Meanwhile, he sent his steadiest lieutenant rearward to inform Gordon about what awaited him.

To Evans' surprise and not a little dismay, a lone regiment hurried up on the 31st Georgia's left. Not enough of a reinforcement to do more than excite the Yankees to take a more active interest in affairs.

Virginians. From Extra Billy Smith's bunch. Haughty as ever. Cocky and quick, they swept forward, calling to the Georgians to get up and join the attack then mocking them, in hard words, when they declined the invitation.

The Virginians swarmed over the crest, met a hurricane volley, and returned with impressive speed.

It was the Georgians' turn to hurl insults.

An order arrived from Gordon to pull back and rejoin the brigade. The Virginians saw the wisdom of following suit, order or no order. But even as the humbled withdrew, another lone Virginian regiment leapt into the cauldron.

The confusion grew worse.

When Evans located Gordon to report, the brigade commander was conferring with General Early, an excitable man. Early flapped his arms and blasphemed to shame Lucifer, his high-pitched voice turning sulfur into sound.

Gordon shot Evans a look that said, *Let him blow off for a minute,* and Evans waited, though not without blushing as Early's tirade turned to accusing the Yankees and then his own men of unlikely, if not impossible, contortions and combinations of human bodies.

Finally, Early ran out of himself. He noticed Evans and, before

Gordon could speak, the general demanded, "Well, Reverend, what the hell's out there that you saw and I can't?"

"Didn't have time to count heads, sir," Evans told him, "but it looked like the better part of a Yankee division. And they seem inclined to stay."

Jubal Early pulled back his soldiers but kept them ready to advance again. This time there would be proper coordination, with no brigade commanders making fool decisions on their own—Extra Billy was farting-out-the-mouth proof that a former governor was not necessarily meant to command a brigade. Or a shithouse detail. Sooner or later, Smith was going to make a mistake that cost them all dearly, but nothing could be done about the man.

There were times when Jubal Early missed the old Army.

Ready enough to fight, though. All he needed was word from Lee that his attack would have support from the west, where McLaws was supposed to do his part and hadn't. Early wasn't about to take on a Yankee corps with a single division. There was a mountain-mile's difference between bravery and stupidity, and he'd already used up the day's stupidity rations.

He spit out his used-up chaw, slopping his beard and drying it with his cuff.

The last orders he'd received from Lee had specified a coordinated attack to crush John Sedgwick. But nothing had happened on the Chancellorsville side of the battlefield. Laff McLaws probably had one paw on his pecker and the other up his ass, as usual.

He did wonder what was taking Lee so long. Tardiness wasn't one of the old man's qualities.

Fight like the devil, that he would. He just needed Robert E. Lee to get things moving.

Uncle John Sedgwick would have traded a full brigade for a single clear and unequivocal order. Hooker wanted him to hold the fords and a bridgehead. But another order granted him the authority to evacuate to the north bank, if pressed. And some damned fool had abandoned the heights behind Fredericksburg—had Gibbon been sleeping? Now those fords were denied him, leaving Banks' Ford more vital than ever.

Amid the orders arriving out of sequence, he'd also been instructed to renew his advance westward toward Chancellorsville—but only given evidence that Hooker was attacking eastward himself.

There had been no sign of that.

Attack? Defend? Remain in place? Recross the river? Eat beans and play checkers?

Awaiting definite orders, he'd done the sensible thing in the wake of Howe's morning scuffle: He'd arrayed the Sixth Corps on good defensive ground that shielded the last fords and the loop in the river.

Flags high, his wearied retinue located Albion Howe again. The first thing Sedgwick asked the division commander was:

"Any word about Longstreet? Any sign? Those prisoners have anything to say?"

Howe shook his head. "All of them were Early's men. Mostly Virginians. Took themselves a good licking. As for Longstreet . . . nothing, sir. Seems more phantom than fact."

That, at least, gave cause for hope. But Sedgwick remained on guard. For all the folderol about honor and rectitude, Robert E. Lee was a wily sonofabitch.

"All right, Albie. Talk."

The division commander understood. "It's fine terrain to fight on, no complaints. Channels the Rebs away from any point of concentration, run of the ground will break up large formations. It may be a division front on the map, but it's going to be a brigade fight on the ground." He gestured toward invisible Rebs. "Come at me from over there—which seems the likely approach—they'll hit a heavy skirmish line. Push that back, they'll encounter Neill's brigade. If Neill can't hold them, they'll meet Lew Grant's Vermonters. Who have a knack for creating Confederate widows."

"All right. Good." Sedgwick looked around. Listening. "Rebs have been awfully quiet. Not sure whether I like that."

"Maybe they're having second thoughts. About attacking."

Sedgwick's face hardened. "Lee never has second thoughts about attacking."

Walter Taylor did not believe he had ever seen Robert E. Lee in such a fury, but a man had to know the general to recognize it, to catch the faintest pinking of the face that signaled an inferno raging within. Lee rarely raised his voice and never shouted, but the air around him turned arctic enough to freeze Lord Franklin twice. As he followed the general from one disordered headquarters to another, Taylor tried to stay hidden behind Lee's shoulder, available if needed, but not an immediate target for his wrath.

Lee had awakened that day in excellent spirits, certain that his subordinates knew their roles and Sedgwick's corps would be destroyed before the day's meridian. Instead, nothing had happened, other than a half-hearted, broken-off effort by Early's Division. McLaws had not moved, and when Lee arrived to find him seated under a tree devouring a chicken, Lee's quiet remarks had cut like a saber.

McLaws had protested that his division alone was insufficient, that his scouts had found the Federals well posted and in strength. So Lee had ordered up the remainder of Anderson's Division, only to find Dick Anderson's slowness an outrage atop McLaws' lethargy. Anderson's men could not just pull off the Chancellorsville line without being replaced by troops from another division. And that took time, it stood to reason. But Lee had passed beyond reason. He wanted an *attack*. And the hours passed.

Behind those silver manners, Lee was a killer. More than once, Taylor had seen the old man's savage will at work. It was not the sort of thing that one discussed, but there it was.

Still, Lee retained the self-control—that icy self-control—to recognize that any attack required coordination if it was to destroy the Federal Sixth Corps, especially after the Yankees had time to prepare. But even with Anderson up and in place at last, there had been more delays, with Early waiting for McLaws to advance, and

McLaws waiting on Early, in a comic performance worthy of a minstrel show.

Taylor longed to say to Lee, "The men are tired, sir, they've been fighting for four days, that's why they're lagging." But he knew that Lee, if he replied at all, would say, in a tone of impatient disdain, "*Those people,* too, are weary. But they can afford to be weary and we cannot."

The afternoon waned.

Lee would have relieved all three, McLaws, Anderson, and Early, if he'd had men to replace them. But he had none with sufficient experience, none who were ready.

Jackson was right: The South could not win through mercy. Hearts had to be hardened, excuses punished, failure forbidden upon pain of death.

Jackson was right. . . .

Now the divisions were in place at last, the final orders issued, and his much-delayed attack would commence at the signal of three cannon shots in succession.

Blessedly, Hooker, a fool's fool, had not lifted a finger to interfere, mesmerized by feints and occasional shelling that masked the depletion of Lee's lines at Chancellorsville.

The equation was simple: Hooker was afraid, while he was not.

Lee drew out his watch. It was five twenty-six. He nudged Traveller toward Alexander's gun line. He would give the order to fire at five thirty.

He longed to ride over a field paved blue with corpses.

It's hot," Jackson muttered, as the wagon jolted along.

"Yes, sir," Dr. McGuire said from his perch above him. "Gets hot under the canvas. But it's worse without it."

"Our wounded must suffer greatly."

"We do our best, General."

Voice much weakened, Jackson said, "I did not mean to chide."

"No offense taken, sir."

"War is a terrible matter, Doctor. It takes us in thrall, a seductress. I do believe the Lord meant to instruct me, with this wound." Then he added, "I do feel warm."

"You need rest. And you'll get it soon, sir."

"I would like . . . perhaps, at the next house . . ."

"Water? There's water right here." McGuire's face spoke of thought and the surgeon added, "Cold well water might be dangerous, General. Given your condition, the shock to the internal system."

"Not to drink. Compresses. Cold compresses. For my head. I would be grateful."

After an awkward delay, McGuire said, "I don't know if that would be wise."

"I have always . . . I have *always* found water treatments to be healthful. I always gained from visiting the springs, the hydrology cure." Jackson tried to smile, unsure if he managed it. The journey was hard, and long, and he did not feel as strong as he had the past evening. "Water, Doctor, is the font of life. It cures much. And cannot hurt us."

Jackson's ears quickened. He believed he heard artillery fire in the distance, serious gunnery this time, not mere teasing. He'd been waiting to hear it all day.

McGuire laid the back of a hand on Jackson's forehead. The wagon creaked and jolted.

"You're a bit warm. But it's likely just the heat."

"Wet compresses would ease me."

Surrendering, the doctor ordered the driver to pause at the next respectable dwelling.

"I suppose the water wouldn't do any harm," he said.

THIRTEEN

Evening, May 4

Micky Deary hammered the hillside with the remains of his brogans, head ducked down to his shoulders and Yankee bullets thrilling the air about him. The slope was an insult that robbed a man of his breath, and the Irish lads of the 6th Louisiana managed but a half-hearted howl as they climbed. The only sweetness of it was that Yankees atop a hill always fired too high, though they fired enough.

Shooting from half a world away, long-range Union guns north of the river hunted their whereabouts.

"Jaysus, it's set to flurry a man," an Antrim banty complained.

Consumed by the calf-burning, knee-rending going-up-ness—after a day of shuttling here and there—Deary had no air to waste on words.

So on they went, as bitter as piss in the porridge, hating for hatred's deliciousness—hate, the poor man's treat.

Above the Yankees, thick clouds gathered to smother the pretty day, called by the guns. By twilight, there'd be rain, any man born of Ireland could tell, and their work had best be finished before that, or the whole commotion would bog down in the clabber.

Hidden Yankees, scoundrels all, fired into the regiment's flank, sudden and savage, but Colonel Forno paid them no attention, for the top of the hill and the ground beyond was precious.

Deary missed his messmate Danny Riordan, for Danny was ever a joy amid a fight. But Riordan was in a hospital bed, claimed by the bloody shits, and Deary felt alone and on his guard. For all the packing and pushing, a field of battle was a lonely place.

The Yankees were stubborn and made them pause a turd-fling from the top. Only a heavy skirmish line they had, by now a man could tell, but the buggers were set up grand as a baronet's footman. They wanted uprooting by force, and they'd get it sure.

The Yankee voices, defiant, offered no music, only an ugly growl of dull obscenities. 'Twas clear there were few Irishmen among them.

Deary delighted to see a blue-belly's head burst and spit brains, for men took their bullets in many a way and pleasing it was to know the dead were dead.

"Forr-udd, Loooz-annah," the colonel called in his taskmaster's baritone.

Up they went in another rush, devouring the last distance, and the Yankees retired, though not in their usual haste.

Gasping, Deary surveyed the scene on the rolling ground they'd gained but not yet conquered. A fresh Yankee battery nudged them and the officers led them along. One or two of the older boyos faltered, either used up or pretending, but the regiment and their half of the brigade showed doughty enough.

Beyond a swale, the main Yankee line was aboil with boys in blue, dark as rotted praties in their multitude.

Deary kept to his swarm and pounded the earth, but he did think on black praties, the mush of death, the memory indelible although he'd been but five, if the counting was sure. And then his father died during the passage, done by the ailment he chose of the murderous many, and they dropped him into the waves, tah-rah, leaving his mother bewildered and lost, with not two coins to jingle. He, a boy, had only seen her rage and he learned the back-knuckled smack of a hand on his face, if ever he dared to whisper about hunger. He'd hated her then, even as he clung, as he'd hated the men who passed her along to New Orleans, where she'd left him at last with the Sisters, who no more wanted Micky Deary, runt-grown, than they longed for a whore's salvation. Bitter, bitter women they were, their mercies short and crabbed.

Yet how the years instructed a man, how misery taught him true! He saw now that his mother had been no more than a child herself, younger by years than he was on this bounty-of-blood day, and he thought of her not without kindness, wherever she might be, if still alive.

'Twas a wonder and sweet, what next transpired, as lovely as free whiskey: They struck the Yankees on the flank while others occupied them, and the blue-bellies ran like rats from dogs and torches.

Full-lunged and riled to a fury, the men about him shrieked like the great Banshee multiplied by a thousand. Of battle lines there were none left, just a mighty mob determined to do harm for the joy of destruction. Had church windows been in their way, they would have smashed them and barely repented on doomsday.

'Twas a killing hour.

But a single Yankee regiment broke in the beginning and Louisiana's transplants from Kerry and Cork slammed into the next bunch, just as the Federals struggled to realign.

Soon the dread came upon them, and the weak peeled fast away.

Leaping a low mound of dirt thrown up, Deary found himself eye to eye with a Yankee born for a brawl. The blue-belly swung his rifle back to club out Deary's brains, but Deary fixed his snout with a fist, for courage might be a noble thing, but quickness was better still.

As the Yankee reeled, Deary tripped the man and shoved him and he fell. But Deary had not survived on Christian virtue: He brought down the butt of his rifle smack on the Yankee's snout, just where the bones shook hands, putting all his cock-of-the-walk weight behind it and catching a glimpse of terrified eyes before he pulped them proper.

The regiment moved on again, in triumph, with the Federal defense ruined. Oh, sweet it was, the glory of the evening!

Weary as he was from head to foot, Deary joined the mass exhilaration, embracing the thrill of conquest that elated the kings of old, the irresistible liquor of revenge and the raw delight of doing harm to others. War didn't bring out the worst in men, Deary didn't think that at all. War let men be themselves without fear of the law.

The officers struggled to reestablish order, but that was folly. The excitement overpowered even captains, and what man didn't want the first peep of the Yankee bounty waiting to be plundered? They dashed ahead, beyond weariness, souls flocking to salvation.

Tonight they would eat their fill, like the warriors whose ancient songs still whispered in the winds of Connemara. Each man his master as in the buried age of Ireland's glory, they swept over another weakling ridge only to find they'd been cheated by the devil.

A Yankee line, the strongest yet, waited behind sharpened abatis, artillery positioned on the flanks to cross their fires and take lives in a muchness.

The grim guns spoke.

The regiment raised a cry of rage and staggered toward the Yankees, with men tumbling. A few boyos reached the edge of the Yankee obstacle, only to be cut down by converging fires. Others took shelter wherever it was to be had. Deary chose his ground and chose his targets.

The 6th Louisiana showed as stubborn as poverty in the Limerick warrens, but worn the lads were and bleeding more each moment. The Yankees hollered, *"Vermont! Vermont!"* and Deary never had heard of the place until war came upon him, nor did he think he was inclined to visit. The North sounded colder of heart than an absentee landlord.

Without orders, Deary and his wronged fellows stepped backward once then twice, men done dirty by fate and through no fault of their own. They did not run but gave ground as a Scotsman gives a penny, ruing the loss.

With a cheer, the Yankees charged.

It was too much. Men with legs of stone found strength to run. And Deary was not the last.

No sooner had the survivors left the fateful crest behind than rifles blazed out from the Confederate rear, confounding all.

Men didn't know which way to flee.

Officers, doing their duty for once, rushed straight into the volleys, waving their gentleman's paws and crying, "Don't shoot! We're

Southrons, cease fire!" Their wiser peers pushed forward flags and had the bearers wave them.

It took a grave lot of minutes to coax the firing to a stop. By then the regiment and the entire brigade was a fear-eyed shambles.

The long-range Federal guns came calling again.

Deary blundered into a grove, called by the treacherous safety of the forest, the old come-hither of trees, only to find himself in a lunatic scramble, where regiments joining the fight had somehow collided, their anger aimed at each other now and the Yankees all but forgotten.

Edging and shoving and threatening his way through the back end of the hooley, Deary made his way across a ravine—recognized from the eternity of half an hour before—and gained a field occupied by Confederate batteries waiting for something to do, forgotten and useless.

He stopped and stood in the open, alone, and shook his head.

It began to rain.

Watching the Louisiana Brigade—"brigands" more like—go up that hill, Jubal Early had grinned like a Methodist witnessing the sufferings of a sinner: A handsome victory was in his grasp.

And then it had all gone unaccountably wrong. Hoke got himself shot out of the saddle, just when he needed to pivot his command. Orders went astray and brigades either split into weakened parts or mingled. In the early dark of the woodlands, his men fired on each other. Then the Louisianans, the demi-brigade that had surged over the hill, came running back.

Goddamned mess.

And there was a drenching rain on the way, his lumbago was never wrong.

The only hope remaining was Gordon's Brigade.

John Brown Gordon felt unstoppable. Aware of the pandemonium on his left, and stung by the heavy guns across the river, the Georgian simply refused to be discouraged, riding before his banners, upright and flaunting his saber, defying fate: A man placed his bets and took the consequences. Bloodthirsty and hollering, his brigade brushed off thin lines of Yankees and hastened toward the fords, the keys to bagging an entire Union corps.

He would not have objected to being the hero of the hour.

Nor would it be such a terrible thing if he alone succeeded while others failed. He never wished harm on his rivals—that was unworthy—but neither did he mind it if they faltered.

And they were faltering now. But they also were keeping the Yankees occupied and stretched to breaking. *Bella fortuna,* where Gordon's Brigade had encountered the first skirmishers, both sides had been unsure of the other's whereabouts. His Georgians had been spoiling for a fight, though—especially Clem Evans and his marauders—and they'd sent the Yankees flying once then twice, barely pausing to spoon up a helping of prisoners. Gordon had sent his captives rearward immediately, with an order to the lieutenant in charge to parade them past Jubal Early, even if he had to countermarch them.

The Yankees did have more artillery on the north bank than was decent. He reckoned that at least a full battery was composed of siege guns, with plenty of rifled batteries to assist.

Didn't slow his men, though. The big shells only made them step out briskly.

Again, he wished his Fanny were magically near. A celebration of private joys would have capped the day most finely, nor would she have had the patience to let him bathe first. Gordon only shook his head whenever a man claimed women found loving unpleasant. Just took the right woman matched with the right man. Or, sometimes, the wrong woman with the utterly wrong man, though that was another tale.

Even in a battle's moments of respite, Gordon could smile about the foibles and follies of the male and the inexhaustible wonder of the female. Life was a banquet, and only damned fools were afraid to eat.

Gordon favored red meat over chicken.

Ignoring the clouds running overhead and the graying of the

light, his soldiers cheered over nothing but sheer delight, like those Greeks raising a ruckus by pounding their shields.

"Drive on, boys, drive on!"

Gordon was not a drinking man, but he'd indulged more times than one. And this was better by far, a higher exaltation than stay-at-homes ever would know. There were times when fighting seemed fully half of the purpose of existence.

He didn't hate the Federals, didn't believe he hated any man. Hatred was wasteful, it ate men up. Gordon just found killing Yankees useful, for the time being, and he didn't rule out befriending them again: After the war they'd still be next-door neighbors, and lives took many a turn. The man who reveled in making lifelong enemies was ultimately an enemy to himself.

There was no reason why you couldn't kill a man and do business with his brother. That sort of thing happened all the time in the Bible.

It made him smile to think of teasing Clem Evans on that point.

Gordon heard cheers from his left rear, unmistakable Yankee hurrahs. That jarred him. He didn't want his fellow brigade commanders to lose outright, just wished them lesser successes. He wanted his people to win, after all.

And he, at least, was winning. He'd struck the end of the Federal lines, there was nothing left in front of him. The Yankees must have misjudged the full extent of their perimeter, or they'd been forced to shift men to other points, leaving a gap. Otherwise these open fields, all but undefended, made no sense.

He'd had the luck of the day, that was the truth. After that not-unembarrassing charge up the heights early in the morning. Those chattering, untidy women, those homespun Fredericksburg belles—add 'em together, the sum wouldn't rise as high as Fanny's ankles.

He was about to dispatch a courier to announce his success when a blue wave rose from the river bend ahead, a surge not of water but of men, flowing forward at the double-quick, Yankees in the thousands.

Gordon halted his brigade. It took a good minute for officers to return order to their lines and prepare for a fight. Given a static target, the Federal artillery across the river found the range and rejoiced.

Soldiers who had been merry moments before disintegrated into pulp and splinters.

Still posted ahead of his lines and unwilling to distance himself from the brigade's colors, Gordon drew out his field glasses. The light had grown frail as the clouds swelled and sank, and he could not identify the approaching flags, but the troops were well-drilled, whoever they belonged to.

A nearby impact prickled his face with dirt and troubled his horse.

He began to worry that those successful Yankees to his rear might close in behind him, upending his plans entirely, the hunted becoming the hunters.

Never show alarm, though: That was his battlefield rule. He refused to display the least hint of concern. Instead, he rode his lines, in front of waiting rifles, smiling, with his good cheek shown to the ranks.

"What a fine day for Georgia! What a grand day! Look there, you've flushed out the last reserves they'd got. Give them a pleasant Georgia welcome, hear?"

The position was impossible to maintain. Not with the pounding from those untouchable batteries. Suddenly, his brigade was exposed in more ways than he could tally.

Steering his horse behind his lines, he rode from colonel to colonel, instructing them to be prepared to withdraw and ordering Colonel Evans to cover the movement.

"We'll give them a brigade volley, but you hold your fire, Clem. Let them have it just when the others pull back." They both eyed the oncoming Federals and Gordon added, "Those boys aren't out to drive us back to Richmond. They're out to restore their line, they'll let you get off."

Evans' eyes shone, delighted by the dangerous work entrusted. One more of life's inexplicable men, Gordon thought. Wanted to be a preacher to poor country folk, but killed them in the meantime. For a laced-up Christian, Clem was amiable. And heathen-good at his work.

Raindrops skirmished, the heavens were set to attack.

Before riding off, Gordon told Evans, "No fool heroics now. Don't want your Allie chasing me with an axe handle."

Clem smiled big as a peach. "That woman wouldn't settle for using the handle."

The day hadn't ended quite the way Clement Evans would have preferred, but he wouldn't write that to his wife. There'd been success enough to allow him to fib and make the success entire. He did long for that woman to think well of him.

The queer thing was that his men had arrived back in their lines in a fine mood. If they hadn't been able to stand up to those Yankees and give them a proper whipping, the 31st Georgia had spanked them nevertheless. In the course of a running fight under a downpour, they'd gotten drenched and muddied up like hogs—and still his men made jokes and laughed, their casualties low and spirits near as high as those trailing clouds.

In fact, the entire brigade was far from dispirited. Unlike the Louisianans and North Carolinians, who hadn't had their best day of the war, the Georgians just shrugged off the evening's setback. Gordon had that effect. He could bust a man's nose with a brick and the fellow would pay him a dollar for the honor.

And Clement Evans was grateful for a gift the Lord had sent His faithful servant: In the final confusion of the day, in near dark and rain that sloshed like a tipped washtub, his soldiers had brought him a handsome horse, courtesy of a very unhappy Yankee.

The rain stopped after warning of what might follow. Wet as a stray dog and hunched of spine, Jubal Early banged through the farmhouse door. Immediately, he sensed the gloom, smelled punishment, and stopped. In the lamplight, Lee sat stiffly, face locked tight. McLaws and Anderson stood before him, waiting for the hangman.

Taking a risk, Early put spunk in his voice:

"Came near breaking them, General Lee. Almost whipped them, we did."

Turning slowly toward him, Lee's face went the Gorgon one better. In a quiet voice that could bring a man to his knees, Lee said:

"General Early, I'm glad to see you. At last."

Lee had to muster all his willpower not to shout his rage. Early, who at least had made a fight of it, had nearly broken Lee's grip on himself when he burst in full of self-congratulation, barking that he had "almost whipped them." Lee had barely refrained from snapping that "almost" is a word no officer should ever use. "Almost" was a word for moral cowards.

Keeping the three division commanders on their feet before him, Lee suppressed another pulse of fury. If Early had fought and failed, Anderson had barely fought, and McLaws had hardly moved. What was wrong with these men? Couldn't they grasp the necessity of sacrifice? The need for relentlessness? The fundamental requirement to impose your will on the enemy and never stop? They'd held a triumph in their fists and let it run through their fingers.

With his voice under strict discipline—he had disciplined his life since his first day at West Point—Lee said:

"Gentlemen, you failed your country today."

McLaws opened his mouth to protest, but Lee stopped him with a raised finger.

"I will not hear excuses," Lee continued. "Excuses are a worthless currency. What I expect, gentlemen, is an advance at dawn by each of your divisions and all of your men. Nor do I wish you to drive those people and General Sedgwick across the river. I expect you to *destroy* them. Here." Merciless and unwavering, his eyes searched downcast faces.

Judging their expressions of fear and regret, of wounded pride and inevitable self-interest, he turned his inner anger toward Jackson.

He had learned further details of Jackson's wounding, appalled. How could Jackson have behaved so foolishly, taken so little care? This day . . . this day and the day before . . . would have had different outcomes had Jackson been present. But the man had played the fool in a junior officer's witless prank, devil-may-care in the dark. And who would pay the price? If Jackson had lost an arm, the army had lost an unrivaled opportunity, perhaps even a chance to end the war.

For the South, incomplete victories would never be sufficient. His army had to strike the Union's heart. Those people had to be shocked into submission, they had to understand they could not win.

Well, tomorrow would be different, if the Lord allowed. How might Jackson put it? Sedgwick and his corps would "suffer the fate of the Amalekites." Then, if Hooker did not flee, the following day would see the destruction of that man's entire army, an end befitting Pharaoh's chariots.

After letting his silence punish the generals standing penitent, Lee told them:

"Alexander has ranged Banks' Ford, the essential point. He will shell the crossing all night, to discourage any thought those people may have of escape. At dawn, your skirmishers will advance and press the attack. No matter the circumstance, not a single regiment will withdraw as long as one man remains to hold its flag." Again, he scanned the faces, though with impatience this time. "I believe you understand me."

Truant from their duty on this day, the division commanders traded looks, waiting for one of the others to break the silence. Finally, Early said:

"Yes, sir. I reckon we understand, all right."

With a doorward cant of his head, Lee concluded:

"Good. Now you may go."

Dan Butterfield was mortified. Upon his arrival to oversee the staff, Hooker had tugged him aside without allowing him time to take a piss.

Joe had concocted a new plan. And it was madness.

The bluster was still intact, but Joe seemed deprived of his senses. When he spoke, his hands grew agitated.

With wet canvas sagging and an oil lamp flickering, Joe rambled on, his great shock of hair greased and dirty, the side of his face puffed up and badly bruised.

"It's brilliant," Hooker repeated. "Can't you see it? If Lee fails to attack me here tomorrow, I'll withdraw the army under cover of darkness and recross where Sedgwick's holding open the fords. Surprise Lee and overwhelm him." Excited and unsteady, he looked at Butterfield expectantly.

Dan Butterfield did not know where—or how—to begin. If the grand plan they'd designed had not led to Lee's defeat, a madcap, impossible scheme of sneaking the army over the river and back again—while Lee, alert now, watched—just made no sense. It was a Chinese opium dream, an invitation to complete disaster.

"Joe . . . Sedgwick was hard-pressed today. And Lee's apt to hit him much harder tomorrow, he wants to gobble the plum at the end of the branch."

Hooker shook his head. "No. Lee *failed* today. Tomorrow, he'll come at *us*, right here. He's *got* to come at us."

Butterfield almost felt that Joe would be better off if he had a couple of whiskeys. His excitement was peculiar and unnerving. And those hands . . .

"Well, Joe, let's look into it . . . tally the numbers, see what can be done." It was the sort of answer Butterfield had learned in the world of business, an answer that was no answer at all. "Meanwhile, I've finally gotten news of the cavalry."

"What does he say?"

"Actually, it's all from the Richmond papers. Smuggled across the lines. Apparently, the Cavalry Corps has been everywhere doing everything, Richmond's been in a panic." Butterfield's features narrowed. "Everything except fulfilling the mission. Stoneman doesn't seem to have annoyed Lee in the least."

"Worthless," Hooker said. "They're worthless. I've relieved Averell, you know. The man couldn't follow orders."

"I know, I know. Joe, we have to talk about that. I have to admit the orders were unclear, it wasn't—"

"The man didn't follow orders. Done is done."

Butterfield would have preferred to wait to raise the next, more sensitive matter, but there was no time. Joe had to see the reality before him, to protect himself.

"Listen, Joe . . . I need you to trust my advice on something."

Hooker's eyes focused as they had not done. "What?"

"Summon a council of war. Tonight. All the corps commanders. Except Sedgwick, of course."

Hooker folded his arms. "I don't believe in councils of war. I'm in sole command." Unsteady fingers troubled an elbow. "Councils of war don't ever make good decisions, they always give in to their fears."

"Joe, that's the point. Look, the campaign hasn't gone exactly as we'd hoped. Frankly, there will be recriminations." He stepped closer, lowering his voice, as if political spies surrounded the tent. "Have them vote. On whether you should withdraw the army or stay and fight. Get them on the record, in front of each other."

"No. No, I've made up my mind. If Lee doesn't attack us here tomorrow, I'll withdraw and then recross the Rappahannock behind Sedgwick, strike Lee there, make a new start."

"Well, we could see what happens." He took Hooker by the forearm and told him, "Joe, you need to have them vote. Trust me."

"And if they vote against me? If they vote to just sit here? Or attack Lee from here, where he's prepared to receive us? And Longstreet could—"

"Longstreet's not here. Sharpe finds no evidence of it."

"But he *will* be. Any day."

Instead of releasing Hooker's arm, Butterfield tightened his grip. "Joe, hear me out. If they vote to stay here and sit, or even to attack . . . the blame will fall on their shoulders, if we fail. We'll make damned sure of that. You'll be the honest chief who welcomed advice, ever willing to hear out his subordinates, wanting only the best for army and country. And if they vote to withdraw, they're the ones whose courage failed." Butterfield sighed and dropped his hand away. "Between us, I've done well backing fire insurance. And I'm telling you that you need insurance now. And this kind's free." He reached for Hooker's wrist again but stopped himself. "Joe, the aftermath of all of this is going to be one self-serving accusation after another. And Lincoln can't be trusted, look at how he treated George McClellan."

"Lincoln . . ." Hooker's voice might have belonged to a sleepwalker.

"We've got to spread the blame, Joe."

"A council of war . . ."

"Don't even call it that, if you don't want to. Don't call it anything. But get them to vote. In front of each other."

"I'm still the army's commander, I'm still responsible. No matter what they—"

"Yes and no. The question is what the newspapers will say, where the factions in Congress will see their advantage. You have powerful friends, but you have to help them help you. Listen to me now, Joe. *I'm* your friend. And I'm going to be honest. The goal at this point isn't a victor's laurels. It's to avoid a comprehensive defeat, the loss of this army you've built—an army still loyal to *you,* even if its generals aren't. Don't be a damned fool, get those vipers to vote. Make them squirm."

Dan Butterfield had bet heavily on Joe Hooker, who had seemed capable of rising to any command, to any office. And Butterfield intended to remain loyal, that was beyond question. But he was a man of business, a realist, and he had to consider that a time might one day come when Hooker would need to be dropped. Not yet, of course.

"Council of war . . . ," Hooker repeated.

* * *

Sedgwick veered between confidence and fear. His men had repulsed the Johnnies handsomely, his line had not failed at a single point. Still, he had pulled back after the fighting, to a snug defensive position above Banks' Ford. He was confident he could hold.

Unless Longstreet truly had arrived or would arrive. Unless Lee piled on still greater force. It would be impossible for the corps to cross the river under fire in broad daylight. And the blasted Confederate artillery was already shelling the only reliable crossing.

The Rappahannock had risen alarmingly, too. That cloudburst had threatened his pontoons, the sudden increase in the current had all but ripped them loose. What if more rain came and he was trapped?

Mightn't it be the wiser course to withdraw tonight? If Hooker could be persuaded to approve it? "Fighting Joe" Hooker . . . Sedgwick had always been skeptical of the man, if privately, and now he distrusted him thoroughly: He could count on Lee attacking the Sixth Corps, all right, but he couldn't count on Hooker to come to his aid. The man had more mouth than brains, that was the problem.

The campaign had been a travesty since the first of the bridges was laid, a classroom study concocted by Hooker and Butterfield, perfect in design and completely impractical. And he was the one about to pay the price.

He turned to McMahon, his chief of staff, again.

"I want another report from the engineers. Water levels, current, bank saturation, pontoon stability . . . you know. Wouldn't do to be caught out and trapped."

"No, sir."

It struck Uncle John Sedgwick that if conditions at the ford demanded a prompt withdrawal, more than a single problem would be solved.

Marty McMahon, chief of staff of the Sixth Corps, had lost another illusion. With a brother gone to an inglorious death of common illness while in uniform and another brother serving at great risk, many a scale had fallen from his eyes. But he had idolized Sedgwick—a splendid man on a battlefield—until now. Given what was essentially an independent command, Sedgwick had failed, paralyzed by the responsibility. Again and again, the corps commander's decisions had been laggard and overly cautious, in McMahon's view, and one chance after another had been lost. Sedgwick had only come into his own this very day, when finally forced to fight. Now he was equivocating again.

Lieutenant Colonel Martin McMahon believed two things. First, that the corps' new position could be defended against Lee's entire army. And second, that Sedgwick was going to find an excuse to retreat across the river that night.

The lesson McMahon took to heart was that responsibility could break a man as readily as any enemy.

He wondered if that had happened to General Hooker.

We're counting on you, Dan," Butterfield told Sickles.

Mud-slopped, George Meade dismounted in front of the headquarters tent. Given the clots of aides waiting idly in the darkness, he suspected that he was among the last of the corps commanders to arrive.

He drew off his riding gloves and thrust them into his belt. Trees dripped, a small rain after the great. A sergeant lifted the flap of the headquarters tent to let him enter.

The instant Meade stepped inside, the stench of wet wool and unwashed bodies struck him. The gathered generals stood around a table that bore a lantern and a map.

Hooker looked up, face swollen. "Ah. The favored son of Philadelphia has joined us, after all." He turned to Butterfield, whom Meade regarded as little more than a pimp. "Slocum? Can we expect Slocum to grace us with his presence?"

Butterfield answered softly, close to Hooker's ear.

Meade surveyed the attendees: Hooker looked as stiff as a

dressmaker's mannequin, while Butterfield had the air of a boxer waiting in his corner; Reynolds looked drained; Howard had on his preacher's face; difficult to read, Sickles lurked on the other side of Butterfield from Hooker; Couch's eyes roamed, judging; and Gouverneur Warren stood quietly at the rear of the crowded tent. Warren didn't belong in the assembly, but Meade never minded having a fellow engineer on hand.

"All right," Hooker said, "let's get started. Since no one can find Slocum—which may say something about the state of this army." He smirked, inviting laughter, but none came. Only Butterfield even smiled. The mood was of waiting to have a tooth drawn and wishing to get the bloody business done.

Meade suspected that Butterfield, newly arrived, was behind the meeting, but he couldn't yet figure out why it had been called. Surely not a council of war—Hooker wasn't that sort.

"The situation, as I see it," Hooker continued, "is challenging. Were we to attack Lee from this position toward Fredericksburg—an attack to the east—our initial moves would be confined to forest roads easily blocked." His eyes settled on Meade. "George has seen those narrow lanes firsthand. To force our way through would be to invite excessive casualties—possibly for naught."

Meade said nothing, didn't nod and didn't change his expression. He wanted to know what Joe Hooker was up to.

"As *I* see it," Hooker said, forcing his posture to the haughty rectitude no man liked, "a frontal attack to the south could involve even greater risks. Lee has been erecting field fortifications."

"As have we," Reynolds put in, his voice verging on crankiness. He looked about to drop right where he stood.

Hooker ignored the comment. "Alternatively, should Lee be reinforced and choose to attack us here, he would, no doubt, pay a heavy price . . . but that downpour earlier . . . I believe it reminded us all that we have our backs to a river and rely on bridges that flooding would put at risk. May can be a rainy month in Virginia, after all." He glanced from face to face, registering doubts, and added, "I merely note that, of course."

Everyone waited.

Fumbling, Hooker drew a paper scrap from his pocket. "I have here the latest dispatch from Sedgwick's headquarters. *He* fears he may be compelled to withdraw across the Rappahannock tonight. I shall know more within the hour, but, at present, he finds his position untenable. Given the river's rise, the possibility of more rain at any time . . ."

"Then Sedgwick could reinforce us here," Howard said. "Were we to advance on Lee."

Hooker's grimace made clear that the suggestion was less than welcome. Meade caught Butterfield turning to Hooker then turning back again without intervening.

Their eyes met and Butterfield smiled at Meade, as if in hoary friendship. The chief of staff took charge of the silence and asked, "Anyone for a cigar? If I brought nothing else to this army, I did bring along good smokes."

Only Sickles took one. When he realized he had been the sole willing recipient, he didn't light it.

Meade noticed a drip through the canvas. It reignited his frequent anger about the shoddy goods supplied to the army.

"Gentlemen," Hooker resumed, "let me share my standing orders with you. At the cost of all else, this army is directed to defend Washington. And, frankly, I worry about the steadiness of some of our regiments, those near the end of their enlistments. I must bear that in mind. In view of our duty to protect the capital."

"Joe, that's an old bugbear," Meade spoke up. "This business of covering Washington at every turn has paralyzed this army time and again." He swallowed fetid air and plunged ahead. "If we hit Lee—hard, with all we've got—he's not about to scamper off to capture Stanton and Chase."

Hooker looked venomous, but he managed to smile. "Now we have the opinion of Rittenhouse Square. . . ."

Meade felt as though, short of that last remark, Hooker had seemed to be reading from a script someone else had written. It sounded like Joe, but it didn't. Butterfield again, Meade was certain.

He reminded himself that they all were worn and short-tempered. Margaret would have taken him up for his lack of consideration, his impatience. At such a moment, clear thought, without prejudice, was essential. The hour demanded fairness, even to men he detested.

In the distance, some ass began to sing, as if he'd found a bottle.

"All right," Butterfield said, speaking up for the first time, "the commanding general puts the following proposition to the corps commanders present. Shall we attack Lee tomorrow and risk a decisive battle? Or should we withdraw the army to the north bank of the river? This isn't about formulating specific plans. It's a straightforward proposition." The New Yorker looked around, a man forever weighing the value of everything before him.

"The commanding general and I will withdraw," Butterfield continued, "so all may express their opinions, unembarrassed by our presence. Warren will remain—with your permission—as an informed resource, should you have inquiries about the state of the field. He knows Uncle John's situation firsthand, as well as our own dispositions in detail." He gathered up papers he had not used, as if they were props in a theater, their purpose served. "Summon us when you're ready with your advice."

The two men left.

The remaining generals regarded each other warily. Meade was the first to speak:

"He's already made up his mind to retreat, that's clear. Well, I vote to fight. To bring every corps in this army to bear against Lee. Without delay. Strike him tomorrow morning."

"Hear, hear!" Howard all but shouted. "My corps . . . I won't minimize the difficulties we created for this army, but my men want to fight, to erase the stain. They'd be eager to lead the attack."

Disappointing Meade—not for the first time—Couch said, "I don't know. I can see both sides."

Reynolds woke from his stupor. "I say fight. I'm with George and Otis. We didn't come down here just to take a stroll." He tottered, slipping a half step back, finding it difficult to remain on his feet. "My corps hasn't made much of a contribution—hasn't been allowed to—so we haven't bled as others have. Thus I can't urge my view to an excess. But I favor an attack on Lee tomorrow." His eyes met Meade's, but Reynolds could not hold the focus. "Sorry, I have to sit down. I'm sorry." He looked about for a camp chair with the ungainly wildness of exhaustion. "If I fall asleep, George has my proxy. I vote as he votes."

Silent until then, Sickles declared, "I don't believe Joe expects a formal vote. Just an informal poll." He shrugged, mustaches fallen and face begrimed. "I believe my corps has fought as well and as long as any here. And I say without shame that I favor a retreat."

That shocked Meade. Sickles had been all blood and thunder since the campaign's first day.

"Dan . . . ," he said. But the needed words didn't come quickly enough and Sickles continued:

"Yes, a retreat would signal a reverse. But while I'm not a professional soldier like the rest of you, I think I can claim experience of the political profession—and speaking as a former politician, the country could bear a reverse of the sort we've suffered, a disappointment but not a disaster." He surveyed the room as if facing a greater crowd and his tone assumed a rhetorician's flourish. "A catastrophic defeat, though? A mass surrender, with our men pressed against the river? Pressed *into* the river? Ball's Bluff magnified a hundred times? Why, the entire Union would lose heart."

He held out his hand, as if to reassure them. "If we withdraw, we will suffer vituperation . . . and Joe, poor Joe will be vilified. But he's man enough to bear the burden, I think. We all can bear the burden." Again, he made a show of searching their faces. "But would any of us welcome the blame for the final dissolution of the Union? If this army is destroyed, that will be our fate."

"That's an exaggeration, Dan, and you know it," Meade snapped. Restraining his anger, he continued, "If Sharpe's right, we still outnumber Lee two to one. He's not about to destroy this army." He snorted. "We might do the job ourselves, but Bobby Lee won't."

Couch leaned into the lamplight, features earnest. "No, George,

I see Dan's point. Oh, we're all fighters here, every one of us. But the potential consequences . . ."

Startled and betrayed, Meade turned to Warren. "Guvvie, what do *you* think? You've seen every position, every line."

"George, I don't command a corps. I'm . . . only here to offer expertise. Such as it may be."

"But you've got a damned *mind*, an informed opinion. Just tell us what you think."

Warren weighed the request. The lantern sputtered. Outside, men laughed.

Beginning with a sigh, Warren said, "I've *begged* Joe to attack. Earlier this evening, I *begged* him." He looked down, already defeated. "I'd hoped something would come of this . . . this meeting. A decision to fight, a plan of battle . . ."

"Well, something *has* come of it," Meade told him. "Five corps commanders present, three in favor of a morning attack."

"Remember, this wasn't a formal vote," Sickles insisted. "Nobody can claim that. It was just an informal poll. Nothing binding."

"Let's see what else Joe has to say," Couch offered. "Tell him what we think and see where it goes." Musing, he added, "I'm not *against* an attack . . . I simply don't favor one."

Meade wanted to vomit. Darius Couch seemed more the politician than Dan Sickles. And Dan . . . what had gotten into him?

Butterfield? They were cronies, of course, Butterfield, Hooker, and Sickles. What *was* Butterfield up to? Whatever it was, it didn't seem to have gone as had been expected. Dan was fidgety, a serving maid suspected of stealing spoons.

He wished he were not so weary, wished he could think with greater subtlety.

Hooker and his chief of staff returned. Hooker listened to each man's views with great solemnity, a dignity pompous and false. After the others had had their say, Meade spoke for Reynolds while the First Corps commander continued to snore in his chair.

Hooker's façade, already weakened, crumbled as Meade spoke.

But he pasted up two-thirds of his bordello grin and concluded by saying, "Thank you, gentlemen. I have decided to withdraw the army. If Lee does not attack us tomorrow, our movement will commence as darkness falls. Orders of march will be provided by the staff in the morning." He gave Meade a killing look. "You are dismissed."

Awakened and accompanied to his horse, Reynolds asked Meade:

"If he'd already made up his mind to retreat, why gather us up at midnight?"

That goddamned Meade," Joe Hooker said. "That bastard son of a syphilitic whore . . ."

"Best to keep your voice down," Butterfield told him.

"Now this." Hooker held Sedgwick's latest message in a trembling hand. "He wants me to authorize him to run away, to recross his corps immediately."

"Let him," Butterfield said.

"But my plan . . ."

"Let him. But don't lose that message, get it in the logs. That's his contribution, another cause of failure. Not your fault, Joe."

Hooker's features took on the innocence of an earnest child. "I *could* have beaten Lee. I could have done it. *They* let me down, all of them."

"I know."

"That piss-cutter Meade . . . I'd like to go at that snot with my bare fists."

"I have a better idea," Butterfield told him. "Designate the Fifth Corps as the rear guard for the crossing. Were Lee to strike while the crossing was under way . . . well, Meade would be responsible for any losses. Wouldn't he? And if, say, there were trouble at the bridges and the rear guard was cut off . . . George wants to fight, so let him."

"I . . . don't want to be vengeful, you understand."

"Of course not."

FOURTEEN

May 5 to May 6

With the morning's revelations, Lee's bridled rage gave way to bitterness and a steady, simmering anger toward his subordinates. He had risen before dawn, barely teased by sleep. He could not recall his dreams, but they had been troubled. A glass of buttermilk and a campfire biscuit did not appease him, and the evening's rain had left behind a morass that soiled his boots. He was curt with the servant who cared for his uniforms and sour toward the groom who saw to his horse. Then a witless soldier surprised him during a quarrel with his bowels. Soon after, the first news arrived from the morning's advance. It gripped him like a cramp.

The Union Sixth Corps had escaped. His advancing skirmishers had discovered only forgotten pickets, bewildered stragglers, a handful of eager deserters, and a wealth of abandoned equipment and supplies. Despite the nightlong shelling of Banks' Ford, Sedgwick had slipped off, retreating with a finesse he had not shown on the attack.

The dilatory actions—the contemptible indolence—of McLaws, Anderson, and even Early the day before had robbed the army of a magnificent prize: an entire Union corps offered for the taking.

With his generals sent off again, smarting and in receipt of explicit orders, he turned to Taylor and said, with unwonted sharpness:

"What is this commotion, Major? Who are those men? I cannot think with this noise."

Taylor nodded, meek as a maid, and said, "I'll see to it, sir." And off he strode to quiet the headquarters hangers-on, the scouts and orderlies, the couriers and commissaries, none of whose behavior had been unusual.

Instantly, Lee was ashamed of himself: Authority abused was authority compromised. All through his career, he had taken pains to be civil, even in distasteful situations. An officer's task—a soldier's duty—was to protect the weak, and, by definition, every subordinate was weaker than his superior.

This war had cost him so much. He must not let it compromise his character. He would not allow it to render him common and spiteful.

Even the innermost members of his staff avoided approaching him. He stepped still farther apart from those who served him, staring northward then lifting his eyes to the heavens. The day could not decide on a course, with a masked sun and sailing clouds showing luminous borders. It must not rain. Not again. Not before he completed his final and greatest task: the destruction of Joseph Hooker's mishandled army.

He had dispatched them, his three right-flank generals, to gather their soldiers and march to join the divisions waiting at Chancellorsville. Before this day was out, the Army of the Potomac would be shattered and captive, no matter the cost in lives.

And the war might end before summer came to the South.

No," Hooker said, handing back the draft order, "I want the wounded moved *now*. And the supply wagons. Then the reserve artillery. I want them across the river before dark, it's going to be hard enough to get the batteries and six corps across in one night. Three bridges or thirty, things go wrong." He nodded to Butterfield. "Other than that, good work."

Butterfield held the pages in both hands, not quite ready to have them copied and distributed.

"Joe . . . I hear what you're saying . . . but if we start moving the wounded now, to say nothing of the trains, it might alert Lee. And it could send the wrong signal to the men."

"I want the wounded evacuated *today*. Starting as soon as

possible. No more discussion, Dan." He stopped cold but then added, "Except for those too badly hurt, of course. Arrange for surgeons to stay behind, look after them. Plenty of medical supplies, don't be parsimonious."

Butterfield could not help but be impressed by the man before him, a fellow who had become all but a stranger over the past few days. Since waking that morning, Joe had been the old Hooker, lucid and decisive, a different man from the addled creature of the day before.

A realization gripped Butterfield, the prospect of a splendid opportunity.

"Joe, you're brilliant," he said. And he meant it. By and large.

Hooker smirked. "I'm glad somebody in this army sees it."

"No, truly. The wounded. Moving them now." Butterfield felt almost hopeful again. "We can push that in the newspapers, it's pure bullion: 'Hooker cares for his wounded soldiers first.' Really, that's good."

"It's not about the newspapers," Hooker said. He sounded uncomfortably sincere.

Butterfield waved his hands. "Doesn't matter. Either way. The folks back home will like it. The voters . . ."

"Speaking of which . . . I'd like you to take care of keeping Lincoln informed. To the degree he needs to be informed." Hooker met Butterfield's eyes. "You know how to put things. In that world. Spoon up the porridge, placate him." He took out a filthy rag and cleared his nostrils, one then the other. "The man saw two Indians once and thinks he's a soldier. Just see to that end of things."

"Sure, Joe. I'll handle it." Butterfield lifted the papers a few inches, calling Hooker's attention back to the order. "Anything else? Before I get this out?"

"No, I think that's all." Hooker straightened his back and lifted his chin. Even with the side of his face bruised and misshapen, he remained the public's model of a general, an inspiring figure even now for the soldiers. "Meanwhile, if Lee's fool enough to attack us today, in this position . . . God help him, because I won't."

"Joe . . . you don't really believe he'd consider attacking? Now? Here? Given the time we've had to entrench, the numbers? He'd be utterly mad. . . ."

"Not mad. Proud. Mark my words, his pride will be Lee's undoing. Today or another day."

Butterfield shrugged. "I'll get this off."

As the chief of staff turned back to his duties, Hooker added, "Send the first copy to Meade. We'll see just how badly he wants to fight, after all."

Through a smudged window, he glimpsed the glory of God's creation. The sky was overcast, that odd gray that could nag the eye with brightness, still he found it beautiful. Turning his head just a little on his pillow, he saw treetops in new leaf, and when he had awakened at dawn he heard birdsong, not artillery. He never had found the words, not even with the few women who had come close to him, to express his wonder at the Lord's generosity, the fruitfulness, or the splendor that awaited a man each day.

He recalled those summer afternoons in the glade across the river, the slow waters cooling the air, the green scent of life, and his unthinking youth.

How long ago that was, and how very fine it had been.

The Lord had given him much upon this earth, so very much. If the Lord had seen fit to take his arm—surely for good reason—his gratitude and soul remained intact.

The only matter pestering his conscience was his lack of eagerness to return to duty. He was obliged to return to the war the moment he felt himself capable. That was as clear as the Lord's own admonitions. Yet he craved a little time apart from those dreadful seductions, the elation of blood-bought victories and the trap of earthly renown.

He wished to go home.

All his days, he had needed to be strong for himself and for others, and now he bore the weight of tens of thousands. And he was tired. He longed for a brief dispensation, for permission to be weak for a little while, to rely on the strength of others, on his *esposa,* to be caressed.

He thought now that the Lord had chastised him not only for his pride, but for the sinful pleasure he took in war. Even in prayer, he had lied to the Lord about the ecstasy he'd come to crave, his lust to slay his enemies and the transfiguring joy he felt at a foe's defeat.

Joshua had done his duty, some of its biddings terrible, but he could not recall the Bible portraying Joshua as delighting in cruelties. Joshua was obedient to and fearful of the Lord, not jubilant amid massacre. His deeds might have brought him satisfaction at doing the work of the Lord, but not pleasure, never pleasure.

He had sinned. And the Lord demanded repentance.

If only he might have a little time, some weeks apart . . .

They told him little of the battle's course and that much only upon his insistence. He gathered that things had been going well but that matters were not yet resolved.

They did not wish to excite him. They wished him to rest. But the rest he needed was not merely of the body.

The body would heal, he was certain. The flesh was the slightest matter. Pain passed, as did pleasures. The body was a transient's habitation.

What was the difference between regret and repentance? How could a man be certain that his faith was true and pure, and not an attempt to bargain with the Lord, to bribe Him with hosannas?

A cardinal, a male, perched on the windowsill, a perfect creature, vivid and wonderful.

Yes, he was thankful to the Lord. For that flitting bird. For everything.

With a quick knock, Dr. McGuire came into the room. The Chandlers had been generous, providing him with a little house apart, with privacy, while their own home ached with the suffering of the wounded.

"You're awake, sir?"

"Resting. As ordered."

McGuire drew a chair to the bedside. "The pain in your side . . . it's gone? You're feeling better?"

"Yes," Jackson lied.

Robinson Crusoe. That's who he'd damned well felt like. Robinson Crusoe, bereft even of his Friday. Nominally the chief of artillery for the Army of the Potomac, Brigadier General Henry Hunt had found himself in charge of just about nothing. Left behind to stew and fret and watch.

In his reorganization of the army, Hooker had pushed not only the batteries but full control over them down to corps and even divisions, maintaining only a grudging army reserve. Hunt had warned him: In a crisis, there had to be one central authority able to shift guns around a battlefield without dickering with generals who didn't want to release a single tube. Hooker hadn't listened and paid the price.

Hooker had even ordered him to remain north of the river. To keep him out of the way, to prevent him from interfering.

Even so, Hunt had stayed busy, shifting batteries up and down the north bank as they were needed, in the saddle so constantly he'd lamed one horse and just about used up another.

Oh, he'd gotten his authority back, returned to him in a panic, but too late. Hunt had foreseen what the Southern guns could do—even though his army had better artillerymen, better cannon, and better ammunition. All Hunt had been able to accomplish was to cover the last withdrawal from Fredericksburg and to shield the flight of Sedgwick's corps from the lunatic mess into which Uncle John had led it.

Now the rest of the army was retreating, with teamsters already crowding the three bridges and a general order issued for a withdrawal after dark—another development he'd anticipated. Indeed, Hunt already had over forty guns in position above and below the crossing site, prepared to protect the army as it returned.

Still, the situation remained a disgraceful mess, and Hunt took it personally. He knew what his guns could have done, had he been trusted. Artillery, well-handled, could decide a battle before either side grasped that its fate had already been determined.

Instead of supporting advances and repelling attacks, he'd been consigned to passivity and embarrassment.

Henry Hunt swore that if ever he was allowed to employ his batteries and battalions as he saw fit, he'd show every last damned infantry officer what massed guns could do.

Again, the afternoon declined while his soldiers moved too slowly. As Lee watched the head of Anderson's column pass by on a march barely begun, he fought an urge to dismount and shove the officers along.

A courier had informed him that McLaws had closed on his new position at Chancellorsville, enabling Heth to join Stuart on the left. But Anderson had been slow yet again at gathering his command and starting his march.

Anderson had excuses, of course. Everyone had excuses. And plans came to naught.

Nor did the weather look promising.

He had hoped to launch an attack on both of Hooker's flanks by two p.m. Now the hands on his pocket watch neared four and it would be at least two more hours before Anderson was in place and set to attack.

But attack they would. Lee didn't care if it would be after midnight and dark as Hades. His army was going to strike. And Hooker and his army would be destroyed.

Nothing was going to stop him.

George Meade continued to hope that Lee would attack while the army was still in place. If Lee proved fool enough to assault the heavily fortified lines, it might yet redeem the campaign, at least in part.

His men waited. He waited. Nothing happened.

Crowding in from the west, the clouds remained swollen. If they didn't pass by, if it rained, the crossing was going to be a wretched affair.

His corps had been ordered to serve as the rear guard. Meade understood the taunt, but if Joe Hooker had meant to punish him, it hadn't worked. One corps or another had to bring up the rear, and Meade believed his men would give Lee a thrashing, should the old traitor interfere with the crossing.

Those clouds, though . . .

Corporal Bill Smith had a presentiment. No more, really, than an unsettling feeling, it nonetheless worked on his nerves. He'd never believed in hocus-pocus doings before the war, but he'd seen too many deaths foretold to rule out the strangest things.

He did not want to attack. Not this time.

But the 12th Virginia stood in line, behind a parapet of earth and logs, waiting for the order to go forward.

As they'd relieved the ragtags of Heth's division, their fellow Virginians had warned them that the Yankees had built themselves a position that passed for a downright fortress, a line of defenses that promised the massacre of any hayseed idiots who approached it.

Normally, Bill Smith allowed for a generous degree of exaggeration from his fellow soldiers, but this time he believed every word of warning.

He did not want to go forward.

But the mood was of inevitability. All that day, he had not seen one officer of rank who hadn't gone mean as a water snake, and the junior officers just put one foot in front of the other, staying quiet.

This was it, then. This was it.

He found himself praying. Without thinking to do it, without deciding.

He had the jumps, no question. His guts felt queasy and watery. He'd never been so shaken.

Didn't want to bust out crying, him wearing corporal's stripes.

Oh, Lord, oh, Jesus, please don't. Just don't. Please don't.

The clouds exploded with rain, as if a dam in Heaven had collapsed.

Lee waved off Taylor's attempt to spread his oilskin cape across his shoulders. He preferred to let the deluge soak him through, rather than cower. The weather had played him a vicious trick, but he would spite the weather. His men would advance the moment the tempest ceased.

The rain fell with a weight that threatened to bruise flesh. Still, Robert E. Lee's expression never changed. Even though the world had gone dark and no man was positioned to see his face.

Strength of character mattered. Even when no man saw it. Especially when no man saw it.

The rain slashed in to blind him.

Hurricanes in Mexico and Texan thunderstorms could not compare. Sheets of lightning bleached the sky and the heavens roared. The rain fell with force enough to knock down a child, to fell a woman. Fields became ponds, and ponds became lakes, and the world closed in and blackened to stop hearts. Then fingers of lightning, the broken bones of the universe, made men gasp again. Lee felt the primitive impulse to take shelter, it was almost overpowering, but he remained in the saddle, fiercely upright. He would not be moved. He would not be defeated. His will would not be weakened. This rain would cease and then he would attack.

Back in his bad years, Hooker had once passed out on the floor and a pair of sluts had overturned a tub of bathwater on him. He'd never known how heavy water could be, not until that rude, aquatic morning.

This rain was harder, heavier. It threatened to play the devil with all of his plans. Already, the engineers had warned of a six-foot rise in the river, with worse to come. It seemed increasingly possible that the army would be cut off.

Ordering Dan Butterfield to follow, the general commanding

the Army of the Potomac led his escort to the bridges and hurried to safety on the northern bank.

Private Benjamin Farmer lay in the mud beside the others who'd suffered the gravest wounds. Rain punched his face, but he could not turn his head to keep the water from clogging his nose and forcing its way into his mouth and throat. He gagged. And he gagged again.

He wanted to live.

He yearned with heart and soul to rise from the slop, but his arms and legs no longer obeyed his commands. Men lying near cried out for help, but Farmer did not dare open his mouth, afraid of choking on the gush of water.

Men cursed or called for their mothers. Others begged, "Help me," over and over.

And all of them waited.

Water cascaded from the cabin's roof and the wounded served as gutters. More water raced down a slope behind the shack, engulfing the patch of yard. All around, water pooled and rose, as if to float men off, but the mud held them fast where hurried hands had left them.

Those who could sit up or at least incline on their elbows were blessed: They shivered and hoped.

Benjamin Farmer could not rise an inch. And no one moved to help him. He wanted to be home, back in New York, warm within walls he knew. They could cut off his arms and legs, if only they sent him home.

Surgeons had not been seen for hours and the orderlies had slipped away, after scouring the pockets of helpless men. Farmer had nothing of material value: He'd already been robbed as he lay on the battlefield.

Still, a man in a bloody smock pocketed the picture of his sweetheart, sealed in a tin frame, the last of his possessions. Even the battlefield thieves had spared him that.

Well, Clara would not have him now, it didn't matter. What

woman would ever want him? He would give her up, release her from her vows. If he could just live.

His Clara faded, dismissed in his mother's favor.

Familiar walls beckoned again, the flowered wallpaper and a bright lamp on the table: home.

I'll be a good boy, Mother, I'll be a good boy always. I'll be such a good boy. . . .

The gathering water reached his ears and continued rising steadily. Lips sealed, he prayed in wild fragments and broken words imagined.

The water smoothed onto his cheeks. Then it lapped the corners of his mouth.

He willed his body to rise, with all the might a man could ever muster. But nothing happened.

Even now, he could not believe that he would not be rescued, that he could be abandoned to die like this.

Wouldn't *anyone* help him?

The water closed over his mouth and flooded his nostrils.

Persuaded at last to take shelter, Lee turned to Marshall, to all of his gathered staff, and told them, "Prepare new orders for an attack in the morning."

Gouverneur Warren finally located Hooker in a house on the north bank, a mile from the crossing site. Heavy with mud and soaked through despite his rubber cape, Warren felt an immense, almost unmanageable resentment upon finding Hooker dry and dozing before a fire, but there was no time to indulge in selfish emotions.

Jostled by Dan Butterfield, Hooker opened his eyes.

"We need to suspend the crossing," Warren told him, dripping on a dirtied, poor-man's rug. "The bridges are ready to tear loose, the water's over their tops. They can't take any more stress, the cables won't hold."

"Well, do something. You're the engineer."

Warren ignored Hooker's tone, the implied insult. "The engineers are doing their best, they all know what's at stake. But the crossings need to stop, at least for an hour or two. Until they can shore things up." After a flush of doubt, Warren decided to explain the effort under way. "There's no hope of maintaining all three bridges. We're taking the weakest one down and using the pontoons and deck to extend the remaining two. It's the only chance."

"We'd only have two bridges. The army needs three, it's all been calculated."

Warren's temper seeped into his voice. "The choice is two bridges, or no bridges. It's been raining like this for, what, seven hours? Eight? The truth is no one can promise even two bridges that will hold. The river's banks are collapsing. But those men out there in the rain are doing every goddamned thing they can."

Hooker stared at him. As if the rain and all else were Warren's fault. Then the stare drooped to a vacancy.

Butterfield stepped in, telling Warren, "We'll signal Couch. If the damned torches will stay lit." He looked down at Hooker, seated and gone distant. "Just a pause. Until the problem's solved."

Butterfield made a discreet sign for Warren to leave.

Captain Bill Folwell felt the bridge give way beneath him. Losing his balance, he toppled toward the river, too startled to react. He fell between two barely tethered pontoons and smacked the water.

The cold and the current hit him a double blow. Stronger than any muscle, the flood gripped him and pulled him away.

By a miracle, he managed to grasp a rope. Hoping it was attached at the other end.

Normally drowsy, the river had awakened to a rage. It took all of his strength just to cling to the line, he could not pull himself back toward the bridge.

The current twisted his body and forced him under, into a heavy darkness, into panic. When he resurfaced, choking, torches dazzled his swamped eyes. He was closer to the bridge than he'd believed. Or the bridge had come to him.

Barely audible in the tempest, a voice called:

"Hang on, sir. Hang on, we'll pull you in."

He gripped the rope to skin the flesh from his palms, hacking up water, fighting.

The river wanted him.

After the longest minute of his life, big hands grabbed his collar then clutched an arm. His soldiers, his engineers, hauled him out of the water, wary themselves of tumbling off the bridge but far more skilled at their labors than was Folwell.

He coughed up more foul water.

"You all right, sir?" one of his sergeants asked.

He had no idea. He supposed so. He nodded.

"Right, boys," the sergeant said, "back to work."

Tarred against the rain's onslaught, the torches moved away, leaving a lantern to sputter on the planks. The rain fought to get at the tiny flame.

Voice made quiet—as much as the storm allowed—the sergeant told him, "Captain, you'd best go back up on the bank now. And do what officers do."

Finding his voice, Folwell gasped, "I want to help. Times like this . . . everyone has to pitch in, even the officers. I . . . want to help."

"Well, sir," the sergeant told him, "you'd help a great deal by not falling back in the river."

To Meade's astonishment, Couch had had yet another change of mind. As the senior general remaining south of the river, Couch was in command in Hooker's absence. Voice raised against the rain, he repeated:

"You were right, George. We needed to make a fight of it. I didn't have my head attached last night."

"Well, we still can. That 'pause' in Joe's signal, it's going to last all night, I'd bet a gold piece. And when the morning comes—when Lee comes—we'll still be here."

Cascades of water bent the shoulders of the two generals and forced down the heads of their horses. Neither man complained.

And after ten hours of the deluge, a soldier just adjusted to the misery.

"Three corps," Couch mused. "That's not bad. Mine, yours, Reynolds'."

"We could hold this bridgehead until doomsday. Warren laid out a line that's close to perfect. A single corps could hold it. And with three . . . and the Johnnies slowed by the mud . . ."

"Warren wants command of a corps, you know," Couch commented.

"If it were in my power, I'd give him one."

"All right. I'll send a signal to Joe. Or try to. I swear to God, Judas Iscariot must have come back as a Signal officer. I'll tell him that we mean to fight it out." He snorted, loud as a horse. "Damned well won't surrender, that's for certain."

Couch turned his mount in the ever-deepening mud and the horse struggled off with the general hunched in his saddle.

Even on duty in Florida, Meade had never witnessed such a storm. His spectacles were useless, his clinging uniform a woolen prison, his rain cape merely adding sweat to the mix.

He gave necessary orders to the drenched, dutiful men who would, in turn, give orders to his soldiers, the men who suffered all and had no voices. Of all the tragedies, great and small, that had broken the campaign, what galled him, what gnawed at him most deeply, was the waste of good men's lives. Hooker hadn't *fought:* He'd staged a parade then quit.

And good men died for nothing.

George Meade swore that if ever such decisions were up to him, he would fight to win when a fight was on and never squander lives in a half-hearted effort.

Materializing from the drown-the-world darkness, John Reynolds found him.

"Took a while to sniff you out, George," Reynolds said. "This rain."

"Couldn't smell a pig's ass in this storm."

Reynolds forced his mount closer. "George, I just wanted to tell you . . . bridges or not, if you stay here to fight, I'm staying with you. To the end."

Meade was touched. "Couch wants to fight it out, too. He changed his mind."

Face a white smear framed by a turned-up collar and cap pulled low, Reynolds said, "You know, George, I'd gladly serve under you, date of rank be damned. If you were in Joe's place."

Meade snorted. "Only the biggest damned fool in the world would accept command of this army."

"No, no, *no!*" Hooker barked. "Answer him immediately. The engineers have two spans open again, the withdrawal resumes immediately." He paced and snarled, "They want to embarrass me, that's all. Couch, what has *he* done on this campaign? Now he wants to strike a heroic pose?" He scanned the floor as if hunting creatures to kill. "Meade's behind it. Meade's gotten to him. I should charge them all with mutiny. . . ."

"Keep your voice down, Joe. Sit down. I'll handle everything," Butterfield assured him.

Orders were orders, and George Meade was an obedient soldier. In the gray of a tardy dawn, he marched his last brigade through the mud and swollen air back to the crossings. He'd left a powerful skirmish line behind, enough to discourage any Confederates able and willing to struggle through the mire.

So far, there had been no sign of Rebel movement.

The last acres by the river were packed with troops, Couch's corps and his own men waiting their turn: Reynolds' corps was already across. The progress over the bridges was constant and orderly, but Meade felt the press of time.

Hooker had ordered them all to withdraw, and the order was explicit. Meade was *not* to fight. He could resist if attacked, but must seek to break contact promptly. There would be no last stand south of the Rappahannock.

Meade watched, alone, as the crowd on the south bank thinned and the endless blue columns finally neared an end. It was time, he decided, to call in the skirmishers. Then he would cross the river himself, accepting defeat.

He wondered what the future held for all of them.

If he'd suffered through an uglier night, Bill Smith couldn't recall it. The feared attack had not gone forward, thanks to that hammer-hard rain, and his presentiment had come to nothing. But the squalor and near hopelessness of that night spent in the open, wrapped in a useless Yankee tent half, had been a discouraging business, enough to make the best of men lose heart.

And he wasn't feeling like the best of men.

The rain had stopped, leaving behind mud to swallow a horse. True, they had captured Yankee rations to chaw on, but even those were wet through and befouled. In air as heavy as soaked towels, men quietly cleaned their rifles, those indispensable fifth limbs, and hoped their cartridges were dry enough.

The attack had only been postponed. Every man knew it, without being told.

Of course, the 12th Virginia was tasked for skirmishers. And Corporal Smith found himself among the anointed.

Still galled him to have built that bridge for the Yankees. Just scalded his innards to ponder it.

No man showed high spirits. Each one a picture of mortal ruination, the soldiers didn't even step far off to flush their guts. Pride might return—it surely would—but for the present it was on the deserters' list.

The only human being on God's damp earth who seemed downright offensively and inexplicably cheerful was Little Billy. Mahone had come by on his too-big horse, kicking up mud and whatnot, cackling about going out to find him some Yankees for his breakfast.

Smith suspected that the Yankees had appetites of their own, not all congenial.

At last, the go-ahead-now order came down, well after the dawn had pretended to come. Unhappy soldiers stepped off under a dirty sky.

Hadn't gone as far as a rifle shot before a man's legs wore out. Down Southside way, you had to go deep in a swamp to find such mud. He had to keep on going, though. His legs just had to do as they were told. And as long as he had arms and strength left in them, Smith intended to hold his rifle high, defying the mud that leapt toward the weapon.

Yankees might catch him out many a way, but they wouldn't catch him with a useless rifle.

"Guess this here's 'the merry month of May,'" a jokester snickered.

No one laughed.

The feel of things grew ominous. Ahead, every man could see the open stretches, freed of all but stumps, where the Yankees had cleared extensive fields of fire. Beyond, layers of abatis announced the presence of field fortifications.

"Going to get it now," the jokester said. "Yes, sirree. Just you wait."

"Shut up," a sergeant told him.

Every man bent his shoulders. Tense as a coward's finger on a trigger.

The only two sounds left in the world were birds at their own doings and the suck-slop of men struggling forward, many barefoot by choice to save their shoes.

What the devil were the Yankees waiting for?

Movement. Ahead. Smith clutched his rifle tighter, thumb set to cock back the hammer.

Waving his arms wildly to signal *Don't shoot!*, a gray-clad figure clambered up from behind the Yankees' earthen parapet. He called the Virginians forward.

The Yankee fortifications were impressive—daunting—but abandoned. A handful of soldiers from a sister regiment had found easier going through a grove and made it inside the Yankee barricades first.

"I'll be . . . ," Smith said to himself.

They held up then, waiting on further orders, which took a fair time to come. By the time they resumed their advance, the hour pushed noon. Here and there, forgotten Yankees or men who'd slept through everything materialized to be taken prisoner—not without enduring some hard teasing and the ritual of having their pockets emptied for the immediate benefit of the Confederacy. Some of the Federals were confused, others were sheepish, and some were plain relieved.

One Yank had dirty pictures you wouldn't believe.

Later, facing another Union line even more formidable, the 12th Virginia was halted for the last time. Other regiments, other brigades, had already gone ahead to clear things out.

Word came back that the whole Yankee army was gone.

Disgusted, Lee retreated into quiet. A victory had been won, indeed, but a great chance had been lost. Still, he believed he had learned a thing of value: The Union army had lost the will to fight. The soldiers in blue might range from brave to indifferent, along with the cowards who disgraced every flag, but the generals—so many of them men he'd known and respected—hadn't the heart for an all-or-nothing fight. They did not lack strength of arms but strength of purpose.

The Union generals behaved like frightened men.

His mood was raw and forbidding, his stomach gone sour, but a vision had already begun to take hold, a course he'd pursued too timidly the year before, when he had crossed the Potomac into Maryland. He had lacked the confidence then to drive any deeper, fearful that he might be cut off and cornered. The price of his caution had been that he'd handed the initiative to McClellan, who, blessedly, had failed to make the most of it. Still, the Army of Northern Virginia had been driven to near destruction outside of Sharpsburg.

He saw now that his mistake had been lack of boldness. It was an error he would not make again.

The North beckoned. Virginia might be spared yet another summer of war. With Baltimore or, better, Philadelphia threatened or seized outright, even the most unforgiving men in Washington would be persuaded that further conflict was useless.

Robert E. Lee was confident that the Union army would remain ill-led, surly, but incapable of stopping him.

And his own army, Lee believed, could not be defeated.

The prospect of marching north demanded much consideration, of course. He would discuss it with Longstreet, when that truculent naysayer arrived, to test its logic and practicability. If a feasible plan matured, he would put it to President Davis.

When Lee turned back to his staff, his face had eased.

After a march that would have undone old Job, confinement in verminous railcars, and more slogging thereafter, Sam Pickens had stumbled across Washington City in a rainstorm that beat all, ending up in what the guards called the "Old Capitol Prison."

At least a man got fed and not so badly. The Yankees were more curious than wicked. A few of the guards put on a swagger that seemed more farce than fierce, but most seemed to know they were high-yella lucky to be guarding Rebs in the rear and not facing them in battle.

Nobody seemed to know how the fight was going or had gone, but some rumors put Marse Robert just outside Washington, while others claimed he'd been driven back on Richmond. Other hearsay, more credible, held that they'd be exchanged in no time at all, since a mighty passel of Yanks had been taken prisoner. True or not, it was pleasant to believe it.

Through all his travails, Pickens had managed to hold on to a silver dollar, and when the guards let the sutlers come braying down the gangway between the cells, he bought his fellows a pie and a jar of molasses, hoarding the change.

A Yankee surgeon or some such like came by to inspect them for smallpox, measles, and fevers. He smelled Pickens' rotten feet before he got near him.

After marveling that those feet were a case for the medical books, the Yankee had his orderly fetch a bottle of liniment then wash down Pickens' feet and bandage them up.

In the U.S. Military Telegraph office in Washington, a haggard man read through the latest dispatches. Then he read them again.

When he rose at last, his broken expression silenced the last whispers in the room, leaving only the tick of the keys and the scratch of pencils as evidence that the world had not come to an end.

Very tall, but bent at the shoulders—as if he bore an invisible hod of bricks—he muttered:

"What will the country say?"

Then he walked back to the house the people had loaned him.

Epilogue

Thomas Jonathan "Stonewall" Jackson died on the tenth of May 1863. Weakened by his wounds and the trauma of amputation, he could not long resist when pneumonia struck. He saw his wife and child before his death, but despite his proximity, Lee made no effort to visit him.

Of the other generals portrayed in this book, Union and Confederate:

John Reynolds died at Gettysburg.

Carnot Posey died from wounds suffered at Bristoe Station.

"Uncle John" Sedgwick died at Spotsylvania.

J. E. B. Stuart died from wounds received at Yellow Tavern.

Robert Rodes died at the Third Battle of Winchester.

Stephen Ramseur died at Cedar Creek.

Ambrose Powell Hill died at Petersburg.

Convinced that his Army of Northern Virginia was invincible, Robert E. Lee invaded Pennsylvania.

George Meade took command of the Army of the Potomac three days before the Battle of Gettysburg. He defeated Lee on an open battlefield with roughly equal numbers, turning the tide of the war.

At Gettysburg, Dan Sickles made an unapproved advance with his division, exposing the Union left flank. His movement led to the battle's gravest crisis. Sickles lost a leg but lost no time in hurrying to tell Lincoln that the Gettysburg victory was due to his sagacity and courage, while any mistakes made on the field were Meade's.

On the third day at Gettysburg, Henry Hunt's massed artillery destroyed Lee's last hope of victory.

Joseph Hooker received command of the Twentieth Corps under Sherman and fought well, only to quit the field when denied another army-level command. After the war, he married, drank, and died.

Dan Butterfield stood by Hooker until 1864, commanding a division in his Twentieth Corps. After the war and to the surprise of many, Butterfield remained in the U.S. Army as a brevet major general until 1870, all the while growing wealthier through private business interests. Maneuvering past the scandals of the Grant administration, he prospered until his death in 1901. His notable legacy to the U.S. Army remains the bugle call "Taps."

Oliver Otis Howard continued to command the Eleventh Corps, which collapsed again at Gettysburg (thanks to a blunder by Francis Channing Barlow), earning him the nickname "Uh-oh Howard." His corps was ordered west for a fresh start under Sherman, and both Howard and his men built a solid record as fighters. Impressed by Howard's battlefield performance, Sherman chose him over Hooker to command the Army of the Tennessee.

Howard's greatest achievements came after the war: A zealous champion of "Negro" rights, he headed the Freedmen's Bureau for nearly a decade. Although his tenure was marred by the corruption of subordinates—as at Chancellorsville, Howard trusted the wrong men—he was instrumental in gaining the vote for former slaves. When other reform efforts failed, it was because he confused the desirable with the possible.

Howard remained on active duty until 1894, with years of frontier service, but he continued to press for the integration of religious congregations and for the foundation of colleges that would educate blacks (as well as founding a college to serve poor whites in Appalachia). Today, the greatest of those institutions, Howard University, continues to bear his name.

Immediately after Chancellorsville, the Northern press vilified Carl Schurz, based upon a false report that his division, not Devens', had been positioned on the Union flank and simply fled. His fellow generals knew better and Schurz continued to lead his division until a falling-out with Hooker in the western theater, after which he campaigned for Lincoln's reelection. Schurz then returned to the battlefield and served in the Carolinas through the war's end.

In peacetime, Schurz founded a newspaper in St. Louis and became the country's first German American senator—and a fierce campaigner against government corruption. Appointed secretary of the interior by President Hayes, Schurz took on the spoils system, shielded the Bureau of Indian Affairs against the War Department, removed corrupt Indian agents, insisted that treaties be honored, and championed what later generations would call "human rights." In the age of the robber barons, he fought to protect public lands, and he always stood up for *der kleine Mann*, "the little guy." He served as the editor for the *New-York Evening Post* and *The Nation* and became the lead editorial writer for *Harper's Weekly*, the most influential periodical of the era. Revered among German Americans, the doggedly anti-imperialist Schurz remained a political force and an outspoken voice for justice until his death in 1906.

Then we forgot him.

Emory Upton earned his general's star for his innovative attack at Spotsylvania. Having commanded artillery and infantry units, he went on to command a cavalry division that crushed Nathan Bedford Forrest's Confederates and tore through Alabama and Georgia in the closing days of the war. In subsequent years, he became the most important reformer in the history of the United States Army. Afflicted with what appears to have been an agonizing brain tumor, he shot himself in 1881.

Initially opposed to the war and no friend to slavery, Jubal Early became the foremost mythologizer of Robert E. Lee and the leading champion of the "Lost Cause" movement.

Fitz Lee survived the war and became the governor of Virginia.

John Brown Gordon became Georgia's governor and a United States senator, adored in the South and respected in the North. He and Fanny shared one of the great love stories of their century.

Clement Evans became a much-beloved Methodist preacher. Resisting all attempts to promote him to higher dignities within the church, he chose to minister to the country folk and small-town citizens who had been his soldiers.

Author's Note

Joseph Hooker's impressive plan for the Chancellorsville campaign failed for many reasons, but three stand out:

First, the plan was too complex for the communications technologies of the era. Hooker's initial moves, including an artful deception plan conceived by Dan Butterfield, went flawlessly, and the plan continued to unfold well until the first significant contact with the enemy. Thereafter, inadequate communications triggered a breakdown of the Union effort. Not only did Hooker have no idea of the location of most of his cavalry, at key moments he lacked awareness of the activities of the nearby Union Sixth Corps, and time-sensitive orders went awry. Still worse, his leadership style all but prohibited initiative. Overall, Hooker conceived a twentieth-century plan for a mid-nineteenth-century army.

Second, Hooker, despite earnest intentions, could not rise to the responsibilities of army-level, independent command. Personally brave and tactically able, Hooker had simply risen above the competencies of his character and skill. Faced with the resolute and implacable Robert E. Lee, he froze and failed.

Third, and not least, there was Lee himself. It does not slight Jackson's gifts, commitment, or ferocity to note that every major decision at Chancellorsville was Lee's. Certainly, Lee made mistakes—he almost made a tragic one at the battle's end, saved only by the weather and Hooker's retreat—but his tenacity, his refusal ever to give in to fear, and his canny appraisals of those who opposed him made him the antithesis of Hooker. Whatever the sources of Lee's unbreakable will, that quality rendered him peerless until Grant came east. Indeed, had Robert E. Lee, rather than Jackson, died at Chancellorsville, the Confederacy would have collapsed by midsummer 1864.

Today, as Lee's statues are torn down by a generation gorged on its self-righteousness, his reputation as a soldier endures. If Jackson was greater than the sum of his parts, Lee was greater by far than the sum of his failings.

This book began with the offhand remark "I've been thinking about Chancellorsville," to which Bob Gleason, my editor, responded: "Jackson!"

I had shied from writing about "Stonewall" Jackson for years because he remains the only major Civil War figure more enigmatic than Grant. Today's culture of internet snark, had it been extant in 1861, would have dismissed the two of them as "a failure and a freak." Yet Grant became the war's visionary strategist and Jackson its finest tactical commander.

I've grown convinced that Jackson suffered from a form of spectrum disorder, which he largely overcame by strength of will. Others will have their own views, and none of us will ever know for certain what made this forbidding, compelling, and contradictory man—who would not have survived in today's politically correct military—the brilliant, beyond-the-rules leader he became. What shall we make of a man who defied his neighbors to open a Sunday school for free blacks and slaves and who disregarded Virginia law to teach them to read, but who advocated killing Union prisoners en masse? Jackson's religiosity is unfashionable; his cause is deemed reprehensible; and his profession is disdained by the fortunate and finely educated. Yet he remains as exemplary to those who defend us as he is anathema to those who know nothing about him beyond the color of the last uniform he wore.

How difficult is it to "know" Thomas Jonathan Jackson? While writing about him I thought, at various times, of St. John of the

Cross (he of the "dark night of the soul"); of Simon de Montfort (he of the Albigensian Crusade); of Erwin Rommel; of John Calvin; of Oliver Cromwell; and of those special souls who delight unconditionally in children.

Yet I do not know him. He cannot be known.

Some readers may have been disappointed that I did not recount the oft recited, drawn-out, high-Victorian version of Jackson's death, with its absence of sickroom smells and lurking archangels. The portrayals of Jackson's final days in hagiographic memoirs and pseudo-histories, in popular novels and films, put me in mind of the most saccharine Baroque paintings of the Assumption of the Virgin. Such frilly, pastel nonsense slights Jackson's suffering, sacrifice, and bewildering complexity, while evoking Oscar Wilde's comment on the death of Little Nell.

Jackson is best remembered on horseback, leading his men in battle, not mooning sentimentally on a tidied-up deathbed.

Joseph Hooker is another matter. He did his best, but it was not good enough. As for the hoary tales of his drunkenness during the Chancellorsville campaign, the evidence from the most dependable sources (not all of them well-disposed to Hooker) is overwhelmingly in favor of his sobriety during that tragic week.

Hooker was indeed a heavy drinker (nor was that his only vice), but he appears to have made a conscientious and firm decision to abstain for the duration of the campaign. Indeed, the wisest contemporary observation may have been that it wasn't Hooker's drinking that impaired him but the sudden withdrawal from alcohol.

As for the reports of him lying about in a drunken stupor on May 3, 1863, they rely on glimpses from a distance. Hooker certainly did take to a cot at times that day, but he'd just suffered an ill-timed concussion—as Napoléon knew, luck, good or bad, matters on a battlefield. And speaking as someone who suffered a concussion, got up, did a television panel, attended a banquet, flew home, and then collapsed, I assure the reader that the effects of concussions are not identical, nor do they arrive on a schedule, but they can be devastating.

Joe Hooker wasn't drunk. He was just too small.

In the ultimately mysterious—even mystical—act of creating life on the page, sometimes a writer is ambushed by ghosts with gripes. This time, Dan Sickles showed up midbook to tell me why he defied expert advice and disobeyed orders to thrust his guns out to the Peach Orchard at Gettysburg. Exhaling a cloud of cigar smoke, the one-legged rascal smoothed his mustaches and snapped, "Hazel Grove, you dunce! Remember what happened when Hooker made me give up Hazel Grove to the Johnnies? I wasn't going to give them the best ground again."

It was no use countering that the no-man's-land position at the Peach Orchard lacked the dominance and defensibility of Hazel Grove. Sickles called me "as pigheaded as George Meade" and disappeared.

He was not about to repeat the same mistake. So he made another.

In every book I have written on our Civil War, I have adhered to the agreed facts. Where there have been unresolved issues, I have applied my own experience as a soldier to make sense of things. I have done my best to reflect characters accurately as I elaborated their thoughts and sentiments. Usually, the only conscious alterations I made were to translate the exaggeratedly formal and purified speeches set down decades after events into realistic dialogue. Few officers in midbattle hold forth in florid sentences and sculpted paragraphs, and soldiers talk as soldiers talk, whether Roman legionaries on a barbarous frontier or enlisted men in Afghanistan today.

Still, there have been rare instances when I found it useful to invent appropriate details, and I feel obliged to alert the reader when I supplement the facts. In this book, I did it twice. The instances may seem minor, but the reader should be aware of them.

First, there is no evidence of Hooker romancing a ranchero's daughter when down on his luck in Sonoma. I inserted that bit for two reasons: first to illustrate how far Hooker, the former officer, had fallen in society—the father is appalled at Hooker's presumption—and also to deepen in yet another way the reader's sense of how complex American society already had become on the eve of the Civil War. Much of this book has that underlying purpose.

The second fabrication is, literally, a footnote: In his illuminating letters home, the "real" Sam Pickens made no mention of suffering from bad feet at Chancellorsville (although the details of his battle experience are rendered faithfully). As a former Army private and, later, a junior officer in an infantry battalion, I have an appreciation of the importance of feet that would outdo the wisdom of any podiatrist. I inflicted that curse on Pickens to drive home, yet again, what campaigning truly was like for the grunts of yesteryear.

I'm allergic to attempts to romanticize war.

My thanks, as ever, to my wife, Katherine, who has a quick eye for the errant word, and to my editor, Bob Gleason, who takes a patient view of errant authors. Thanks also to the troops of all ranks at Forge; to Sona Vogel, the most talented copy editor I have encountered; and, not least, to veteran mapmaker George Skoch. I also am indebted, not for the first time, to Peter G. Tsouras and John Horn for sharing their research with me.

On the administrative side, I chose to spell out the numbers assigned to Union corps this time—"Sixth Corps" rather than the traditional "VI Corps," for example—because I've found that younger readers, especially, have not been taught Roman numerals (as they have not been taught history, either). The "correct" numerals are assigned on the maps.

As always, it's essential to recognize and recommend key books that shaped my interpretation of Chancellorsville, but even obeying my rule not to cite books praised in previous works of mine, I can include only a small selection of the hundreds of volumes exploited over a near lifetime of study. My apologies to anyone whose work I appear to have slighted.

Beyond the indispensable *Official Records of the War of the Rebellion,* countless books bear on Chancellorsville in full or in part. Of the available campaign accounts, three stand out as enduring. First, Major John Bigelow, Jr.'s compendious account, *The Campaign of Chancellorsville,* published in 1910 (within the lifetimes of many veterans), will remain a Civil War classic, its fine maps unrivaled. Later historians may have corrected minor points, but Bigelow's remains the seminal work.

Of later campaign histories, Stephen W. Sears' *Chancellorsville* unsurprisingly remains the best single volume for the modern reader. (Any work by Sears is well worth reading.) That said, I also found great value in *Chancellorsville 1863: The Souls of the Brave,* by Ernest B. Furguson. To me, the two books complement each other.

The U.S. Army War College battlefield guides are always useful and instructive, and the *Guide to the Battles of Chancellorsville and Fredericksburg* equals the best.

Under the Crescent Moon with the XI Corps in the Civil War, volume 1: *From the Defenses of Washington to Chancellorsville, 1862–1863,* by James S. Pula, fills an inexcusable gap in Civil War history. Despite a near lifelong interest in the unlucky Eleventh Corps and its colorful assortment of generals and colonels, I learned much from Dr. Pula's book and turned to it often. Overall, his academic crusade to give fair credit to the various immigrant groups who ultimately won the war for the Union has been as revolutionary as the men about whom he has written. He's a myth buster and a booster of justice.

Of the countless books on Jackson, two recent accounts are not only masterful but a pleasure to read. Coming in at 950 pages, *Stonewall Jackson: The Man, the Soldier, the Legend,* by James I. Robertson, Jr., is exhaustive but never exhausting. For those particularly interested in the military aspects of Jackson's life, this book is the choice. General readers can turn to *Rebel Yell: The Violence, Passion, and Redemption of Stonewall Jackson,* by S. C.

Gwynne, which comes in at a mere 672 pages. Gwynne is a fine writer and he captures Jackson the man with consummate skill. But this is quibbling: Each book offers a full and enthralling picture of this unique figure. I profited from both.

For those inspired to search even deeper into Jackson's psychology and the environment that shaped his maturity, *The Life and Letters of Margaret Junkin Preston,* compiled by Elizabeth Preston Allan, is an excellent window into a lost world and gives a glimpse of Jackson's "impossible" love.

Beyond that, many who touched Jackson and survived the war left written accounts of the man and their experiences serving under him. I have listed the best of those memoirs elsewhere.

On Hooker, the best available account is *Fighting Joe Hooker,* by Walter H. Hebert. It's a first-rate book about a second-rate man.

On Carl Schurz, of whom I am a pronounced admirer, there is a dearth of modern biographies, but *The Autobiography of Carl Schurz: Lincoln's Champion and Friend*, edited by Wayne Andrews, and the *Intimate Letters of Carl Schurz, 1841 to 1869,* compiled and edited by Joseph Schafer, serve as excellent and inspiring portraits of a genuinely good man.

For more details on O. O. Howard's eventful life, the best choice is *Sword and Olive Branch: Oliver Otis Howard,* by John A. Carpenter. For more on Howard's postwar campaign for minority rights, see *The Good Man: The Civil War's "Christian General" and His Fight for Racial Equality,* by Gordon L. Weil.

M. Gambone's *Major-General Darius Nash Couch: Enigmatic Valor* is a valuable work on that largely forgotten leader, while Darrell L. Collins' *Major General Robert E. Rodes of the Army of Northern Virginia* pays suitable tribute to a leader the South could not afford to lose but did.

Finally, there were two books from which I took particular pleasure. The first was *Voices from Company D: Diaries by the Greensboro Guards, Fifth Alabama Infantry Regiment, Army of Northern Virginia,* edited winningly by G. Ward Hubbs. Sam Pickens was not the only neighborhood boy to write wonderful letters home.

Likewise, *Sharpshooter: The Selected Letters and Papers of Maj. Eugene Blackford, C.S.A.*, volume 1, edited by Fred L. Ray, offers a vivid sense of a very American life. In the end, I did not feature Blackford as a leading character, but he would have served well in those ranks.

Again, many other works related to this campaign have been cited in the notes to my previous Civil War books. All deserved to be named a second time, but even the most generous publisher applies the brakes at some point.

I remain in debt to many, living and dead.

—Ralph Peters
August 24, 2018